THE STRONGEST WEB

The Detective Inspector John Cahill Series, Volume 3

John O'Donovan

Published by Castley & Fox Publishers, 2024.

THE STRONGEST WEB

First edition. August 20, 2024.

ISBN: 979-8227444219

Written by John O'Donovan.

Also by John O'Donovan

The Detective Inspector John Cahill Series
The Deadly Steps
Alibi for an Alibi
THE STRONGEST WEB

Watch for more at https://johnodonovanbooks.blogspot.com.

For the few that worked on Guillotine. What a difference it made!

Epigraph

L aws are like <u>cobwebs</u>, which may catch small flies, but let wasps and hornets break through.
Jonathan Swift 1667-1745

MAP OF IRELAND

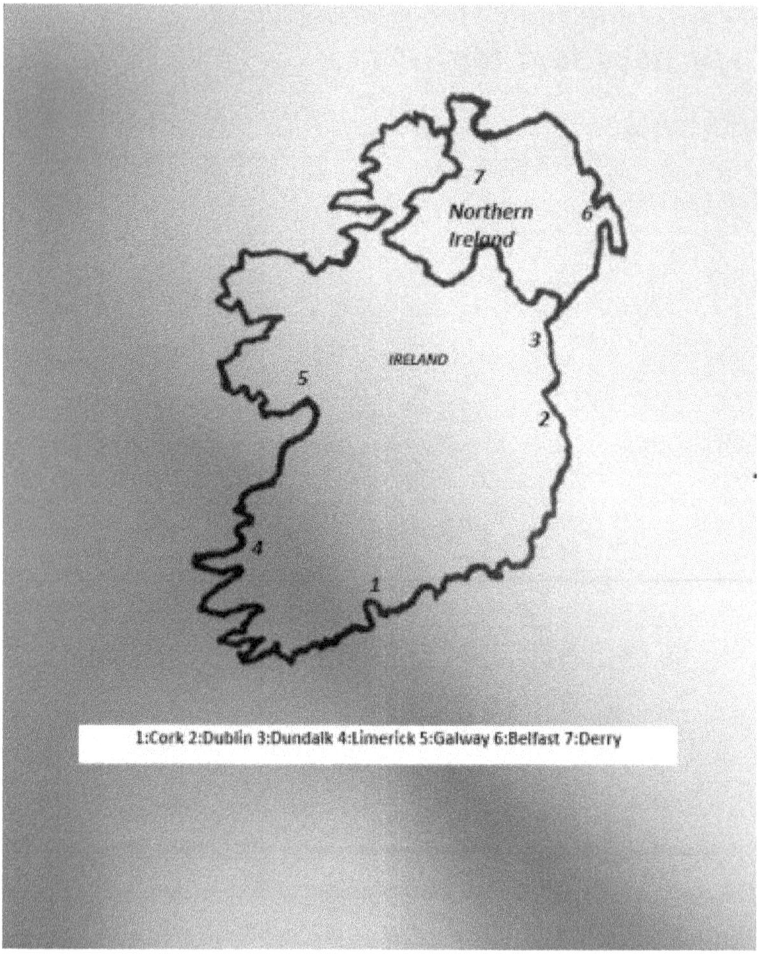

1:Cork 2:Dublin 3:Dundalk 4:Limerick 5:Galway 6:Belfast 7:Derry

CONTENTS

Prologue

B ackground: Detective Inspector John Cahill.
From Volume 1, 2 and 3 of the D.I. John Cahill
series:

Volume 1: THE DEADLY STEPS
Volume 2: ALIBI FOR AN ALIBI
Volume 3: THE STRONGEST WEB

John Cahill grew up in one of Cork City's oldest neighborhoods, Blackpool, situated in the heart of the North Side. Unlike most kids in the Blackpool area, John did not play the traditional sports of hurling and Gaelic football. Instead, at an early age, he got involved with horses and ponies. In his late teens, John Cahill entered the world of horseracing. John and his wife, Jules, operated a small-scale horse training establishment at Inchydoney's twin beaches on the west coast, near Cork City.

Volume 1 *(The Deadly Steps)*: *After sustaining a life altering injury* on the racecourse at Down Royal, Northern Ireland, John Cahill needed a new career with a secure future for his family. While recuperating in hospital in Belfast, he formed a close bond with fellow patient, Constable Fred Nesbit of the Royal Ulster Constabulary. Fred convinced John to become a police officer, but in 1994 at the age of thirty-three, he was too old to join Ireland's national police force, 'An Garda Siochana.' So he crossed the border into Northern Ireland and joined the Royal Ulster Constabulary.

- *R.U.C. Constable John Cahill* was promoted to detective constable in 1997 and assigned to the Criminal Investigation Division (C.I.D.) in Belfast.
- *The Royal Ulster Constabulary* was rebranded in 1999 after the Good Friday Agreement and became the Police Service of Northern Ireland. John Cahill's career flourished in the new police service.
- *After working on his first* homicide investigation, Detective Constable John Cahill was promoted to the rank of detective sergeant and transferred to the Serious Crime Unit in Belfast.
- *Detective Sergeant John Cahill* successfully investigated many complex cases while assigned to the Serious Crimes Unit. These included homicides, kidnappings, robberies, and the case of an international gun-runner and bombmaker. It wasn't long before he was promoted to the rank of detective inspector.
- *With promotion came transfer* within the Police Service of Northern Ireland. Detective Inspector John Cahill was assigned to the Professional Responsibilities Unit, the force's Internal Affairs unit.
- *During this assignment*, D.I. Cahill ruffled some feathers with some senior ranking officers and the police union when he investigated two officers for failing to carry out their duty. The officers' negligence led to the death of young man from a marginalized community.
- *With the assistant chief constable* as an ally, Detective Inspector Cahill was transferred again. He was seconded to an Integrated Fugitive Squad, working with An Garda Siochana in his native Cork City, south of the border in the Republic of Ireland.
- *John and Jules Cahill moved back* to their homestead in

Inchydoney in West Cork. After two extremely successful years leading the Integrated Fugitive Squad, D.I. Cahill was parachuted back into the world of Serious Crime when his boss in the Garda, Superintendent Paddy Collins, asked him to lead a difficult and complex homicide investigation.

- *Using extraordinary investigative techniques*, D.I. Cahill led a small, dedicated team of investigators in the newly formed Serious Crime Unit in Cork City, tackling the notorious street gangs, the Independent Posse and the Mahon Warlords.

- **Volume 2 *(Alibi for an Alibi)***: *Detective Inspector John Cahill* investigated three homicides that occurred during New Year's celebrations. With dozens of witnesses who 'saw nothing,' Cork City's Serious Crime Unit used every tool in their kit to solve these atrocious crimes that were carried out at the behest of the gang leaders.

- *D.I. John Cahill hoped* that the level of violence would subside if the leaders of this loosely structured gang were taken out of the picture. Fear was the strongest weapon that the gang had and Mikey Galvin knew how to inflict fear on everyone that knew him.

- With the strongest gang council members locked up, Cork City should have been a safer place.

- **Volume 3 *(The Strongest Web)***: *Detective Inspector John Cahill* realizes he could not have been more wrong. The new gang leader is an ambitious sociopath, with a propensity for violence, known only to the worst war criminals in history. The gangs employ child soldiers to do their dirty work and convince these children that they are untouchable due to their young age. Only luck and the perseverance of the detectives of Cork City's Serious Crime

Unit can end the reign of terror, not seen since the days of the Black and Tans.

- **Read on** to find out how the Serious Crime Unit turns to new tactics to bring peace to Cork City

Chapter 1

The north wind howled down Blarney Street on a cold, wet, windy Friday night in mid-October. It was just after midnight and Anthony Woodsworth left the bar on Blarney Street and headed for home. As per usual for a Friday night, Anthony had had a skinful of beer and was slightly the worse for wear as he half staggered along the sidewalk. He pulled his heavy winter parka around him to block the biting north wind. Winter was starting to take an early grip on Cork City. On his way home, Anthony stopped in at the Fish and Chip Shop and ordered himself a snack. It was closing time at most of the bars in the area so the shop was busy with eight ravenous customers ahead of him.

Most of the customers were happy to wait in line for their food but Anthony was a messy drunk. He called out to the woman behind the counter, "Would ya ever hurry up there, Josie? Me stomach thinks me throat has been cut. And it better be feckin' hot too, not like last week."

"Enough of your oul guff now, Anthony! Keep it up and you'll be barred and you can feck off home hungry to Caroline," the woman yelled back, not taking any nonsense from Anthony.

Anthony quietened down after being put in his place, shuffled through the queue and eventually received his food. He got his usual order: a bag of chips, a sausage in batter and a hamburger. He ordered a chicken supper for his wife, Caroline. As Anthony made his way home to Harbour View Road, he ate his snack out of the paper wrapping. His kept his wife's offering sheltered by wrapping it up tightly in its own paper packaging and placed it in the inside pocket of his thick parka.

As Anthony walked along Harbour View Road, he balled up the paper that wrapped his snack and threw it on the sidewalk. He pushed open his garden gate and made his way to the front door. He pulled the key from his pant pocket, took aim with it and got it in the keyhole on the first attempt. Anthony turned the key and *bump*! The door was bolted from the inside. Anthony hammered on the door and rang the doorbell. He stepped back from the door, looked up at the upstairs windows and returned to the door again, ringing the bell frantically.

Then the upstairs window flew open and an angry woman stuck her head out. "You're drunk again, aren't you? I told you last week that if you came home langers drunk again, I'd lock you out!"

"Ah Caroline, I only had a few pints. I'm not that bad, I swear. And I bought you a chicken supper," Anthony pleaded as he fished the warm package out of his pocket and held it up for his wife to see.

"You can stick the chicken supper up your arse and feck off up to your mother's house for the night! Come back here in the morning when you're sober," Caroline hollered angrily as she slammed the window shut. She turned the lights off and the house was in darkness.

Anthony knew there was no point in trying to reason with her. After all, she had given him fair warning last Friday when he came home late, pissed as usual. He turned around and headed out the gate, pulling his parka in around him. He took the paper package from his pocket, opened it and started on his wife's crispy fried chicken, mushy peas and chips.

Using his fingers as cutlery, Anthony picked away at the lukewarm food as he passed through Knocknaheeney on his way to his mother's home in Manor View Estate.

It was now after 3:00AM. Anthony had sobered up slightly after his fill of greasy food and the cold air. He walked up to the porch at the front of his mother's house. The house was in darkness; only the porch light shone brightly. The street was dead quiet. Anthony knocked on the front door, somewhat more calmly than he had knocked on his own front door a couple of hours earlier. When there was no answer, he rang the doorbell and knocked again. Still no answer.

Anthony walked around the back of the house and peeked in the windows. Darkness and nothing moving within. He walked back to the front street and noticed that his mother's car wasn't parked there. "Ah fuck it anyway," he said to himself. "I forgot she's babysitting for me sister tonight."

Tired, cold and still feeling a few of the effects of several pints of stout, Anthony decided to lie down in his mother's porch and get some sleep. Before doing so, he unscrewed the bulb from the porch light, making it much darker. He carefully placed the bulb in the corner of the porch. Sheltered from the cold wind inside the porch and using a black doormat to block the rising damp from the concrete floor, Anthony Woodsworth drifted off to sleep.

At 4:30AM, Anthony woke to the sound of four gunshots. The sound of the shots appeared to have come from the back lane at the other end of the block. He then heard a vehicle race down the street and off towards Knocknaheeney. "Jesus, almighty! This is a terribly dangerous place." Anthony thought as he shook his head.

Anthony stood up. He was shivering from the cold. He knocked at his mother's front door again. Still no answer. He walked to the front gate in the garden and looked up and down the street. All quiet and still no sign of his mother's car. He walked into the garden, unzipped his fly and pissed up on one of his mother's rose bushes. He went back inside the porch and settled down on the floor mat again.

An hour later, Anthony was woken by a young man standing over him. The man was tall and athletically built. He had short dark brown hair, parted in the middle. He was dressed in all black except for a red bandana around his neck. The young man kicked Anthony to rouse him saying, "What the fuck are you doing hiding in here?"

Anthony, suddenly wide awake, looked up at the man. "I'm not hiding. Who the fuck are you anyway?"

"Who are you down with?" the man asked in a demanding and menacing voice.

Confused, barely awake and somewhat sober, Anthony responded, "Down with? I'm not down with anyone."

"What do you think of the I-P?" the man insisted on an answer as he towered over Anthony.

"What?" Anthony asked, his voice full of confusion as he scrunched his eyes and wrinkled his brow.

"The Independent Posse!" the man replied, even more intimidating as he leaned over Anthony.

"Ah fuck that shower of eejits." Anthony dismissed the man with a wave of his hand.

"Wrong answer!" the man said and he calmly produced a black semi-automatic pistol, held it two centimeters away from Anthony's face, just below his right eye. Then he pulled the trigger.

The hollow-point bullet made a hole nearly five centimeters in diameter as it tore through Anthony's face. He slumped to the ground. There were some involuntary spasms from his body for a few seconds. Then nothing. Anthony Woodsworth lay dead at his mother's front door in Manor View Estate in the heart of Independent Posse territory.

Chapter 2

After Anthony stopped twitching, the assassin leaned in to see if he could find the shell casing that had been ejected out the right side of the slide of his black pistol. The gunman's ears were ringing from the loud crack of the gunshot. When he could not find the silver-coloured shell casing, he started to panic; he was afraid that someone had called the police after the shot rang out. The young man stood up, turned and walked out of the garden. He pulled the red bandana up above his nose, covering half his face. Once out on the sidewalk, he broke into a jog and then ran faster towards a waiting car at the end of the block.

A few people living in Manor View heard the gunshot. Just like they heard the four shots an hour earlier. However, nobody dared to call 999. It wasn't that they did not care. They did, but the regular people who resided in Manor View Estate were terrorized by the gangsters who lived among them. The reality was that they were too scared to get involved.

At 6:45AM, Brenda Woodsworth parked her little yellow FIAT in front of her home in Manor View Estate. She picked her purse up from the floor by the passenger seat and exited the car. She retrieved her overnight bag from the back seat, locked the car and walked towards her front door.

As Brenda walked along the short garden path, she saw the shape of a person lying in her front porch. Instantly, she knew something was not right. Brenda's chest tightened and there was a sinking feeling in the pit of her stomach.

Brenda instinctively knew that this was Anthony lying by her front door. She stopped walking and called out to her son. She had not yet seen the pool of blood. "Anthony, is that you luv? I'm home now. I'll open the door for you." There was no reply.

Brenda took two more steps forward and could now see the thick pool of dark red congealing blood. "Oh Jesus, Mary and Joseph. What happened to you, Anthony?" Although it was not quite daylight, Brenda could plainly see her son's face. Anthony's eyes were wide open, staring at nothing. Brenda started to panic and breathe rapidly. She shook her son and called out to him. There was no response. She did not focus on the hole below his eye; she saw it as only a cut.

When she did not get a response from her son, Brenda ran to the rear of the house and unlocked the back door. She immediately picked up the telephone in the hallway and called 999. Brenda told the call-taker how she had found her son on her front porch. She reported that he must have fallen and cut his head. Now he was unconscious. In her wildest dreams, Brenda would never have guessed that her son had been shot.

In less than ten minutes, the blue flashing lights of the ambulance came to a sudden halt outside Brenda's house. Brenda met the paramedics at the gate and ushered them in to her son. "He must have fallen and split his head open. I can't wake him. Please, for God's sake, help him," she begged as the tears rolled down her face and her voice trembled.

The two paramedics rushed to Anthony's limp body. As soon as they saw his face, they knew he was dead. They also knew this injury was not the result of a fall. "What happened to him?" one of the paramedics called out to Brenda.

"I don't know. I only came home a few minutes ago and found him here. He must have fallen. Will he be OK? Oh, please God, let him be OK!"

The paramedic turned back to Anthony. She pulled the radio from her shoulder and clicked the button on the side. "C-A One-One," she spoke into the radio.

"Go ahead One-One," the dispatcher answered.

"One-One, we have an adult male victim, possible G.S.W. to the head. We require the police here as soon as possible. Copy?"

"Copy that. The Garda are advised and attending," the calm dispatcher replied.

By now, the neighbors were starting to peek out their windows and a few had ventured to their front doors to see what all the commotion was about. A police car stopped abruptly behind the ambulance and two young uniformed officers ran to the front yard.

One of the officers stopped to speak with Brenda and the other proceeded to Anthony and the two paramedics. The officer shone his flashlight onto Anthony's face and stopped dead in his tracks. The young policeman's eyes were as large as saucers when he saw the hole in the dead man's face. The two paramedics were deep in conversation. They had cut Anthony's shirt open and had electrodes stuck to his chest and legs, checking for signs of life.

"I think we should take him to C.U.H.," the one who had called dispatch said.

"What's the point? He has a huge hole in his head. He can't survive. He's dead," the other whispered loudly.

"I don't see any exposed brain matter! He is still somewhat warm. We must transport! He's going to C.U.H.," the woman responded quietly. She stood up and walked to the ambulance to retrieve a stretcher.

"What happened?" the young Garda officer asked the other paramedic.

"I don't know. It looks like he's been shot in the head. His mam says she found him twenty minutes ago and she thinks he fell and hit his head on the step."

The policeman turned, looked at Brenda and then turned back to Anthony. "Does she know that he is likely dead?" he asked in a low voice.

"God love her, no. We'll transport him to Cork University Hospital now. Maybe they can work a miracle, but I would say they'll be lucky if they can harvest some organs."

At this point a Garda sergeant arrived and took control of the scene. He directed the officer who was speaking with the paramedics to go with Anthony in the ambulance and report back with an update from the hospital as soon as possible. He called for reinforcements to guard the scene and directed the other officer to take Brenda to Garda Headquarters on Anglesea Street, where she could be interviewed by detectives. The sergeant then called the duty inspector at headquarters. Duty Inspector Bob Keating was a senior officer who oversaw all Garda operations within the district, outside regular business hours.

"Hello Bob, you'll have to call out the Serious Crime Unit for this one. We have a young male, shot in the head in front of his mother's house in Manor View," the sergeant reported.

"Is he deceased?" the inspector enquired.

"The paramedics will not pronounce him here. But Bob, he has a hole the size of a two-euro coin on his face. He can't have survived that." The sergeant provided the inspector with the few facts that he had and terminated the call.

Bob Keating's next task was to notify Superintendent Paddy Collins, who was in charge of Investigations, and have him assign one of his units to take over this case.

Chapter 3

At 8:15AM on that Saturday morning, Detective Inspector John Cahill was having a well-earned lie in. He purposely did not set an alarm as he had no intention of rising early. Nevertheless, he always kept his phone close by as he never knew when the next call-out was coming. And at 8:15 AM, the call-out came as the phone lit up on the bedside table. It vibrated violently a second before it rang.

Jules, John's wife, shot up in the bed and looked across at the lit-up phone next to her husband. "What now?" Jules sighed, as she guessed her husband would have to go to work. She was worried how long he would be gone for.

John reached out from under the covers and grabbed the phone. He looked at the call display and saw it was 'Superintendent Collins.' "Oh Jesus, can't I get one fucking day off?" John muttered under his breath.

John answered the phone as he rolled out of bed and put on his housecoat. "Hey boss, what have ya got?" He spoke softly as he walked into the kitchen and switched on the electric kettle. He sat at the kitchen table and grabbed a notepad and a pen. In doing so, he had disturbed his two greyhounds. As usual, they were sleeping in their huge wire crates in the kitchen. Lucy, the older and larger of the dogs, started to whimper. She wanted to get outside. John covered the speaker on the phone and shushed the big red dog.

"I'm sorry to ruin your weekend, John, but we have new business in the city. Some fella has been shot in the head in front of his mother's house in Manor View Estate. His mother found him on the doorstep around 6:45AM," the superintendent said apologetically.

"Not Manor View again!" John responded with frustration in his voice. "This has to be gang related. That entire place is a rat's nest full of gangbangers."

"I'm afraid I haven't much more information for you. There are no witnesses, except for the victim's mother who didn't see anything. She only found him."

"Not your fault boss! I'll be in within two hours," John answered, resigning himself to another long day.

Jules walked into the kitchen and started to make two cups of instant coffee. "Are you going in?" she asked, knowing what the answer would be.

John nodded as he opened the dogs' crates, led them to the back door and took them to the back paddock. It was an unremarkable, overcast day. But when John stepped around the side of his house and was greeted by the view of the Atlantic Ocean, as always, it took his breath away.

JOHN AND JULES CAHILL had lived at Inchydoney Beach in West Cork when they married in the early 1980's. Back then, John was a moderately successful racehorse trainer and jockey. They had six stables at the rear of their house and John used the two long sandy beaches as his training ground. However, in the early 1990's, he suffered a career-ending fall from one of his horses at Down Royal Racecourse in Northern Ireland. He spent several months in the Royal Victoria Hospital in Belfast where he met his closest friend, Fred Nesbit. At that time Fred was a constable with the Royal Ulster Constabulary and was recovering from life altering injuries that he sustained in a bomb blast. Both men made miraculous recoveries. Fred was unable to return to regular police work and went to work in the R.U.C.'s training college. Although fit for most things, John was unable to train and ride horses again.

Constable Fred Nesbit convinced his friend to move with his family from Cork to Belfast and join the R.U.C. John joined the R.U.C. in 1994. He eased into the unfamiliar territory of police work, with such ease, that he soon progressed through the ranks.

As the R.U.C. evolved into the Police Service of Northern Ireland, people like John Cahill, with a Republican, Catholic background, became more acceptable. John's career took off. After being promoted to detective inspector, he was transferred to the Professional Responsibilities Unit. John caused upset with the police union and some senior officers when he investigated two police officers who neglected their duty and left a young man, from the marginalized Traveller Community, to die.

In order to protect John from the wrath of some 'old school' beliefs, the assistant chief constable arranged a secondment to the Garda across the border in the Irish Republic. John and Jules moved back to their homestead in Inchydoney. His original assignment with the Garda was to lead an Integrated Fugitive Squad; however, the Garda bosses in Cork soon realized his potential as an investigator and put him in charge of the newly formed Serious Crime Unit in Cork City.

JULES JOINED HER HUSBAND at the front garden of their house and handed him a steaming hot cup of coffee. "How long can you keep this up?" Jules asked, squeezing his hand. She wondered how long he could punish his body and mind working the extremely long hours and seeing, first hand, the carnage and evil that came with being a homicide cop.

"I can't retire for another few years. I hope they'll let us stay here until then. But my five-year secondment is almost up. I really don't want to go back to Belfast. Do you?" He took a sip of his coffee, looking over the horizon of endless ocean. "I'll suck it up as long as I have to in order to stay here. Lucy, Molly, come on inside!" he called to the two greyhounds and headed for the house.

"Yeah right!" Jules replied as she slapped him on the butt. "You love the work. I don't know how you're going to retire."

JOHN SHOWERED AND DRESSED, grabbed a couple of slices of toast and hopped in his car and began the forty-five-minute drive to Cork City. As he approached Bishopstown, on the west side of the city, he started to phone his team. He left it until now to give them at least an extra hour at home with their families.

At Garda Headquarters on Anglesea Street, John made his way to his office on the second floor. He fired up his computer and got the bare facts of this latest incident. Then he moved next door to the incident room from where they would run the investigation.

At the top of the whiteboard, John wrote the incident number assigned to this case. He then wrote the victim's name and underneath, 'G.S.W. to the head.' Next, he wrote the address at Manor View Estate where the incident occurred. Then he wrote the victim's mother's name and the time that she called 999. At this point he had nothing further to add.

His team were now arriving. Detective Garda Pete Sandhu, the team's analyst, looked at the whiteboard and delved into various databases. Within minutes, Pete had Anthony Woodsworth's age, date of birth, his address on Harbour View Road and Anthony's wife's name.

Next to arrive were Detective Garda Eddie Jenkins and Detective Sergeant Mike Williams. Both were among the most accomplished interviewers that John had ever worked with. Detective Sergeant Jeff Rafter and his partner Detective Len Benoit arrived seconds later. The last to arrive was the youngest member of the team, Detective Garda Tim Warren. John partnered with Tim most of the time and they had developed an understanding of each other, especially when interviewing suspects. This had led to numerous confessions.

As the members of the Serious Crime Unit settled in for what looked like it would be a long day, John debriefed with the first officers at the scene and gathered as many facts as he could from them. Then he spoke by phone with the sergeant at the scene in Manor View and requested a canvass of the immediate neighbors, in case anything suspicious was seen or heard.

Pete Sandhu updated the inspector on what he had learned about the victim. Pete had also discovered that Darryl Lyons and his girlfriend lived directly across from Brenda Woodsworth. Lyons was one of the top men in the Independent Posse street gang. Lyons was usually in the company of Tyson Rolland. Rolland had assumed the leadership of the Independent Posse gang after the Serious Crime Unit took Mikey Galvin and his brother Georgy out of the picture following an extremely complex homicide investigation almost two years earlier.

"That's interesting," John commented as he read the information on Darryl Lyons. "What are the chances that somehow the I-P are involved in this?" he asked Pete in a hushed voice. "Does Anthony have any ties to gang life?"

"As far as I can see, he has no connections to any of the gangs in town, but I'll dig a bit deeper to confirm that. He's come to the attention of the police a few times but it's all domestic- related. It appears he has a nasty side to him when he's been drinking. His wife, Caroline, calls 999 when he starts acting up." Pete handed the inspector several pages of reports that he had printed.

John stood at the front of the incident room and immediately his team stopped what they were doing and looked at him, pen at the ready and notebooks open. The briefing started.

"Thank you everyone for coming in on a Saturday morning. I'm sure you all had other plans for the weekend but here we are again," John greeted his team with a smile. Then he continued with the serious business. "We believe our victim is Anthony Woodsworth, thirty-four years old, living on Harbour View Road. He was found this morning at 6:45AM by his mother. Mr. Woodsworth was lying in her front porch at Manor View Estate. He had been shot in the head. He was conveyed to Cork University Hospital by ambulance and has since been pronounced deceased." John's team were making frantic notes as he presented the facts of the case.

"Mike, Eddie! Head to his address on Harbour View. His wife's name is Caroline. You'll have to notify her of Anthony's death. Find out what he was doing at Manor View at his mother's." John assigned his first task of the investigation while Pete kept notes on who was to do what.

"Jeff, Len! You guys make your way to Manor View Estate and canvass the area. Be vigilant in that neighbourhood. Just be aware that the infamous gangster, Darryl Lyons, lives directly across the street from our murder scene. And a block away lives the lovely Trish Langford, the bride of Georgy Galvin so that's another Independent Posse stronghold. Be careful. Tim and I will interview Brenda Woodsworth, the deceased's mother. She's here now. Uniform brought her in this morning after she called 999." John closed his notebook, bringing the briefing to an end.

Chapter 4

"What do you think this lady can tell us? Detective Tim Warren asked his boss as they made their way to Interview Room # 1. "Maybe she did it."

"When has it ever been that easy?" John sighed. He knew this investigation was going to be anything but straight forward.

When John opened the door to Interview Room # 1, he saw Brenda Woodsworth sitting in the corner on a black plastic chair that was bolted to the floor. Brenda was distraught. Her eyes were wet and red from crying. Brenda was a robust woman with dark brown short curly hair. John saw how fragile she looked as he introduced himself and Tim. "Brenda, I'm going to record our entire interview with you so you do not have to go over it again."

Brenda nodded and muttered something inaudible as Tim left the room to turn on the video and audio recording equipment. Once John explained that he needed Brenda to give a full account of her morning, she sobbed and asked, "How is Anthony? Did he wake up in the ambulance?"

John sat opposite the woman and slowly blinked his eyes. "Let's cover everything that you can remember first. It is very important that we understand how you found Anthony and it may help us find out how this happened." John hated himself for ignoring the woman's plea.

Although very upset, Brenda described her evening babysitting her grandchildren at her daughter's house in Ballyphehane. She stayed overnight but left very early in the morning because she wanted to be home to do some chores. Brenda went on to describe how she found Anthony. She told the detectives that he probably came over to her place during the night because his wife would not allow him in the house if he had 'drink taken.'

Brenda was convinced that Anthony had fallen and hit his head on her front step. She asked many times during her statement if he was OK. John agonized about not telling Brenda that her son was dead and that he had been shot. But it was important that he got her statement now, while it was still fresh in her mind. John also questioned Brenda about any possible criminal or gang associations that her son had. As far as she knew, there were none. Nevertheless, once he was sure that Brenda had told them everything that she knew, he had to tell her the bare facts.

"Brenda, I must tell you this and it's going to be difficult to hear. Anthony did not fall and hit his head on your step. Anthony was shot and unfortunately died. Anthony is dead," John said while he held Brenda's hand. The wording he used sounded callous but he had to ensure that there was no doubt in Brenda's mind that her son was dead.

Brenda gasped for air. She tried to say something but then wailed, "Noooo!" She cried uncontrollably as she tightly gripped the inspector's hand.

John let her cry as he and Tim exchanged glances. Tim felt like crying himself. No matter how many times he had witnessed this scene play out, it still hurt him.

After several minutes, Brenda started to process what she had been told. "How could he have been shot?" she asked between sobs. "Who would shoot him at my front door? Anthony was good boy. He was a bit fond of the drink but he had a kind heart. Who would do such a thing?" Brenda begged for an explanation.

"I have no answers for you at this time," John said. "Right now we just don't know what happened to Anthony. But I promise you that we'll do everything possible to find who did this and put them in prison where they belong for a long, long time."

"Where is Anthony now?" Brenda asked as she began to cry again.

"He's at the morgue at Cork University Hospital. I will get someone to take you back to your daughter's in Ballyphehane. Unfortunately, you can't go back home for now. I'll make sure his wife knows how to make arrangements for Anthony, later on today. Tim will sit with you for a few moments while I plan to get you to your daughter's place." John was somewhat relieved that he was able to get out of the awful atmosphere in the interview room.

Minutes later, he returned with a uniformed officer who was going to drive Brenda to her daughter's home. When she was gone, Tim turned to his boss, "She didn't see that coming, did she? She couldn't believe it when you said Anthony had been shot."

"I hate doing that, Tim. I despise myself for trying to advance our investigation while the poor woman is pleading with us for information about her son. We can be so callous. Sometimes I hate this fucking job!"

Mike Williams telephoned his boss to update him on the meeting with Caroline Woodsworth. Caroline described how Anthony had come home inebriated. She had locked him out and refused his peace offering of a chicken supper.

"What time did Anthony leave Harbour View?" John asked the detective sergeant.

"It was between 1:15AM and 1:30AM. She is pretty good with the time because she looked at the clock when he first knocked," Mike answered.

"Was he on foot, or driving or did he take a cab to his mother's?"

"He was on foot. She had control of the car and he wouldn't spend money on a cab, according to Caroline. She sounds tough but she's really very upset about his death," Mike said, slightly relieved that he had answers to the inspector's questions.

"Mike, can you or Eddie walk from Anthony's house to his mother's place on Manor View so we can get an idea of what time he arrived? Don't march like soldiers. Stroll along like a drunk," John requested.

"It's pissing rain boss!" Mike hoped the inspector would change his mind.

"Use an umbrella or tell Eddie to do it," John said with a smile as he hung up the phone.

Eddie Jenkins looked across at his partner as the rain spattered on their windshield. "What does the boss want?" he asked Mike.

"He wants you to walk from here to Manor View to see how long it takes for a timeline on Anthony's movements," Mike said with a glint in his eye.

"For fuck sakes! It's lashing rain. Can't I do it this afternoon when it stops raining?" Eddie groaned while pulling up the collar of his coat, getting ready to brave the rain.

"He wants you to walk it slowly too, like a drunk would." Mike was enjoying himself as his partner had taken the bait... hook, line and sinker. "I'll see you at Manor View Estate. I'm going to head up there and help out with the canvass."

Eddie stepped out of the car into the rain and Mike started the engine and drove off.

Jeff Rafter and Len Benoit attended to C.U.H. and spoke to the emergency room doctor who attended to Anthony when he was brought in. "There was nothing we could do for the poor man," the doctor said as he tut-tutted. "He died as soon as the bullet struck him. I think the ambulance crew were extremely optimistic when they brought him in."

"Is there anything else that you can tell us, maybe a time of death?" Jeff asked.

"He was dead for maybe an hour. The pathologist should be able to tell you much more after the autopsy." The doctor turned to walk back to his department. "Oh, hang on a second! When we cut off his clothing, we did find something that may be useful." The doctor told the two detectives to follow him.

The doctor stepped into a small office in the ER. He unlocked a desk drawer and retrieved a small brown transparent pill bottle. He handed it to Jeff Rafter.

Jeff held the bottle up to the light and looked inside. It contained a silver shell casing from a pistol round. "Where did you find this?" he asked.

"When the patient was moved from the ambulance gurney to the bed, we cut off his coat and his sweater and this fell onto the floor. It was hung up inside his coat. It's probably from the bullet that killed him." The doctor was quite pleased with himself for presenting this piece of evidence.

Jeff called his boss to report as soon as he could. John told him to bring the shell casing to forensics right away.

Sergeant Jennifer Martens was in the forensic lab at Garda Headquarters on Anglesea Street when Jeff Rafter delivered the shell casing. Sergeant Martens donned a pair of latex gloves and carefully opened the pill bottle. She removed it by placing a pencil inside the opening at the end of the casing. Sergeant Martens examined the markings at the base of the shell. "S&W .40cal" was stamped into the base of the shell casing. She told the officers what she had found.

"That's the same type of ammunition that we use," Jeff Rafter said. "There's a lot of power inside that little shell casing."

"I'll do some further tests and take a closer look at this. I'll update your inspector later today," Jennifer commented, dismissing the detectives.

An hour later, Sergeant Martens walked into the incident room, holding the transparent pill bottle in her hand. She sat in a chair in front of the inspector's desk and placed the pill bottle in front of him. John picked up the bottle, held it up to the light and looked into it. "It looks familiar," John said, shaking the little container. "It looks like the ammunition that we use."

"It probably is," Jen Martens replied, taking a breath as she was about to launch into one of her expert opinions. "I went to look at the deceased at the morgue. She placed a brown envelope on the desk and pushed it towards the inspector who opened the envelope and looked at four printed photographs inside. "What do you see when you look at these photos of Mr. Woodsworth?" the sergeant asked.

"That's a big hole in his face!" John said, scrutinizing the photograph. "Close range too. I can see the blue stippling around the edges of the wound."

"Very good. I would say the gun was fired only a couple of centimeters from the skin. I also think it was a hollow-point round." The sergeant paused, waiting for the inspector to ask her why.

John was not in the mood to play her games today. "Yeah, you're probably right," he agreed in his flat North Side, Cork City accent. "A regular round would have a much smaller entry wound and there would be a huge exit wound. The deceased does not have an exit wound."

"How do you know? You can only see the front of his head in these photographs," Jen Martens quizzed the detective.

"Ambulance would not have transported him with two holes in his head. That's classified as an obvious death," John answered, without making eye contact, as he was staring at the photograph of the dead man's face.

"The autopsy is scheduled for tomorrow at 9:00AM at C.U. H. Will you send someone to attend?" the forensic sergeant asked.

"No Jen, I'll leave it with you and your team. The cause of death is going to be a gunshot wound to the head. Call me if there are any surprises."

When Sergeant Martens left the incident room, John put one of the photographs of Anthony Woodsworth on a notice board next to the whiteboard.

"Tim! With me. We'll head up to the scene and see if they need help with the canvass." John opened his desk drawer and retrieved his Glock 27 snub-nose pistol. He picked up a full magazine from the drawer and walked to the loading station in the corner of the incident room. He pulled the slide back on the pistol, locking it in place. He snapped the magazine into the handle of the gun and pulled the slide back, let it go and slide forward again, engaging a round in the chamber. He placed the gun in his holster. Tim Warren walked to the Kevlar lined bucket at the loading station and did likewise, with his Glock 23. Both men grabbed their coats and headed out to their unmarked patrol car.

Tim drove out the rear of the Garda Station onto Eglinton Street; he turned onto Albert Street and headed north across the bridge that spanned the River Lee. He drove across the quays to Mulgrave Road and towards the North Side. Tim drove up Cathedral Road, through Gurranbraher and turned right on Bakers Road and then left on Harbour View Road. This was where Anthony Woodsworth started his last journey. Tim turned on Knocknaheeney Avenue and finally into Manor View Estate.

John and Tim looked at some of the houses in Manor View Estate as they drove. Most were townhouses in rows of four, six or ten. Many of the blocks had at least one derelict house on them, with boarded up windows and gang graffiti painted on the boards. The estate was built in the early 1970's, among much fanfare, when the Taoiseach, the Irish prime minister, cut the first sod. There was no manor to view, only the large ugly concrete water reservoir in Knocknaheeney. Manor View Estate was built to provide affordable housing for working class families, in the hope of establishing a strong sense of community. However, many people looked at the estate as a public housing experiment that went horribly wrong; terrible social and economic problems existed in the estate. As time progressed and unemployment in the area grew, the gangs and the drug dealers were the only ones who were thriving.

When they pulled up in front of Brenda Woodsworth's house, both were pleasantly surprised. Brenda had a lovely garden with rose trees and other shrubs. There would be colourful flowers blooming in the spring and summer. She kept a tidy lawn and her house looked bright and cheerful.

The uniform officer, guarding the entrance to the front garden, raised the blue and white police tape for the detectives. Once they had passed under the tape, he jotted a few words in his notebook, '*Serious Crime, inspector and detective on scene, 2:45PM.*' John stood back and looked at the large pool of dark red congealed blood on the step of the porch. "Jeez, that's a lot of blood," he said to the forensic officer, dressed in all white overalls, who was taking photographs and measurements around the step.

"There's always lots of blood from a head wound," the officer replied.

"What's that?" Tim asked as he pointed to an object in the corner of the porch.

"That's the lightbulb from the porch light. It's been screwed out. I don't know if it was done to conceal the body or what. We'll test it for fingerprints and DNA later," the forensic photographer replied as he refocused his camera and continued with his task.

"That's odd," John remarked as he walked around the side of the house to the back yard.

Mike Williams and Eddie Jenkins showed up outside the police tape and were joined by John and Tim. "Two hours," Eddie said rather sourly as he looked up at the sky, waiting for it to rain again. "He may have done it quicker than that, depending on how drunk he was, but it wouldn't have taken Anthony any longer than two hours to walk from Harbour View Road to here."

"He should have arrived here around 3:00AM," Mike Williams added, grinning. "I don't think it was raining when Anthony made his journey. You didn't get too wet, did you, Eddie?"

"Fuck off," Eddie replied, rubbing his hands together and stomping his feet to warm up.

John smiled; he knew exactly how Eddie ended up walking in the rain. "What's the update from the canvass?" he asked the others. Mike Williams shrugged his shoulders. "Send Jeff and Len a text and have them meet us at Gurranbraher Garda Station. We'll have a coffee there and debrief. Eddie can have a bowl of soup." John winked at Mike and walked to his car.

Chapter 5

The Serious Crime detectives met in a vacant incident room at Gurranbraher Garda Station at Bakers Road and Cathedral Road. This was one of the busiest stations in the region. It was in the heart of Cork's North Side and was in Independent Posse gang territory.

The six detectives sat around a table, drinking stale coffee from Styrofoam cups. "The first house we canvassed was Darryl Lyons' place, directly across from the crime scene," Len Benoit said, reading from his notebook. "Some skank who looked like she was fifteen opened the door. All she wore was a filthy short T-shirt. She had spiky hair and her eyes were sunken into her skull."

"Charming," John commented, encouraging Len to continue.

"She said she was at home all night with Darryl but Darryl went out this morning when he saw the police cars across the street," Len continued as he turned the page in his notebook for the next update.

"That's something. At least we know Darryl Lyons was in the area when the shooting occurred," Tim Warren added, making a note in his own notebook.

"Nobody else in the immediate area claims to have heard anything all night until the ambulance came blaring up the road at around 6:45 AM," Len said, again turning the page for the next update.

"Unbelievable," John remarked, shaking his head. "Nobody even heard a gunshot. A .40 caliber shot would be like a cannon going off in the middle of the night."

"If I lived in Manor View, I wouldn't tell you if I heard anything either. Most of these people live in fear," Jeff Rafter said smiling, although he was being truthful. "Something has to be done about this."

"We went all through the estate until we got to Trish Langford's house," Len went on, pausing for effect.

"Let me guess. Trish invited you in and made tea and biscuits," John responded sarcastically.

"Yeah right! Trish Langford is an ignorant bitch. Before we even asked a question, she said she knew nothing about nothing and didn't see or hear anything and then slammed the door." Once again Len paused. "Nevertheless, the next-door neighbours have a different story. Trish, her sister, you know, the one with the squint, and another girl, probably Samantha Brady, were sitting in the front yard around a fire last night. They were playing loud music and drinking. They quietened down around 4:00AM and about half an hour later there were four gunshots, followed by a vehicle taking off at high speed."

"Now that's interesting," John said. "Are they sure of the time, around 4:30AM?"

Len nodded.

"Our victim was only struck once and there are no signs of any other shots, no ricochets or other shell casings. And 4:30AM is at least an hour too early." John was trying to figure out the significance of this new information. "I don't know what the connection is, but it's not a coincidence."

John picked up his cell phone and called Jennifer Martens, the forensic sergeant. He asked her to send a team to the area of Trish Langford's house and check for signs of a shooting. Then he called Pete Sandhu in his own incident room. John asked Pete to check the traffic cameras in the area for a vehicle driving at high speed around 4:30AM in the Knocknaheeney area.

It was mid afternoon when John and Tim returned to the incident room at Anglesea Street. Pete Sandhu greeted them with some positive news. "I may have the speeding vehicle at 4:30AM. A white Nissan saloon went by the camera on Kilmore Road by the football club at ninety-five kilometers per hour. Here's the plate number and the owner's information." Pete, efficient as usual, handed his boss a couple of sheets of paper.

John and Tim didn't even hang up their coats; they turned around immediately and headed out to find the owner of the white Nissan. They drove to the opposite end of the city from Manor View Estate to a house in the Ravensdale Estate in Mahon. It was an end house in a row of four houses and had a pretty front garden. An innocuous looking white Nissan was parked in the front driveway.

Tim knocked on the door and it was answered by an attractive middle-aged woman. "Yes?" the woman asked, as she looked at the two men wearing suits.

John identified himself, showing his police badge and warrant card. The woman immediately opened the door back and invited the officers in. She led them into a tidy sitting room at the front of the house. In the sitting room was a sofa and two matching armchairs that appeared to be used only on special occasions. A coffee table stood in the center of the room. On it was a family photo of the middle - aged woman, an adult male and two teenage boys.

"What can I help you with, Guard?" the woman asked appearing quite worried.

"I hope you can help us, ma'am." John's Cork City accent took the woman by surprise as most of the cops stationed in Cork City were from other parts of the country. John used his accent to put people at ease and gain their trust. "That's your car in front?" He turned his head to the window.

"It's my husband's car really, but he's working on a gas field off the coast."

"Who was driving it last night?" John asked.

"Jesus, Mary and Joseph! What did he do?" The woman crossed herself and quickly switched from a worried look to an angry one.

"Who had the car?" John asked again.

"My youngest, James. He's next door. I'll call him now. What did he do?"

"Maybe nothing. But we need to talk to him about where he was." John did not want to give too much away in case this woman stopped cooperating. "What time did he come home?"

"It was before five. I heard him and I looked at the clock, 4:55."

A few minutes later eighteen-year-old James Molony entered the living room after receiving a text from his mother. When introduced to the detectives, James was visibly nervous and uncomfortable. John asked to speak with the kid alone and Mrs. Molony reluctantly left the room.

"We want to know more about what happened last night, James," John said. It was a demand, not a request.

James looked down at his feet and started to shake. "We were just driving around and all of a sudden this fella stood out in front of us, in the middle of the road, and started shooting at my car," James answered, his bottom lip trembling.

John and Tim exchanged glances. There was obviously much more to this story than James had told them. "Right James, you need to tell us everything! Leave nothing out, starting with why are you driving your mam's car around Manor View Estate at the other end of the city."

"We used to live in Knocknaheeney until we got this place last year," James continued, his lower lip still quivering. "I was telling some of me mates that I knew where a few of the top dogs in the Posse live." James stopped and looked at the detectives.

"Keep going, James. Don't leave anything out," John said very seriously.

"One of the fellas that was with me is with the Mahon Warlords and he wanted to see the houses. So we drove up to the North Side and drove past Georgy Galvin's place a few times. Then we drove past Darryl Lyons' place." James stopped again.

"You didn't just drive past a few times, did you?" John asked, probing further.

"No." James now looked embarrassed. "We were yelling out the windows at them, calling them slobs," James said as a slight smirk formed on his face.

"Did you see any gangsters?"

"There was nobody at Lyons' place and there were three women at a firepit in front of Galvin's house."

"How many times did you drive by the houses?" Both John and Tim had taken a step closer to James, making him feel extremely uncomfortable.

"About ten times," James said sheepishly. "The last time we drove by Galvin's place, the women had gone inside. Then this big fucker stepped out in the middle of the road and fired three or four shots at us. They hit the windshield and bounced off it. I thought we were going to be killed. Then I booted it out of there," James added, opening his eyes wide as he relived the incident.

Tim Warren turned and left the room. He went outside and inspected the windshield of the white Nissan. Sure enough, there were three chips in the glass in front of the steering wheel but no cracks or breaks. Tim returned to the sitting room and told the inspector what he found.

John called Sergeant Martens on his cell phone. He asked her to send someone to photograph the white Nissan and the chips on the windshield. He then called Mrs. Molony back into the sitting room. "Thank you, Mrs. Molony. James has been very helpful. However, we may need to speak with him again. What you need to know is James is hanging around with members of the Mahon Warlords street gang and he was driving them around in Manor View last night, harassing members of the Independent Posse. I can tell you now that is not going to end well."

Mrs. Molony covered her mouth with both hands. She looked down at her son, now sitting in one of the armchairs. She was both shocked and angry. "That's it! You're not driving that car again until you're twenty-one." James got a clip around the ear and knew better than to argue with her.

When John and Tim returned to the incident room, the rest of the team were there. "We haven't made a lot of progress today, gentlemen. This is going to be a tough one. We'll reconvene tomorrow at 9:30AM. Go home and get some rest." John then dismissed his team.

Chapter 6

It was 7:00PM Saturday night when John returned home to Inchydoney. As usual, he was met at the back door by the two retired racing greyhounds that he and Jules had adopted in Belfast, before they moved back to the Republic. Lucy, the big red dog, came bounding past her master and into the paddock behind the house. Seconds later she was followed by the smaller dark brindle dog, Molly. The two dogs ran around the paddock as only greyhounds can run and then back to John, stopping as if they had slammed on the brakes directly in front of him. John greeted his dogs with a huge smile and several pats on their heads and rumps. It made him happy to see them and no matter how bad a day he was having, they were always happy to see him.

After a shower and supper, John and Jules took the dogs to the beach. It was a cool overcast night and the West Beach was dark with no moonlight to brighten it. The tide was in so the East Beach was inaccessible from the road. They kept the dogs on their leashes as they strolled along the deserted beach. As usual, Jules asked about John's day and the latest investigation.

"It's going to be a tough one. We didn't get much accomplished today, apart from identifying the victim and most of his movements during the night before he was killed." John went on to tell his wife about the shell casing found at the hospital and the other shooting outside Trish Langford's house. He always discussed his cases with his wife. He knew she would not breathe a word about them and she often had good ideas on how to proceed.

"Do you think the two incidents are related?" Jules asked.

"They have to be. I just don't know the connection yet."

"Are you going in tomorrow? You do know it's Sunday?" Jules worried about the long hours that her husband worked and was concerned about his mental and physical health.

I told the lads to be back for 9:30AM. We'll clean up a few loose ends and if nothing new develops, I should be home by suppertime."

"9:30! Ah, you're getting soft in your old age. There was a time you would have them back at seven," Jules teased as they headed home. She knew this was a sign that he needed the rest as much as his team.

THE NEXT MORNING STARTED, as usual, with a briefing in the incident room. John recapped the events of the previous day and ensured everyone was aware of the shooting in front of Trish Langford's house. Sergeant Jen Martens of the Forensic Identification Unit sat in on the briefing. When he had concluded his synopsis of the investigation, John asked the sergeant if she had anything to add.

"The autopsy on Anthony Woodsworth started this morning at C.U.H. I got some X- rays of the injury yesterday." She handed the inspector some photographs of an X-Ray of the victim's head. "As you can see, the bullet is near the back of the victim's skull but did not exit. I believe this is because it was a hollow-point round. I will confirm that later when the projectile is removed." Jen scanned her audience to make sure they were all keeping up with her. "The victim's fingerprints are on the lightbulb that we found in the porch near his body, suggesting that he removed the lightbulb." She paused again for a few seconds.

"As for the second shooting, there's no physical evidence of shots fired in front of the Langford residence. In simpler terms, no shell casings or ricochet marks were found anywhere." Jen paused yet again, this time for effect, "However, we examined the white Nissan and swabbed the marks on the windshield. All the marks tested positive for traces of lead. The indents on the glass also suggest an upward direction of travel, suggesting that the van was hit by a lead projectile. It glanced off the windshield and travelled up and over the roof." Jen closed her notebook, signalling that she was finished.

"How come the bullets didn't go through the window?" John asked. It was what everyone else on his team was thinking. "Have you ever seen anything like this before?"

"We did some ballistic testing on vehicles with the military at Kilworth Range a couple of years ago. It happens more than you think. If it's a less powerful round, like a .22, it can happen. Or if it is a sawed off or damaged barrel it can happen as the round may tumble towards its target rather than travelling in a straight line," Jen answered somewhat smugly.

"She may be a bit odd but she really knows her stuff," Mike Williams said when the briefing was over and Sergeant Martens had left the incident room.

John handed out the day's assignments to his team and started to catch up on the written reports and statements in case he had missed something.

Sunday was less productive than Saturday in the investigation into the killing of Anthony Woodsworth and by mid-afternoon there was nothing more to be done. The entire area had been canvassed and not one person had come forward with information. As they recanvassed the area, all the investigators observed a subdued atmosphere when they asked the residents if they had seen or heard anything around the time of the shooting. It was obvious that the people were scared.

There were no new developments and John sent his team home. He almost felt guilty about racking up the overtime on a Sunday... but not quite. After all, it was the cost of doing business.

On Monday morning after the briefing, Detective Sergeant Ken Scott from the Criminal Investigation Unit walked into the incident room. He spoke to John directly but loud enough for everyone else to hear. "We had a shooting in Mayfield last night. I thought I would be turning it over to you this morning. The victim was circling the drain for a few hours but he seems to have survived the surgery," Ken said in a strong Dublin accent.

"He's out of danger?" John asked, dreading the thought of back-to-back homicides.

"For now. Believe it or not, he was shot in the heart, or at least the slug touched his heart, and the bullet is lodged at the edge of it. It's a small caliber round, possibly a .38. The surgeon isn't going to remove it. It's too dangerous. She said if it had gone any deeper into the tissue it would have killed him instantly."

"Is it gang related?" Jeff Rafter asked.

"Oh yeah," the sergeant said with a snigger. "The victim is Tommy Herschel. He is muscle for the Mahon Warlords. Looks like he was leading a raid on an Independent Posse crack shack but it didn't quite work out for them."

"Who shot him?" John asked.

"Don't know, but it looks like Herschel got a round off too. We found an old World War II 9mm Luger next to him and a spent 9mm shell casing on the ground."

"Fuck, I hope we don't find another dead body," John said, shaking his head. "We discovered another shooting a block from our homicide yesterday. A carload of M-W supporters was driving around the I-P houses in Manor View and someone fired a few rounds to scare them off. Looks like the M-W are starting to come into I-P territory more and more. This could get ugly. The last thing this city needs is a gang war."

THE MAHON WARLORDS and the Independent Posse were both street gangs. Unlike the structured drug cartels that operated mostly out of Dublin and Europe, the street gangs were less organized and, for the most part, made up of younger members. Their territory was traditionally divided by the River Lee that ran through the center of Cork City. The ongoing rivalry between gangs was fierce.

The Independent Posse's domain was on the North Side of the river, their strongholds being Knocknaheeney, Gurranbraher, Farranree, Blackpool, The Glen and Mayfield. The Mahon Warlords, like their name suggested, were based on the Mahon Peninsula, but they reached into Blackrock, Douglas, Ballyphehane, Togher, Wilton and Bishopstown. They also did business in the satellite towns of Carrigaline and Ballincollig.

Both gangs sold drugs, mostly crack cocaine. However, they also sold heroin, crystal meth, fentanyl and of course marijuana. The preferred point of sale was a crack shack or a trap house. The shack was usually a house or apartment where a drug addict lived. The gang would move in and sell from the residence and piece off a few rocks of crack for their host to keep them happy. The shacks were manned by a manager, a security guard and kids to run the drugs out to a vehicle and collect the money. The trap houses were the same, except some of the addicts would stay and use their poison on the premises. The gangs also used Dial a Dealer operations, where one could phone in the order and have the drugs delivered to the door either by car or a BMX bike.

MONDAY WAS FRUSTRATING and uneventful. The Woodsworth homicide investigation was at a standstill. John sent his team home at the end of the day and stared at his computer screen. "Nothing, not even a whisper. Nobody is saying anything. This isn't good," John told Superintendent Paddy Collins who had come into the incident room for an update.

"You're sure this Woodsworth fella isn't a gangster?" the superintendent asked.

"Definitely not! He worked at the brewery on Leitrim Street. He has had a couple of minor domestics but nothing serious. He was only charged once. His history is all alcohol related," John sighed and stared at the computer screen, hoping for inspiration.

"Do you think he was in the wrong place at the wrong time?"

"Fuck it! That's all we need. No motive, not targeted, just a mistake. We'll never get to the bottom of this unless someone breaks silence," John answered, not sounding very hopeful.

IT STARTED TO RAIN as John drove home to Inchydoney. By the time he reached the town of Bandon, the rain was pelting down and the wind had picked up to gale force. Once he crossed the Causeway Bridge onto Inchydoney, the waves were splashing over the coast wall along the road. When he got home, John looked down from his driveway to the Virgin Mary Bank, the rocky outlet between the East and West Beach. The breakers were almost ten meters tall as they lashed off the rocks, sending spray hundreds of meters inland. John ran to the house. The dogs knew better; they didn't want any part of this early winter storm and did not even try to get in the back paddock when the door opened. "No walk tonight, girls," John told the dogs as they met him at the back door.

The remainder of Monday evening was relaxing for John and Jules. They watched some television and listened to the storm raging, with all its might, in from the Atlantic Ocean. They barely discussed the Anthony Woodsworth homicide investigation.

THE ATMOSPHERE WASN'T as relaxed in Tyson Rolland's house in Churchfield in the North Side of Cork City. Tyson had taken over the leadership of the Independent Posse after Mikey Galvin was convicted of accessory to murder and locked up in Cork Prison. Mikey Galvin, or Mikey G as he was known, was a great business man and had developed a successful drug sales network throughout Cork's North Side. Once Mikey G was taken out of the picture by the Garda Serious Crime Unit, under the direction of Detective Inspector John Cahill, Mikey G had no option but to relinquish the leadership and turn over the reins to someone else.

Tyson Rolland was the obvious choice. Like Mikey G, Tyson was a ruthless, vicious, greedy gangster. Tyson was an absolute sociopath with no conscience. If Mikey G had not appointed Tyson as his successor, he would have taken over anyway.

This Monday evening Tyson was plotting with his closest friend, Darryl Lyons. Tyson liked Darryl because Darryl was also ruthless, but he was loyal to Tyson and he lacked ambition. He was not a threat to the leader.

"We got to show those Guppies that they can't show their faces in the North Side," Tyson said, while lining up two lines of cocaine on the coffee table in front of him.

Tyson referred to the gangsters in the Mahon Warlords as Guppies, that is, small fish in the big pond. In turn the Warlords referred to the I-P gangsters as Slobs because most of the membership dressed like slobs and looked like they had been dragged through a hedge backwards. This name calling was childish and something from a grade school playground. Nevertheless, in Cork City's gang land, this name calling was about total disrespect and often ended with serious consequences.

Tyson and Darryl were discussing the raid by the M-W on the I-P crack shack in Mayfield where Tommy Herschel was shot. "Who the fuck do they think they are?" Darryl asked, as his leader leaned forward and sniffed up the line of cocaine with a rolled up 100 euro note.

"The news said that fella didn't die," Tyson replied. His eyes were now watering and his voice was at a higher pitch than usual, as he shot up straight after his snort. "I'm going to make sure they get the message about what will happen if they cross the river again."

"What do you have in mind?" Darryl leaned forward to snort the remainder of his line of cocaine.

Tyson waited until his friend had snorted the line and the initial buzz had settled. "Get those two young fellas to come here around midnight. You know... Olly Sullivan and the skinny African, what's his name?"

"I don't know what his fucking name is, I can't pronounce it. Everyone just calls him Burnt Toast or B.T." Darryl's eyes were bright red and full of tears and some snot was running from his nose down to his chin.

"Go and pick up two straps. Be back here before midnight," Tyson ordered, dismissing his colleague.

When Darryl Lyons returned, he was carrying two semi-automatic pistols, an old Colt, Model 1911 .45 caliber and a Tokarev, in a black backpack. "What are we going to do with these?" he asked Tyson as he took the guns out and placed them on the coffee table.

"We're doing sweet fuck all with them. That's what we got child soldiers for," Tyson sneered.

Chapter 7

Seconds later, two fifteen-year-old kids knocked on Tyson's back door. Tyson opened the door and waved Olly Sullivan and Herbie Okereke, also known as Burnt Toast, into his living room. Both boys had short tight haircuts and wore red tracksuit pants along with red and white running shoes.

"How are ya?" Olly said to Tyson and Darryl.

"I got a job for ye," Tyson replied, looking down at the guns on the coffee table and waving his open hand towards them.

The kids' eyes opened wide with excitement as they stared at the guns.

"Are ye up for a serious mission?" Tyson asked.

"Yeah man, we're good for whatever you need," B.T. answered in his thick East African accent.

Darryl Lyons picked the two handguns off the table by their barrels. He handed the Colt .45 to Olly and the Tokarev to B.T. "Don't lose them and for fuck sakes, whatever you do, don't shoot yourselves," Darryl sniggered. "Do you know how to use them? All you have to do is point them and pull the trigger. Whatever you point at will die," he added to his version of a firearms safety lecture.

"Listen up now lads," Tyson said, looking seriously at the two kids. "You're going to go down to one of Bertie Flynn's crack shacks in one of the lanes between Dominick Street and John Redmond Street. One of the Guppy's Dial a Dealer will pull up on Dominick Street thinking he has a delivery there. I want you two to waste him. Can ye do that?" Tyson stared into the eyes of the two fifteen-year-old kids.

"Fuckin' eh! You bet we can do that, can't we B.T.?" Olly was bursting with excitement. B.T. grinned and nodded.

"Be down at Bertie's crack shack in twenty minutes and just sit there and wait. Don't fuck this up now!" Darryl warned, wagging his index finger at the boys. "I'll text you when to go to Dominick Street and when it's time, I'll text one word, 'NOW'. Then you go and waste that fucker. What's the word that I'll text?" Darryl asked, like a teacher giving a lesson.

"NOW," both boys answered while they brimmed with excitement and stroked their pistols.

"When it's done, run off in different directions and Darryl will get the straps off ye later on. Don't get caught!" Tyson gave the boys their final instructions, and both boys shook their heads, about getting caught. "If ye do get caught, remember you're both young offenders so all you'll get is a slap on the wrist," Tyson said with a laugh and the kids and Darryl laughed with him.

The two young assassins left Tyson's house, mounted their BMX bikes and took off towards Bakers Road, heading south towards Dominick Street. No doubt about it, they were child soldiers. It wasn't long before they arrived at the crack shack in one of six narrow lanes between Dominick Street and John Redmond Street. The lane was too narrow for a vehicle to drive down but the boys had no problem riding their BMXs to the door. Bertie Flynn, who was in charge of the crack shack, looked at the boys when they walked in.

"What are ye doing here?" Bertie asked suspiciously.

"We're on a mission for Tyson," Olly replied, barely able to control his excitement.

"Tyson will text us when he needs us. We're to sit here and wait for the signal," B.T. added, desperately trying to sound important.

"Keep out of my fucking way," Bertie said, dismissing them both.

Around the same time, Tyson Rolland yelled up the stairs in his own house, "Jenny, come down here. I need ya to do something."

A gaunt looking girl came downstairs and walked into the kitchen. Jenny was Tyson's squeeze and was the mother of his son. Jenny spent her time between her parents' house in Parklands near Upper Fair Hill and Tyson's home. Jenny was a good mom. She would have done anything to get away from Tyson but she was too scared to make the break, especially now that they had a baby together.

"I want you to call one of the Guppy's Dial a Dealer and ask for four rocks to be delivered to Dominick Street. Ask him what he's driving and when he'll be there," Tyson said. Darryl handed Jenny a burner phone that he had already dialed the number on.

Jenny took the phone and a male answered, "Yeah?"

"Can you come across the river for four rocks?" Jenny asked, sounding very convincing.

"Where are you?" the male asked.

"Halfway down Dominick Street. It's only across the river. When will you be there?" Jenny asked.

"Ten minutes," the male answered and hung up.

Graham Hogan, a newer member of the Mahon Warlords, was selling crack cocaine from his mother's car when he got the call from the Independent Posse. Graham was alone in the car, which was unusual, because Dial a Dealer sellers generally travelled in pairs. He pulled a U-turn near the Capwell Bus Depot on Summerhill South and headed towards the river. Graham did not suspect this was a setup. He thought it would be really cool if he got a sale in the North Side.

Darryl texted the two assassins who were waiting in the crack shack. Both boys looked at their phone screens and saw "*Go and wait there*." "Yeah!" they both said together as they got up from the floor where they were sitting and ran out the door.

The boys ran the short distance down the lane to Dominick Street and pulled the pistols from their waistbands. The two kids were almost dancing with excitement as they hopped from foot to foot. A couple of minutes later, Graham Hogan pulled up in his mother's Civic hatchback. He stopped in the middle of the narrow street and honked the horn.

The two boys looked at him from the shadows. "That's him. I bet you that's him," Olly said and B.T. nodded as he regripped his pistol.

Graham hit redial on his cell phone and called the phone Jenny had used. "Where are ya?" Graham asked.

"I'll be there in a minute. What are ya driving?" Jenny asked.

"Blue Civic. Hurry up!" Graham replied impatiently.

Darryl Lyons took the phone from Jenny and texted "*Blue Civic NOW*" to the two kids.

Olly and B.T. looked at each other and without saying another word stepped out of the shadows. They ran towards the front of the blue Civic, one on either side of the car.

Olly fired first. A split second later B.T. fired. Olly fired again and then both boys kept firing until they were out of bullets.

Graham Hogan didn't have a chance. He was shot twice in the head and five times in the chest and shoulders. He slumped forward, head down over the steering wheel, with the seatbelt holding him up.

Olly and B.T. looked at each other. Their eyes were wide open and the adrenaline was pumping fast through their veins. "Let's scatter," Olly yelled and he ran south towards Mulgrave Road and down the steps to Devonshire Street.

B.T. ran back up the lane they had come down and ran inside the crack shack, still holding the pistol in his hand.

"What the fuck?" Bertie Flynn yelled when he saw the kid and the pistol.

"We did a mission," B.T. answered in his heavy African accent, as he trembled with excitement from head to toe. "Me and Olly killed a Guppy delivery man."

Someone had called 999 after the sound of gunshots rang through the neighborhood and the sirens were starting to flood into the area.

"Don't tell me that! I don't want to know," Bertie yelled as he quickly assessed the situation and decided on his next move to protect his crack shack. "Up to the attic!" Bertie pointed to the ceiling and ushered B.T. up the stairs. Bertie grabbed the gun from B.T. "Don't make a fucking sound until I come and get you." Bertie shut down the crack shack, sending everyone who was there out into the night. "The cops are on Dominick Street. Find another way home." Bertie slammed the door shut and hid the Tokarev in a secret compartment in a step on the staircase.

B.T. dragged himself through the attic hatch and crawled along the musty space until he found a hiding spot behind the chimney. He sat in the dark, shaking as he thought about the shooting.

Olly Sullivan ran down the steps off Mulgrave Road along Devonshire Street and went to cross Leitrim Street by the builder's yard. He was in the middle of Leitrim Street when a black SUV came up Carroll's Quay. The occupants of the car saw the handgun in Olly's right hand.

The driver slammed on the brakes and activated the blue and red strobe lights on the front of the vehicle. Both driver and passenger leaped from the vehicle. They were members of the Armed Support Unit. Dressed in their grey uniforms, both men drew their Glock pistols from their tactical holsters and challenged Olly.

Olly froze and stared directly into the headlights. For a split second he thought about pointing his empty pistol at the police but the streetwise fifteen-year-old knew how that would end. Olly dropped the pistol and lay down, face first on the road. Seconds later, he was in handcuffs and in the back of the SUV.

AT 4:00AM, THE CELL phone on John Cahill's nightstand lit up; half a second later it rang. Almost immediately John answered it, "Hang on a second," he said, his voice barely above a whisper. Jules turned over and groaned but did not wake. John staggered out of the bedroom into the kitchen. He pulled his housecoat around him and sat down with a pen and paper. He let out a long breath. "Go ahead boss."

"The duty-inspector just called me. There's been a shooting on Dominick Street. Some fella sitting in his car has been shot several times. He is well and truly dead," Superintendent Paddy Collins said, very much awake for the early hour.

"Who is he?" John asked.

"The car is registered to a Mary Hogan from Mahon. It's not reported stolen," the superintendent answered. "But all is not lost. I have some good news for you. An Armed Support Unit were attending to the call and they almost ran over a young fella running across the road holding a handgun."

"Where is he now?

"He's at headquarters, waiting for you."

"OK, I'll be in, in an hour or so." John yawned and scratched his stomach as he ended the call and fell into his usual routine for such a call - out. He switched on the electric kettle, put two teaspoons of instant coffee into a cup and headed to the shower. At 4:20AM, he was dressed and drinking his coffee. The two greyhounds looked at him from inside their wire crates. They were used to this routine and made no attempt to get up. John retrieved his pistol from its lockbox, loaded it and put it into the holster on his right hip. He grabbed his coat and headed for work.

The storm of the previous night had calmed and the rain had stopped. He drove the first four kilometers of the journey at a sedate pace, due to the winding road, but once he reached the town of Clonakilty, it was clear sailing on the N71 and at this time of the day the highway was all but deserted. When he reached the Wilton Roundabout in the city, he called his team in.

THE FIRST THING JOHN did upon arrival at Garda Headquarters on Anglesea Street was to locate the Armed Support Unit crew that happened upon the gunman. "Is he our shooter?" John asked the young Garda officer.

"More than likely. He ran in front of our car holding this in his hand. No more than 600 meters from the scene," the officer replied, holding up a clear plastic evidence bag with the Colt .45 semi-automatic pistol inside.

"Who is he?" John was frantically typing his notes on his computer.

"Oliver Sullivan, fifteen-years-old, Independent Posse hang around," the officer stated, looking at the inspector for a reaction.

"Fifteen! Are you kidding me? Fifteen?" John's astonishment showed.

"He asked for a lawyer. Duty counsel is sending someone down," the Garda replied.

"Good, maybe the fucker will grow up while he's waiting." John shook his head, disgusted by what he had learned.

When the rest of the team arrived, John assigned Mike Williams and Eddie Jenkins to interview Olly Sullivan. He then headed to the scene with the rest of the men.

John and Tim Warren pulled up at the perimeter of the scene and put on their paper shoe covers. They were met by Jen Martens, the forensic sergeant.

"This is a bit of a shit-show," Jen said, leading the two detectives towards a makeshift screen around the vehicle.

Graham Hogan, still slumped over the steering wheel, looked even more eerie as the early morning daylight began to seep through the night clouds.

"We'll be moving him to the morgue soon, if that's OK." John nodded in agreement. "He's been hit at least seven times. I'll know more after the autopsy. But look at this." Jen moved away in front of the vehicle. "Two shooters, one at each side. Fifteen rounds in total, so far."

"What do you mean so far?" Tim asked.

"We've located fifteen shell casings so far. Seven from a .45 caliber gun and eight are an unusual size, 7.62x25mm."

"What are they?" Tim looked puzzled.

"Russian," John said quietly. "I came across them in Northern Ireland a few years ago. Lots of those guns and ammo came out of East Germany and Czechoslovakia when the Iron Curtain fell." Both Tim and Jen Martens looked at him in disbelief.

While canvassing the area, Jeff Rafter knocked on the door of the crack shack in the lane that ran off Dominick Street. Up in the attic, B.T. heard the knock. He knew it was the police. He huddled down behind the chimney, hoping he would not be discovered.

Bertie Flynn sat in the kitchen at the back of the small house. He did not make a sound. He had no intention of answering the door.

After several more attempts to get someone to open the door, Jeff moved on and tried the house next door.

An old man, with a scrap of grey hair and a grey unshaved stubble, answered the door. He wore an old sweater with holes in the elbows and dirty brown pants. "What?" the man asked Jeff, as the spittle flew from his lips, because he had no teeth and wasn't wearing his dentures.

Jeff asked if he had seen or heard anything about the shooting during the night.

I didn't see or hear nothing," the man responded, as Jeff stood back, trying to avoid the shower of spit.

Jeff asked if he knew who lived next door, pointing to the crack shack.

"Sure, people come and go from that place at all hours of the day and night. Then sometimes, it's empty for days at a time. I don't know who they are. They don't bother me and I don't bother them." This time the man seemed to be in a hurry to get away from Jeff.

At Anglesea Street, Olly Sullivan told Mike and Eddy that he shot the 'Guppy,' but he wouldn't elaborate on why or who was with him. All they got from Olly after his admission was "No comment."

Jen Martens found a driver's license in Graham Hogan's pocket and John and Tim went to see his family. It was 11:00AM when they pulled up in front of the row house. John rang the doorbell and Mary Hogan answered, holding a mug of coffee in her right hand and a cigarette in her left.

John asked about the blue Civic.

"My son Graham has it. He should have been back hours ago. He better be back soon because I go to work at noon."

Once inside the home, John had the woman sit down and put her coffee cup aside. Mary Hogan fell off the chair and collapsed on the floor when John told her that her son was dead. She cried uncontrollably and hammered the carpeted floor with both hands. When she slightly composed herself, Tim asked her if there was anyone they could call to be with her. In between deep sobs, Mary suggested her next-door neighbour. Tim ran next door and quickly briefed the neighbour on the news Mary had received. The neighbour sat with the distraught woman and the detectives danced around most of the questions that the two women had. An hour later, John and Tim left the residence. All they had learned was that Graham was hanging around with a 'rough crowd' and some of them were in a gang called the Warlords or something like that.

"That never gets easy," John said to Tim as they drove back to the station on Anglesea Street. "Nobody ever expects to be told that their healthy young son has been brutally killed. It makes me feel so helpless when they go to pieces like that."

"You are anything but helpless. You're doing everything you can to find out who is behind this," Tim replied, trying to be supportive of his boss.

When they returned to the incident room, Sergeant Martens came over to update them on the forensic side of this latest homicide. "You stole my thunder, Inspector," the sergeant said, grinning as she scanned the room. "It is Russian ammunition and most likely fired by a semi-automatic Tokarev TT30. This model of gun has been around almost as long as the Colt .45, which is probably the pistol the other shooter used."

"What else can you tell me?" John asked.

"Not much, fifteen rounds fired. The victim was hit seven times. Anyone of them could have been a killing shot. From the trajectory lines that we have produced, I am certain that both gunmen hit the victim. I'll confirm that after the autopsy and we retrieve the slugs," Jennifer continued, searching her notes for anything else that could help the detectives. "We did find a baggie with four rocks of crack in the consul and a bag with sixteen other rocks inside the glove box."

"Any stray bullets hit any of the houses on Dominick Street?"

"Thankfully, no. We checked everything on both sides of the street and it looks like all fifteen rounds are accounted for. The eight that missed the victim are in the vehicle."

"Thank God for that. The last thing this town needs is some innocent granny or a kid getting shot by a stray round while they're sleeping in their beds." John said, thinking about the worst-case scenario. "Is there any point in going back in to talk with Olly Sullivan?" John asked Mike Williams.

"I don't think so boss. He told us almost right away that he was the shooter but completely shut down after that. If it were fifteen years ago, two swift smacks across the head and a kick up the arse and he would tell us all we want to know. He's a snivelling little fucker who is only a tough guy when he has a gun in his hand." Mike slammed his notebook down on his desk in frustration. "Eddie is almost finished the paperwork to lock him up."

"He's sitting in there with his solicitor like butter wouldn't melt in his mouth. And, because he's a youth, there's no point in going hard on him. We'll look bad at the end of the day," Eddie Jenkins added, equally frustrated, while finishing his report.

"Right! We are done for the night. Thank you all for coming in early. We'll get back at it tomorrow. It's not a total loss. We have one of the shooters. We'll take what we can get," John concluded, noting that his team of investigators were completely frustrated with the lack of headway in the last two homicides.

IT WAS 8:00PM WHEN John arrived home, sixteen hours after the initial call from Superintendent Collins. He was relieved that Jules had already walked the greyhounds and he didn't have to go out again.

"You're unusually quiet," Jules said while John ate his reheated supper.

"These gang murders are getting tougher and tougher to solve. I'm sure Anthony Woodsworth's death is somehow gang related. And today's one has all the hallmarks of a setup. I would bet the M-W Dial a Dealer was lured over the bridge and shot. Probably in retaliation to the raid on the crack shack in Mayfield a couple of nights ago," John replied, eating quickly as if he was worried that he would have to go back to work.

"It's like a gang war. What are you going to do about it?" Jules asked.

"I don't know. This new fella Tyson, with the I-P, he is way worse than Mikey Galvin. Mikey was only interested in easy money. Tyson likes the power. He's very dangerous. I think if we can take him out of the picture, things will calm down. I just don't know how we're going to do it but we must find a way to take out the leaders. The rest will crumble if we do that."

"He sounds really treacherous. You all better be careful." Jules worried about how this would play out.

It was midnight when John finally got to bed. His mind was racing and he tossed and turned for what felt like an eternity before he finally fell asleep. In the early hours of the morning, John woke with a gasp. His recurring nightmare had returned. The victims of all the killings that he had investigated lined up in his bedroom and down the hallway to speak to him. In the dream, John was standing at the foot of the bed and now there was a line up of the deceased, all through the house. They walked up to him one at a time, in single file. All the victims were in the state that they had been found in after they were killed. This night the outlandish procession was led by Graham Hogan, followed by Anthony Woodsworth. Graham Hogan slumped forward as he walked, with bullet holes in his head, face and chest. Anthony had a single large hole in his face, under his right eye. When the corpses reached John, they leaned into him and muttered something. No matter how hard he tried to listen, John could not grasp what they said. As soon as he woke up, he realized it was the usual bad dream. John had been having this nightmare since he started in Cork's Serious Crime Unit. He did not know what scared him more...the grotesque pageant of corpses or the fact that he did not know what they were saying to him.

JOHN YAWNED AS HE WENT to start the briefing the next morning in the incident room on Anglesea Street. In typical Irish fashion, John never told anyone about the nightmare, not even Jules. Although it disturbed him, he knew it wasn't real.

The detectives sat up and listened as John addressed them. "We have taken both these killings as far as we can right now. Hopefully, we get something back from forensics, DNA off the shell casings or something that we can work with. Anybody got any other ideas?"

"I touched base with the confidential informant that we used in the past with the Independent Posse, but he hasn't the same connection since we put Mikey G away," Jeff Rafter said, not really adding anything positive.

"Thanks for that, Jeff," Tim Warren replied sarcastically and drew a sharp look from the inspector.

"There's an I-P crack shack in one of those lanes between Dominick Street and John Redmond Street," Len Benoit announced, getting everyone's attention. "None of the residents will say which house it is, but I am pretty sure it's one of the ones Jeff canvassed yesterday and didn't get an answer from."

"Jeff, Len, keep going back to all the houses in the lanes, where no one was home, until you can figure out which one is the crack shack. Then maybe we can lean on someone," John stated, grasping at straws but trying at least to do something.

The day remained unproductive. It felt like the secrets surrounding the murder of Anthony Woodsworth and Graham Hogan were never going to be discovered.

IT WAS UNUSUAL BUT John was home from work by 5:00PM. When he entered the house, he instinctively knew something was wrong. Jules was sitting in the living room; it was obvious that she was upset and had been crying.

"What's wrong?" John asked as he walked in and sat next to her.

Jules held her cell phone in her hand. She looked at him as tears ran down her cheek. "Fred called. Janet's had a stroke!" Jules started to cry again.

Janet Nesbit and Jules were best friends. They met in the early 1990's when John was in the Intensive Care Unit at The Royal Victoria Hospital in Belfast, while John was recovering from the horrific injuries he received after crashing through a fence during a steeplechase horse race, and his mount fell on top of him. The injuries included: crushed vertebrae, a punctured lung, a fractured skull and a severe brain bleed. Janet's husband, Fred, then a member of the R.U.C., was also in the same intensive care unit with similar injuries, recovering from a bomb blast, while trying to clear a shopping mall when the explosion occurred prematurely.

Later, John and Fred shared a room on a ward and became close friends during their rehabilitation. It was Constable Fred Nesbit who encouraged John to join the Royal Ulster Constabulary in 1994 as his horse racing career was over.

When the Cahills moved to Northern Ireland, Janet helped Jules settle into the police community in Belfast. When John and Jules moved back to Cork, the Nesbit's were regular visitors to Inchydoney. This was earth- shattering news and Jules could not bear to think about losing her best friend.

"Oh my God, NO!" John felt helpless and devastated with this news. He knew nothing about strokes or the treatments that were available. Like most people, he thought the worst when he heard the word.

"She's gone in for emergency surgery. Fred is heartbroken. He doesn't know what's going to happen. I should go up to Belfast to help her after the surgery," Jules said as she wept for her friend.

"We'll both go. Next week! The surgery seems very quick. Is that usual?"

Chapter 8

"Fred was off for the day and they went out for lunch. Of course, Janet went out for a smoke and never came back in. Fred went outside to check on her. He found her sitting or rather slumped on a bench. She was almost unresponsive and Fred thought she had been attacked or something," Jules recounted, as John walked to the kitchen to make her a cup of tea. "I don't know if it's usual or not to have surgery so quickly but I suppose the doctors want to act fast."

"Was she sick? Did she have any symptoms? Are there any symptoms?" John asked. He felt so ignorant about this dreadful illness and felt awkward asking these questions, although his entire livelihood was about asking questions.

"No, she was fine, but you know Janet. She never complains. She has high blood pressure but that was under control. There were no other symptoms. It was a complete surprise. She felt completely fine at lunch!"

John considered his next question carefully; he didn't want to upset his wife more than she already was, but Janet was his friend too and he had to know. "So what does this mean? Can she survive this? Will surgery help?" Immediately, he tried to ease the harshness of his questions. "I'm sorry but I don't know anything about strokes. I know I had a brain injury but it's not the same." John felt helpless, and cruel asking these questions.

"I don't know. Fred called an ambulance and when the paramedics arrived, they knew immediately what was wrong. They took her to hospital. Treatment within the first four hours is critical.

They performed some type of procedure on her. Fred said he'd call back later. I don't know what I should do for her," Jules answered between deep sobs.

John put the tea in front of his wife, sat next to her and put his arm around her. She rested her head on his shoulder and wept. "Right now, all you can do is be at the other end of the phone line and listen. If they want you to go up and help her, then go. You're only part-time at the school now so it won't be a problem taking time off. If you want, I'll go with you." John tried to support Jules as best he could.

The mood in the Cahill household was somber for the rest of the evening. Even the evening walk on the beautiful beaches of Inchydoney was quiet.

"If Fred doesn't call back tonight, I'll phone him in the morning. I'll organize some time off and go to Belfast to help her with her recovery. I hope she'll want me there, "Jules said, still close to tears.

"Of course, she'll want you there. Who else is going to help her? Fred is as useless as me. But I'll go with you if you want me to.".

"No, you don't need to come," she replied, as she put her arm around her husband and patted Molly, the smaller greyhound, on the head with her other hand.

BACK AT GARDA HEADQUARTERS the following day, there was still no progress made in the two recent homicides. There was an air of shock in the entire police service that a fifteen-year-old boy had been arrested for murder. Once that story hit the media, it would become national news and that meant more pressure for the investigators.

Olly Sullivan was one of six kids. He lived with his mother in Knocknaheeney. Jeff Rafter and Len Benoit interviewed Olly's mother. She was a single parent and could not believe that her son would do such a thing. Olly was the oldest and the woman hadn't a clue what he did when he left the house. She had no idea he was in a gang and didn't know any of his friends. She could not get Olly to attend school regularly and hoped that he would find a job and finally grow up. Len Benoit thought he could sense the woman's relief when she realized that she didn't have to provide for Olly anymore. Maybe it was one less worry for her.

Pete Sandhu checked all the social media sites for Olly Sullivan; the kid didn't have his own profile on any one of them. His picture appeared on a few other sites but he was always in a group with other kids, showing off gang signs and looking the 'tough guy.' Pete thought it sad that he couldn't find Olly in any school or football team photos.

JOHN LEFT WORK EARLY. He wanted to get home to be with Jules when she next spoke to Fred. After supper, John took the greyhounds to the beach while Jules remained at home, waiting for the call.

The phone eventually rang. The news about Janet was slightly better and although Fred's voice quivered as he spoke, he held it together and explained her condition to Jules. Janet had suffered an ischemic stroke. A clot had stopped the blood flowing to her brain. The medical team at the hospital had saved her life. They gave her a series of intravenous injections that had to be administered within the first three hours. Janet had a larger clot than usual and the doctors couldn't dissolve it with the medicine delivered by injection. They had to perform a surgical procedure using a device attached to a catheter to remove the clot from the blocked blood vessel.

John returned with the dogs as Jules was ending her conversation with Fred. The dogs raced into the kitchen and lapped up water from their water dishes as if they had been denied water for days.

"She had surgery today? That's quick, isn't it?" John asked, thinking this is the worst-case scenario.

"This is actually a good thing," Jules said. "Fred sounds very optimistic. According to the surgeon, this was a straightforward surgery and if everything is as it appears in the M.R.I. and the C.T. scans, they can just remove the clot and she will be home in a couple of days."

"Are you going up there?".

"Yes, Fred was thrilled when I said I wanted to go up. He's hoping she'll be better in no time."

"So is that it? Just surgery? Will she need any rehab or physical therapy?" John couldn't help feeling stupid. Like most people, he only had heard the horror stories associated with a stroke.

"I don't know. It probably isn't as straightforward as that. You know what Fred is like. He's in a daze at the moment and didn't think to ask any questions like that."

"Do you want me to go with you? I can do whatever you want. I can drive, cook, clean and keep Fred occupied."

Jules smiled at the thought of him cooking and cleaning in someone else's house, let alone his own. "No, it's OK. Fred and I can take care of her. You stay here and take care of the dogs and your gang war." Jules smiled through her tears. "Maureen and Leo can pop over during the day and let the dogs out if you're going to be late. Remember to call them when you're delayed. Just drive me to the airport on Thursday."

Maureen and Leo were their neighbours in Inchydoney. Both were retired teachers and Jules had worked with Maureen for several years before retirement. They were a fantastic couple who had fully embraced their retired life after years of devotion to educating the country's kids.

The next day, Jules arranged to be away from work for a while and began packing. She didn't know how long she would be away but was determined to help Janet and Fred get through this horrendous hand that they had been dealt.

Chapter 9

Early on Wednesday evening, Darryl Lyons, the Independent Posse lieutenant, had to leave his comfort zone and cross the River Lee. He was only going to Hibernian Buildings, just across the river near Albert Quay and Victoria Road but still considered the South Side. This trip was not gang related; it was an errand for his girlfriend's mother.

Darryl called Bertie Flynn, "Hey, watcha doing? I need a ride to Jewtown. Can you pick me up?"

Hibernian Buildings is a neighbourhood of red- bricked terraced houses built over a hundred years ago. The area is known by most Cork people as Jewtown. It was settled in the late 1880's by Jewish people who were forced by the invading Russian army to leave their homes in Lithuania. These settlers flourished in this neighbourhood for generations and set up a thriving community including a synagogue. Now, in the twenty-first century, almost all the descendants of the original settlers had left the area.

"Eddie is doing deliveries in Farranree so he can slide by and pick you up in Manor View. Does that work?" Bertie asked.

"That's grand, call him up," Darryl ordered as if he was calling a taxi.

"I'm in my shack in the lane off Dominick Street. Eddie was supposed to collect me and bring me to my shack in Mayfield when he's finished his deliveries," Bertie said.

"We can pick you up on the way. I won't be long in Jewtown. I only have to do an errand for Tracy's mam. We can go to Mayfield on the way back."

Twenty minutes later, Eddie Flynn, in a red SEAT Tarraco, stopped outside Darryl Lyons' house in Manor View. Eddie honked the horn four times as he sat impatiently. Darryl left his house, carrying a black garbage bag that appeared to be full of old clothes. He opened the rear passenger door and threw the garbage bag onto the seat and sat next to Eddie.

"Go easy on the horn, will ya! All you're doing is drawing attention to us," Darryl scolded the large man behind the wheel.

Eddie looked down at the floor, like a child who had been reprimanded. "Are we picking up me brother?" he asked.

"Ya we are. Now hurry up," Darryl instructed his minion.

Eddie Flynn drove in silence through Knocknaheeney and Gurranbraher until he arrived on Dominick Street, stopping at almost the exact place where Graham Hogan had been shot a few days earlier. Darryl texted Bertie Flynn and a few minutes later, he walked out of a dark lane and hopped into the back of the SUV.

"Did you get rid of the lot?" Bertie asked his brother as soon as he got into the car.

"The phone was hopping. I only had twenty-five rocks. I could have got rid of double that. You should have given me more," Eddie replied, looking at his brother in the rear-view mirror.

"Cash," was all that Bertie said and held out his hand.

Eddie reached into the center consul, picked up a brown paper bag and handed it back to his brother. Bertie opened the bag, took out a wad of banknotes and stuffed them into his coat pocket. Although Eddie Flynn was the older brother, Bertie was the business man and tried to keep a tight leash on his sibling.

Eddie drove down Penrose Quay and across the Michael Collins Bridge. He then drove over the DeValera Bridge, spanning the south channel of the river. Eddie parked the SUV on Montenotte View and all three men got out. Darryl gave Eddie the black garbage bag to carry and they crossed the street and walked into Jewtown. Darryl checked the house numbers as they walked down the narrow street. He stopped and knocked on a white door with a frosted glass window in the center.

Seconds later, a tall thin man, wearing a black sleeveless vest and grubby jeans, answered the door. "Darryl, how are ya boy? Come on in. How'rya lads?" the man said looking at Bertie and Eddie.

The three gangsters walked into the small house. Eddie put the black garbage bag on the ground.

"There's the coats that Tracy was talking about," Darryl said as he kicked the bag on the floor.

The man opened a cupboard and produced half a bottle of Irish whiskey and four glasses. He poured a generous measure into each glass and asked if they wanted water or ice. All three took their drinks neat.

They sat around talking about nothing in particular and worked at polishing off the rest of the bottle until Darryl announced it was time to go. By now it was dark and the only light was from a dull street lamp. On the way back to the SUV, they walked through a gauntlet of six young men leaning against a parked car and a house. Eddie Flynn was walking along the narrow sidewalk in front of his brother and Darryl. Of course Eddie couldn't help himself.

"What are you fucking looking at?" Eddie growled, getting right in one of the men's faces.

"You, ya fat fuck'n slob!" the man and his pals all laughed.

Eddie grabbed the man by the throat and the fight was on. Two of the other men grabbed Eddie and started to punch him around the head. Bertie and Darryl stepped up to help Eddie and now the three gangbangers were giving way more than they got. The Flynn brothers were huge men and didn't flinch when they got a kick or a punch, but when they struck their opponents, their adversaries knew they had been hit. Darryl Lyons was tall, wiry and as tough as nails.

He didn't stop to think; he just punched and kicked anyone that he did not recognize as a Flynn.

The fight didn't last long and the six young men ran off towards Albert Road.

"What the fuck was that all about?" Darryl asked as he dusted himself off and straightened his jacket and shirt.

"They called us a bunch of slobs," Eddie lied.

"Are you sure about that, Eddie?" Bertie asked as he straightened himself. Bertie Flynn was a full member of the Independent Posse but, unlike many of the other full members, he was not a fan of violence. Bertie had a head for business and was one of the gang's most successful drug dealers. Having said that, Bertie was not against using violence when he needed to.

When the three men reached their SUV, the original group of six was standing at the top of Montenotte View and Albert Road, blocking the exit. The group of six had now grown to ten. A few started jeering the I-P trio and calling them 'Slobs.'

"We could just drive straight down Marian Terrace and avoid them," Bertie suggested as he opened the driver's door of the Tarraco.

"Or we could go up there and kick seven different types of shite out of them," Darryl sneered.

"Fuck ya!" Eddie's eyes lit up like a kid on Christmas morning.

Bertie Flynn let out a slow breath. He was smart enough to know that no matter how tough they thought they were, they were not going to win this one by fighting fairly. The odds were against them.

Darryl Lyons reached into his pocket and pulled out a red bandana. He tied it around his face, covering his nose and his mouth. All that could be seen were his eyes, a faint birthmark under his right eye and his short-cropped hair. "Eddie, you come with me. Bertie, drive up behind us and pick us up."

On seeing Darryl put on the bandana, Eddie Flynn did likewise. Bertie got in the car, started the engine and began a three-point turn in the street as the other two walked towards the jeering group. Bertie shook his head; he would have been happier taking the long way around.

Like a couple of gunfighters from the OK Corral, Darryl and Eddie walked up the middle of the street towards Albert Road. "Hang back Eddie. I got a surprise for them," Darryl said in a low voice.

"Huh?" Eddie answered.

Darryl reached behind his back and pulled out a Tokarev semi-automatic pistol. He then produced a sawed-off rifle from the inside pocket of his coat. The rifle, a Cooey Ace, .22 caliber single shot, was only 26 centimeters long; it had been sawed off at the stock and the barrel. This deadly weapon didn't even look like a gun. It had a short wooden stock, wrapped in black electrical tape and a barrel less than 5 centimeters long, attached to the action. Darryl passed the sawed-off rifle to Eddie.

When they were about five paces from the group, Darryl raised the pistol, pointed it towards the crowd and squeezed the trigger. There was a loud pop and the bullet shot from the barrel struck one of the opposing group in the right shoulder. Suddenly, the rest of the bunch knew that Darryl had fired a shot. Panic set in and all ten of them turned and scattered down Albert Road, including the injured man. Eddie decided to fire his weapon at the retreating men. The shot wasn't as loud and the tiny projectile tumbled through the air for several meters and crashed into the road, smashing into several fragments. Seconds later, Bertie pulled up in the Tarraco and Darryl and Eddie hopped in. Bertie didn't waste any time and took off at warp speed. He raced up Victoria Road and down Albert Quay. He sped across the two bridges spanning both channels of the river and disappeared back into the North Side.

The other group ran back into The Buildings where one of their number collapsed. Only then did most of the others realize that he had been shot. 999 was called and police and an ambulance showed up at the scene.

The injured young man, not one of the original six who started the fight with the I-P gangbangers, was transported to Cork University Hospital in unstable condition and was treated for his gunshot wound. The 7.625x25 caliber bullet had struck him on the right shoulder and hit the bone. The bullet then splintered into three smaller pieces of shrapnel and ricocheted inside his body, ripping through flesh, until one piece lodged in his right lung. The young man underwent emergency surgery. Luckily his life was saved.

When the C.I.D. detectives interviewed witnesses, none knew why the three gangsters were in the housing complex or who they were. The red SEAT Tarraco was described as everything from a brown pickup truck to a green four- door saloon. Another senseless gang crime growing colder by the minute.

Chapter 10

John drove Jules to Cork Airport. They had breakfast at the restaurant and said their goodbyes outside the security gates on the second floor. With tears in her eyes, Jules made her way through the maze of barriers. She worried about what may be waiting for her in Belfast. Her flight was due to depart at 9:30AM. She was still over an hour early but by the time she had gone through security, she was comfortably on time.

WHEN JOHN ARRIVED AT Garda Headquarters, the atmosphere in the entire place was buzzing. He made his way to his office in the incident room on the second floor where he learned about the previous evening's shooting at Hibernian Buildings. Thankfully, the victim hadn't died and the Serious Crime Unit did not have to take over the investigation.

Superintendent Paddy Collins walked into John's office, pulled back a chair and flopped down. The superintendent raised both hands to his face and rubbed it vigorously. "Jesus, Mary and Joseph!" Paddy said letting out a huge sigh. "This fucking town is gone to hell. It's as bad as Afghanistan. I suppose you heard about another shooting last night?" the superintendent queried in his strong Kerry accent.

"I just heard about it. I was late getting in. I had to drop Jules at the airport. She's flying up to Belfast. One of our friends is very sick and Jules went to help out."

"I'm sorry to hear that boy."

John nodded, acknowledging the superintendent's commiserations. "I suppose it's another gang shooting?" John asked, while scrolling through his latest emails on his computer screen.

"It sounds like it. I don't think the victim was in a gang but it looks like he and his pals got into it with some Posse fellas. The assistant commissioner has called an emergency meeting this afternoon. She wants to come up with a strategy to curtail the violence. The two latest murders are bound to come up. Is there anything I can say?"

John took a deep breath and let it out slowly as he thought of an answer. "I got nothing boss. There isn't a word on the street about either of them and you shouldn't be surprised at that. We were lucky we caught one kid for the Dominick Street killing. The Independent Posse are sending out a strong message to the other gangs and telling everyone that they're not to be fucked with. It's our own fault. For years, every high-ranking cop in the country has looked at street gangs with disdain." John sounded somewhat despondent.

"What do you mean?" Paddy asked.

"You don't take them seriously. I'm not saying you should show them respect but because they're not the big Dublin cartels, you write them off as just a bunch of thugs. They are organized, they are moving a lot of product and they are very, very dangerous." Right then, an idea struck him. "What kind of strategy are you thinking about?" John asked the superintendent.

"I don't know." Paddy Collins shook his head. "I suppose there will be all sorts of suggestions, everything from putting more cops in the school, blaming the parents and putting it down to a public order issue."

"Why don't you suggest that we reinvent the wheel? Flood the problem areas with cops and make it real difficult for the gangs to do business. Keep arresting the small timers and catch as many of the bigger fish as we can," John was suggesting a simpler solution.

"Sure, with the way bail and the courts are set up, they'll be out before the ink is dry on the paperwork," the superintendent replied, sounding negative.

"So what? Who cares if we keep arresting the same people over and over? Clog up the courts! They will eventually have to keep some of them in and then we fill up the jails! Sooner or later, Joe Soap on the street is going to figure out that it's not the police at fault but it's the system. Then they'll complain about the politicians and not the cops. And every time we arrest some low-level street dealer, we're seizing product. Even if the charge doesn't stick, the product is gone."

"That might work alright. I don't know how long we could keep it up for. We would have to strip resources from other areas. Let me think about that." Paddy Collins was pondering the idea.

AT NOON, JOHN DECIDED he would drive to Inchydoney and let the dogs out. He asked Tim Warren if he wanted to join him. They set out in an unmarked Nissan Rogue and turned right on the N71 at the Bishopstown Roundabout, known locally as "The Magic Roundabout," because there were so many lanes and traffic lights that it was extremely confusing for many drivers. John drove through Innishannon and Bandon before he arrived on the east side of Clonakilty. He then took the coast road to Inchydoney.

Tim had never been to Inchydoney before and was in awe as John drove across the causeway next to the ocean. The tide was out and the mud flats were exposed with deep channels running between them. "This is where you live?" Tim asked as he stared out at the vast ocean.

"Yeah, there's not much to see around here," John joked as he waved his hand, showing off the scenery. He drove up the hill and the steep driveway to his house. When the car stopped, Tim stepped out, raised his hand over his eyes to block the glare and contemplated the horizon in silence. "If you keep staring out to the west, the next land mass that you'll see is Newfoundland in Canada." John stepped out of the car. "Come on, I'll show you around and introduce you to the girls."

They walked around the side of the house into the back paddock. "They look like stables over there," Tim said as he surveyed the property.

"They are or at least they were. There hasn't been a horse or a pony in there for nearly seventeen years." John sounded somewhat nostalgic, remembering his old life which seemed so much simpler than life as a police officer.

Tim walked towards the stables as John unlocked the back door and went inside. He released the hounds from their crates. Seconds later, the door opened again and the two greyhounds came bounding out into the paddock and galloping towards Tim. Tim froze, not knowing what to expect, but the speeding dogs stopped centimeters from his feet and immediately started to lick him.

"Tim, meet the girls. The big red one is Lucy and the brindle is Molly. They wouldn't harm a fly so don't be a bit worried about them." Tim petted the dogs and scratched behind their ears. He was now officially a friend for life.

John invited Tim into the house and made coffee while the dogs remained in the paddock, sniffing and running about. Tim looked at some old photographs of the Cahill family on the walls and shelves; he was astounded when he saw a photo of John sitting on top of a racehorse as the horse jumped a solid steeplechase fence. "Is that you?"

"Yeah, that was September, 1991 at Listowel Races." John told Tim how he used to train and ride racehorses but his career ended after a fall at Down Royal in Northern Ireland. This was how he came to join the Royal Ulster Constabulary and later the Police Service of Northern Ireland. Tim listened in disbelief.

"I knew you were a cop with P.S.N.I. but I didn't know anything about the racehorses," Tim responded, standing at the front window and mesmerized by the view.

"Well now that you know where we are, you must come down here with the family during the summer. This is truly a beautiful place. Jules is away for a few days so if I get stuck at work, I might ask you to pop down and let the dogs out or feed them if our neighbours are away. Our next-door neighbours are excellent and are only too happy to help out with the dogs, but when bad weather rolls in, this place can be very inhospitable."

"No problem boss, anytime you want, just ask." After coffee, the dogs went back in their crates and John and Tim drove back to the city.

BEFORE THE END OF THE working day, Superintendent Collins returned to the incident room. He had just left the executive meeting. John and Tim met him in the hallway as he walked towards his office.

"How did it go sir?" John asked.

"Ah Jaysus, I went with your suggestion and of course they couldn't just go with the simple plan. They had to complicate it. I'll fill you in soon. I have a couple of calls to make first," Paddy Collins answered as he walked by, more flustered than usual.

A half hour later, when Superintendent Collins walked into John's office, he closed the door and sat down, looking quite serious. "Everyone is going to have to get involved in this. We are going to hammer down on the gangs and spot-check them every time they step out onto the street. We are going to do this all over the county. In every small town and village, each and every druggie and dealer are going to get the attention they deserve," the superintendent said.

"When you say everyone, does that really mean everyone? Are you going to pull people from personnel and other admin jobs?" John asked sceptically.

"We are going to go hard for a month. I am pulling them out of offices and the schools and anywhere else I can find people. Unless you have only one leg or one arm, you're going to be on the beat checking people, taking names and kicking their arse!" The superintendent slapped his folder on John's desk.

"That's great, when do you want to start?"

"There will be an order out in writing tomorrow for everyone and we will start on Monday. We'll be keeping records to make sure that everyone is pulling their weight. It would be easier to manage if we were keeping it only in the city but the entire county is going to be a nightmare." Paddy Collins let out a long breath.

"If everyone buys into this, it will work out. You know some of those small towns are full of drugs and some of them are on the pipeline for bringing drugs into the city. I'll make sure my guys buy into it and even if we get new business, we'll keep up the harassment on the side as well," John added as the superintendent stood up to leave.

"I have no concerns about you and your lot. It's some of the office dwellers that I'm worried about. Sure, some of them haven't been outside these four walls in years. And listen! It's not harassment. It's a spot-check!" Paddy Collins grinned as he walked out.

AT THE END OF THE WORK day, John was preparing to head home when his cell phone beeped. He looked at the text on the screen; it was Jules. She was at Fred and Janet Nesbit's home in Belfast and now that Janet was home from hospital, Jules was in full nursing mode. John said he would call her from the car.

As he drove out the Wilton Road, towards the N71, John called Jules. "You can never get home on time when I'm there," she teased, saying it loud enough for Janet to hear and smile at the comment.

John told her about the new scheme that the Garda were going to launch the next week, for a month, to try to stem the gang violence that was getting out of control in the city.

"Will it work?" Jules asked.

"If we hit them hard enough the first week, it should make a difference. Especially if we get some drugs and guns off the street. That should keep them underground for a while. There was another shooting last night. Not far from the headquarters, Jewtown," John said, as he drove under the old viaduct.

"Was anyone killed?"

"Some kid got very lucky. A small caliber bullet that didn't hit any vital organs. But I looked at the C.I.D. report and it was definitely gang related. How are Janet and Fred?" John asked changing the subject.

"Fred is fine. He's very worried but he's being strong for her. I feel so bad for Janet. She's very worried and scared. It's a lot more serious than I thought. Her mobility is affected and her speech isn't great," Jules whispered, as she had left the room and was now standing in the front hallway.

"Janet needs a lot of time to recover. Hopefully it all goes well. Are you able to help with the rehab?"

"I hope so. But we don't know what's in store yet."

When John hung up, he was driving through Ballinascarty, the birthplace of Henry Ford's father and grandfather. He looked at the old Ford Model T that was on permanent display in the center of the village. Within six minutes he arrived in Clonakilty. Not wanting to make dinner when he got home, he stopped at a fast-food take-out restaurant. After picking up some hard-core deep-fried cuisine, which he knew he shouldn't be eating, he drove another ten minutes along the coast road to Inchydoney. Once home, he let the dogs out and ate his comfort food. When the dogs were fed, he took them to the West Beach for a walk. He missed not having his wife with him and could not help feeling bad for his friends, Fred and Janet Nesbit, who must be going through hell after Janet's close brush with death.

THE FOLLOWING MORNING, John told his team about the month-long crackdown that was about to start. He expected them to be on the streets as much as possible and spot-checking everyone who looked like they may be associated to a gang.

"We should spend as much time as possible in Manor View. Who knows, maybe we'll get some new information on Anthony Wordsworth's murder," Mike Williams said.

"Good idea, Mike. We should spend all our time in Manor View, Knocknaheeney and Churchfield," Len Benoit agreed.

"That's great lads, but let's come up with a rota. We'll split up and some of us will go to Mayfield, Ballyvolane, Blackpool and The Glen and the rest can go up the hills to Manor View, Knocknaheeney, Farranree and Churchfield. We can switch it up if the locals are getting used to seeing us. Keep shaking the trees. You never know what will fall out. Mike is right. This is a great opportunity to gather some intelligence on the gangs," John suggested.

"When are we starting this?" Jeff Rafter asked.

"It's officially starting Monday but there's no time like the present. Let's start now. We'll show them that our gang is bigger than theirs," John said, bringing the briefing to an end.

During the next week, the Independent Posse and the Mahon Warlords were under pressure. Their crack shacks were either being raided by the police or officers would park outside them in plain view, forcing them to shut down. The street dealers were getting spot-checked and they were losing product and weapons hand over fist. Tyson Rolland was furious.

"What the fuck is going on?" Tyson yelled at Darryl Lyons.

"I don't know boy! All the junkies still want their shit from us and they're calling all the time but half the time we try and deliver, the cops are pinching us. We have more runners in Cork Jail than we do on the street," Darryl answered.

"Are there any shacks that are still open for business?" Tyson asked.

"Bertie Flynn has the one near Dominick Street and another one in the Flats near Glenamoy in Mayfield. But Bertie called me a while ago and said he is running out of product. Who do you want to reload him?"

"Give his brother Eddie an ounce of crack for each of the shacks," Tyson said, as he was deep in thought.

"An ounce? That won't last very long," Darryl replied, questioning his boss.

"If he loses one or two ounces, it won't be too bad. He can come back and get more and keep going back and forth." Tyson was trying to keep up with his supply and demand problems.

Darryl Lyons made his way to one of the stash houses in Manor View and picked up two ounces of crack cocaine. He then met up with Eddie Flynn and instructed him to deliver one package to his brother's shack near Dominick Street and the other to the shack in Mayfield. "Call me when you're done and I'll reload you to go again."

Eddie made both deliveries without being stopped by the police and he went back and picked up another two ounces. This also went off without a hitch. He met up with Darryl Lyons for the third reload and delivered the first ounce to the crack shack near Dominick Street and then headed off across the North Side to Mayfield. When he got as far as Dillons Cross, instead of continuing along the Old Youghal Road, Eddie took a detour and drove down into Glen Park.

Eddie Flynn opened the package, pulled out a glass pipe and put a rock of crack cocaine into the pipe. Eddie lit the pipe and inhaled the illicit smoke deep into his lungs. It happened almost instantly; the cocaine was absorbed into his blood stream and, within seconds, he felt the crazy strong buzz in his brain. One piece of crack led to another and yet another. Eddie looked at the package and knew there was no point in delivering it now.

Eddie Flynn lay low for the next three days and smoked the rest of the crack cocaine he had stolen from the gang. When he finally surfaced, he went to Tyson's house in Churchfield and told Darryl Lyons and Tyson that he got pinched by the cops and they seized the ounce of crack he was supposed to deliver to the shack in Mayfield.

Tyson took one look at Eddie and knew he had been on a three-day bender. Eddie looked rough. He had sunken eyes and his short greasy hair was standing on end. His clothes were filthy and he looked like he had lost ten kilos in weight.

But Tyson did not challenge Eddie. "Where did they hold you?" he asked.

"Mayfield Garda Station. They just questioned me a few times and let me go. They said they would summons me to court later on," Eddie answered, but he couldn't hold Tyson's gaze and looked down at his boots.

"That's OK boy," Tyson said, "I need you back here in two hours."

"No problem, I'll be back in two hours," Eddie said, happy at the thought that he had lied his way out of a big dilemma.

When Eddie left, Tyson turned to Darryl. "Get hold of two more full members but not his brother. He's going to be D-Boarded when he comes back."

Darryl picked up his phone and made the calls.

Eddie returned on time. He still looked like hell but he was feeling good about himself. Why wouldn't he? He thought he got away with stealing the crack cocaine. But when he walked into Tyson's house, he stopped dead in his tracks and took a deep breath.

Tyson spoke, "This is a disciplinary board hearing, Eddie. We are going to ask you some questions now so don't fucking lie to us. Got it?"

Eddie nodded and blinked several times.

"Now sit there!" Tyson pointed to a wooden chair in the middle of the dimly lit kitchen.

"I won't lie," Eddie said, knowing he had been caught and, if he lied now, it would be much worse for him.

"What happened to the ounce that you lost?" Tyson asked sharply.

Eddie took a deep breath and looked down at his feet like a beaten man. "I stole it, Tyson. I'm sorry. I know it was for me brother but I took it."

"What did you do with it?" Tyson yelled and the other three board members stared menacingly at Eddie.

"I smoked the whole lot me self. I didn't sell any of it or give it away. I just went on a bender for three days. I wasn't arrested, I swear, Tyson. I smoked it all me self," Eddie was pleading for forgiveness and understanding. "I couldn't help it. It was, like, calling out to me." Eddie tried a grin, attempting to lighten the mood. It didn't work.

"Wait out in the hall." Tyson pointed to the door behind Eddie.

Eddie went out into the hallway and stood near the closed door. The hall was dark. The only light was from a single bulb, high up on the ceiling of the stairs. Eddie could hear the other four talking and wondered what his fate would be.

"What do you want to do with him?" Darryl Lyons asked.

"Do you think he smoked the whole ounce himself?" one of the others asked.

"Take one look at him! Of course he went on a bender for three days. He's fucked! I suppose we need him around because everyone else is getting locked up. How about we give him a few digs and make him do a mission?" Tyson said, like the chairman of a panel of judges. "Come back in, Eddie!" he yelled.

"Eddie, you're a fuck up." Tyson pointed to the chair and Eddie sat, like a trained dog.

"I know I am. I'm sorry Tyson. I won't do it again. I swear to God."

"Ten punches to the face and then you have to do a mission for us." Tyson made his ruling as he looked at the others.

Eddie looked relieved. "Thanks Tyson, what's the mission?"

"I'll let you know in a few days. Take that chair out in the back yard, sit down and don't try and block us."

Eddie carried the chair through the kitchen and into the back yard. He sat on the chair and faced the others. Then he sat on his hands and closed his eyes tight. Tyson put on a pair of leather gloves, stood in front of Eddie and punched Eddie four times, as hard as he could, on the side of his head. He took off the gloves and handed them to Darryl. Darryl punched Eddie twice and then handed the gloves to one of the other men who did the same.

Eddie Flynn took the ten punches to the face. When the punishment beating was over, Eddie's eyes were swollen, his nose was bleeding and his lips were cut. He also had a couple of loose teeth. He went to stand up but was dizzy and staggered, holding onto the back of the chair.

"Are ya all right?" Tyson asked, not really caring if he was or not.

"I'm grand," Eddie said as he steadied himself and went to leave.

"I'll let you know about the mission in a few days. Go on, fuck off now." Tyson dismissed the thief.

Eddie gained some composure when he started to walk but still felt dizzy as he made his way to his brother's crack shack in the lane near Dominick Street.

When he walked into the shack, Bertie froze and stared at him. "What the fuck happened to you?"

"I'm sorry Bertie. I had to meet with Tyson and Darryl. I was D-Boarded. I stole that ounce of crack. I wasn't arrested."

"Ya fuckin' eejit, what am I going to do with you?" Bertie said, shaking his head.

Chapter 11

During the late afternoon after Janet had received her rehab schedule, Jules called her husband. "Fred went with her today for the first appointment. He says that everything went very well. But she's exhausted and although she won't say it, she's in terrible pain. By all accounts, she is on the road to recovery."

"Well, that's good news. What happens now?"

"I'll know more tonight when I speak with Janet. She's sleeping now. I have to keep her talking when she's up. Her speech isn't good and she's embarrassed, but I don't mind. The last thing we want is her withdrawing into herself. Her speech will improve."

"Is that part of the therapy as well?" John asked.

"Oh yes, she has to go for speech therapy and physical therapy and she has an occupational therapist assigned. In fairness, they're taking great care of her. Fred is worried about her memory loss but the occupational therapist isn't too concerned. She says it's early days."

"Hmm, the brain does have a way of fixing itself." John remembered his own brain injury many years earlier. "So she's not out of the woods yet?"

Jules didn't answer; she could not as she was too upset. John did not ask again.

IN HIS HOUSE IN CHURCHFIELD, Tyson Rolland had to make alternative arrangements to keep his illicit drug trade operating. "I heard there are cops all along the M8 Motorway on the road from Dublin. We need to get a shipment through," Tyson said to Darryl Lyons and his number one drug dealer, Bertie Flynn. "We don't want to run dry or the Guppies will take our customers."

"I heard the cops are clamping down on them too. Do you really want to risk five kilos coming in from Dublin?" Bertie asked, weighing up the risks and being the voice of reason, with a strong head for business.

"What do you mean?" Darryl asked.

"With all the heat on us at the moment, wouldn't it be safer to bring in smaller amounts more often? That way if the courier gets pinched, we're not losing so much," Bertie said.

"Good job you're not as thick as your brother," Tyson sneered. "That's not a bad idea. Who can you get to do a run to Dublin for a couple of kilos? And don't say your brother because he'd disappear for a month."

Bertie glared at Tyson. He didn't like the jabs that Tyson was throwing out about Eddie even though Eddie had earned his bad reputation. Nevertheless, this was not the time to speak out against Tyson. "Archie Cambridge will do it. I'll give him my car," Bertie said, keeping his hard stare on Tyson.

If Tyson felt there was tension, he certainly did not show it. "Tell Archie to go up to Dublin tomorrow and I'll set up a meet. Tell him to come back during rush hour. So he better be leaving Dublin around 3:00PM and be in heavy traffic the whole way back."

Bertie Flynn left Tyson's house and met up with his friend, Archie Cambridge. Archie was in his mid-twenties. He was tall and fit. Archie always dressed in black; today he wore a black bomber jacket over a black hoodie and black tracksuit pants. A black baseball cap covered his short brown hair. He had a red bandana in his pocket, sporting his gang's colours.

"Will you go to Dublin tomorrow morning and bring a package back for Tyson?" Bertie asked.

"No problem. Will I take the train or the bus?" Archie responded.

"No, they're watching the train station and the bus stops. There are fucking cops everywhere! Take the Tarraco."

"How much will I have?"

"I'd say no more than two bricks. Anyway, if you get caught with a small amount, you won't be locked up for long." Bertie grinned slyly.

Archie Cambridge didn't care about going to prison. He had been in and out of custody since he was fourteen years old. Prison was part of his life. Sometimes it was inconvenient but always inevitable.

"I might turn off at Mitchelstown on the way back and take the N73 through Mallow. It's a bit longer but it's off the main motorway." Archie, a street-smart criminal, thought about his route.

"That's a good idea." Bertie agreed with his friend, forgetting Tyson's instructions about staying in heavy traffic. He handed Archie a torn twenty-euro banknote and a semi-automatic pistol. "That's Darryl's gun. He wants it back when you get home."

The next afternoon Archie Cambridge pulled into a service station on the Naas Road on the outskirts of Dublin. It had rained but now there was a watery sun shining on the damp ground. He pulled up next to a white hatchback, got out, stepped around a puddle and walked to the driver side window of the car. "How's it going?" Archie said to the driver.

The driver didn't answer; he just blew a steady plume of smoke from his cigarette out the open window.

Archie handed the man half a twenty euro note. The driver looked at it, reached into his glove box and pulled out another half of a twenty euro note. The two halves were a match. The man got out of the car and opened the hood. He reached in behind the car battery and retrieved two small bricklike packages, wrapped in cellophane.

He handed the bricks to Archie, closed the hood, got back into the hatchback and drove off.

The entire transaction took less than two minutes. Archie stood there holding almost one hundred and fifty thousand euros' worth of cocaine. He smiled to himself as he lifted the cushion on the back seat of the Tarraco and placed the two packages there. Archie headed south for Cork.

Traffic was steady and Archie didn't want to break any traffic laws. It took him two and a half hours to reach Mitchelstown. He took a left turn onto the N73 instead of continuing on the M8, the more direct route to Cork City.

Traffic was a little lighter and Archie had picked up the pace a bit. The roads were dry and the sun was shining. He was feeling very comfortable until he noticed a Garda patrol car in his rear-view mirror, just outside the small town of Kildorrery. Like any guilty person, Archie slowed down considerably and drew unnecessary attention to himself. The uniformed officers saw this and immediately ran a check on the license plate of the red Tarraco.

Archie was nervous and he gripped the steering wheel tightly. He kept checking his mirrors and the cop car was still there.

The registered owner came back as Martina Fitzpatrick. Further checks showed that Martina was the girlfriend of Bertie Flynn, a known Independent Posse gang member.

"Light him up!" the driver of the patrol car said to his partner, who immediately switched on the emergency lights and siren.

Archie Cambridge's heart missed a beat when he heard the siren. There was an agonizing knot in his stomach. He knew he was caught. For a second, he thought about making a run for it but knew there was nowhere to go out here in the country. He would be boxed in, in no time. He turned on his turn signal and pulled over at the side of the road.

"Maybe they won't search the car." Archie thought to himself as he waited for the cops to approach him.

Archie gripped the steering wheel as a cold sweat broke out on his forehead. He saw the tall lean Garda officer, in the bright yellow hi-vis jacket, walk towards his car. The Garda tapped on the driver's side window and Archie hit the power button to open it.

"Driver's license and insurance please," the officer said, staring at Archie.

He pulled out his wallet and handed the officer his driver's license.

"And the insurance certificate?"

"I don't have it but I know the car is insured," Archie replied, his voice crackling with worry. He unconsciously looked at the glove box. He did not want to open it. He knew Darryl Lyons' handgun that he had brought for protection was in there.

"Shut the engine off and step out of the car," the Garda ordered. By now the second Garda, the driver of the car, had also approached the vehicle. For a split-second Archie thought again about taking off. But he knew he would be caught so he obeyed the officer's command. "Who owns the car?" the officer asked.

"Me friend's oul doll, Martina is her name," Archie muttered. For the life of him, he could not remember Martina's last name.

"And who is your friend?"

Archie let out a long breath and sighed, "Bertie Flynn."

"Take a seat in the back of our car, Mr. Cambridge. I'm going to look inside your car. Is that OK with you?" the Garda said, standing about half a meter from Archie's face.

"Do you have a warrant?"

"Do I need one? I can get one easily," the officer answered, as the other officer took hold of Archie's arm and led him towards the police car.

"Go on so." Archie sounded defeated.

Once Archie was secured in the back of the police car, the officer opened the glove box and immediately found the semi-automatic handgun. "GUN!" he yelled out. His partner immediately ran towards Archie's car. The officer pointed into the glove box and at the black pistol.

The Garda officer reached for his radio and pressed the button on the side. "North Cork Zero-Eight."

"N-C Zero-Eight, go ahead," the calm and reassuring voice of the police dispatcher replied.

"We require a tow truck at our traffic stop. We have located a handgun inside a vehicle. We will need it towed to Mallow Garda Station where we will continue the search. Copy?"

"Copy that! Do you require any more units at your location?" the dispatcher asked.

"That's negative. We have one male in custody, nobody outstanding. We will follow the tow truck to Mallow," the Garda replied, elated after their unexpected seizure.

In less than an hour, the red SEAT Tarraco was towed into a compound at the rear of Mallow Garda Station and Archie Cambridge was placed in an interview room.

The uniform officers briefed the C.I.D. detectives on their traffic stop outside Kildorrery and told them where the pistol was. The detective sergeant in charge obtained a search warrant to search the rest of the car and it didn't take long to find the two one-kilo bricks of cocaine in the trunk.

The handgun was photographed and placed in the Garda stores where it would be sent to the National Laboratory for testing.

"That's a strange looking gun you had there, Archie," the detective sergeant said, sitting across the table from Archie and tapping a photograph of the gun.

"No comment!" Archie responded, staring at a spot on the wall.

"A Tokarev! I had to look it up on the internet. That's from Eastern Europe. How did you end up with it?"

"No comment."

When questioned about the cocaine, Archie gave the same "No comment" answer. Archie knew how to play this game; he wasn't going to say a word. He would leave all the talking up to his lawyer in court. Archie knew what was in store for him. Because of his past record, Archie was denied bail and remanded to Limerick Prison until trial.

THAT EVENING JULES called home. "Janet fell at home this afternoon." It was all too much for her and Jules started to cry again. "She has a walking frame but she refuses to use it. She was walking around the dining room, hanging on to the table and down she went!"

"Were you there?" John asked, trying not to sound accusing.

"I was in the kitchen when I heard the thump! She's OK. We laughed about it afterwards and then we cried. Janet told me that she's getting terrible headaches and when she does fall asleep, she wakes with blinding lights flashing. The doctors said that's normal and it's the brain healing. She won't have to have any more surgery," Jules said. The sadness in her voice was consuming.

"That sounds good, doesn't it? That they don't have to do any more surgery?" John was unsure of the facts and almost in tears as well.

"I suppose so. Right now, she's finding the rehab difficult and exhausting. They're making her do more every session and it's very hard work. Either Fred or I go with her for her clinic appointments and I help her with the in-home sessions."

"How's that going?"

"Good! She's cranky as hell but some of that is because she has had to quit smoking. Like she needs that on top of everything else."

"It's better than the alternative," John remarked, trying to be positive for his wife. "Quitting smoking can only be a good thing in the long run."

Jules told John that she would stay in Belfast for at least another couple of weeks and maybe longer if Janet needed her.

"Maybe Janet and Fred can come here for a change of scenery, when she doesn't have to go to the clinic for rehab and if she feels up to it," John suggested.

"I'll mention that. She might be glad of a distraction. How's work? Any new business?" Jules asked, changing the subject briefly.

John told his wife that the crackdown on the gangs seemed to be paying off. The police had seized a lot of drugs and weapons and the street level violence appeared to have calmed down.

Chapter 12

Tyson Rolland was furious when he heard that Archie Cambridge had been arrested. "He lost a strap and a couple of 'keys.' Why didn't he stick to the main road like he was supposed to? He wouldn't have stood out in the rush hour traffic!" Tyson punched the wall and kicked a chair in his kitchen while he ranted on to Bertie Flynn. "I don't know. I suppose he thought he was being clever," Bertie said, shrugging his shoulders. He was not about to tell Tyson that he encouraged Archie to take the detour.

Tyson felt he was losing his grip on the gang. The others were looking to him for direction during this crisis that had brought the police to his door. He had no answers. On top of that, his girlfriend, Jenny O'Callaghan, had taken their son and moved back to her parents' house in Parklands in Upper Fair Hill. Jenny was fuming; Tyson had used her to entice the Guppy Dial a Dealer and make the phone call that lured him to his death on Dominick Street. Jenny was scared that she would be charged as an accessory for facilitating the murder.

"Get someone else to pick up another 'key' in Dublin. This time make sure they come down the M8 during rush hour. Otherwise, I will fucking kill them myself," Tyson raged, as spit flew from his lips. "Where's your half-wit brother? Is he still around?"

"Yeah. I have a tight rein on him," Bertie said. He hoped that Tyson wouldn't suggest sending Eddie to Dublin to pick up a kilo of cocaine.

"Tell him to come by tomorrow. I have a job for him," Tyson ordered and turned and walked out of his own kitchen.

Bertie looked at Darryl Lyons. He didn't know if the meeting was over and he was supposed to leave. Darryl just shrugged his shoulders. Bertie stood up and left.

When Eddie Flynn showed up at Tyson's the next day, the swelling on his face had reduced considerably. He still had a proper shiner on his left eye. The eye itself was bloodshot and the skin surrounding it went from light orange to dark purple. It looked painful.

"Bertie said you have a job for me?" Eddie said to Tyson when he opened the front door.

Eddie Flynn was really starting to annoy Tyson. In fact, Tyson couldn't stand the sight of him. He opened the door wide, turned and walked down the dim hall into the kitchen. Eddie followed. For some reason, the room looked more bleak than usual. As always, Darryl Lyons was there. Tyson stood up on a chair and retrieved a sawed-off shotgun from the top of one of the kitchen cupboards. Eddie Flynn just about shit his pants. He thought he was about to be executed.

Tyson saw the look of terror on Eddie's face. The cruel bastard loved it. For a few seconds, which felt like an hour to Eddie, Tyson said nothing. He just stared at Eddie while holding the gun by the short stock. Then he stepped off the chair and spoke. "Time for your mission, Eddie." Tyson smirked as Eddie Flynn let out a sigh of relief.

"Here's the address." Darryl Lyons handed Eddie a piece of paper. "You can't miss it. It's one of those narrow streets between Fairfield Avenue and Popham's Road. The third house in on the north side of the street. Your target is Liam Mahony. He's a big fat fuck with foxy red hair and a beard. He's always sitting on the step."

"What do you want me to do?" Eddie asked.

"Shoot the fucker! What do ya fuckin think?" Tyson said, firing Eddie a dirty look. "He's been warned. He's selling crack out the front door and he was told he had to pay a tax. He needs to learn the hard way." Tyson was still holding the shotgun. "Do you have a problem with that?"

"No, no problem," Eddie answered and Tyson handed him the gun.

Eddie was driving another one of his brother's vehicles; this time it was a white Ford Fiesta, also registered to Martina Fitzpatrick. Eddie had no issues finding the address. He knew the North Side of Cork City better than any cab driver because he was a regular Dial a Dealer for his brother's business. Eddie drove down Fairfield Avenue and turned right onto the narrow street. He looked into the front yards and up the steps leading to the front doors of the first few houses and, sure enough, he saw his target. Eddie drove twice around the block to make sure he had the right place. He passed the house again and parked.

Eddie pulled up his hoody and picked up the sawed-off shotgun from the car floor. He checked that the safety button was off and walked towards the target address, holding the shotgun behind his leg. The large red-headed man was sitting on the step at the front door. He looked up when Eddie walked up the steps from the street.

"Hey Liam!" Eddie called out.

"How're ya?" Liam Mahony replied, thinking he had a walk-up customer.

Eddie raised the shotgun, turned his head away and pulled the trigger. 'BOOM!' a round went off. As Eddie raised the shotgun, Liam Mahony raised his left hand with his palm up. The shot went wide and to the right but some of the blast caught Liam Mahony's left hand, blowing away three of his fingers. Mahony let out a loud yell.

Eddie slid the action forward, ejecting the spent shell casing and placing another live shell in the receiver. Eddie fired the second round as he turned and took a step. This shot also went wide and blasted the wall of Liam Mahony's house. A few pellets broke a downstairs window pane. Eddie ran back to his car, threw the gun on the floor behind the passenger seat and drove off, squealing his tires.

Liam Mahony managed to make it into his house; his son called 999 and emergency services were dispatched. Mahony was taken to hospital by ambulance. He gave the police the best description he could of his attacker, stating he was a 'tall heavy-set male wearing a black hoody with the hood up.' It could have been anyone. Mahony also told the police that he saw a small white hatchback drive by two or three times just before the shooting.

Liam Mahony knew why he was shot. He knew the I-P had shot him but was not about to tell the police this.

"WE WERE DOING REALLY well until the shooting in the North Side yesterday," Paddy Collins said to John Cahill when they met for coffee the following day. "The violence was really slowing down."

"No doubt this was gang or drug related," John surmised.

"If it was, the victim is saying nothing. There were a few anonymous calls to Crimestoppers in the last month, complaining about him selling drugs out of the house while children were playing on the street, but nothing proven," the superintendent answered.

"This morning, I got DNA results back on the shell casing from the Woodsworth homicide," John said, looking into his coffee cup.

"Oh yeah?"

"Nothing. Not even a hint. The heat from the gases in that gun when it's fired usually gets rid of all traces of DNA." John was totally dejected. "I hate to say it but this one might go unsolved."

"I'm afraid you might be right."

JULES CALLED THAT EVENING. She was in higher spirits this time because Janet was feeling a bit better. The therapists were forcing her to work hard but it was paying off. Janet's speech was improving daily; she was now swearing like a trooper. Her mobility was getting better as she had moved up from the walking frame to a cane. Her short- term memory had been restored. Janet was becoming more and more independent.

THE STRESS WAS GROWING by the hour in the small house in Churchfield. Tyson Rolland was raging when he found out that Liam Mahony was still alive. He had a diabolical look in his eyes and his face was beet red. "Can't that fucking eejit do anything right!" he screamed and threw his beer can out the back door into the yard, while pacing around his kitchen. "At least he got the message, I suppose. Did dumb-ass shoot his fucking hand off?"

"I heard he lost three fingers," Darryl Lyons sniggered.

Still pacing back and forth, Tyson picked up his phone and pressed the speed dial for Jenny, his girlfriend. It went straight to voicemail again. "I'm sick and tired of that fucking bitch. She needs to answer her phone and get back here with the kid." Tyson didn't like being ignored. "I'll fucking fix her once and for all."

Darryl Lyons didn't ask; he didn't want to get mixed up in Tyson's domestic problems. Feeling awkward, he made his excuses and left a few minutes later.

After several more drinks and two lines of cocaine, Tyson called Jenny for the twentieth time. And again, after just one ring, the call went straight to voicemail. "Fucking cunt!" Tyson yelled and threw his phone across the kitchen. He stomped up the stairs to his bedroom. Staring into the dark room, he opened the closet. He picked up the shoes that were on the floor and threw them across the room. Then he lifted a false bottom on the closet floor, reached into a hidden compartment and retrieved a black pistol. He put the pistol in his waistband, ran down the stairs and headed into the back yard. Tyson pulled his hood up and mounted an innocuous looking old mountain bike that was lying in the grass and headed off towards Parklands.

He pedalled past the Fair Field soccer grounds on Upper Fair Hill. It was exactly 2:00AM when Tyson cycled past Jenny's parents' house in Parklands. The house was in complete darkness. Tyson stopped and glared at the two-storey semi-detached house. The garden was well kept and two newer model cars were parked in the driveway. "Fucking bitch," he muttered. He stared at the smaller window on the second level, knowing that Jenny and his child were sleeping in that room.

Tyson started to cycle again. He stayed on the same street and stopped outside another well-kept semi-detached house, with a low ornate pebble dashed wall in the front. There were two closed decorative wrought iron gates hanging from the wall, protecting the property. Jenny's best friend, Lisa Doyle, lived here. Tyson got off the bike and stood outside the low wall, facing the house. He pulled the black pistol out of his waistband, slid the slide back halfway and looked to see that he had a round in the chamber. He let the slide back down slowly and pointed the gun at the house. There were fifteen windowpanes in the front of the house, including the front door; Tyson fired fifteen rounds and shot out each one of them. When his magazine was empty, he looked at his handiwork and grinned. Tyson saw a light go on in a neighbour's house. He got back on his bike and disappeared into the darkness.

Luckily, nobody was hurt. Peter Doyle, Lisa's father, woke up when the shooting started and he heard the glass breaking at the front of his house. Peter didn't know what was happening and at first thought he was having a nightmare. He instantly realized that something was very wrong and called 999.

Peter Doyle worked as an electrician and had no connections to any criminals. He believed the same of the rest of his family. The C.I.D. detectives, assigned to investigate, were stumped as to a motive, and believed it may have been a case of mistaken identity. However, when Jenny heard about her friend's house getting shot up, she knew what happened; it was a message to her from Tyson. She knew what she had to do to keep her friends and family safe. Later that day, she packed up her baby and her belongings, getting ready to head back to Tyson's house in Churchfield. Jenny called Martina Fitzgerald, Bertie Flynn's girlfriend, and asked for help moving. Bertie called Tyson and asked for permission to help.

"Yeah, bring the fucking bitch back," Tyson said with a satisfied sneer. "I unloaded a clip into her pal's house. I knew she would get the message." Bertie Flynn was shocked but not surprised. It did alarm him, just how dangerous Tyson Rolland really was.

Martina and Bertie loaded up the white Ford Fiesta and helped Jenny and the baby move back to Tyson's place in Churchfield. "Why are you going back there if you don't feel safe?" Martina asked as they made the short drive.

"I don't know what Tyson will do next. I'm sure he shot up the Doyles' house last night, just to warn me. Whatever he does, I know he won't harm this fella," Jenny said, snuggling her baby close to her as Bertie watched in the rear-view mirror.

Chapter 13

"We're going to keep the pressure on the gangs for at least another week," John told his team at the morning briefing. "There have been two shootings in the last few days. Thankfully, nobody was killed in either of them so C.I.D. are working both of them."

"That Liam Mahony who got his fingers shot off is a player. I came across him when I was in the drug squad," Jeff Rafter said.

John always encouraged input from his team during briefings. He was a firm believer in sharing as much knowledge as possible. There was no place for secrets within the team in a unit like this; however, what they discussed in the incident room was only known to a handful of people.

"That's what we're hearing. Maybe he wasn't paying the I-P for the privilege of selling drugs on their turf," John answered.

"What about the shooting in Parklands? That sounds odd. I was talking to the guys in C.I.D. and they have no leads. "This looks like a very ordinary family," Mike Williams commented, looking perplexed.

"The superintendent says that the family is as clean as a whistle. The dad, Peter Doyle, is an electrical contractor and the mom works in a supermarket. They have two kids, both girls in their early twenties. One of them is at college in Limerick and the other is a student at the Technological Institute in Bishopstown. Maybe it was just some junkie going crazy smashing windows." John shrugged his shoulders and was very happy that this wasn't his investigation.

"Now get out there and fight crime and make some miserable gangbanger's life more miserable than it already is!"

The guys laughed and strapped on their Glocks and headed out. They had planned on meeting for breakfast before the day's work. John knew their plan; he didn't intend to tag along. They needed time to vent to each other away from the boss. If the venting was serious, he would hear about it soon enough.

Around lunchtime, Jeff Rafter and Len Benoit came into the office. "We were following a couple of fellas in a car and they sped up and dumped a baggie out the window. They thought we didn't see it. We picked it up and look what we got." Len held up a small sandwich bag with forty rocks of crack cocaine inside. "Someone is going to be pissed off." Len laughed as he sat at his desk to start the paperwork for the seizure.

"Do you know who they were?" John asked.

"Not a clue. They were long gone. We couldn't read the plate number on the car. That's why we were following it," Jeff Rafter replied.

"Oh well! We got their drugs. Somebody is probably going to get a beating for it." John smiled as he continued his own paperwork.

The next few days were more of the same. A major crackdown of street gangs and street-level drug dealers. The initiative was having the desired effect, although the courts were getting backed up and the remand side of Cork Prison was filling up.

JULES CALLED JOHN AND said she was returning home the following morning. "Janet is feeling much better. She's exhausted from the treatment, both the physical and speech therapy, but we manage to go for a short walk every day. She and Fred are going to come and stay with us for a few days next week."

"That's excellent, what time are you getting in tomorrow morning? I'll pick you up."

"I land at eleven. Will you be able to get out?"

"No problem, there's nothing much going on here. All we're doing is harassing the gang-bangers and making their life difficult. I might take the rest of the day off," John said, thinking Jules would probably like the company after being in Belfast helping her friend.

"That would be nice. You can help clean the place up before Janet and Fred come to visit."

"Or maybe I'll stay at work." John chuckled.

IT WAS AS IF HE JINXED things by saying he would take a day off. At 3:30AM, John's cell phone lit up on his night table. Seconds later the shrill ring woke him. Before the second ring, he grabbed the phone and looked at the call display, 'Superintendent Collins.'

"Hey boss, what's up?" John sat up in bed; he didn't have to leave the room as Jules wasn't sleeping next to him.

"New business, that's what's up," a sleepy sounding superintendent said.

"For fucks sakes," John muttered as he threw back the covers, put on his housecoat and walked to the kitchen. He picked up a pen and pad and sat at the kitchen table. "OK, what have we got?"

"Well, I don't really know for sure what we have. I just got off the phone with the duty inspector and we have new business. It's not a gang thing. It appears to be a family matter. A young girl, seventeen years old, staying with her auntie and uncle, was stabbed to death by her cousin," the superintendent said in his strong rural Kerry accent.

"Is he in custody?"

"Yes! He also slashed his father. It's bizarre," the superintendent added, stifling a yawn.

"Are there any witnesses?" the inspector asked as he made his way to the sink to fill the electric kettle.

"There were seven people in the house. I don't know who saw what but they're all on their way to headquarters, except for the man who was slashed. He's on his way to hospital."

"Where did this happen?" John asked, as he balanced the cell phone between his shoulder and his ear, while filling the kettle.

"In Wilton, one of the streets across from the hospital."

"That's a nice area and not the usual places we attend for this kind of thing. I'll stop by on my way in to work." John scribbled down the address. "I'll be in, in about an hour and a half. I have to look after the dogs. Jules is still out of town."

"No problem. I don't think there's any rush with this one. It looks like everything is under control and everyone involved is with us," Superintendent Collins replied, again yawning. "I might catch another hour or two of sleep before I go in."

"You may as well. See you in there," John said as he ended the call.

John took a few sips of the steaming hot coffee and let out a huge sigh. He walked over to the two large crates where the greyhounds were sleeping. They were used to his getting up in the middle of the night and going to work. They made no attempt to be let out of the crates. "Sorry girls, but Jules is still away. So she can't let you out in the morning. You gotta go now."

Lucy stood up, stepped out of her crate and stretched her long lean body; she shook herself, sending drool flying across the kitchen floor. Molly also stepped out of her crate and arched her back like a cat and yawned. Both dogs walked across the kitchen to the back door. John turned on the outside lights and let the dogs out in the back paddock. He stood at the door, drinking his coffee and watching them as they sniffed their way around the paddock, eventually relieving themselves. When he let them back in the house, the dogs made their way to the living room. Lucy, the big red girl, hopped up on the sofa and lay on her back, with her four legs pointing up towards the ceiling. Molly, the smaller brindle, had a stunned look on her face after being woken up in the middle of the night. She looked at Lucy on the sofa and lay on a rug in front of the television. John smiled at his two old retired athletes and made his way to the shower. He would put them back in their crates before he went to work and ask his neighbours, Maureen and Leo, to let them out around breakfast time.

FORTY-FIVE MINUTES later, John turned at the Wilton Roundabout and turned in at Wilton Court to a well-kept housing estate. He easily found the crime scene; it was the one with four police cars parked in front. He retrieved a pair of shoe covers, a medical mask and a pair of latex gloves from the trunk of his car and walked to the front door.

"Good morning, sir," the young Garda officer, who was standing guard at the front of the house, said.

"It's not that good," John replied, smiling at the young officer. "Have you been inside?"

"No sir, everyone was out when I got here and the sarge posted me here until I'm relieved."

At that, the sergeant walked around from the rear of the house. John reached out to shake his hand. "John Cahill, Serious Crime Unit."

"Ah! You're the fella from the R.U.C.," the sergeant said with a grin.

"Something like that." John smiled. Some people still had not figured out that the R.U.C. was disbanded and replaced by the Police Service of Northern Ireland. "Have you been inside?"

"I have. We cleared the house to make sure there were no other bodies or people hiding. 'Tis a nice house, well kept," the sergeant answered.

"Get masked and gloved up and put on a pair of shoe covers and give me a quick tour of the inside."

The sergeant walked to one of the police cars and put on his personal protective equipment. They walked in the front door. The sergeant stopped in the hallway and pointed into the sitting room, off to the left. "In there is the main scene. It's really bad." The sergeant made no effort to walk into the room.

John looked at him; he could see the reluctance in the sergeant's eyes. John knew that violent death was difficult to look at. He would never force his colleague to go into the room nor would he think any less of him for not wanting to do so. "Wait here. I'll take a quick look." John stepped into the sitting room. The other officer looked relieved.

John found the teenage girl behind the door, lying on a sofa, face up. Her eyes were open, staring blankly towards the ceiling. The cushions on the sofa and the floor were soaked in dark, almost black blood. Her nightdress had been ripped open by the knife. The girl had been eviscerated. The wound ran from her neck to below her navel. "You poor, poor child." John thought. He could feel the emotion rising inside him. He closed his eyes to get it under control. He took a deep breath, let it out slowly and said, "Why did this happen to you?"

John scanned the room. Nothing else seemed out of place. There were no signs of a struggle. Just the extreme violence that took place on the sofa. He backed out of the sitting room and looked at the sergeant.

"I've never seen anything like that," the sergeant said.

"You said this is the main scene. Is there another one?" John asked, without commenting on what he had just seen in the sitting room. He had to compartmentalize it in order to do his job.

"Through here to the kitchen." The sergeant pointed down the hall. The two officers walked through the house and John stopped at the open kitchen door. "This is where the suspect attacked and stabbed his father," the sergeant said. "Definite signs of a struggle here." John looked at the upturned chairs and the kitchen table pushed out of place. "There's a fair bit of blood. Where did he get stabbed?"

"He got slashed on the arm. He got a bad cut but he managed to hang on to the young fella until the uniforms got on scene. It was the boy's mam called 999," the sergeant replied. This time he had no problem looking at the scene.

"And the suspect? What has he got to say for himself?" John asked.

"Nothing at all! I saw him in the back of the car. I'd say he is out of his mind on drugs. He was just muttering away to himself. I told them to get him away, out of here, and down to headquarters," the sergeant answered.

"How old is he?"

"He just turned nineteen, according to his mother."

"OK sarge, thanks for the tour. Nobody else goes in or out of here until the forensic team takes control. I'll let them know we were in there." John headed back to his car and started to phone his team, asking them to come in early for another gruesome day.

When he arrived at headquarters, John made his way to the incident room. He switched on his computer and got down the basic details of the event. Once he had his investigative summary started, he called the uniform division on the third floor and asked the sergeant in charge to send down the first crews that attended the scene, so that he could interview them.

It was 5:00AM when the first crew sat in front of the inspector. He didn't know either of the officers and could not believe how young they looked. "These two look like a couple of kids. Either I'm getting old or they're getting younger." he thought. John began the interview by introducing himself to the officers; then he asked them their names, immediately putting them at ease.

Both officers had made excellent notes and related how they were let into the home by the female homeowner and found the suspect, standing in the kitchen holding a bloody knife, while his father was backed into a corner, using a chair to hold the young man back.

They yelled at the suspect several times, telling him to drop the knife. They were about to taser him when he turned, looked at them and dropped the knife.

"He looked stoned. He never said a word that made any sense. He just muttered and groaned, when we handcuffed him," the young Garda said.

His partner then spoke up. "I went into the front room then and found the other victim. I checked her for a pulse but I knew I wouldn't find one. He must have stabbed her while she slept."

John noticed how pale the officer who discovered the deceased was. She also had a quiver in her voice when she recalled the scene. Nevertheless, John was impressed by how professional these two young officers were, although he knew they would be affected in some way by what they had discovered. He thanked them and commended them for their professionalism, "Write up your reports and scan your notes before you retire from duty this morning."

"Yes sir," they both replied.

"Before you go, remember what you both dealt with this morning is not normal. Make sure you talk about it between yourselves. If it really bothers you, there is lots of help. There's nothing wrong with asking for it."

The officers thanked him as they left his office. John interviewed another crew and got the names of everyone who had been brought into the station and their relationship to the victim. Then he wrote the names on the white board in the incident room.

By 6:00AM he was ready to brief his team. "The deceased victim is seventeen-year-old Agatha McSweeney. Her uncle, Padraig McSweeney, is the surviving victim." John stood in front of his team as they jotted the information in their notebooks. "The suspect is William McSweeney, Padraig's son. Padraig is currently at Cork University Hospital and William is in custody here. We have four witnesses here also." John was interrupted by a frantic knock on the incident room door.

John answered the knock and found another fresh-faced Garda officer, "I'm sorry to interrupt sir, but the suspect is acting really strange!"

"What do you mean strange?" John tried not to sound annoyed with being interrupted.

"He's after ripping off his disposable clothing. He pissed on the floor and now he's sitting in a pool of piss and splashing it." Then they heard a high-pitched wail from the corridor. "That's probably him now, howling like a hound," the officer said in a Dublin accent.

"We'll finish this in a few minutes." John turned to his team who all heard the commotion and they followed their boss to the area where the interview rooms were situated.

John slid back the metal window cover in the center of the door. He could not see the suspect because he was sitting against the door. But John could hear him. Detective Pete Sandhu had gone to the video monitor room and called his boss.

John looked at the video monitor. "What the fuck!" he said to nobody in particular.

The young man, now completely naked, was sitting against the door in a pool of liquid. He was staring at the ceiling and howling.

He held his arms in front of him and every few seconds he would push the air and slap the palms of his hands on the wet floor.

"What the fuck is he on?" Mike Williams said and a few of the others laughed. John looked around the room and the laughing stopped.

"Get me another paper suit," John ordered and few seconds later Tim Warren produced a disposable suit. John walked out of the monitor room and back to the interview room where the suspect was. John unbolted the door and tried to push it open. He couldn't due to the weight of the young man on the other side. "Give me a hand here," he said as he stepped aside. Eddie Jenkins, Tim Warren and Mike Williams put their shoulders to the door and forced it open enough for John to step inside.

"William!" John called out in a loud stern voice. The suspect did not react and kept pushing the air with his outstretched hands. "William, look at me!" John spoke a little louder this time. William stopped and looked up at John. It was as if it he just realized there was someone else in the room. "Stand up, William!" John ordered. The young man stood up. He looked at John, but John felt as if the man couldn't see him. However, at least he was following direct orders.

"Sit down over there!" John said loudly, pointing to the plastic chair that was bolted to the floor. William obeyed the command. "Put this on," John ordered as he handed William the paper shirt. William took the shirt and held it in his hand. He looked at it as if he didn't know what to do with it. John took the shirt back, opened the clasp-buttons and helped William put his arms in the sleeves. Then he buttoned up the front of the shirt. John next put William's legs in the pants. "Pull them up now!" William stood and pulled up his pants.

John turned and looked out the door. There were about eight cops standing outside, ready to rush in, if William attacked the inspector. "Turn the video on in another room and put him in there. Get a caretaker to clean this mess up. Come with me, William." John guided William out of the chair, holding him by the arm and leading him to another room. "I want three of you to stay in there with him. If he starts up again, tell him to stop and call me," John informed three of the uniform officers. He went back to the incident room, followed by his team.

"What do you make of that?" Jeff Rafter asked.

"I don't know what to make of it. It's got to be drugs, doesn't it?" John took a deep breath and blew it out slowly, composing himself. "We have four witnesses here. William's mother, his brother and two sisters. Let's interview them, find out what they know about what happened earlier and what the fuck he's taking."

John assigned Mike Williams and Eddie Jenkins to go to the hospital to check on Padraig McSweeney and interview him if he was up to it. Jeff Rafter and Len Benoit were assigned to interview the siblings and John and Tim Warren interviewed William's mother.

When Mike and Eddie walked into the emergency department at Cork University Hospital, they found Padraig McSweeney lying on a stretcher in the busy hallway. There were three other people lying in stretcher beds in the packed hallway. Padraig had been treated by the trauma team who had stopped the bleeding and stabilized him. All colour had drained from his face; he looked bewildered and terrified.

Mike Williams spoke in a hushed voice. "Hello Padraig, we are detectives from the Serious Crime Unit. Can we ask you a few questions?"

Padraig looked at the detective and nodded. "Ask away."

Mike looked around. The other people lying in stretchers were sleeping. Mike could see that Padraig was both in shock and heavily medicated. He would try to keep the questions short and simple. "Who did this to you?"

Padraig's eyes immediately filled with tears. He tried to blink them away but couldn't. He turned his head away for a few seconds and then turned back to the two detectives. "My own son William did this. Oh, sweet Jesus, what has got into him? I think he is after killing Aggie." Padraig gulped back a breath and started to cry. He just could not believe what he had said.

"Who's Aggie?" Mike asked, keeping his voice calm and low.

"Aggie or Agatha is my niece. She stays with us when her dad is away."

Mike didn't need to know any more at this point. The other investigators would get all Aggie's background from her family members. He wanted to know more about the suspect. "Why would William do this?"

"Jaysus boy, I don't know. Sure, he was always a great young fella. He is in his first year in U.C.C. He wants to be a teacher." Padraig was genuinely puzzled.

"Is he into drugs or does he drink much?" Mike was pushing gently for more answers.

"God no! But he started acting strange a few weeks ago. We all thought he might be trying some weed. He denied it when I asked him. But he would anyway, wouldn't he?" Padraig lay back and wiped his eyes with his uninjured hand.

"What do you mean acting strange?"

Padraig thought about the question for a moment. He was doing very well for a man who had been traumatised and heavily medicated. "We would see him staring at something, like he was seeing things. And he'd be talking to himself. To be honest, we thought it was kinda funny." Padraig started to tear up again.

"Did you see him stab Aggie?" Eddie Jenkins asked.

Padraig closed his eyes and breathed heavily. "I heard her screaming and I ran into the room. William was standing over her with the knife in his hand. I saw all the blood on the floor," Padraig replied, keeping his eyes shut the entire time.

"What happened then?"

"He turned around and looked at me. Then he lunged at me. I ran down the hall into the kitchen and I picked up a chair to hold him back." Padraig stopped and took a few more deep breaths. He opened his eyes and continued. "He kept looking at the top of my head. I called out to him but I couldn't get him to look at me. He was determined to get at my head. Sheila called 999, and in fairness, the Guards were there very quickly. I don't remember much after that." Padraig looked exhausted after revealing his ordeal.

At that moment a nurse came by to check on Padraig. "He really should try to get some rest," she said to the detectives. Eddie Jenkins agreed and tapped Mike on the arm as he jerked his head towards the exit.

"We'll come back and talk to you again when you're a bit stronger," Mike said.

"Is William OK?" Padraig asked.

"He's not injured," Eddie said, smiling at the wounded man.

"I think he's doing more than smoking weed," Eddie announced as they drove back to headquarters.

John's phone dinged as he and Tim walked towards the interview room where Padraig's wife waited. He checked the text message. It was Jules. Her flight was delayed. "Thank God, I had forgotten all about that," he said aloud. Then he looked at Tim. "Jules is coming back from Belfast today. Her flight is delayed. She'll text me when they're taking off. I hate to say it but I hope it's a couple of hours."

Sheila McSweeney told a story similar to her husbands about their son's recent behavior. William had been a really good kid and had never given them an ounce of trouble while growing up. He was acting a 'bit odd' for the last few weeks but she thought it might just be pressure from his course at university. Sheila also told the detectives that Aggie, her husband's niece, stayed with them when her dad went to work in Europe. Aggie's mother had died a couple of years before. Aggie suffered from severe asthma so she stayed with the McSweeneys when she needed to. Aggie had just recovered from an asthma attack the day before William attacked her. Sheila said she didn't know why William did what he did. He always got on well with Aggie and his dad.

When Mike and Eddie returned from the hospital and all the family members had been interviewed, the Serious Crime team shared what they had learned in another briefing. John asked Jeff Rafter and Len Benoit to arrange to take Sheila and her other children to a relative's home while he and Tim would attempt to interview William McSweeney.

William sat in silence in the interview room with three uniformed Garda officers. He just stared at a spot on the wall. John and Tim entered the room. "Any more problems?" John asked.

"No sir, not a sound out of him since he came in here," one of the officers replied.

"Thanks lads, we'll talk with him now. Maybe you can wait outside in case we need you again," Tim said, holding the door open.

John pulled a chair up and sat directly in front of William. He was less than a foot from his face. John told William that he may be charged with the murder of Agatha and the attempted murder of his father. William said nothing. John told him his rights and asked him if he wanted to call a lawyer. Again, William said nothing.

"William, can you hear me!" John said loudly, looking directly at him.

"Yeah," William nodded as he answered in a low dull voice.

"William! Why did you hurt Aggie?" John asked sternly.

William looked at John for the first time. He angled his head slightly. William was thinking. "ZARO!" William shouted.

John looked at Tim. Tim shrugged his shoulders. "What's zaro?" John asked. "Tell me William, what does zaro mean?" William didn't answer. He stared away at the wall.

John glanced at Tim, looking for inspiration. Tim appeared extremely uncomfortable. John looked back at William. "William, why did you attack your dad?"

William responded again to the question. He definitely understood what was being asked. "No, not Dad. Zaro was on him," William answered in a low, primeval voice. Immediately William turned away from the detectives towards the wall. He started pushing the air with the palms of his hands by extending his arms. "Go away! Go away Zaro!" William chanted.

John instantly shivered. For the first time in his career, he felt frightened in the interview room. Tim and John looked at each other. Tim tried a weak smile. "Is Zaro here?" John asked.

William continued pushing the air for a few more seconds, stopped and turned back to the detectives. "Zaro is gone now."

John now believed that William was not on drugs but hallucinating for some other reason. "William! Was Zaro on Aggie?" William did not respond. John asked again, even louder this time, "WILLIAM, WAS ZARO ON AGGIE? TELL ME!"

William continued to stare at the top of the table. He was breathing heavily. Then he answered with one word, "Inside."

John asked William, three more times, if Zaro was inside Aggie but William had shut down and didn't respond. When Tim and John left the interview room, John asked the three uniform officers to sit with William but not to engage with him.

Tim looked at his boss, "What the fuck was that all about?"

"I have no idea, but if that Zaro fella was in there, he was sitting right across from you." John smiled as he walked back to the incident room as a shiver now ran down Tim's spine.

Back at the incident room, John assigned Len Benoit to complete the paperwork to detain William McSweeney. He called a senior lawyer at Public Prosecutions and relayed the events of the incident. John told the lawyer that he didn't believe William was high on drugs but had suffered some kind of mental breakdown and was possibly in a state of psychosis. He was going to recommend that the Prison Service take William to hospital for a psychiatric evaluation. The lawyer agreed and instructed John to charge William with one count of murder and one count of attempted murder.

John walked out of his office and spoke to Len Benoit, "Put in large bold letters at the beginning and at the end of your report: 'THIS PRISONER IS TO BE TAKEN FOR A PSYCHIATRIC EVALUATION.'" He then went to the superintendent's office to tell him about the interview. As he sat down, Jules texted. She had boarded the plane in Belfast and should be in Cork in an hour.

"You don't think he was putting it on?" Paddy Collins asked.

"If he was, he should be in Hollywood. He scared the crap out of Tim and me. I don't know what happened to him but that kid is really, really ill.

Chapter 14

At 2:00PM, Jules walked down the steps of the twin-prop De Haviland Dash 8 and onto the tarmac at Cork Airport. She walked into the terminal and was waved past the passport control desk. When she walked out of the baggage area, she saw her husband waiting. They kissed and hugged. "You look tired," she said to him.

"It was a long night. I'll tell you about it later but you look great as always," John replied, hugging her again.

"Ya, right." Jules shrugged her shoulders.

On the drive back to Inchydoney, they spoke about Janet and Fred in Belfast. "Janet is doing well, considering what she's been through." She seemed to be determined to get through this once she put the initial surgery and the worst of the therapy behind her." Jules told her husband some of the details of Janet's surgery and how brave Janet was, going for the rehab treatment day after day.

"Will Janet and Fred come and stay with us for a while?" John asked.

"They hope to come down in a week or two for five or six days."

"I hope they do. Maybe I can take some time off and we can all relax." John realized that Jules was shaken by her recent stay in Belfast. Although, because of his job, many of their conversations were never far away from the subject of sudden violent death, Janet's illness had struck a chord deeper than any of the homicides. It made Jules think of their own mortality.

When they arrived at their homestead at Inchydoney, the greyhounds were thrilled to see Jules. Lucy ran around the living room, jumping over cushions and anything else that was in her way.

Molly started 'break-dancing,' by spinning around on her hind legs. Later, John and Jules took the dogs to the deserted beaches for a walk. The evening was cool and there was a strong breeze blowing in, off the ocean. The tide was fully out and the dogs were able to run ahead as far as they wanted through the wet hard packed sand. John told his wife about the McSweeney homicide and how another family had been destroyed. Jules could see that this incident was different from all the others that he had investigated and he was shaken. This tragic case had the hallmark of a homicide that was likely caused by mental illness and there was no intent involved. The couple and their dogs crossed the rocky bank from the East to the West Beach and continued their walk in a sad silence.

BACK IN INDEPENDENT Posse territory, Big Eddie Flynn had messed up again. Twos eight-balls of crack cocaine (or a quarter of an ounce) belonging to Darryl Lyons had gone missing. Eddie had stolen it and consumed it all, while on another uncontrollable binge to satisfy his desperate addiction.

Eddie was summoned to another disciplinary board hearing at Tyson Rolland's house.

"How fucking stupid are you, Eddie?" Tyson yelled.

"I must be very stupid. Sorry lads," Eddie answered, looking down at his feet, as he stood in front of Tyson Rolland, Darryl Lyons and two other members of the Independent Posse.

"You are on very thin ice, Eddie. Do you know that?" Tyson continued. Eddie didn't answer but just nodded, indicating he understood. "This is your last fucking chance, Eddie. Twenty fucking punches to the face this time. Obviously ten wasn't enough the last time. And another mission!" Tyson spit as he yelled.

"OK Tyson, I'm sorry. I'm sorry Darryl," Eddie said, grovelling. "You know I'll pay you back!"

"There'll be more consequences if you fuck up this mission. Got it?" Tyson sneered, jabbing his pointer finger at Eddie. Tyson stood up, put on his black leather gloves and walked over to Eddie. "You know the drill! Go out in the yard and sit down. Don't try and block any shots."

Eddie carried his chair to the yard, sat down on his hands and closed his eyes, waiting for the punishment to begin. Tyson stood in front of him, flexed his shoulders and punched Eddie five times in the head. Eddie's head jerked back after the first punch but he straightened up and was ready for the rest. By the fifth punch, the blood was streaming from Eddie's nose and he had a sizeable cut to his lip. Then the other members of the board lined up and they all punched Eddie until he received twenty punches to the head. When they were done, Eddie's face was unrecognizable. His eyes were swollen shut and the rest of his face was a bloody mess. Darryl instructed the other two gang members to help Eddie up and take him some place to recover. Tyson, grinning, threw a couple of buckets of water over the blood-stained ground.

Eddie Flynn ended up crashing at his brother's crack shack. "What did you do now?" Bertie asked, looking helplessly at the battered mess that had been delivered to him.

"I can't help it bro. I took a couple of eight-balls. I knew they'd catch me but I couldn't resist," Eddie answered, spitting blood from the many cuts inside his mouth.

"You have to pull yourself together, Ed. You're as bad as some of the crackheads that come to buy from us."

"Ah, I'm not. Am I?" Eddie was despondent and knew he was in trouble. "I'll try and stop.".

Later that day at Bertie Flynn's crack shack, Burnt Toast showed up to work as a runner for a few hours. Eddie was up now and moving around. He walked up to the kid and towered over him. "Hey B.T., I heard you're a rat!"

B.T. looked furious. Although much smaller than Eddie, B.T. wasn't afraid of him. He knew Eddie by reputation and had no respect for him, "Fuck you, you fucking crackhead!" B.T stood up for himself.

"Hey! Cool it!" Bertie Flynn stepped in. "What's he talking about?"

"I don't know. Ask your crackhead brother." B.T. smirked.

Bertie looked at Eddie, "Well?"

"I heard he called the cops on someone." Eddie sounded like a big child. Bertie looked to B.T. for an explanation.

"My mom's boyfriend was slapping her around. Yeah, I called the cops. It was either that or stab him," B.T. said in his strong African accent.

"That's not being a rat," Bertie responded. "Get back to work." Bertie pointed to the kitchen and said to his brother, "In there, you."

"Watch your fucking mouth. You're in enough trouble. You can't go around calling people rats for no fucking reason!" Bertie stood inches away from his brother's face, making sure he got the message.

The next day Eddie was summoned to Darryl Lyons' for his next mission. "Bring your brother's strap," Darryl told him.

When Eddie showed up at Darryl's house in Manor View, he threw his mountain bike in the front garden, went around the back of the house and knocked at the door. Darryl answered, "Did ya bring the strap?"

Eddie nodded. Darryl opened the door and Eddie walked into the kitchen.

"Show me," ordered Darryl.

Eddie reached behind his back and pulled out an old .38 caliber break action Webley revolver. The gun was a dark blue steel with a wooden handle. It looked old and heavy. Eddie snapped it open at the cylinder to show that it was loaded.

"Good, let's go," Darryl said, grabbing his coat from the back of a chair. Seconds later a cab pulled up at the front of the house and honked the horn. Darryl Lyons used cabs all the time to get around. He always used the same few drivers and knew that he could trust them. They never turned on the meter. They didn't need to; Darryl paid them well for their discretion.

Darryl sat in the front passenger seat and Eddie right behind him in the back. "Ballincollig," was all that Darryl said to the driver, who put the car in gear and drove off.

Ballincollig is a sizable suburb on the western edge of Cork City. It used to be a small village with a military barracks embedded in it. The military were long gone; the village had grown into a large town and now it had been encompassed by the city, with over 18,000 people inhabiting the area. Like any other suburb with a sizable population, Ballincollig had its fair share of social issues, including drugs. No particular gang had a stronghold in the suburb. The Mahon Warlords supplied a few independent drug dealers and the Independent Posse had a few members living in the town who oversaw business for their gang.

Today, Darryl was going to settle a score with an independent drug dealer who had not paid money that he owed to the I-P for almost half a kilo of crack cocaine. The dealer had switched over to the M-W as his supplier in order to keep his business going.

"Drop us off at the pub beyond the Tesco. Wait for us there and we'll be about half an hour," Darryl told the cab driver.

"No problem," the driver replied. There was no more conversation for the entire trip. The cab drove through Sunday's Well and crossed the bridge onto the Western Road. The driver then turned west and drove out the 'Straight Road' to Carrigrohane, around the roundabout and into Ballincollig.

The watery sun was setting and dusk was settling in quickly. The main street in Ballincollig was busy with people coming home from work. Eddie Flynn looked out the cab window. He was fascinated how one side of the street resembled an old Irish village and the other side was ultra modern. He looked at the new Garda Station and smirked to himself. Then they drove by the limestone wall and gate from the old military barracks; it now housed a shopping center. Soon they were out of the traffic jam of the town center and the cabbie pulled up in front of a pub on the west side of town.

"Let's go," Darryl said, looking at Eddie as he opened the passenger door and stepped out of the car.

Darryl walked back towards the town and turned down what looked like a country road. Eddie kept up, about a half step behind.

"There are townhouses at the end of this road. I'm going to point one out and you're going to knock on the door. When the fella inside comes out, you're going to shoot him. Got it?" Darryl ordered.

"Who is he?" Eddie asked.

"Frankie Spillane. Do ya know him?" Eddie shook his head. "He's tall and skinny with short spiky hair. Sometimes he wears glasses. He thinks they make him look clever." Darryl laughed.

As they arrived at the end of the road, there were farmers' fields on one side and nice tidy whitewashed townhouses on the other. The two gangsters walked into the housing complex. They passed a few blocks of four single storey houses and Darryl nodded and pointed his head at one house. "That's it, there in the middle, 10111 is the number." They walked back, near the fields and Darryl handed Eddie a black balaclava. "I'll stay back and stand six. Put this on when you go up to the house. Don't fuck this up. We want this fucker dead! OK?"

Eddie's heart was racing and his hands were shaking as he pulled out the revolver from the back of his waistband, "No problem," he gasped, barely above a whisper.

Big Eddie Flynn stepped out of the shadows and made his way back to the housing estate. He pulled his hood up and walked, head down, with a purpose. It was now dark but the street lights cast an eerie shadow. Eddie stopped across the street from the target address. He patted his waistband confirming to himself that the gun was there. There were lights on inside the house and he could see the flicker of a television.

Eddie crossed the street, walked past the low, red-bricked wall and down the short driveway. He had already formulated a plan; however, in true Eddie Flynn fashion, it wasn't the greatest plan. He wasn't going to knock on the front door and ask for Frankie Spillane. Eddie decided to bang on the front window and when Frankie looked out, he would shoot him.

Eddie pulled the balaclava out of his coat pocket, took his hood down and put the mask on. He straightened the mask, making sure he could see through the eye slots. Then he pulled the revolver from the waistband at the small of his back. He walked through the wet grass and a muddy flowerbed to a large picture window. Eddie hid next to a creeping rose tree. He could hear the television through the window. It was a cartoon show. He slapped the window with the palm of his gloved hand and waited.

It felt like an hour, but in reality it was only a few seconds until a tall skinny man with short, spiked hair came to the window and looked out. Eddie stepped out from behind the rose tree. His balaclava caught on a branch and pulled across his face, blocking the view from his left eye. "Ah shit!" Eddie said. He straightened the mask somewhat and raised the heavy revolver. Frankie Spillane was motionless at the other side of the glass. In a moment frozen in time, the two men stared each other in the eye. Then Eddie strained to pull the heavy-duty trigger. BANG! A shot rang out and shattered the window. He jerked the trigger again and fired another shot. This time he knew he hit his target. He saw Frankie's head jerk and the blood spatter from his cheek

Eddie didn't waste any time hanging about. He turned around and legged it out of the front garden and back towards the farmers' fields. Darryl Lyons was already halfway up the road and briskly making his way back to the taxi. Eddie was sweating and he ripped off the balaclava and threw it over the ditch. A minute later he caught up with Darryl.

"I heard the shots. Did ya get him?" Darryl asked.

"Yup, I shot him right in the head. He's done!" Eddie said, out of breath after the run and the adrenaline rush.

"Did he come to the door?"

"No, I banged on the window and he came and looked out. I shot him twice."

Darryl looked over at Eddie and rolled his eyes upwards, "Why didn't ya just knock on the doorlike I told ya?"

"I don't know. I didn't think of it." Eddie shrugged his shoulders, sounding more stupid than ever.

The gangsters walked back to the main street and the cab, waiting for them outside the pub. The driver had his seat back and a baseball cap pulled down over his face. He snoozed with his hands behind his head. When Darryl grabbed the handle of the front door, the driver sprang up in his seat and his hat fell off. He flicked the switch on the panel next to him and the door unlocked. "Back to my place," Darryl said, as Eddie slid into the back seat. The driver started up the cab, found a place to turn around and headed back to the city.

Chapter 15

The following morning, Tyson Rolland listened to the radio for a news update. "*A man is in critical condition after a shooting last night in a quiet housing estate in Ballincollig,*" the news reader said in a calm, posh voice.

"Critical! What the fuck is that?" Tyson scowled as he picked up his phone and started to search for the news report.

Seconds later, a text came through from Darryl Lyons. "Check out the news. He fucked it up again."

Tyson texted Darryl back and an hour later, he showed up at Tyson's house, riding an old battered ten-speed bike. He threw the bike on the ground in the back yard and walked into the kitchen.

AT GARDA HEADQUARTERS, John and his team were catching up on reports and the never-ending paperwork and disclosure requests for the public prosecutor. Superintendent Collins walked into the incident room. "Another shooting last night," the super said, sitting down at John's desk.

"Are they going to die?" John asked, sounding callous but really only thinking about having to start another major investigation.

"Probably not, at this stage. Some fella got shot in the head out in Ballincollig. Maybe he'll be brain damaged. Sure, we might never be able to tell," the superintendent said with a mischievous grin.

"Who's the victim?"

"Spillane is his name. He's a player. Sells cocaine and meth in the suburbs," Collins answered.

"So it is gang related then. Shit! I thought we had a handle on this and slowed things down," John sighed, shaking his head. "How did this one happen?"

"It was brazen! Someone banged on the front window of his house and when he went to look out, Bang! Right in the face! I'm going to leave it with the detectives in Ballincollig for now. They have a really good handle on things out there. That is, unless he dies. Then it's coming your way." Paddy Collins stood up to leave.

John blew out a long slow breath and thought to himself, "I hope this fucker survives."

IN TYSON ROLLAND'S house in Churchfield, he and Darryl Lyons were discussing the non-fatal shooting of Frankie Spillane. B.T., Tyson's loyal child soldier, showed up at the back door. "What do you want?" Darryl asked when he opened the door.

"Come on in boy," Tyson yelled when he saw who was there. Tyson liked B.T. He saw a ruthless streak in him.

"Someone called me a rat," B.T. said, "and I wanted you to know that I'm no rat!"

"Who called you a rat?" Tyson was curious and concerned. He was a believer that there was no smoke without fire and if someone was calling this kid a rat, there just may be something to it.

"It was Big E," the kid replied, looking affronted.

"Eddie Flynn called you a rat?" Darryl slapped the table with both hands.

"Why would Big E say something like that?" Tyson scowled.

"I called the cops on my mom's boyfriend. He was slapping the shit out of her. I had to do something. He's twice my size. If I had a strap, I would have blown his fucking head off," B.T. said, clenching his jaw and looking determined. "I'm not a rat, Tyson. I had to do something."

"Who heard Big E call you a rat?"

"His brother Bertie and some other crackhead that was in Bertie's shack."

"What did Bertie say?" Darryl Lyons asked.

"He told Big E to shut the fuck up and I was no rat," B.T. said grinning.

"Bertie's right. You aren't a rat. You're a good soldier so don't worry about it, little man. Go on, off you go," Tyson assured him, nodding his head towards the back door. B.T. turned and left the house.

"What are we going to do about that?" Darryl asked Tyson.

"Big Fuckin' E!" Tyson shook his head as he grimaced. "He just doesn't learn. We could punch him in the head all day long and he still won't learn." Tyson was angry and the more he thought about Eddie Flynn, the angrier he got. "You and B.T. will take him out!" Tyson finally made up his mind about Eddie Flynn.

"I'm down with that," Darryl said. "Do you want us to shoot him?"

"He's not worth a fucking bullet. Shank the bastard!" Tyson clenched his jaw and shook his head. "Do it tomorrow before he fucks anything else up or steals another 'eight-ball.'"

Darryl Lyons didn't blink an eye. "Consider it done."

The next morning B.T. showed up at Bertie Flynn's crack shack near Dominick Street. He told Eddie that he had to come and meet Darryl Lyons at a vacant house in Mahon. Eddie rolled his eyes; he thought it was another D-Boarding because he did not kill Frankie Spillane. "He's got another mission for you in Warlord territory," B.T. told the gangster. Eddie shrugged his shoulders. He thought this was better than another twenty punches to the head. Eddie's imagination began to run wild. He firmly believed that he had been selected to assassinate one of the leaders of the Mahon Warlords and if he could pull this off, all would be forgiven.

B.T. and Eddie took a cab to the Cork County Council estate in Mahon. When they walked into the vacant house, through the back door, Darryl Lyons was waiting. The house was derelict and had been destroyed when the last tenants had left. All the cabinets had been ripped off the walls, the toilet had been smashed and anything of value had been removed, including all the copper piping and electrical wires. The house was on a list of houses to be renovated by the council; they just hadn't got around to it. In the kitchen, on top of an upturned blue five-gallon bucket, sat two large butcher knives.

Eddie looked at Darryl. "How's it going?" Eddie asked. He hadn't noticed the knives on the bucket, or if he did, he didn't say anything.

"Alright," Darryl answered. "In there," he said, nodding his head towards an open doorway, leading into what used to be a living room. When Eddie walked through the doorway, Darryl turned his head and nodded towards the bucket. B.T. stepped towards it and picked up one of the butcher knives. Darryl Lyons picked up the other.

Darryl and B.T. walked with a purpose behind Eddie. Then Darryl raised his knife, holding it with both hands and plunged it, with a downwards strike, between Eddie Flynn's shoulder blades.

Eddie let out a scream as his knees buckled and he tried to reach behind his back with both hands. Eddie fell face first onto the floor. "Finish him off now!" Darryl ordered, as B.T. stepped up with his knife, clenched in his hand.

Stabbing someone was not as easy as shooting someone from six meters away. Stabbing was up close and personal; B.T. was squeamish to begin with. He stabbed Eddie three times in the lower back but barely broke the skin. He grimaced each time as he felt the sharp blade slice through the big man.

Although fatally wounded, Eddie tried to get up and was on his hands and knees. Instinct told him to run away but his lungs were filling with blood from Darryl's initial stab wound. "Ah for fucks sakes!" Darryl shoved B.T. aside and thrust the knife into the big man's side, all the way to the hilt. "That's how you do it! Come on now, finish the fucker off!" Darryl yelled, encouraging the kid.

And B.T. did what he was asked. He raised his knife with both hands and drove it into Eddie Flynn's neck. Eddie collapsed on the ground and let out a final breath. But B.T. did not stop there. He yanked the knife out of Eddie's neck and flew into a frenzy. He stabbed Eddie over and over again, until one of the rivets holding the blade to the handle broke; the blade slid up, forming a V shape. B.T. held up the broken knife, looked at it with disgust, and threw it into the corner. Then he kicked Eddie's corpse as it lay on the floor.

Darryl Lyons stood back and looked at B.T. with admiration. "Nice work boy. Come on, let's get out of here."

Chapter 16

Two days after Eddie Flynn was murdered, a couple of workmen from the council walked into the vacant house in Mahon to prepare for refurbishment. They stopped suddenly at the damaged back door when the foul stench hit them. Neither of them was familiar with the odor and they forced themselves to walk through the door. They stopped dead in their tracks when they walked into the living room and found Eddie Flynn's lifeless body lying face down on the floor. His left arm was stretched above his head and his right arm was tucked in under his body. Eddie's face was drained of all color and his open eyes stared blankly towards the wall.

One of the workers reached down and shook Eddie's shoulder and called out to him to see if he was alright. The other man turned and ran from the derelict house. Seconds later the other worker ran into the rear garden. They called 999 and then called their supervisor. Five minutes later a Garda patrol car pulled up, followed by an ambulance.

The two workers told the young uniformed Garda officer what they had discovered inside and the officer walked around the back of the house and entered the kitchen. Although a junior officer, he was familiar with the unforgettable stench of death, once he stepped over the threshold.

The officer covered his nose and mouth with his gloved left hand, walked through the kitchen and into the living room where he found Big Eddie Flynn's corpse.

Seconds later the paramedics came into the house. They quickly assessed Eddie; when they saw the lividity, they knew immediately that there was no helping this man. "He's deceased. There's nothing we can do for him. Looks like he has been dead for a couple of days. Rigor has set in and it's starting to wear off and look, lividity," one of the paramedics said to the police officer. He pointed to the dark red skin where the deceased's blood had pooled at the lower points of his body, causing the skin to redden.

"Looks like he was stabbed or hacked," the officer said and the paramedic nodded in agreement.

The officer reached for the microphone on his left shoulder and keyed the switch on the side. He turned his face towards to the microphone and called his dispatcher. When the calm voice of the dispatcher answered, the young officer told her that he had a deceased male in the vacant house and there were signs of violence at the scene. The officer then escorted the paramedics out of the house and waited for reinforcements.

Inspector John Cahill was sitting in his office when his phone rang. He looked at the call display and saw it was his boss, Superintendent Paddy Collins. "Hi, what's up?" he answered the phone.

"New business! A deceased male in a derelict council house in Mahon. Two council workers found him about an hour ago. It looks like he may have been stabbed. It's all yours. Let me know how it goes."

"Do we have an I.D. on the victim?" John asked.

"I don't think so, at least I wasn't told. I'm assuming we don't know who he is yet. It's a derelict house in Mahon so I'm fairly sure his fingerprints will be in our system." Paddy Collins sounded jaded.

"Alright, I'll muster the troops and we'll get stuck into it." John called his team together and he looked up the details of the call on the computer. Then he texted Jules, *We got new business! I won't be home for a while.* He placed a heart emoji at the end of the message.

"*K, eat proper food and don't stay there all night xxx.*" Jules texted back.

Before he addressed his team, John spoke with the sergeant who was managing the scene in order to learn some basic facts. Then he started his briefing in the usual manner. He wrote the incident number at the top of the whiteboard in the incident room and the address of the scene underneath. He put a big question mark where he would usually write the victim's name. He left the area for witnesses blank. The investigators of the Serious Crime Unit did not look impressed when they saw the details in front of them.

"We're just waiting for Sergeant Martens, from forensics to join us," John said, checking his watch. And as if on cue, Sergeant Jen Martens walked into the incident room. "Thanks for joining us, Jen. I'll bring you up to speed and you can get out there and work your magic." Sergeant Martens smiled and sat down.

Jen Martens replied in her usual confident manner, "I have already assigned someone to attend the scene. We are testing a new portable fingerprint scanner so I'm hoping to have a tentative I.D. on the deceased very quickly."

"Jeez, Jen, that would be great. The sooner we find out who this fella is, the sooner we can find out what he was doing in the derelict house," John responded.

"Mike and Eddie, you two head to the scene and start canvassing the neighbours. Find out if anyone saw anybody going in or out of the scene. Also, check for CCTV. Hopefully someone along the road has it. Jeff and Len, go wide on the area. See if you can find any other CCTV from stores or businesses in the area. We don't know what we're looking for yet but let's secure the video footage now, before it's lost. We can look through it later. Tim and I will wait and see who the victim is and we'll do the notifications and see if we can learn anything else." John sent his team out in the cold damp afternoon.

"Sorry, Jen, I don't have anything else for you. The uniforms at the scene say it's a derelict house that has been vandalized over the last few months so I expect it will be an ugly scene. Lord knows what you'll find in there," John told the forensic sergeant.

Jen Martens smiled back. "I'm sure we'll find something useful." Just then her cell phone buzzed in her pocket; Jen answered and smiled. "I'm glad you like it," she said to the caller and ended the call. "Our victim's fingerprints are on file," she said smugly, as she drew out the anticipation. John let out a long breath and a sigh. He allowed her to have her moment of glory. "Twenty-six-year-old Edward Flynn. You will have to run him on PULSE. He obviously has a record."

Before John could turn to his computer, Detective Pete Sandhu, the unit analyst, was punching in the name to PULSE, the Garda database. "That's odd," Pete said, and John walked behind him to look at his screen. Edward Flynn, also known as Big E, is Independent Posse. What is he doing in Mahon?"

"Good question Pete," John said. "That's probably why he is dead. He crossed the River Styx." John shook his head. "Print out his profile, Pete. And make sure we have a next of kin. Tim and I will make the notification."

"What's the River Styx?" Tim Warren asked.

"The river of the dead," John answered philosophically. "It appears to be what happens when these gangsters cross the River Lee."

"His next of kin is his younger brother Bertie. Bertie is also flagged as an I-P member. Neither of them has a proper address but Bertie is associated with Martina Fitzpatrick. Looks like she has a couple of kids with him. She lives in The Glen." Pete handed the inspector the profiles for both Eddie and Bertie Flynn.

"These two look like a right couple of thugs." John passed the papers to Tim Warren. John opened his desk drawer and took out his pistol and a fully loaded magazine. He walked over to the unloading station and loaded the snub-nosed Glock 27 with the ten-round magazine. Tim did the same with his regular sized Glock 23. "I wonder what this fella knows," John said as they walked out the door.

"Didn't we talk to the Flynns after the New Year's murder, a while back?" Tim asked as he drove down Glen Avenue and turned onto Mourne Avenue. The inspector didn't answer but nodded, remembering the very complex investigation after another shooting in Manor View Estate.

After a few more turns, Tim pulled up outside a neat red-bricked house in the center of a row of six houses. The garden was nothing special but it wasn't overgrown. There were some children's toys hiding in the grass; all in all, the house was in good condition. Tim knocked on the front door. John turned and looked out over the street. The view was astounding. In the distance the green hills rolled out all the way to Rathcooney. "That's a million-dollar view," John said. Tim turned around and was taken aback by what he saw.

Just then, the noise of the lock turning on the door sounded. A menacing looking Bertie Flynn stood, holding the door. Bertie was wearing a black 'wife-beater' shirt and baggy blue jeans that hung low on his hips. "Yeah?" Bertie said, as he stuck his chin out in an intimidating manner.

"Hi Bertie, I'm Inspector John Cahill and this is Detective Garda Tim Warren of the Serious Crime Unit. Can we come in and speak with you?"

"No, you can't. What's this about?" Bertie was not giving an inch.

John was very tempted to say something like, '*Your asshole brother is dead. Someone killed him. Can we come in now?*' But, he didn't. Instead, he said, "I got some bad news for you, Bertie. It's about Eddie. We really shouldn't do this on the front step with all the neighbours watching."

Bertie Flynn held his pose for a few seconds but the officers could see that he was shaken by what John had told him. Then he took his hand off the door and stepped aside. "In there." He pointed to the kitchen at the end of the hallway.

"You should really sit down," Tim said to Bertie.

"No, I'm OK," Bertie replied. He had a terrible feeling in his gut. He knew something bad had happened. Bertie Flynn was scared.

Tim looked at his boss. John nodded at Tim and then John started to speak. "I'm very sorry, Bertie, but your brother Eddie has been found dead."

Bertie gasped. His eyes were burning as the tears formed. He was a tough gangster but he was having a normal human reaction to this terrible news. "Did he overdose?"

"No, it looks like he has been stabbed. He was found in a vacant house in Mahon."

"Mahon? What the fuck was he doing in Mahon?" Bertie said, his eyes wide open with shock.

"We were hoping you might be able to answer that for us. When was the last time you saw him?" Tim asked.

"I haven't seen him for a couple of days." Bertie paused and let out a long breath. "That's not unusual though." Bertie told the officers that he had no clue as to why his brother would venture down to Mahon. "Eddie knew better. It wasn't safe for him to go there."

"Look, Bertie, I know you and Eddie are I-P. I don't care about that. Right now, that doesn't matter to me. All I want to know is who killed your brother. If there is anything at all that you know, you really should tell us." John hoped Bertie Flynn would open up.

"Ya, right!" Bertie shrugged his shoulders and wiped the tears from his eyes.

"I mean it Bertie. We're not here to judge you or your brother. That's someone else's job. Our job is to find out who killed Eddie."

Bertie Flynn stared at the inspector. "I don't know anything," was all he managed to say. The tough gangster was rattled and close to tears.

Bertie walked the officers to the door and closed it behind them. As soon as the door shut, John and Tim heard an anguished wail as Bertie Flynn wept bitterly for the loss of his brother. Inside, Bertie sat on the floor with his back to the front door and cried bitter tears.

"What did you make of that?" Tim asked as they drove down Ballyhooly Road towards the city center.

"I would love to have a long chat with him. I'm sure he knows lots," John said as he stared out the window at the old toll booth house at Saint Luke's Cross.

At the end of a long day of canvassing the neighbourhood in Mahon and scouring for CCTV footage, John briefed with his crew. "Somebody please tell me we have a lead on this one," John was pleading with his team but knowing the answer.

"The canvass drew a blank," Mike Williams answered. "That place has been vacant for months and everyone and his dog have been in and out of there. The neighbours don't even call in anymore when someone goes in. Every scrap of copper wire and pipe have been stolen from it. Just about every neighbour said they weren't surprised this happened; it was a disaster waiting to happen."

"What about CCTV?"

"Not much to go on. One person on the street has a doorbell camera. I suppose we can go over it and maybe we'll see something. We also gathered CCTV footage from everywhere we could find it in a three-kilometer radius. Do you want us to get the traffic cameras as well?" Len Benoit asked.

"You may as well. I don't know what we're looking for but it may be useful. Pete, can you start looking at the doorbell camera tomorrow? Go back three, no four days. Just log everything that you see." John felt dejected at the prospect of another difficult case ahead of him. "Alright! Go home. Get some sleep and be back tomorrow for nine."

"Nine?" Tim Warren piped up.

"What's wrong with nine?" John asked.

"It's already midnight. Nine is a bit early," Tim answered sheepishly.

"Well, I think it's pretty clear that you're not getting enough beauty sleep, Tim. And you obviously need more. Let's push the start time back to ten." John smiled at his partner.

"Thanks boss, but it won't help him. He's still an ugly fucker," Mike Williams said from the back of the room.

JOHN DROVE HOME THROUGH the rain, all the way to Inchydoney. As he hit the coast, the rain intensified and it hopped off the roof of the car; the windshield wipers could barely keep up. When he entered the house, he was met by the sweet scent of recent baking. He followed the aroma to the kitchen and found a baking tray of imperial shortbread cookies, left to cool. There was a note next to the cookies, "ONLY ONE," and a heart- shaped drawing. He smiled as he picked up two. He walked past the dogs' crates and raised his index finger to his lips. "Shhh," he said to the greyhounds as he ate the first cookie.

After a quick shower to wash away the grime of the day and the stench of death, John slipped into bed next to his wife. Jules stirred when he put his arm around her waist. "How many cookies did you have?" she mumbled.

"Only one," he lied.

"How many?" She knew him too well.

"Two," he answered sheepishly. She turned and kissed him.

Chapter 17

The following morning there was no great improvement in the weather. It was grey and quiet and full of all the damp sweetness of an early Irish winter. Over coffee, Jules asked John about the latest case. "It's ugly! It looks like an I-P gangster was in M-W territory and got killed. We're already behind the eight-ball here. It looks like he's been dead for a couple of days."

"With any luck you'll get something today that will help wrap it up quickly," Jules said.

"Yeah, I hope so. You know what it's like. You're only as good as your last investigation. It won't be long before they start looking at the stats and saying the solve rate is dropping!"

"Surely Paddy Collins will have your back?" Keep pushing ahead. You'll get the break you need in the end."

"I hope you're right because, as it stands, I have two-and-a-half unsolved murders."

"Two-and-a-half?" Jules asked, grinning at the odd number.

"First, there is Anthony Woodsworth who we found in his mother's porch. We haven't a clue who killed him. This latest one, Eddie Flynn, God knows where that will go. And we only arrested one of the shooters who killed the Mahon Warrior delivery driver, Graham Hogan, on Dominick Street. We don't know who the second shooter is." John stared into his coffee cup. "We have done everything we can in the Woodsworth and Hogan cases. We'll go out today and beat the bushes in the Flynn case. I really don't know if we'll be any further ahead when we're finished."

"That's all you can do right now. Just do your best as you always do. You'll get a break, just stay positive!" Jules hugged her husband, supportive as always.

"I hate these gang related killings. Although Anthony Woodsworth had no ties to any gang, he was killed in the heart of Independent Posse territory, and his murder has all the hallmarks of a gang slaying. Graham Hogan's death is definitely gang related. He was stupid enough to sell M-W drugs in I-P country, and it looks like Eddie Flynn did the same thing, but the other way around."

John drove the forty-five minutes from his beach home in West Cork to the city. He knew Jules was right; he had to stay positive. If he started to show signs of defeat, what chance did his team have.

John addressed the team at the morning briefing. "The autopsy on Eddie Flynn is this morning. We will find out more when that's concluded. Sergeant Martens is attending." Everyone had a look of relief on their faces; nobody liked attending an autopsy. "Pete has compiled a list of Eddie Flynn's associates. They are all gangbangers! Do whatever it takes to get every single one of them in here for an interview and find out what they know about Eddie Flynn." John paused and looked at his audience. They were busy making notes and studying the list of names to see if they knew any of them. "Tim and I will talk to his brother again."

"What if we get nothing from any of them?" Eddie Jenkins asked, keeping his head down and not making eye contact with the inspector.

"What if? What if it's on a Tuesday and it's raining? There is no what if." Although John was exasperated and about to lose it, he held his cool. "We do what we're good at, Ed. We dig and dig until we find something even though we don't know what we're looking for. That's why you guys are here. You're the best in the business. Now get out there and get some fucking answers." John smiled at his crew.

"We're on it boss," Eddie Jenkins said, with a new lease of positivity.

It was early afternoon when Sergeant Jennifer Martens walked into the incident room. She sat in front of the inspector's desk. "What ya got?" John asked.

"Well, Eddie Flynn was stabbed to death. You'll win a prize if you can guess how many times he was stabbed," Jen said with her usual mischievous grin.

"Fifteen?" John played along.

"Try again."

"Twenty-five?"

"Higher."

"I don't fucking know, fifty times."

"Try one more," Jen said.

Alright, one hundred stab wounds."

"Almost correct. The pathologist stopped counting at ninety-seven. There were a few more shallow ones, almost hesitation marks, or they were just too tired to continue the frenzy," Jen reported now quite seriously.

"Ninety-seven? That's a bit of overkill," John said as he made a note on his investigative summary.

"There were two killers or at least there were two knives used. We recovered two knives at the scene. Both run-of-the-mill kitchen knives. One of them is broken at the handle. It probably hit a large bone," Jen read from her notes. Then she looked across the desk at the inspector. "Before you ask, there are no fingerprints on the knives. We've swabbed the handles for DNA. We may get lucky if the assailants weren't wearing gloves."

"Anything else from the scene?"

"Nothing jumping out. We have seized a few cigarette butts and got a few fuzzy fingerprints that we are trying to develop. However, there's been a thousand people through that dump in the last couple of months. If we get any hits, it will not be definitive." Jen Martens was as stoic as ever.

For the rest of the day, the investigators from the Serious Crime Unit brought in all of Eddie Flynn's friends and associates. John and Tim brought Bertie Flynn in for an interview.

"Me and my big brother Eddie were raised by our gran in Buttevant. When she died, we moved to the city. Eddie was the only family I had left," Bertie Flynn said, his eyes red from mourning his dead brother.

"Tell me about Eddie," John asked calmly.

Bertie picked up on John's North Side accent and looked across the table at him. "You don't sound like a cop."

"It's a long story how I came to be sitting here, Bertie. Maybe we'll talk about it some day. But you're right. I'm originally from Blackpool. North Sider, born and bred," John said smiling back at the now vulnerable gangster. "I'm really with the Police Service of Northern Ireland but I've been working with the Garda for a few years now."

Bertie Flynn liked John Cahill. He felt at ease talking to him. "My brother, Big E was as tough as nails. He had a heart of gold and would fight to the death for you." Bertie choked back the tears. "His weakness was crack. He fucking loved crack. He even stole it from me!" Bertie knew he should not have said that and looked across at the inspector. John didn't blink an eye and let the silence hang in the air, waiting for Bertie to carry on. And Bertie did carry on. "Eddie was loyal to the core. He would do anything for me and there were some other people he really wanted to impress. But if you ask me, what was he doing in Mahon, I really haven't a clue."

"If you were to guess what he was doing in Mahon, what would you say?" John asked.

Bertie Flynn looked at the inspector and smiled. "Eddie probably went there to rip someone off. He would get a great kick out of ripping off some Warlord in their own backyard. Then he would brag about it for the next couple of months."

John walked Bertie Flynn to the front door of the Garda Station. He shook his hand as the big man was about to leave. "I'm very sorry for your loss, Bertie." Bertie saw the sincerity in the inspector's face, as tears flowed down his cheek. John handed Bertie his business card. "If you hear anything at all or want to talk with me again, just reach out." All Bertie could do was nod. The lump in his throat wouldn't allow him to speak.

When he returned to the incident room, John briefed with the rest of his team. They were no further ahead. Eddie Flynn's friends and associates all told the same story. Eddie was a tough guy but also a raving crackhead who couldn't be trusted to hold a stash of drugs. Every single one of them believed that Eddie would only cross the river and go that far into enemy territory to rip off a Mahon Warlord drug dealer.

"Tomorrow, we'll delve into the CCTV and analyse every second of it," John said, trying to keep positive as he dismissed the team.

BERTIE FLYNN DIDN'T go home after he left Garda Headquarters on Anglesea Street. He knew something was off. Bertie drove to Churchfield and to Tyson Rolland's home.

Tyson and Darryl Lyons were in the kitchen when Bertie knocked on the back door. Darryl let him in. Bertie sat at the kitchen table across from Tyson. Darryl stood strategically behind Bertie in case there was trouble. Bertie eyed the other two and knew something was up. But he kept calm. His heart was pounding. Despite his suspicion and the anger that was building inside him, Bertie was scared. "You heard about Eddie?" Bertie said.

"Yup." Tyson nodded his head.

"Do you think it was the Guppies got him?" Bertie couldn't help the tremor in his voice.

Tyson stood up and walked behind Bertie's chair. Bertie felt a cold shiver go through his body. Tyson grabbed Bertie's left shoulder with his left hand and squeezed it. Bertie couldn't see it but Tyson had his right hand behind his back, grabbing the handle of his Glock pistol. "You know that your brother was a liability. In fact, he was a fucking disaster," Tyson said with venom, not sympathy in his voice.

Bertie felt like running out the door. But he did not. He just nodded his head, wanting Tyson to continue.

"Eddie was on thin ice all along. He went too far when he called someone a rat! He got what was coming to him." Tyson squeezed Bertie's shoulder harder. "You know what happens when you step out of line?" Tyson was mocking Bertie. It was as if he was baiting him to fight back. "That kid is no rat. B.T. and Darryl told Eddie that," Tyson said mockingly.

Bertie Flynn, the shrewd businesslike drug dealer, shut his eyes tight. This wasn't the time to fight back. These two were looking for a reason to kill him too. "Yup," Bertie said, relaxing his body. Tyson let go of his shoulder and loosened his grip on the pistol. There was silence in the kitchen for a few long moments; then Bertie stood up and walked out the back door. "See ya," he said. He stared Darryl Lyons in the eye who, for after a second, couldn't hold his gaze. Bertie walked out of the house and to his car.

Bertie drove to the industrial park near the computer plant in Holly Hill. He pulled over and started to sob uncontrollably, knowing that his brother Eddie had been killed by his own gang. And there was nothing he could do about it.

Chapter 18

Senior members of the Independent Posse street gang, on 'D' Range in Limerick Prison, sat around a table in the recreation area. From a distance, the sterile institutional scene looked like they were playing an innocent game of cards. In reality, this was a council meeting and the gangsters were deciding someone's fate. The rest of the prisoners mingled around the noisy hall. It was full of men who made the best of their situation, laughing, shouting and trying to pass the time away.

Archie Cambridge, the drug mule, was not invited to this meeting; he was much too junior. Nevertheless, he was standing six for the gangsters and supposed to whistle if any of the jail guards came too close.

The guards rarely came on the floor. Most of the time they sat in their impenetrable glass room, known as the 'fish bowl,' monitoring their charges on the CCTV that covered most of the floor. There was also a gantry hovering above the floor where the guards could keep a watchful eye. However, due to a shortage of manpower, this platform was rarely used.

Ray-Ray Daniels, the most senior member of the gang, chaired this council meeting. Daniels was serving four years for causing harm, when he should have been serving ten years for attempted murder. His victim was persuaded not to be too cooperative with the police.

"The issue here is Walter is out of line and he has to go," Ray-Ray said, looking around the table.

Walter Sheldon, another senior Independent Posse member who was serving time for manslaughter, had recently been transferred from Cork Prison and was trying to take over leadership of the gang in Limerick. Ray-Ray Daniels didn't like the competition.

"What are we going to do?" asked another one of the gangsters. "Walter and Mikey Galvin go way back."

"Mikey is maxed out in the Midlands Prison. He can't make any decisions. Walter knows that and it's up to us to decide. I say Walter must go! We roll him off the range today." Ray-Ray looked menacingly at the rest of the men.

Ray-Ray Daniels was one of the meanest, toughest and most violent people in Limerick Prison. He had a short fuse and could snap at any moment. He had an extremely violent record for disturbing serious offences. The only thing missing from his pedigree was a conviction for murder. Although the other men who sat around the table with him considered themselves friends and business associates, none of them had any intention of crossing him. "Let's take a vote," Ray-Ray continued. "All in favor of rolling Sheldon off the range today?" Ray-Ray looked menacingly around the table. All the others raised their hands in support of the motion.

Ray-Ray called Archie Cambridge over to the table. "Tell Walter we want to speak to him here," Daniels barked.

Archie walked around the range, looking into various open cells, until he found Walter Sheldon. "Ray-Ray wants to see ya at the table," Archie said, trying to sound tough but obviously a little intimidated.

"What the fuck does he want?" Walter asked.

"I don't know."

Walter got up from his bunk and walked down the range. His grey tracksuit bottoms hung down low on his waist. His tough guy swagger looked over exaggerated as he swung his arms and shoulders as he moved.

"Sit down Walter," Ray-Ray demanded.

Walter sat down and slowly looked around the table, staring for a few seconds at each of the other men. Then he looked at Daniels. Walter didn't speak.

"Walter, since you got here three weeks ago, all you've done is piss everyone off. You've been asked to stop, but no. You're still acting the maggot. We have a good thing going here. You're not in Cork now. We've decided that you have to leave our range today!" Ray-Ray said in a low controlled threatening voice.

"You've decided! Who the fuck are you shower of shites to decide that I should leave the range? I'm an O.G. An original fucking gangster, one of the founding members of I-P. You can all go and fuck yourselves." Walter was not afraid to speak his mind and not in the least bit scared.

"The council has voted. You have two hours to request a move." Ray-Ray slapped the palms of his hands hard on the table, signaling that the meeting was over. Walter stood up and walked away.

Jeffrey Brady, another senior gangster, was first to speak. "He's not going to go."

"He'll go! One way or another, he'll go," Daniels said as everyone else got up from the table. "There's a blind spot at the end of the hall. If he doesn't make a move in the next two hours, get everyone up to the blind spot and we'll get Walter into Cell 22. That's in the blind spot too."

Two hours came and went. Walter Sheldon made no attempt to request a move to another range. Jeffrey Brady approached Archie Cambridge. "Something is going to go down in a minute. You have to be outside 22 and stand six. If any of the bulls show up, raise the alarm. Got it?"

Archie Cambridge made his way to Cell 22 and stood outside, looking down the range towards the fishbowl. At that point, Brady, Daniels and the rest of the I-P council got everyone to casually move to the area of the blind spot. Walter Sheldon was forced into Cell 22. Five men stood around him in the cramped space, large enough for only two. "You were warned!" roared Ray-Ray Daniels.

"Fuck off!" Sheldon yelled back, taking a fighting stance.

The powerful Ray-Ray Daniels was not to be messed with. He lunged forward and grabbed Walter Sheldon by the throat and squeezed tightly. Walter tried to fight back but the space was too cramped. It took less than a minute for Walter to pass out.

Daniels did not let go of Walter's throat; instead he shook him. "You'll go now, won't ya?" he mocked. Archie Cambridge stole a look over his shoulder and saw what was happening inside Cell 22.

When Ray-Ray finally eased his grip on Walter's throat, Walter slumped to the ground. "Get up," Jeffrey Brady said, kicking Walter's leg. There was no response. "Ah for fuck sakes, you're after killing him." Brady was high with excitement.

"Ah shit! I only meant to choke him out." Daniels laughed. "Anyways, we'll make sure everyone is solid." Ray-Ray turned around and grabbed a towel near the stainless-steel sink. He wrapped the towel around Walter Sheldon's neck, tied it in a knot and pulled both ends of the towel. "Now everyone, pull on the towel, that way we all killed the fucker."

Jeffrey Brady stepped up and pulled both ends of the towel. Then the other three did the same. Archie Cambridge had stolen another couple of glances and was terrified he also would be ordered to pull the ends of the towel. However, the council members did not even consider him. They stepped out of Cell 22 and walked down the range. Everyone else walked back into view of the cameras. The entire incident took less than five minutes.

Two hours later, right at lockdown for the night, Walter Sheldon's body was discovered by the jail guards. The police were called; the entire prison was put in lockdown and a major investigation was initiated.

Detectives from Limerick City attended the jail. They conducted exhaustive interviews with everyone on D Range and, of course, nobody saw or heard anything. They looked at hours upon hours of video surveillance and again drew a blank. It was impossible to tell who went into Cell 22 with Walter Sheldon because everyone on the range was mingling in the blind spot. The detectives knew that it had to be one or more of the fifty men on D Range, but they could not ascertain who actually was responsible for killing Walter Sheldon.

A couple of days later, after the lockdown had been lifted, Archie Cambridge made a call to his friend, Bertie Flynn, in Cork City. "Did ya hear about Walter?" Archie asked.

"I saw it on the news. Someone got to him, I suppose," Bertie replied, hoping to hear more of the scandal.

"They were rolling him off the range for acting the prick! The whole council voted him out," Archie said, excitement building in his voice.

However, Bertie was an experienced campaigner and shut his friend down before he said anymore. "You better shut up now! They're going to be all over the phones."

"I didn't see nothing," Archie caught himself. "I'm just saying what I heard from everyone else in here."

THAT EVENING, ON THE twin beaches at Inchydoney, John and Jules walked the greyhounds. The tide was fully out and the moon lit up the cloudless sky. As the tide was out, they decided to stroll on the East Beach, easier to access. Halfway down the steps, John undid the dogs' leashes and they immediately took off. They jumped a pool of seawater at the foot of the steps and raced along the beach until they were almost out of sight, half a kilometer away. John whistled and both dogs made a wide turn towards the ocean and then galloped back towards John and Jules. They were now closer to the water and the sea spray was flying all around them. "Oh, that was bright!" Jules said. "We're going to have two wet dogs around the house all night."

"Ah sure, they're enjoying themselves. Look at them." John smiled at his two dogs running with such determination.

The dogs pulled up at the base of the rocky bank that separates the East and West Beaches and started to sniff the seaweed.

"Any developments at work?" Jules asked.

"Nothing. We're just going through the motions but there's nothing new. We can't get a break on anything."

"But the bosses must realize that this is typical of gang stuff. It was the same in the North, wasn't it? Nobody would talk about the paramilitaries or the breakaway drug gangs. They were too scared." Jules tried to reassure her husband.

"I know that. And you know that and Paddy Collins knows it, but there are a few people above him who would love to see us fail and send us, cap in hand, back to Belfast. There is always animosity in the higher ranks. They're always trying to get one over on each other and get the favour of the chief."

"That's a shame., They should all be pushing for the common goal, to solve the crime," Jules added, shaking her head.

"On the surface, that's what it looks like. But when you stop and look at them, they are all building their own little empires and will step on anyone that gets in their way to get to the top. Oh well, the worst they can do is transfer me back to the North."

Before they knew it, they had walked over a kilometer and had reached the channel. They stopped and looked over at the lights of the small fishing village of Ring. The dogs had followed them, sniffing their way along the beach. The wind picked up and they decided to walk back along the sand dunes where they could find some shelter. As they dropped down into the dunes, John turned and looked across the Atlantic. He could see the lights of a large container ship, sailing across the horizon, headed to Europe or Africa.

"Have you heard anything from Janet and Fred?" John asked.

"I keep asking them to come and stay with us for a few days. Janet said she would let me know tomorrow."

When they returned to their home, John dried the dogs off with an old bath towel and Jules made some popcorn for a snack before bed. At 4:00AM, John shot up in bed. He gasped for breath as he looked around the room. Then he settled; he knew it was only a dream. The parade of dead bodies had come to visit him once more. This time they were led by Eddie Flynn, with his ninety-seven stab wounds. Then came seventeen-year-old Agatha McSweeney. In the dream, she stood in front of John. Her head was to one side and there was dried blood all over her face. She had been cut open from her neck to her hips. Just like Eddie, Agatha leaned forward, whispered something to John, turned and disappeared. Graham Hogan was next, with bullet holes in his head, face, and chest. Hogan also whispered something to John before disappearing. Then came Anthony Woodsworth, with the five-centimeter hole under his eye.

John could swear that Woodsworth had grabbed him by the shoulders when he went to whisper in his ear. This is what jolted him back to reality. Although he knew it was a dream, it had scared the living daylights out of him, especially because he actually felt Woodsworth touch him. And of course, as always, he had no idea what any of the cadavers had whispered in his ear.

He couldn't fall back asleep and an hour later, John watched the clock turn five. It was time to get up. When he got to work, he opened the file on Anthony Woodsworth, hoping that he would find something that he had missed. Maybe this is why Woodsworth had grabbed him in his nightmare. No such luck. There was nothing new; nothing had been missed. They had done everything they could and reached a dead end.

During the morning Jules texted, "*Fred and Janet are coming next week. They will stay for a few days.*" "*Excellent, can't wait,*" John texted back. "Well, at least that's something to look forward to." he thought. Meanwhile he was reading an internal bulletin about the murder of Walter Sheldon in Limerick Prison. He called Roxboro Road Garda Station in Limerick and learned that Walter had been killed on a range that was predominantly controlled by the Independent Posse gang.

John walked the few steps from his office to the incident room. "I think we might be in for some busy times," he said, holding up the bulletin for all to see. "Walter Sheldon, an old-time I-P gangster, has been killed in Limerick Prison."

"That's not such a bad thing, is it?" Mike Williams piped up.

"As long as it doesn't overflow into Cork Prison. Walter was killed on an I-P range so there is either some in-fighting or the gang war is going to another level." John worried that this could get worse before it gets better.

"Is there any point in reaching out to 'our informant' with the Independent Posse?" Len Benoit asked, looking at his partner with a sly grin.

"That fucking eejit is a liability! The last time we used him in the New Year's murder investigation, he made a right cock up of it. He almost stabbed the suspect," Rafter replied, horrified as he remembered the scene that played out in the hotel room at the casino. "I can reach out to him, if you want."

John thought about it for a few seconds. "Go ahead, call him up. See if he still has his three-way phone call business going." John turned to head back to his office, stopped and faced his team. "Where are we on interviewing the associates of Eddie Flynn?"

His answer was in the blank looks on the faces of the investigators. There were no new developments. "It looks like Eddie had a chronic crack habit and, rumor has it, he ripped off everyone and anyone including his own brother. He probably went to Mahon to rip off someone there and finally got his comeuppance," Eddie Jenkins said, breaking the silence.

"You're probably right." John shook his head as he turned and walked into his office.

Chapter 19

Bertie Flynn sat alone in the kitchen of his crack shack near Dominick Street. The house was quiet; he hadn't opened for business yet and he was enjoying the solitude. Bertie sipped a steaming hot mug of tea. He wasn't a serious drinker and, apart from a few pills now and again, he rarely used drugs. A mug of tea suited him just fine. Bertie was into making money. He was happy with the arrangement he had with the Independent Posse gang, cutting them into his deals and keeping a share for himself. He always had plenty of cash on hand. There was never a time when he did not have at least 60,000 euros in a shopping bag in his closet.

But now Bertie felt threatened. Tyson was behind his brother's murder and he knew if he did something about it, he would be next. "I hate that fucking bolix," Bertie said aloud. He thumped the table and the mug jumped, spilling drops of the hot liquid over its edge.

Bertie picked up his phone and scrolled through his contacts. He found the number he was looking for, an acquaintance in Drogheda. Drogheda, a city in County Louth about forty kilometers north of Dublin, was another troubled city with a gang problem.

Bertie called the number. "How are ya? It's Bertie Flynn in Cork."

"Bertie fucking Flynn! How the hell are ya?" the deep voice replied. "Hey, come 'ere, I was sorry to hear about your brother."

"Thanks, the poor fucker got stabbed nearly a hundred times." The sadness seeped through Bertie's voice.

"Do ya know who did it?" the deep voice asked.

"I have my suspicions. Nothing I can do about it right now." Bertie sounded completely defeated.

"Anyway, what do ya want with me? I'm sure this isn't a social call."

"I want to do some business on me own. What would a key cost?"

"I can't help ya right now. I have diversified into some other yokes but I can put you in touch with some people in Dundalk. They got some good connections across the border. I'll reach out to them and introduce you. Can they get you at this number?"

"Yes, they can. But don't take too long and listen! This can't get back to anyone in Cork. OK?" Bertie's voice had risen a couple of octaves.

"Don't worry. That crazy fucker Tyson won't hear anything from this end of the country. He does all his business in Dublin."

Bertie ended the call and sighed. He picked up his mug and drained what was left of his tea.

LATER THAT AFTERNOON, Jeff Rafter walked into the inspector's office. "I tried to get hold of our friend," he said.

"Which friend is that? Gerry Campbell?"

Rafter nodded. "He didn't answer his phone so I checked in case he was in custody. And, of course, he is."

"What did he do now?" John enquired.

John had arrested Gerry Campbell years earlier when Campbell was a high school student in Belfast. Back then, Campbell had confessed to his part in a homicide but agreed to testify against his co-accused and was convicted of a lesser crime. After his release from prison in Northern Ireland, Campbell had relocated to the Republic and set up a lucrative drug network in Limerick City. He regularly did business with the Cork gangs. Like a lot of criminals, Gerry

Campbell also provided information to the police. His handler was Jeff Rafter and his secondary handler was Inspector John Cahill. In the last few years, Gerry Campbell had provided information on two gang related homicide investigations.

"He lost a fight at the Cliff Top Bar in Ennis Town. After he was thrown out on his arse, he went to his car and picked up a Mac 10 automatic pistol and fired it at the bar. He lost control of the gun and it sprayed bullets all over the place. I don't know how he did it but he managed to shoot out a window in a house across the street. Luckily, the old lady living there went to bed early and wasn't killed," Jeff said, trying not to laugh.

"He'll do a couple of years for that. We can't use him as a jailhouse informant. He is too unreliable. Don't even bother trying to contact him," John replied, going back to the report he was reading. When Rafter left the office, John sighed and shook his head. "We're spinning our wheels here." he thought to himself. Seconds later he found himself checking out houses for rent in Belfast. He feared his secondment to the Garda was coming to an abrupt end because they were unable to solve these recent murders.

THE NEXT FEW DAYS DRAGGED on with no progress being made in the current investigations. Jules could see how it was bringing her husband down. He was quiet on their evening walks and was always deep in thought. "Janet and Fred are coming tomorrow. I hope you're in better form than you've been in the last few weeks. Janet is coming here to recuperate, not to get depressed," Jules said, poking John in the ribs as they walked along the beach.

"I'll be fine. It will be a great distraction to have them here." He tried to sound positive.

The following morning John and Jules drove to Cork Airport to collect Fred and Janet Nesbit. Fred and Janet breezed through passport control and picked up their bags from the luggage carousel. They were waved through customs and their faces lit up into broad smiles when they stepped through the sliding door and saw John and Jules waiting for them.

After hugs all around, John found himself tearing up when he saw Janet. She looked tired. The colour had drained from her face and she had aged several years in the few months since he last saw her. "You look well," he said to her.

"I do not! I look like a shit after a shower," she answered with her familiar laugh.

John took the spinner suitcase from her and Jules and Janet walked towards the exit while John and Fred took up the rear. Janet still used a cane but was walking well.

"How's things?" Fred asked in his thick Belfast accent.

"Same shite, different flies," John answered in his sing-song North Side Cork City accent. "Thank God you got here between showers. Let's get to the car before it starts raining again," John joked as he walked faster towards the car park.

They took the scenic route back to Inchydoney. Instead of going through Cork City, John turned left out of the airport and drove to Kinsale. Here they stopped for a coffee. After coffee, they took a short stroll through the gorgeous scenic town, wandering up and down the narrow streets and along the seafront wharf and back to their car. From Kinsale they followed the coast to Garretstown and Garrylucas beaches; they stopped briefly to watch a couple kitesurfing on the waves. They drove over the green hills, where the occasional horses and cattle shared some winter grazing, to Coolmain and Kilbrittan. It was time to stop again for a very fancy lunch at a gorgeous pink- coloured restaurant.

After lunch John drove along the coast road to Timoleauge. As they entered the picturesque village, John pointed out the ruins of the old abbey. "Some of my ancestors are buried in there. There are headstones dating back to the 1500's," John said, sounding like a tour guide. He glanced in the rear-view mirror at Janet. She looked worn out but happily taking in the beautiful surroundings. "We'll be home soon, only about twenty minutes away," he added. Janet saw him looking at her and smiled.

Another ten kilometers and they were in Clonakilty. After weaving their way through a bit of traffic, they were on the road to Inchydoney. This wasn't Fred and Janet's first visit but, as always, the drive along the coast was spectacular. "You're never coming back to Belfast, are you?" Fred said, waving his arm across at the view.

"We'll talk about that. I don't think I am the flavour of the day at the moment." John looked at Fred in the rear-view mirror and Jules stole a glance at her husband's face.

When they arrived at the homestead, high on the cliff overlooking the twin beaches of Inchydoney, Fred and Janet stood in awe as the vast Atlantic Ocean lay in front of them. Once they entered the house, the two greyhounds ran directly to the guests, ignoring their owners. Janet knelt and hugged the dogs, both lapping up the attention. Jules showed the visitors to their room and encouraged Janet to lie down and rest. She resisted the suggestion but only for a short while, and accompanied by a hot water bottle, Janet headed off for a nap.

"Why don't the two of you take the dogs to the beach and get out from under my feet while Janet snoozes?" Jules said, picking up the dogs' leashes and rattling them, knowing that the men couldn't refuse now even if they wanted to.

John smiled at his wife. He fetched the dogs' light raincoats from the closet in the hallway. Now the dogs were dancing around him. He put the pink coat on Lucy, the bigger of the greyhounds, and the purple one on Molly, the smaller brindle. "Here, you take Lucy, in case we see a cat." John handed Fred the leash.

"Molly can spot a cat from half a kilometer away and loses her mind. She goes from gentle and placid to raging anger in a split second. We think she was live baited with cats to teach her to race," Jules explained, patting the greyhound on the head.

"That sounds awful," Fred said.

"It is, but it happens. Greyhound racing is a big business and, as you know, money talks and speaks the truth!" John answered as he took hold of the leash and headed out the door. "So, how are you really?" John asked as the two men were walking down the long driveway to the road above the West Beach.

"I'm grand," Fred said quietly. After a few seconds of silence, he spoke more. "This has been the worst couple of months of my life. I thought I lost her. This is way worse than the bomb blast in '93." Fred's voice cracked as he opened up for the first time since he found Janet outside the restaurant after the stroke. He took a few deep breaths and carried on. "I felt so helpless. I knew nothing about this vile condition. Sure, all we ever knew about a stroke is you have one and that's that! You die or you're disabled for the rest of your life."

John looked at his friend and could see his pain. He knew this was hard for Fred. Therapy for Irish people is to 'bottle it up or bury it deep' and cops usually didn't share their feelings, let alone their problems.

"When the ambulance showed up, the paramedics knew exactly what was happening. They put me somewhat at ease and explained everything in plain language that even I could understand. They said the timing was in our favour because it had only just occurred," Fred spoke freely now that the flood gates were opened. "At least now, when we got to the hospital, I knew that it wasn't an automatic death sentence. There was hope and lots of it."

They had walked as far as the end of the hill and the entrance to the hotel carpark. "So far so good, no cats today. Let's walk both beaches. There's hardly anyone around and the tide is out," John said, knowing it would take the best part of an hour. They headed down the steps to the East Beach. At the foot of the steps, John stopped and took the leash off Molly; Fred did likewise for Lucy. The two dogs raced ahead of them for about five hundred meters before abruptly stopping and investigating a bunch of wet seaweed.

"Then the neurologist came to see me. She was a wonderful person." Fred continued his story without prompting. "She had all the M.R.I's, C.T. scans and X-rays in her hand and immediately put me at ease. Janet was in the resus room at this point. The doctor told me what had happened and the treatment Janet would have. She explained what the medication would do and why she wanted to remove the clot instead of waiting for it to dissolve. However, there were no guarantees until surgery. Then she pulled up her calendar and said, '*I've administered the injections and will do the surgery in a few hours.*'" Fred paused and took a deep breath. "I was in shock. I didn't think it would be so soon. I thought it would be a few days or even the next week or maybe in a month or so, but no, the surgeon was giving us a few hours. They move very quickly with these things."

"I suppose they don't hang about with something like this." John was fascinated by the details that Fred was providing.

"I didn't really have time to think about it. Before we knew it, it was the evening. Janet was still sedated. I felt that I should be asking questions but didn't know what to ask, let alone who to ask. But as you well know, the staff were amazing. They were very kind and if I did think of a question, they answered it right away. Before I knew it, they were wheeling her off to the theater."

"Where did you go then?"

"I sat in the Day Surgery Family Waiting Room. It was the longest few hours of my life, I think. I sat next to this older fella whose wife was having some varicose vein surgery. He was quite amusing. He said that her surgery would get him out of having to go ballroom dancing." Fred smiled at the memory. "I was only half listening to him. I was scared shitless that the outcome was going to be grim and our life as we know it was over. If that was the case, I didn't know what I was going to do." Fred took another deep breath and swallowed hard. "A nurse eventually told me that Janet was out of surgery and in the recovery room but I couldn't see her yet because they had to wait for her to come around. And of course, Janet being Janet, she did that in her own sweet time."

By this time, they had reached the east end of the beach. They stood at the channel and Fred stopped to survey his surroundings. It was as if he only just realized where he was. "Jesus, this place is fucking heavenly," he said as he looked across the channel to the little fishing village of Ring. John smiled in agreement. Molly had ventured into the water and was wading up to her underbelly as her long tail trailed in the water. John called her over and took her raincoat off. They turned to head back to the Virgin Mary Bank, the rocky outcrop that separated both beaches, when Molly ran through the water. She stopped next to the two men and shook violently, sending spray everywhere.

As they walked back towards the headland, Fred continued his story; he didn't need prompting. "When I eventually got to the recovery room, Janet was sitting up. The effects of the anesthetic hadn't worn off but she was feeling OK until she tried to speak. She couldn't. We were both terrified. I wasn't prepared for that. I know one of the nurses had said something about Janet's speech but it went in one ear and out the other. I'm sure I scared Janet as much as I scared myself with the look on my face. Then the surgeon came by and she said the operation went well and the clot was successfully removed. The injections they gave her when she arrived at the hospital had dissolved most of it. It sounded so routine."

Fred stopped and surveyed the beach; he looked out to his left at the Atlantic. The wind had picked up and the spray was blowing off the tops of the waves as they crashed on the shoreline. Then he looked to his right at the wild sand dunes, with the long spiky grass shaking in the wind. "My first impression of the occupational therapist was that she was about nineteen-years-old. But she knew her stuff! She was awesome in the way that she explained everything. This was a well-oiled machine because she had all the reports from the surgeon at hand. She said there was no need for in-patient rehab. That was a relief because Janet didn't want to stay in hospital. So she recommended a vigorous physical rehab program and an equally vigorous speech therapy program, and, of course, the stop smoking lecture. After a couple of days we were off to see the physical therapist. Do you know how we always hear in the media about people waiting for appointments? That's not the case at all! Our appointments were bang! bang! bang! One after the other, only a day or two apart. We were looking at weeks of daily appointments." Fred paused and blinked away his tears. "That's when Jules came in. She was fantastic! Those physical therapy sessions were very tough at first and they kicked the crap out of Janet. She's only just getting over them now. Janet suffered so much both mentally and physically. I really don't know how she took it all. She is much stronger than me, that's for sure."

They had finally reached the beginning of East Beach where they started. John called the dogs over and put their leashes on them. They walked up the concrete lifeboat launch which was still high and dry as the tide hadn't yet reached it. On top of the bluff, they walked towards the edge, watching the waves break high over the rocks and the spray reaching them, thirty meters from the edge. "How were they at work?" John asked.

"Oh, they were great. No problem taking time off. I have so much time banked that I could take a year off," Fred said, now smiling and relieved that he had unburdened himself.

"I'm glad it all worked out for ye. Janet will be fine," John assured Fred, patting his friend on the shoulder.

"Wait until I tell ya! I was told I should apply for an assistant chief constable position that's opening up next month," Fred said. There was obvious excitement in his voice and he was relieved to be able to change the subject.

"Are you going to apply?"

"Janet says I should. It's a contract position. Five years and then that's that, retire."

"You better apply. That way you can keep me here until I retire."

"If I had your ability to lead, I wouldn't have any doubts. Your achievements are well known back home." Fred looked admiringly at his friend. "Your team would run through a brick wall if you told them to. But you'd never tell them to do that. They would only have to follow you because you'd be first through that wall. Do you know the difference between a leader and a manager?" John shook his head, waiting for the answer. "A manager manages things, like policy, budgets and overtime. A leader leads his people. You have that rare talent and that's why some of the best managers dislike you. They're jealous because they want to be leaders and they just don't have it in them."

"If you get the assistant chief's job, will you retire after it or will you aim higher?" John asked.

"I would have to retire. I'll never be chief. That's a political appointment," Fred answered.

"You could always apply for the top job down here in the Republic." John laughed.

"Oh yeah, a P.S.N.I. officer running the Garda, like that will ever happen," Fred answered but he wasn't laughing.

They headed down the steps to the West Beach. The strand was similar to the one behind them, but not as long when the tide was fully out. At the far end, there was another channel where the tidal waters flowed into the harbour. At the foot of the steps, John unleashed the dogs. A small black and white Jack Russell terrier ran over to inspect them. Lucy danced in front of the terrier, challenging it to a race. Then all three dogs dashed off along the beach. The terrier, gamely trying to keep up, was fifty paces off the leaders. Fred laughed at the spectacle. "They're showing off now," John said.

"So things are good here? You don't want to come back anytime soon?" Fred asked.

"Things are great when we are solving cases and making arrests. Not so great right now. These gang killings are hard to close." John told Fred about the recent spate of gang violence in Cork City and the difficulty he was having in making any form of headway in the investigations.

"Hang in there. Keep pushing forward every day and you'll eventually get a break. You have the luck of the devil!" Fred laughed. "And fuck the begrudgers! There's a lot of jealousy in this game. I see it at my level all the time. There are people who would rather you fail to solve a murder than see you get some praise for pulling off the impossible." John shook his head but he knew his friend was right. When they arrived at the channel at the west end of the beach, a gentle mist was beginning to fall. John leashed the dogs, who, by now, had lost their short-legged opponent.

"We best head back to the house. This mist will turn to a downpour in a few minutes," John said, looking at the sky.

When they arrived back at the house, Janet and Jules were sitting in the kitchen, laughing, and nursing a glass of wine.

Chapter 20

Bertie Flynn tapped his waistband, feeling the .38 caliber Webley revolver that he had concealed there, as he walked into a bar overlooking the Boyne River on Meat Market Lane in Drogheda. Once inside, his eyes adjusted to the dimmed lighting and he saw his associate. The two men locked eyes and Bertie walked across the barroom to his friend who was seated in a booth. The men shook hands and Bertie sat down opposite the other man. "Will ya have a pint?" he asked Bertie.

"I'll have a coffee," Bertie replied, getting a suspicious look from across the table. "What? I don't drink much and the last thing I need is a D.U.I. up here.

Mark Chapman raised his hand and, catching the barman's eye, called out, "Coffee for your man here." Chapman sipped his pint of stout, licked the white froth from his upper lip and looked across the table, sizing Bertie Flynn up. A few seconds later a middle-aged woman brought a mug of coffee and some cream and sugar on the side to Bertie. "You're thinking of branching out on your own, are ya?" Chapman said.

"I think I should disappear for a while. Things are getting out of hand in Cork. I can easily afford a kilo of coke and that would set me up." Bertie snapped open the little cup of cream and poured it into his coffee.

"Be careful. The country is tied up pretty tight. If you move in on someone else's territory you could end up like your brother."

"I was thinking of going to Scotland or Holland."

Chapman nodded in approval. "What about meth?" Chapman said in his deep voice, holding his stare on Bertie all the time.

"Are you in that game?" Bertie asked, sounding surprised. There was no reaction or answer from Chapman. "That shit turns people into zombies. They lose their fucking minds completely and start to rot from the inside out. I hate dealing with people who are fucked up on that stuff."

"It does fuck people up, alright. But they keep coming back for more. There's a crew up in Dundalk that can hook you up. They're bringing in product from Newry in the North. I'll put you in touch with them. However, if you fuck them over, they'll cut you up into little pieces and scatter you all over the country. Trust me. They've done it before!" Chapman winked at Bertie and took another swig of his pint.

"How much?"

"Fifty-five, that's a one-off price, mates' rates, and all that. Take it or leave it."

Bertie Flynn let out a deep breath and looked up at the ceiling. "I'll take it."

Chapman handed Bertie a small piece of paper with a phone number written on it. He drained his pint and stood up to leave. "It's great to see you, Bertie. Again, I'm sorry to hear about Eddie. He was alright. Tell them fellas that you talked to me. They're expecting your call. All the best now." Chapman stepped away from the booth and tied up his coat. Before turning to walk away, he looked at Bertie, "If you change your mind about the meth, let me know," and as if they had been chatting about the weather, Chapman walked out of the bar.

Bertie Flynn studied the phone number as he finished his coffee. He took a couple of deep breaths, pulled out his cell phone from his coat pocket and punched in the number. "Yeah?" a Northern Ireland accented man answered.

"I'm Bertie from Cork. Mark Chapman gave me this number."

"Drive north to Dundalk and call me when you get there." Chapman's contact ended the call.

"How the fuck do you get to Dundalk?" Bertie thought. He left the bar and returned to his car. He checked the maps app on his phone and saw that Dundalk was only about thirty kilometers north on the M1 Motorway. Bertie drove north and half an hour later, he turned off at the Carrickmacross Road and drove into Dundalk. He pulled over to the side of the road and called Chapman's contact back.

"Where are ya?" the man asked.

"I'm in Dundalk. I pulled in off the Carrickmacross Road. Are we going to do this or are you going to have me running around like a fucking eejit all day?" Bertie sounded annoyed.

The man laughed, "You're OK. Go back to the M1 and continue north to Carrigdale. Take Exit 20 to the old Dublin Road, heading for Newry. It's only about fourteen kilometers from where you are. You'll see a huge red barn on your right. Pull in there and we'll meet ya. Fifty-five is the price, ya?"

"Sounds good, I'll be there in half an hour." Bertie ended the call. Bertie checked his mirrors, looked all around and reached under his seat. He pulled out a red and white striped plastic shopping bag. There were six bundles of bank notes in it. Each bundle held ten thousand euros. Bertie counted out five thousand euros from one of the bundles and put it into the glove compartment. He replaced the bag of cash under his seat, patted the Webley revolver on his hip and started up his car. Bertie turned around and drove back to the M1 and headed north. The M1 turned into the N1. At the roundabout at Dromintee he saw a signpost for Belfast and another for Jonesborough. Only then did he realize how close he was to the border of both the Republic and Northern Ireland.

A few minutes later, Bertie pulled off the road into a farmyard with a huge red barn. The yard was full of farm machinery and trailers. There were two wrecked trucks at the rear of the yard near a five-bar gate that led into some muddy fields. Bertie spotted a man wearing light blue overalls behind one of the wrecked trucks. The man peeked out from behind the truck at Bertie's car.

Then, from behind Bertie, another man, wearing dirty red overalls, walked up to the car. Bertie let the window down, "How's it going?" Bertie said.

"Are you lost?" the man in the red overalls said sounding unfriendly.

"Chapman sent me." Bertie tried to sound calm but there was a definite quiver in his voice.

The man in red waved to the fellow in the blue overalls; he then stepped out from behind the wrecked truck carrying a plastic shopping bag. The man in red had both hands in his pockets. Bertie knew he was armed. "Come into the barn," he said to Bertie. "Bring your stuff with you."

Bertie reached under the seat to get his bag of cash. Only when he moved, did he think he had moved too quickly and saw the man in red flinch. "I'm getting me money!" Bertie called out, the pitch in his voice slightly higher than usual. He stepped out of the car, holding the bag of money out from his side, in his left hand. Both Bertie and the man in red let out a sharp breath and they smiled.

'Blue overalls' came into the barn and threw the plastic bag on an old work bench. Bertie threw his bag of cash on the bench, reached over and picked up the other bag. He opened it and saw it had a neat, pressed brick of cocaine wrapped in several layers of clingfilm. 'Blue overalls' picked up the bag of cash and inspected the contents, "Fifty-five?" he said.

"Fifty-five G's, as agreed. Count it if you want."

"Oh, we will, don't you worry," 'Blue overalls' said. "We'll find you if it's short."

"OK, are we good?" Bertie asked. The man in red nodded and Bertie walked to his car. He did not look back but the hair on his neck was standing up as he listened intently for the sound of something suspicious. Nothing happened. Bertie got into his car, headed back to the road and drove south.

Chapter 21

Bertie Flynn was elated as he drove south. He had purchased a kilo of cocaine and knew if he cut it properly, he could easily triple his money. He could get the hell out of Cork and away from Tyson Rolland and the Independent Posse.

In his excitement, Bertie got confused at the roundabout at Dromintee and took the wrong exit. He didn't know it but he was almost in the heart of the village of Jonesborough, County Armagh, five hundred meters inside the Northern Ireland border.

On the outskirts of the tiny village, Bertie saw the yellow and blue Land Rover Defender in his rear-view mirror. The police vehicle lit him up, with its blue strobe lights and Bertie pulled over. Bertie looked confused when he saw the police officer wearing a dark green uniform and holding his hand on the handle of a semi-automatic pistol on his hip. It was at that moment that he realized his mistake and had accidentally entered Northern Ireland. He was so used to seeing the unarmed Republican Garda in their blue uniforms.

"Shut the engine off and step out of the car, sir," the young police officer said to Bertie. Bertie stepped out of the car and saw another police officer, standing by the passenger side of the Defender. "Before I pat you down, is there anything that I'm going to find on you?" the officer asked.

Bertie let out a long breath and looked down at his feet. "I've a gun on my right-hand side, he muttered."

The young officer stepped back and to the left and, as quick as a flash, drew his service pistol and pointed it directly at Bertie. Bertie raised his hands. The other officer dashed forward and Bertie was ordered to lie prone on the ground. The old .38 caliber Webley was removed from his waistband; Bertie was handcuffed, stood back up and was led to the back of the Defender. It didn't take the two officers long to find the kilo of cocaine.

Although he was only five hundred meters out of his way, Bertie Flynn was in custody in the United Kingdom. A joint task force of customs officers from both sides of the border had seen him drive in and out of the farmyard. Whether Bertie Flynn drove into Northern Ireland or stayed in the Republic, he was destined to be stopped by police.

Bertie was taken to Ardmore P.S.N.I. station in Newry. His car was towed to a secure search area in the same compound. His eyes opened wide as he approached the police station on the Belfast Road. This place did not look like any police station he had ever seen. It was surrounded by a twenty-foot-high brick wall, with another eight-foot metal fence on top of the wall. It was a fortress. Bertie swallowed hard. His heart was pounding. He knew he was in big trouble. He was led to a sparsely furnished room, searched and had his name, date of birth and background information taken. Then Bertie was led to a cold dark concrete bunker, the usual holding room, the same the world over. He sat on the cold concrete bench, put his hands to his face and felt like crying like a baby.

After what felt like a lifetime, a detective came into the holding room. "Mr. Flynn, would you like to consult with a solicitor," he asked in a somewhat harsh Northern Ireland accent.

"Is there any point?" Bertie looked up at the detective.

"You may as well. It probably won't help your circumstances very much but she can tell you what's in store. You were caught with a loaded handgun and a substantial amount of cocaine."

"So you're saying I'm fucked!"

"Pretty much." The detective, cracked a smile.

Bertie called the duty solicitor who told him that she would see him within the hour.

Bertie was led to an interview room where he met with a middle-aged woman. She had shoulder length salt and pepper hair; she was dressed in a grey suit and wore brown tortoiseshell glasses. After the introductions, Bertie explained his predicament. The solicitor told him that the best he could do was take full responsibility for the drugs and the gun and hope that the courts would be lenient.

The next morning, Bertie appeared before a magistrate and was remanded to Maghaberry Prison near Belfast. He had never done serious time before. When he walked onto the range in Maghaberry, he was scared and it showed. As soon as he spoke, the local thugs knew he wasn't from The North and Bertie found himself having to fight to stay safe.

After a day in custody in this foreign prison, Bertie called his girlfriend, Martina Fitzpatrick in Cork. He told her that he had been arrested in Northern Ireland and was looking at serious time. "What about the Fiesta?" Martina asked, not wanting to be left without a car with two young children to run about.

"It's impounded. I can't get it back. They'll probably sell it off."

"This gets better by the fucking minute! No car, no money and you're not around to make any money. How am I supposed to come and see ya? That's if I want to." Martina didn't know whether to cry or yell at him.

Bertie could hear one of his kids crying in the background, "Wait until I know what's happening. My solicitor is going to talk to the Crown prosecutor and see how much time I'll get if I plead guilty. It's been set down for trial in three months so I should know well before that," Bertie said, cringing, trying to keep calm but the fear of the unknown was eating at him.

THE POPULATION OF MAGHABERRY Prison hovered around a thousand inmates. Nobody there had ever heard of the Independent Posse and Bertie ended up in the general population, where he didn't have the protection of the violent gang behind him. Bertie was not a small man. Although he didn't like to fight, he was well able to. Soon he earned the respect of his fellow prisoners and, for the most part, was left alone. The courts appointed another solicitor to assist him but the future was bleak. He was looking at six years. Guns and drugs were not a good combination to be pinched with.

It didn't take long for word to get out in Cork's gang scene that Bertie Flynn had been pinched by the police in Northern Ireland. Tyson Rolland was furious. He knew Bertie had used gang money to buy a kilo of cocaine and planned to skip town. Tyson could care less about the money; it was the fact that someone had dared to double-cross him that bothered him. "I'll be talking to the Dublin lads to see if I can send a message to Bertie so nobody else decides that it's OK to rip me off," Tyson said to Darryl Lyons.

JOHN AND JULES ENJOYED spending time with their visitors. They had taken them to all the scenic areas and had driven along the Wild Atlantic Way for a couple of hundred kilometers, all the way to the Beara Peninsula. "I have to say Northern Ireland is a beautiful place but West Cork is like another planet," Fred remarked, looking across at the Galley Head Lighthouse, only minutes away from Inchydoney. Janet was looking and feeling better too. The mild Atlantic air was definitely agreeing with her.

It was now the middle of March and springtime was well in hand. "We should go to the races again. We had great fun when we did that the last time you both were in Belfast," Janet said. "Jules can put the mortgage payment on a horse and we can all go out to dinner."

Everyone laughed at the memory of Jules' big win at Down Royal races. "There's racing in Mallow tomorrow." John always knew where there was racing and regularly watched it on television. "Or we could go to a point-to-point on Sunday, if you don't mind watching some quality racing on farmland."

"I think Janet would like a little bit of comfort at the racecourse and not eating greasy warm chips with our fingers, up to our knees in mud on the side of a hill." Jules gave her husband a look for his suggestion.

The following morning, they made the sixty-five-kilometer cross country journey to Cork Racecourse in Mallow. They all backed an outsider in the feature race of the day; the horse was trained in a stable at Innishannon, a West Cork village close to Inchydoney. The mare looked like she was going to have to settle for third or fourth place when the leader unexpectedly tripped at the final hurdle and brought down his closest challenger. They were all elated when the mare won by a short head, coming home at 10/1. Once again, Jules made the most money, having placed fifty euros to win on the local horse.

On the way home, they stopped at Jules' aunt's bar in Bandon. Nan was expecting them and had her usual Irish stew, made from prime Irish lamb, ready on the stove. Nan promised a more lively night of entertainment the next time Fred and Janet came to visit. She was well known for the live Irish music sessions that were regularly held in her bar. But not tonight. Janet was exhausted but very happy. It was almost time for her and Fred to return home. For the first time in a long time, while visiting with her friends in Inchydoney, she had felt normal and was able to forget about her close brush with death.

Chapter 22

Bertie Flynn met with his solicitor in the legal room at Maghaberry Prison. "The Crown is going to ask for eight years," the lawyer said.

"Eight years! Eight fucking years! I wouldn't get that for killing someone in Cork!" Bertie said, no doubt he was quite frustrated.

"They can ask for eight. However, I think we can get you off with six." The lawyer sounded very pleased with himself. "You did have a loaded handgun and a substantial amount of cocaine when you were stopped by the police." Having seen Bertie's face, the lawyer was backpedalling and trying to justify himself.

"What if we go to trial? Is there a chance I could get off?" Bertie asked.

"Look, Mr. Flynn. The traffic stop was both legal and justified. Of course, it is your right to plead not guilty but I must advise against it. You run the risk of getting a higher sentence if convicted after a trial. The judge might decide to give you ten years." The solicitor left it up to Bertie to ultimately decide his fate.

"Give me a chance to talk to my 'old lady.' I'll let you know but she'll probably tell me to plead out." Bertie blew out a long breath, shook his head and stood up to return to the range.

Bertie went to his cell, lay on the bunk and folded his arms across his face. He thought about his options; he had none. Usually when a gang member went to jail, his family might get some assistance from the gang. But Tyson would know that Bertie was branching out on his own and Martina would not get any help from the I-P. The future was looking bleak.

Bertie fell asleep for an hour and when he woke up, he went in line to use the phone. Martina answered almost immediately. "Did you meet the solicitor?" she asked.

Bertie explained his options, as they were presented by the lawyer. Martina started to cry. Bertie felt frustrated and didn't know what to say or how to console her. "Tyson came here last night," she said between sobs.

Bertie perked up immediately, "What did he want?"

He made me go with him to Darryl's house in Manor View. I had to get me mam to come and watch the kids." Martina was in floods of tears now and Bertie, on the other end of the phone line, was very anxious.

"What did he want you for?" Bertie asked, a little harsher than he intended.

"There was a mess in the utility room by the back door. He made me, Jenny and Christina Carney clean it up."

"What kind of a mess?"

"A bad mess, lots of blood," Martina whispered.

"How much? Bertie asked frantically.

"Fucking lots! The whole floor was flooded with blood. I'm not saying any more over the phone." Martina wasn't stupid and knew when to shut up.

Martina ended the call. Bertie returned to his bunk and lay down, staring at the bunk above him.

IN INCHYDONEY, FRED and Janet's holiday was coming to an end and they were preparing to fly back to Belfast. Fred went for one last walk on the beaches with John and the dogs. "You're in no hurry to come back to Belfast, are you?" Fred asked.

"I think I would stick it out for six months and retire. I might just retire from here anyway," John said, as they headed past the hotel towards the East Beach.

"Why would you retire?" Fred was surprised at the notion.

"Because I'm too old for this shit. Take one look at me. I used to ride racehorses up and down these beaches. I couldn't ride a plow horse now." John patted his stomach. "We work for days on end, dealing with the worst of society and for what? A good pension? You have to survive to enjoy it."

"You love this stuff. You won't retire."

"You're right there. I do love it but I also know I can't do it forever. It's taking its toll on both me and Jules. If I get sent back to The North, there is no guarantee I would end up in Serious Crime again. I don't know how I would adjust to working at anything else. And, even then, it would be the same shit, different flies." John was being completely honest.

"I think I can guarantee you would go to Serious Crime if you came back, if that's what you wanted. I'm also pretty sure that nobody up North is going to force you back. If that happens, it happens from this side of the border."

"Then I better get solving some of these latest killings," John said, as he undid the dogs' leashes and they took off at a ferocious gallop.

At the house on the cliff top, Jules and Janet sat, admiring the view. "Are you going to be OK when you go back?" Jules asked. The concern in her voice showed.

"I have to be, don't I? I should be over the moon because the prognosis is good but I'm not. I'm scared and I hate being scared and I feel...I don't know how I feel." Janet started to cry. Jules moved next to her and put her arm around her shoulder. She didn't know what to say. Nobody did.

"There must be support groups for women who have gone through this. Would it help to talk about it with someone?"

"I can't do that. I don't think it would help me, talking to other people about their illness. I'm afraid it would make me worse."

"You're talking to me now," Jules said.

Janet smiled. "That's different," she answered softly. "I talk to Fred too, but I don't want to burden him. He's been amazing and I love the bones of him but this thing! It's changed everything."

"Give it time. It will get better." Jules hugged her friend.

IN MAGHABERRY PRISON, Bertie Flynn had made a decision. He was going to try to bargain his way out of prison. He had asked to make a private call to the police. Half an hour later, Bertie was escorted to the security office where he spoke on the phone with a detective from Lisburn P.S.N.I. Station.

Bertie explained who he was and why he was in custody. "I have some information on an unsolved murder," Bertie said.

"What murder?" the detective's interest was piqued.

"It happened in Cork, five or six months ago. I know who did it," Bertie said.

"If you want to tell me who did it, I'll gladly pass the information on to the police in the Republic but there is nothing we can do for you," the detective said. "Do you want to give me a name?"

Bertie thought about it. He was discouraged but was trying to think quickly. "Do you know Inspector Cahill?" he asked.

"Who?" the detective answered.

"He's one of your lot but he's working with the Garda in Cork. Can you tell him I want to talk to him?" Bertie was trying to play one last card. He heard the clicks of a keyboard in the background and said nothing, waiting for a reply.

"John Cahill. Yeah, he's an inspector from Belfast. I see here he's is on special assignment in the Republic. I can get a message to him to call you. Will that do?"

Bertie let out a sigh of relief. "Yes please, tell him it's urgent."

"Sure, but you got to give me something more. I have to tell him something more specific to make sure he's interested."

Bertie thought about it for a second. "Tell him it's about a fella who was shot in the head in Manor View five or six months ago. It was Tyson did it. I met him about an hour..."

"Whoa, whoa, slow down. I'm trying to write this down. Give me a chance to catch up. OK, it was Tyson," the detective said, in the now familiar harsh Northern Ireland accent.

"I met him an hour after it happened and he told me about it," Bertie said. The excitement in his voice was very noticeable.

"OK, what else?"

"That's enough. Tell him to call me or come to see me. I'll tell him all about it." Bertie said, cutting the conversation short.

" Fine, I'll send him an email. How long are you going to be there?" the detective asked.

"About six fucking years," Bertie answered and the policeman laughed.

Bertie returned to the bunk in his range while the detective looked up the email address for John Cahill. He sent a detailed email to the inspector, describing the conversation with Bertie Flynn. At the end of the email the officer added, *'Flynn sounds desperate and this could be all a load of rubbish. I would be happy to go and see him and sound him out for you, if you want.'*

EARLY THE FOLLOWING morning as Fred was putting their suitcases in John's car, John checked his emails on his laptop. He saw an email from Detective Sergeant Charlie Brennan, Lisburn P.S.N.I. John read the email with interest. "Hey Fred, do you know a Charlie Brennan, stationed in Lisburn?"

"I do, he's in the Criminal Investigation Division. Nice guy and a clever copper too. We have about 7000 officers. You get to know all the idiots but I try and get to know the really good ones too. Why?" Fred asked.

John showed Fred the email he received from the Lisburn officer. "Do you think he'd go and speak with this fella and do a good job?"

"I've heard good things about him. Let's give him a call," Fred said, taking out his cell phone and calling Lisburn Police Station. He was put through to D.S. Brennan in the C.I.D. office. Fred introduced himself as Superintendent Nesbit and told Brennan that he was actually in Cork with Inspector Cahill.

Brennan sat up straight in his chair and listened intently as Fred passed the phone to John. "I'll go and see him this morning, sir. I will call you right away after I speak with him. I'll also write up a report and have it restricted to you, me, and the superintendent so nobody else can go snooping into it." Brennan was looking forward to doing something different and assisting a couple of higher-ranking officers. He didn't know what John Cahill was working on in Cork but guessed it was some super, top-secret assignment, especially when a superintendent was there too.

Janet and Jules said their good-byes in the kitchen and John drove Fred and Janet to the airport. There was a heavy mist but no fog on the Kinsale Road where the airport was situated. John parked at the drop-off area and went inside the terminal with his friends. They left their luggage at the baggage-drop counter and headed to the escalator. John hugged his friends and they headed up to the security gate on the second level. He stood watching them until they were out of sight. He felt sad to see them go. He hated goodbyes. He returned to his car and headed to work.

Chapter 23

John met with Superintendent Paddy Collins at Garda Headquarters on Anglesea Street. He told him about the call from the detective at Lisburn P.S.N.I.

"That's going to be a political nightmare, sending someone up there to talk to him if he has some useful information." Paddy sighed at the thought of the paperwork involved.

"What nightmare?" John said. "Did you forget that I can go over the border anytime that I want and conduct interviews, make arrests and carry a gun. I'm P.S.N.I.!"

The superintendent looked up and smiled. "Jaysus, you're right! I forgot all about that. You've been around so long, you're like part of the furniture. Do what ever you need to do. Just keep me informed." John laughed at this and headed back to his own office.

At the morning briefing he told his team about the email and subsequent phone call from Detective Sergeant Brennan from Lisburn. "Do you think there is anything to it?" Mike Williams asked.

"Brennan says Flynn was caught with a kilo of cocaine and a loaded revolver. That will get him a few years. Maybe he's making the whole thing up, just to get out," Eddie Jenkins said, joining in the debate.

"It doesn't make sense!" Jeff Rafter added. "I-P have always got their drugs from the cartels in Dublin. Why would Flynn be in 'Bandit Country' in South Armagh picking up drugs? And only one kilo? I don't know. Something's off here." Jeff Rafter was the only member of the team who had previous drug squad experience.

John was happy to see the team deliberating over this latest development, even if it turned out to be nothing. It was raising them from the slump they had been experiencing after all the dead ends.

"I agree with Jeff," Pete Sandhu added in his thick Punjabi accent. "I've looked through all of Flynn's record and any intel associated to him and he's not a courier. He's a dealer. Something is not right here."

"I suppose we will have to wait for Charlie Brennan to get back to us. He's supposed to see Flynn this morning," John said.

At almost the exact same time, Detective Sergeant Charlie Brennan had made the ten-kilometer trek from his police station in Lisburn to Maghaberry Prison, west of the city. He drove down the long driveway from Old Road. After parking, he made his way to the administrative buildings, outside the main prison perimeter. He requested to see Bertie Flynn at the duty office and was led to a secure office where he deposited his cell phone, service pistol, ammunition and handcuffs. Then he waited in an interview room. Charlie looked around. It was typical of all such rooms; the walls were painted a thick cream colour and the floor tiles were a black, white and red pattern. There were two small windows with a metal grill on both the inside and the outside, attached to the window frame. On the wall was a sign that read 'Smoking is strictly prohibited.'

Charlie sat on one of three chairs in the room, next to a table that was bolted to the wall. He waited almost half an hour. He was bored without his phone to browse and took to pacing in the room, looking out the window at the grey buildings and a corner of the carpark. Finally, Charlie heard a door open and close and then footsteps approaching the interview room.

The door opened. Charlie Brennan saw a tall, well- built young man, with black hair cut close to his scalp. He was dressed in a grey sweatsuit and was wearing white socks and dark blue flip-flops. The man had his hands cuffed in front of him and was flanked by two prison guards.

"Bertie Flynn?" Brennan asked.

"Yup," said one of the guards. "Do you want us to stick around?"

"We'll be fine," Brennan said, taking a seat at the table.

"Cuffs on or off?" the guard asked.

"Off please." Brennan said.

Bertie's cuffs were removed and the guard handed Brennan a pager about the size of a box of matches, telling him to press the call button when he was ready to leave or if the prisoner caused trouble.

When the guards left, Bertie sat at the table. Brennan introduced himself and was upfront with Bertie when he told him that he couldn't do anything to help him. He was only there to listen to what Bertie had to say and then report back to Inspector Cahill in Cork.

"Do you think he can do anything for me?" Bertie asked.

"I don't know. I suppose it depends on what you can tell him. I don't know him but I do know he is well connected." Brennan opened his notebook and took out his pen.

Bertie told Brennan that he was involved with a street gang in Cork. He said that he was hanging out in a crack shack on the night, a few months ago, when a fella got shot dead in Manor View. Bertie claimed that Tyson Rolland came into the crack shack sometime before daybreak and he was all jacked up. Rolland then told Bertie that he just shot a hater in Manor View.

Brennan looked sceptically at Bertie Flynn. He tried to ask some clarifying questions but Bertie said he would save his answers for Inspector Cahill. Bertie also claimed to know a lot more about the gang but would not elaborate.

Detective Sergeant Brennan told Bertie that he would report everything back to Inspector Cahill in Cork and he would only come back to see him on the request of the Garda. Bertie was escorted back to his range inside the prison.

Charlie Brennan pulled in on the Leckey Road, before he hit the highway, and called John Cahill in Cork.

"I don't get a good feeling about him, sir," Brennan said. "He makes this Rolland fella seem like Jimmy Hoffa and I think he's spinning a bit of a yarn here."

"But he's certain that this happened five or six months ago and definitely in Manor View?" John asked.

"That's the one thing he is set on."

"We do have an unsolved murder in Manor View, back in October. Whether it's true or not, this is the only piece of information we've received. I will let you know if I decide to come up and speak with him."

After ending the call, John sat and stared across the room. He wanted to speak to Bertie Flynn and find out, first hand, what he had to say. He knew he couldn't make a deal with Bertie, not without the backing of the Office of the Director of Public Prosecutions.

He picked up his phone again and called Brian McCarthy, a senior prosecutor with the D.P.P. John had worked high profile cases with McCarthy before and knew if he could deliver a favourable result after an interview with Flynn, McCarthy would move heaven and earth to get Flynn a deal. However, he also knew that if he told McCarthy that Charlie Brennan had doubts about Flynn, he would shut it down right there and then.

John was correct; McCarthy was interested. He knew the Independent Posse were causing havoc in Cork City and believed Tyson Rolland was behind most of the violence. "It will be very difficult to work something out with the Crown prosecutors in Northern Ireland," McCarthy said.

"Hmm," difficult but not impossible." John smiled; he knew he had the lawyer hooked.

"There are avenues for such arrangements but only if the information is completely corroborated and serves the public's interest," McCarthy said. "Leave it with me until tomorrow. I have to check on a few things."

John was not surprised by this. He knew it wouldn't be straight forward. Even though Brian McCarthy was a brilliant lawyer, he was not one to jump into a dodgy situation, feet first, without giving it his full attention.

THAT EVENING, AS USUAL, John and Jules walked the dogs on the beach. The tide was coming in so they kept to the West Beach, rather than getting cut off from the steps on the East Beach by the rising water. "How were Fred and Janet at the airport?" Jules asked.

"They were great. I think they had a good time. Janet didn't look as drained as she did when she arrived last week."

"I think they enjoyed the break. She's not as strong as you think she is and is very fragile at the moment," Jules said.

"So is Fred. We had a couple of long chats. This thing has kicked the crap out of the two of them," John answered and they continued to discuss their friends.

"Any news at work?" Jules changed the subject.

John told her about Charlie Brennan's interview with Bertie Flynn and his opinion of Flynn. He also told her about the conversation he had with Brian McCarthy.

"You spoke with Flynn after his brother was killed, didn't you?" Jules asked and John nodded. "I think you should go and speak with him yourself. It sounds like he badly wants to talk to you."

"I probably will go and speak with him. But I hope McCarthy is on board to offer him something."

"Why does Brennan think he's shifty?" Jules asked.

"He doesn't get a good vibe from him. I must respect his opinion. Fred says he has a good reputation as a detective. If Flynn is desperate enough, he's likely to make up anything to try and get out of a jam," John said, going over all the possible scenarios in his head. "I think I'll go up and speak with him. Maybe I'll bring Pete with me. He'll be able to muddle through any bullshit Flynn spouts and confirm it on the computer. We'll figure out if he's telling the truth or not."

JOHN WAS DEEP IN THOUGHT when Brian McCarthy called from the Office of the Director of Public Prosecutions the next morning.

"Brian, thanks for calling back. Are we ready to head up to Northern Ireland?"

McCarthy sighed loudly, "When do you want to speak with Mr. Flynn?"

"I can go tomorrow. I'll bring one of my guys along. Do you fancy a trip over the border?" John sensed that the lawyer was interested in hearing more from Bertie Flynn.

"I can't. I'm preparing for a trial that's scheduled to start next week. I've asked Nancy O'Dwyer, one of our senior lawyers, to go with you.". I'll tell her to expect your call and that you plan on going North tomorrow."

John knew Nancy O'Dwyer; she had prosecuted some of his cases in the past and was a very capable lawyer. Nevertheless, he couldn't help feeling that maybe Brian McCarthy was putting a little bit of distance between himself and the upcoming Bertie Flynn interview, just in case it didn't work out.

John called Nancy O'Dwyer and arranged to meet her at Cork Airport, bright and early the following morning. Then he asked a clerk from Travel Services to book the tickets and three rooms in the hotel near the Titanic Museum in Belfast.

"The Titanic Museum?" Paddy Collins said. "There must be a cheaper hotel in Belfast!"

"Ah, don't be such a tight arse! That's where I always stay when I go up for training or meetings. They'll give us a government rate. Pete and Nancy can go and see the museum. It's pretty spectacular." John smiled because he knew his boss was just teasing.

"Oh! I didn't know it was a bit of holiday too. Maybe I should go," the superintendent said, playing along.

"I'll call Travel Services and tell them to book another seat on the plane."

"Ah feck off out of that! Sure, who would run this place if I was missing for a day?" the superintendent waved his hand, dismissing John.

John called Charlie Brennan in Lisburn; he asked him to get word to Bertie Flynn that they would see him tomorrow. John suggested that Flynn have his solicitor with him for the meeting. Brennan said he would go to Maghaberry Prison in the morning and bring Bertie Flynn to Lisburn P.S.N.I. station. It would be easier to conduct an interview there. John agreed that it was a good idea.

As usual, Pete Sandhu thought of everything and packed all the essential office equipment from laptops to red pens in his briefcase. The two cops and the lawyer met on the ground floor of Cork Airport. They ascended the escalator to the second floor where Nancy O'Dwyer made her way through the security screening process. John and Pete went into a side office. John presented a receptionist with several forms and both he and Pete showed their police identification. The receptionist checked and photocopied the forms and handed them back to John. She called one of the security people and gave him the photocopies.

"Are you wearing your guns or are they in your hand luggage?" the security officer asked.

We're wearing them but they are unloaded," John answered, opening his coat, showing the small compact Glock 27 on his hip.

"That's grand so." He led the two detectives out of the office and around the security screening area where nobody would know that they were carrying firearms on the commercial flight.

Pete and John met with Nancy Dwyer at the departure gate and they sat and chatted while waiting to board their flight to Belfast.

The flight to Belfast was quick as they travelled on an Airbus A320 jet, rather than the usual twin prop planes that often serviced the short route. Once they landed in Belfast, John sought out the P.S.N.I. office in the main terminal. He picked up the keys to an unmarked police car that was waiting for him.

John drove into Belfast city center and took the M1 Motorway south to Lisburn. "How do you want to play this, Nancy?" John asked as they drove the twenty kilometers from the airport to the police station.

Nancy was sitting in the front seat; Pete was in the back behind John. She looked back at Pete and then at John. "Start by telling this fella that if we catch him out on one lie, that's it! We walk away from him and he gets nothing, no matter what else he tells us." Nancy was scribbling some notes in her notebook. "You can also tell him that he has to disclose to us every single criminal act he has done in his lifetime, especially while with the gang. And," she paused for effect, "he has to tell us everything he knows about the gang and the other members."

John looked in the rear-view mirror at Pete who was also frantically making notes. He turned off the M1 and into Lisburn's city center. As he drove along Laganbank Road, John pointed to a high red-bricked wall with an eight-foot-high chain-link fence on top of the wall. "This is where we're going," he said.

Pete stared out the window. "I thought we were going to the police station, not the prison.".

"This is the police station. We like to keep them safe and secure up here," John said, grinning slyly.

Pete let out a sharp whistle. "What's the fence on top of the wall for?"

"It makes it difficult to fire a missile over it," John answered.

"That's what I was afraid of!" Pete whispered, staring out the window.

Chapter 24

John drove in the main entrance to a secure forecourt. Here he presented his P.S.N.I. identification to the guard and was allowed entry to the main carpark. The trio made their way into the building and to the front counter. Pete had relaxed now that he was in the somewhat familiar surroundings of a police station. John identified himself to a young officer at the counter and Detective Sergeant Charlie Brennan was summoned.

A few minutes later, Charlie Brennan arrived in the foyer. After introductions all around, he led the three visitors to a stairwell. "The elevator is giving trouble again," Charlie said and they hiked up the stairs to the second floor.

"Just like home," Pete said with a laugh.

They walked down a corridor towards the C.I.D. offices. Charlie stopped and pointed to a door on his left. "He's in there. The room is wired for audio and video but nothing is recording at the moment. Do you want to pop your head in or do you want to come into our office first?"

"We'll go to your office first," John replied. "He'll only ask us for something!"

Charlie Brennan sniggered, "The first thing he asked for this morning when I took him out of the prison was a burger."

"Is his legal advisor here?" Nancy O'Dwyer asked.

"I called his solicitor and he's on his way," Brennan answered.

Charlie Brennan led the Cork crew into a small room off the video monitor room. Here he had a laptop computer and headphones set up on a desk. He also had provided two notepads and several pens. "If you're not all going in the room, whoever is staying outside can monitor the interview from here. I can get more headsets if you need them," Charlie informed them.

"I'm not going in the interview room. I don't even want to see this fella in person right now," Nancy added. "But I will speak with his solicitor, as soon as he gets here."

John was impressed with Brennan as he had gone out of his way to have everything ready for them. He made a mental note to send a follow-up email to Brennan's immediate supervisor, thanking him for the assistance and Cc it to Fred.

While waiting for Bertie Flynn's lawyer, Charlie Brennan's inquisitive nature got the better of him. "You must be doing some top-secret work in the Republic, sir. You had one of the top brass with you when we spoke on the phone."

"Not top-secret, Charlie. I was seconded there a few years ago to work in an Integrated Fugitive Squad, but I kinda got sidetracked into the Serious Crime Unit in Cork City. And I've been there ever since."

"And you're from the Republic?" Charlie asked.

"I'm from Cork City. I joined up here, in the R.U.C. in 1994. I was here for the end of the 'troubles' and the transition to P.S.N.I., the whole works." John smiled as he reminisced.

"So how come Nesbit was with you? Do you answer to him? Rumor has it, he's next in line for the assistant chief constable spot," Charlie said, prying deeper.

John didn't mind the prying; after all, it was the sign of a good detective to ask all the questions. "Fred and I go way back. I knew him before he went to the Training Division after his injury in the mid-nineties.

Charlie Brennan was just about to ask another question when he was interrupted by his cell phone. Bertie Flynn's solicitor was downstairs.

"Do you want to speak to the lawyer alone?" John asked Nancy Dwyer when Charlie left the room.

"No, I only want to make sure he knows what we're doing here. After I speak to him, we should allow him to speak with Flynn, in private, so he can advise him on what to do."

Moments later, Charlie Brennan returned with Flynn's solicitor. The man, who looked to be in his late forties, was out of breath from keeping up with Charlie after they had quickly climbed the stairs. There were beads of sweat on his forehead and under his unkempt wispy hair, long overdue for a haircut. The jacket of his charcoal grey suit was too large for him and the pants were too tight. "Hello," he said in a cultured Belfast accent, "Angus Tighe, solicitor for Mr. Flynn." Tighe shifted his briefcase from his right to his left hand and shook hands with John.

John, in turn, introduced Angus Tighe to Nancy and Pete. It was as if there was no one else in the room except Nancy as Tighe directed all his focus on the other lawyer. Nevertheless, Nancy O'Dwyer was not flattered by the attention; she saw Tighe for what he was, pompous and out of his league.

"Mr. Tighe, we are here at the request of your client who claims to have information about an unsolved homicide in Cork City in the Republic of Ireland that occurred last October." Nancy immediately took charge of the meeting.

"I'm aware of that," Tighe said.

"I expect you will want some time alone with your client before these police officers interview him. Please let him know that under no circumstances, at this point, will he be offered any consideration on his current situation. He must tell us the truth and must answer ALL our questions. After that, his statement will be analyzed and if believed to be useful, he may be offered judicial consideration." Nancy was taking a hard stance and looking directly at the defense lawyer.

"I would like to be present for the duration of the interview," Tighe responded.

"Of course, you are welcome to sit with your client throughout. I will not be sitting in as I do not want to be classified as a witness in any proceedings that may come from this interview," Nancy replied, planting the seed in Tighe's mind that he may not want to be present during the interview. "After all, we are interviewing him as a witness. He has no jeopardy during this interview."

Angus Tighe left the monitor room and went to speak privately with Bertie Flynn. After he repeated everything that Nancy O'Dwyer told him, Angus reminded Bertie that once he crossed this line, there was no going back. "You will not be able to fool them so if you are going to go ahead with this, I suggest that you tell them the entire truth or you're going to burn all of your bridges and find yourself on your own." Angus stared at Bertie looking very concerned.

"If your information is good and they can use it, there is a chance that you will get some sort of a deal. If you pull out now, you may get six years and maybe, with parole, you can walk away after four or five. Once you start this interview, there is little I can do," Angus Tighe said, looking extremely serious at his client.

Bertie took a deep breath and let it out slowly. He closed his eyes for several seconds and when he opened them, he spoke. "I need to do this. I can't sit here for a few years while my wife and kids need me."

"Alright!" Angus Tighe stood up and knocked on the door. Charlie Brennan opened it. "He's ready to speak with the officers from Cork," Tighe said to Charlie.

With that, Charlie closed the door again and went to get John and Pete. Nancy O'Dwyer turned on the monitor and put on her headphones. "Let the games begin," she said to herself.

Chapter 25

John and Pete walked into the interview room. "How are ya, Bertie?" John said, shaking Bertie's hand. He introduced Pete and they both sat down. John explained to Bertie that they would take a sworn witness statement from him and if he were found to be lying about anything, he may be charged with a criminal offence, like perjury or perverting the course of justice. "This is no time for bullshit, Bertie. This is going to be a long day. You must agree to answer all our questions truthfully. If you tell us a hundred things and ninety-nine of them are completely true and one is a lie, guess what? No deal! And, I will still use the information in the ninety-nine things you told me. Have you got that?"

Bertie looked fairly stoic. He glanced at Angus Tighe and then looked back at John. "Yup, I got it."

Pete then went over a sworn statement declaration form with Bertie, who affirmed to tell the truth, and signed the document. There was no going back now.

"Bertie, before you start, you are being treated as a witness here today. That means, I expect you to tell me all the criminal offences that you yourself did. But because we are treating you as a witness, whatever you tell us will not be used against you. Do you understand that?"

Bertie nodded his head and answered, "Yeah."

"The reason I want to know about all the bad things you have done is so I can assess your credibility. The prosecutors in Cork also will want to see what kind of person you are. If you hide something now and any of this goes to court, I can guarantee that the defense lawyers will dig it up. You'll look like a liar and our case will be down the toilet. Got it?"

"I understand." Bertie nodded and grinned slightly.

"I'm going to tell you what Detective Sergeant Charlie Brennan told us. He said that you met Tyson Rolland in October, in a crack shack, and Tyson told you that he had just killed a hater. You also told D.S. Brennan that Tyson was all hyped up." John paused and took a breath. "What you told D.S. Brennan was enough to get Pete and me up here to speak with you. If that story changes now, that's absolutely fine. From here on in, I just want to hear the truth." John continued, holding Bertie's stare.

Bertie Flynn looked down at the floor. The only sound in the room was Bertie's breathing; it was louder than the three other people who were present. He looked up at John and began. "I remember that Friday night in the middle of October very well. It was actually on Saturday morning at around ten o'clock that I was told about the shooting. It happened at a house directly across from where Darryl Lyons lives. A fella was shot in the face, in the doorway of that house." Bertie paused and looked around the room. "I was in a crack shack that I was in charge of, in a lane off Dominick Street, when I was told about it by the person who shot that man."

"Who told you this, Bertie?" John asked, letting the silence settle again.

Bertie physically squirmed in his chair. He took a deep breath and blew it out quickly. It was plain to see that he was struggling with himself. "It was my best friend told me. My best friend shot that man," Bertie replied, his voice low but clear.

John waited; the silence was almost painful but he let Bertie sweat. Bertie finally continued, "It was Archie Cambridge. He's my best friend and he told me all the details on the Saturday morning after he killed that man."

Angus Tighe stopped writing in his notebook and looked across at Bertie. Pete actually saw beads of sweat on the solicitor's forehead.

"OK, tell me exactly how that conversation came about." John was feeling much better about this revelation rather than the one Bertie had made about Tyson claiming to be the assassin.

"I was chilling at the shack near Dominick Street on the Saturday morning. There was nobody else there when Archie showed up. He was shaking. I knew that something was up." Bertie stopped and fidgeted with his hands. John sat back and let Bertie go on in his own time. Bertie took a few deep breaths and started again. "Archie said that he was at a house party in Knocknaheeney. I knew that was true because I was at the same party earlier in the night and saw him. Archie said that Darryl had called Tyson. Darryl said that there were a bunch of M-W haters outside his house, harassing him. Then Tyson called Archie over and told him to go and whack the haters."

Pete Sandhu was making some notes; John just sat there and listened, waiting for Bertie to continue. At this point, Angus Tighe was the most uncomfortable looking person in the room.

"Archie said that Tyson handed him a gun and he went to Darryl's house with Alfie Hastings and Alfie's old lady. Do you know Alfie Hastings?"

"I know who he is." John remembered that Alfie Hastings was another long-time member of the notorious gang.

"Archie said he sat in the back seat of Alfie's BMW. Alfie's old lady, Lily Crawford, drove, and Alfie sat in the front next to her. They drove past Trish Galvin's house and then up past Darryl's place. They saw a fella in the garden across the street from Darryl's house." Bertie took another deep breath but now he looked committed to keep going. "Alfie parked at the end of the street and Archie got out and walked back to Darryl's house. He found the fella hunkered down in the porch of the house. Archie walked up to him and asked him who he was down with."

"What do you mean 'down with'?" Pete asked. At the same time, he got a scolding glance from John for interrupting.

"Like, 'what gang are you supporting?'" Bertie answered. He took another deep breath and continued. "Your man said he wasn't down with anyone so Archie asked him what did he think of I-P." Bertie now paused for effect, but all he got was a nod from John to continue. "Then, your man said, 'Fuck the I-P, they're a shower of cunts,' or something like that. Then Archie pulled out the gun and shot him point-blank in the face." Bertie stopped there. He looked at the faces around the room.

Angus Tighe looked like he was going to be sick. "Can I have two minutes in private with my client?"

"Really? Right now?" John said, quite frustrated. "OK, we'll be back in two minutes." He and Pete stood up and left the room.

"You don't need me here. There's nothing I can do for you now. It's between you and the authorities in the Republic," a defeated looking Angus Tighe said to Bertie.

"Fair enough!" Bertie replied and the solicitor stood up and left the room. Once outside he told John that Bertie was ready to continue. Tighe walked down the hall towards the monitor room where Nancy O'Dwyer sat listening to the interview. She heard him approaching and closed the door before he reached it. Charlie Brennan appeared and escorted the scared solicitor from the building.

John and Pete returned to the interview room. "OK Bertie, I guess you scared him off," John said. "The last thing you told us was that Archie found this man who was in a porch across from Darryl Lyon's house and then Archie shot him in the face. Carry on from there, with what Archie told you next."

"Archie said that he tried to find the shell casing and take it with him but he couldn't find it. He was starting to panic so he legged it. He ran down the street and Alfie and his old lady were waiting for him. He jumped in the car and Lily drove them back to the party," Bertie said, looking like that was all he had to tell.

But John needed more, much more. "What happened then?"

"Tyson asked him how it went. And Archie told him he found one M-W hater and shot him in the face. Tyson took his gun back and that was it really. When Archie came to see me a few hours later, he was really jacked up."

"What else did Archie say? I know he said more, especially if he was jacked up." John was pushing for more clarity.

"Archie said that Tyson was worried that me and him were well respected within the gang and we might be a challenge to him. So Tyson sent Archie on that mission to have something over him."

"You said that Tyson took HIS gun back. What type of gun is it?" John asked.

"It's a Glock. Just like the ones that you fellas have. It's his pride and joy. He loves that gun. He has two clips for it too and hollow-point ammo," Bertie said.

"And Archie told you that this was the gun that he used?" John asked.

"Yeah, he told me that Tyson gave him the Glock because he didn't have a gun himself and I was gone by that time so he couldn't borrow mine. I told you Tyson loves that gun. It's the same gun he used to shoot up a house in Parklands a few weeks ago. He shot every single window out of the front of the house."

Pete was frantically making notes while John quickly thought about the random, unexplained shooting in Parklands a few weeks earlier. "Why would Tyson do that?"

"Tyson's old lady, Jenny, was on the outs with him. Jenny's best friend lives at that house in Parklands so Tyson shot it up to send a message to Jenny to come back to him. She got the message and I moved her back."

"OK Bertie, you're doing great, but before we keep going and talk about some other stuff, how come you got so much detail from Archie? The way you tell it, it's like you were there with him," John said. Pete turned to a fresh page in his notebook and Bertie took another deep breath.

"Me, Archie and Eddie all grew up together. We all joined I-P at the same time and shared everything. He was like our third brother. We're really close. When Archie is jacked up, like he was that morning, that's what he does. He relives it when he's telling you about it. But he would only do it for me. If Eddie was around, he would have dummied up. Eddie liked to brag," Bertie replied sadly as he remembered his dead brother.

Chapter 26

"Did you ever talk to Tyson about this? Did he ever mention it?" John asked.

"He popped into the shack the next day. Business was good so we couldn't talk much."

"What did you talk about?" John continued to probe.

"Tyson said that he sent Archie on a mission last night and he did good! He said Archie followed his orders to the tee and merc'd a Guppy hater," Bertie replied.

"Hang on a minute, what does merc'd mean to you? And what's a Guppy hater? I have to apologize. I'm an old fart and my street slang isn't what it should be." John smiled at the man across the table.

Bertie sniggered, "Merc'd means killed and a Guppy hater is a Mahon Warlord gangbanger."

"I just looked it up on an urban dictionary." Pete held up his phone. "Merc'd comes from the word mercenary and it means to kill."

"Thanks for that, Pete. OK, continue! You said that Tyson was worried about you and Archie taking over from him. Did he ever send you on a mission so that he could keep you in your place?" Bertie had a troubled look on his face. John had to get him to open up; he had to get the full story. "You mentioned that you were at the same party as Archie and Tyson. Where was it?" John asked, cautiously taking control of the interview.

"It was just a house party on Killiney. One of the lads threw a party for his birthday. It was nothing special." Bertie looked away quickly when he answered.

John suspected there was more to this party than Bertie was saying. "Remember Bertie, we are in this for the long haul. You must tell us everything and it has to be the truth. Now tell me, what else happened at this party?" John sat back in his chair and stared at Bertie Flynn.

Bertie looked at his feet. He closed his eyes for a few seconds. John figured Bertie was deciding what to do and how much he should say. Then he began. "Tyson sent me on a mission too. I'm pretty sure I killed someone." Bertie raised his head and stared at the detective who showed no reaction and remained silent. Bertie felt that he had to continue. "Earlier in the night, Tyson said there were some haters harassing Trish Langford. Do you know her? She's Georgy Galvin's old lady."

"I know Trish," John said nodding. "A lovely lady," he added sarcastically.

"He told me to go and take care of them. I went up to Manor View and found these assholes driving around Trish's place like maniacs. They were doing handbrake turns and honking the horn around her house." Bertie paused and took a few breaths.

"Go on, you're doing great," John said, encouraging the gangster to continue.

"I stayed in the shadows. I'm pretty sure they didn't see me. They were driving this little white four-door Nissan and when they were coming back to Trish's house, I stepped out in front of them and fired four rounds at them, directly at the front windshield. I must have hit the two in the front seats. I saw them flinch." It was clear from his face that he was reliving that incident; Bertie put his hands up to his face when he said the word 'flinch.'

John looked across at Pete and stole a quick smile. He knew this was the same car that was shot at a couple of hours before Anthony Woodsworth was killed. This was dynamite information; nobody knew about this shooting. It was never reported to the police and it was never mentioned in any media report.

"Why do you think you killed someone?" John asked, keeping his voice very calm and even.

"I must have. I saw the bullets strike the windshield. I had to hit them. And I saw in the newspaper the next day that there was more killing in Cork's North Side."

"Did you read that article?" John asked.

Bertie shook his head. "Just the headline. I was too sick to read anymore."

"Just to be clear, Bertie, was this the same night that Archie was sent on the mission across from Darryl Lyon's house? And it was definitely a small white Nissan that you shot at?"

"Yeah, the exact same night, only a little bit earlier."

"What happened immediately after you shot at the white Nissan?"

"I jumped out of the way and the car swerved and mounted the footpath and drove off like a scalded cat."

"Did you go back to the party and report to Tyson?" John asked.

"No, I was too fucking scared. I legged it back to the shack near Dominick Street and phoned him. I stayed at the shack all the next day before I eventually went to our place in The Glen."

"Did Tyson give you a gun too?" John asked.

"No. I have my own. It was the same gun that I had when I got pinched a few weeks ago."

"What kind of gun is it?"

"It's really old but it works well. It's an old .38 caliber Webley. You won't be able to compare the rounds. I ran a file down the barrel a couple of years ago to prevent any C.S.I. stuff," Bertie said sheepishly.

"The P.S.N.I. have that gun now?" John asked. Bertie nodded. "Let's take a fifteen-minute break, Bertie. Do you want to use the bathroom or have a tea or coffee?"

"Can I have a cup of tea and a biscuit?" Bertie asked.

John and Pete left the room. Pete rustled up a cup of tea in a Styrofoam cup and two chocolate-covered biscuits; he left them with Bertie and went to hear what John and Nancy O'Dwyer were talking about.

"What do you think so far?" John was trying not to look too excited.

"I don't know what to think. What he has told us about the guns is easy to corroborate. Do you know what type of weapon was used to kill Woodsworth?" Nancy O'Dwyer asked.

"It was a ten-millimeter round, most likely fired from a 40 caliber Glock or similar weapon. The casing was found in the victim's clothing at the hospital. I haven't a clue what type of gun was used to shoot up the house in Parklands but I remember hearing about the incident."

"Hmm," Nancy muttered. "What about this other shooting? Has he just admitted to a murder? That's going to make him difficult to deal with," Nancy said, reading from her notes.

"Now here's the interesting thing, Nancy." John pulled his chair closer to the solicitor. "That shooting happened exactly as he said. A small white Nissan was cruising around Manor View the night that Woodsworth was killed. There were four occupants, all from Mahon. They were tormenting Trish Langford and probably driving by Darryl Lyons' house too and causing him grief. Someone, most likely Bertie Flynn, jumped in front of the car and fired a few rounds from an old gun and hit the windshield. The ammunition was very old and it didn't even break the windshield."

"That is interesting. Who else would know about this?" Nancy asked.

"It was most likely a revolver used in that shooting too because we didn't find any shell casings at the scene," Pete added.

"Apart from the occupants of the car, who were scared shitless, the only other person is the one who fired the shots. This incident wasn't even reported to police. We found out about it, when somebody reported hearing the shots, during our canvass for the Woodsworth homicide," John said, as Nancy made more notes. "This fella is being sincere. He thinks he just confessed to a murder. Let's get back in there and see what else he has to say." John and Pete stood up to head back to the interview room.

"One thing you have to ask, sooner or later, is what exactly does he want and why is he doing this," Nancy said, without looking up from her notebook.

"Are you going to put him out of his misery and tell him he didn't kill anyone?" Pete asked John, before they entered the interview room.

John stopped and looked at his partner, "What do you think we should do?"

"If we tell him now, he may relax some more and keep talking but it could also work against us."

"Let's keep him sweet and tell him nobody died," John suggested.

When the interview resumed, John told Bertie that nobody inside the white Nissan had died or was even injured. Bertie could not believe his luck and actually teared up when he heard the good news. "I can tell you about other murders and shootings that Tyson is behind. I have proof too," Bertie said, his eyes lighting up now.

"That's good. I want to hear about everything. If you need a break or a cup of tea at any time, let me know." Bertie nodded. "But one thing that I want to be clear about...why are you telling me all of this now?" John asked.

Bertie breathed loudly through his nose, and his eyes were red and full of tears. "Well obviously, I want to get out of this fucking place. I can't sit here for five or six years. But if I get a deal from you it has to include my old lady and our kids."

"Everything depends on how much of everything that you tell us is proven to be true and correct." John again reaffirmed the need for Bertie to be completely truthful. "Now what else?"

Bertie paused and looked at the ceiling before turning his gaze to the inspector. "They killed my brother," Bertie said, with a mixture of rage and sorrow.

"Your brother, Eddie, Big E?" John asked.

I think it was Darryl Lyons and a kid called B.T., but it was Tyson ordered it."

"Why?" John asked.

Bertie went on to explain how his brother had stolen drugs on more than one occasion. He told them about the disciplinary board hearings, the punishments that Eddie received and the missions he was sent on. He described the shooting of Liam Mahony near Popham's Road and how Eddie failed to kill Mahony but did shoot off a couple of his fingers. "He used a sawed-off shotgun on that one."

Bertie went on to describe Eddie's second mission in Ballincollig where Eddie went with Darryl Lyons to shoot Frankie Spillane, a rival drug dealer. Again, Eddie had failed to kill his target. "He used my revolver for that one. Yeah, the same gun that the cops have here." John nodded, trying not to smile and Pete made frantic notes.

"How do you know these 'missions' went down like this?" John asked.

"Eddie told me. Eddie told me everything. He even told me when he stole drugs from me. He was my big brother but I was the one looking after him. He was like a big kid, always trying to impress." A tear escaped from Bertie's eye and ran down his cheek.

"And this is why Tyson had him killed? Because he fucked up the two missions?"

"No, the final straw was when Eddie called B.T. a rat. B.T. is like Tyson's pet. He calls him his number one child soldier." Bertie described the time that Eddie called B.T. a rat for calling police on his stepfather.

"And how do you know this for sure?" John asked.

"Tyson told me. He said Eddie had been on thin ice all along because of the thefts and the fucked-up missions. Calling B.T. a rat was the last straw. They lured him to Mahon to make it look like it was the Guppies did it."

"What exactly did Tyson say?"

"He said, 'That kid is no rat. B.T. and Darryl showed Eddie that.' Tyson was threatening me when he said it. He wanted me to do something then but he would have killed me. I know that." Bertie said, still with a mixture of sorrow and anger in his voice.

John liked this. It was a solid reason for Bertie Flynn to turn on the gang. To get revenge was one of the main reasons that criminals spoke to the police.

John looked over at Pete who appeared to be up to date with his notes. "Who is this B.T.?"

Bertie Flynn smiled and his eyes lit up. "Let me tell you a few things about B.T. We all call him Burnt Toast or B.T. He's an African kid. I think he lives on Shandon Street. His real name is Herbie Okie Dokie or something like that. Nobody can pronounce it so we all call him Burnt Toast." John laughed; this was so typical Cork.

Bertie continued, "Do you remember after Archie shot that fella in Manor View? A few days later there was another murder on Dominick Street. A Guppie Dial a Dealer was shot in his car."

John nodded; he wanted to hear more. Pete started writing again.

"Olly Sullivan was arrested for that. B.T. was the other shooter." Bertie had a smug look on his face now.

"How do you know?"

"I run a crack shack in one of the lanes off Dominick Street. They came to my place before the shooting and said they were on a mission for Tyson. Olly had a Colt .45 and B.T. had one of Darryl's Tokarevs."

John blinked. He didn't want to smile. He had to hold his poker face and not let Bertie know that his description of the guns used to kill Graham Hogan was bang on!

"B.T. came back to my place after the shooting and hid in the attic. I kicked everyone out and turned the lights off before the cops came around. I still have the gun!"

"The Tokarev?" John asked. At this point he found it impossible to hide his excitement.

Bertie smiled a sly grin. "Yeah, I took the gun from him and sent him to the attic. Then I hid the gun in a secret compartment in one of the steps on the stairs."

"Which step?"

Bertie thought about it for a few seconds, counting in his mind. "The fourth step from the floor.".

"Why did they kill this fella?" John asked.

"I don't know. Tyson probably wanted to send the Guppies a message that they shouldn't cross the river."

"Did B.T. say anything about the shooting when he came back to the crack shack?"

"He said that him and Olly just wasted a Guppy delivery man. He was all jacked up and shaking with excitement." Bertie did his best to recall the conversation.

"You said that B.T. had one of Darryl's Tokarevs," Pete said. "How many does he have?"

Bertie smiled that sly grin again. John knew there was more to come. "He has two. He calls them the twins. I don't know why he had them. They were very hard to get ammo for. I can tell you about the other one. You guys have that one too." Bertie paused for effect.

John had to smile at him. If everything he was saying was proven to be true, Bertie was a superstar witness. "Go on," he said to Bertie, knowing he didn't need the encouragement.

"There was a shooting in Jewtown a few months ago. Me, Darryl and Eddie went to a house down there. Darryl had to drop something off for some oul fella. We got in a fight with a bunch of assholes when we were going back to my car and Darryl and Eddie shot at them. Darryl had the other Tokarev and Eddie had a sawed off .22 rifle. One of the assholes got shot, probably by Darryl, because Eddie's gun was useless. It was like a pea-shooter."

"Where were you when this happened?" John asked.

"I was getting the fucking car but I saw the whole fucking thing." Bertie went into detail about what had happened before the shooting in Jewtown.

"So how do we have that gun?" Pete asked.

"Archie Cambridge went to Dublin to pick up a couple of bricks. It was around the time there was loads of heat on everyone so we started bringing the coke in, in smaller batches. Archie got picked off on the road between Mitchelstown and Mallow. He had Darryl's Tokarev in the car," Bertie said. "He was driving my car when he was stopped."

John knew that sometimes it could take years, if ever, for bullet casings found at different crime scenes to be matched to other crimes, unless the investigators asked for a comparison. It was a flaw in the system.

"Where is Archie now?" John asked.

Bertie chuckled. He was prepared for this question and knew his answer would be of great interest to this cop. "Archie is in Limerick Prison. He's going to apply for bail on the trafficking charge but he knows he won't get it."

"Hmm," John said, thinking about this. "You have implicated him as the trigger man in a homicide. He's probably going to be charged with that. You realize that, don't you?"

That wiped the smile off Bertie's face. "Yeah, but he might want a deal too. We spoke about this a long time ago and knew that this day would come when we had to look out for ourselves."

"So you think he'd be willing to talk?" John asked. "He would have to implicate Tyson and Alfie Hastings as well as Alfie's old lady."

"He would. I know he would if he got the right deal. Do you know that Archie was on the range when Walter Sheldon was killed?" Bertie knew that he had the policeman's full attention again.

"Was Archie involved in that?" John asked.

"He knows something about it. He called me and said a few things but he shut up before he went too far."

"When was that?"

Bertie thought about this and was calculating the time frame in his head. "It was about a week after Walter was killed. They were locked down for a few days and Archie called me just after they got out of lockdown."

"Did he actually mention the murder?"

"Oh yeah, he said the council voted Walter off the range. Then I reminded him that the guards would be all over the phones so he shut up."

"Pity you reminded him of that," John said in a low voice.

"If I approach Archie, can I tell him that we've spoken and you recommended that I speak with him?" John asked.

Bertie thought about this for a few seconds. "I have no fear of Archie. He's like a brother to me. You can tell him that I'm cooperating. Make sure you tell him what I told you about Eddie's death."

"What else can you tell us about the Independent Posse?" John asked.

Chapter 27

B ertie smiled, "I can tell you lots. Do you remember the shooting in Manor View on New Year's Day a couple of years ago?"

"Yes, I do," John answered. He knew that investigation very well. It had been one of the most difficult investigations he had ever been involved in, starting with dozens of witnesses to be interviewed after a young man was shot dead, during a free-for-all brawl in the middle of the street in Manor View Estate, shortly after the New Year countdown. "We made three arrests in that case."

"Do you know how it all started?" Bertie took a breath as if he was going to lead into a long monologue and Pete Sandhu flipped to a new page in his notebook. "Georgy and Mikey Galvin held a New Year's party at Georgy's place." John nodded; he knew all of this. "Me and Eddie were outside having a smoke when we saw a few young fellas coming out of a house across the street. They were wearing red soccer jerseys. Eddie called them out for wearing the red jerseys. They told us to go and fuck ourselves and Eddie gave one of them a licking."

John knew this was exactly what had occurred; however, he didn't know that it was Eddie and Bertie Flynn who started the fight. "What happened then?" John asked.

"A load of fellas came out of the other house and then the I-P supporters came out of Georgy's house and we had a huge fight in the middle of the street. It was like Friday night in Rathkeale." John smiled. Rathkeale in County Limerick had been the scene of ongoing violence for years between different factions of the community. "I was almost killed." Bertie started to raise his prison

208

issued sweatshirt. "I got knocked to the ground by one huge fella and he jumped on top of me and tried to stab me. He had a huge hunting knife and was leaning on it with all his weight. I was wearing a thick leather biker jacket and the knife pierced the leather and was sticking into my skin, right here." Bertie pointed to a tiny scar on his breast bone. "I thought I was a goner. I couldn't hold him off any longer when suddenly Mikey G came running up and booted the fella in the head with a full out soccer kick and he rolled off me."

"Were you there when the shooting started?"

"Yeah, I saw Johnny shoot into the crowd. He didn't give a fuck who he hit. He was just blasting. Then he ran into Trish Langford's house. Mikey and Georgy got the gun away from there before the cops arrived.

"It's a pity that you didn't tell us this when it happened. You could have saved us a lot of work," John said. Georgy and Mikey Galvin, along with Johnny Johnson, were all convicted for the killing of Jason Kimberly. That occurred when Johnny Johnson fired several rounds from a sawed-off shotgun into the mob.

This case was well and truly closed but it was good to hear the eyewitness description of what had happened and also to get the background on what started the altercation that day. John knew that this would help with Bertie Flynn's credibility.

"There's one other thing you should know about that night," Bertie said.

"What's that?"

"Mikey and Georgy organized that party as an alibi because Mikey had ordered the killing of two young fellas that used to work for us. They ripped us off and Tyson's brother was contracted to come to Cork and kill them both on New Year's Eve."

John and Pete immediately perked up. They were also involved in the double homicide investigation into the murders of Alvin

Pomeroy and Julian Hodnett, both killed the same night that Jason Kimberly died at Manor View.

"What do you mean they organized it as an alibi?" John asked. Although all three murders had been solved and those responsible were locked up, John did not know that the three killings were all connected.

"Mikey knew that Pomeroy and Hodnett had ripped him off and he ordered their assassination. Tyson was tasked with getting it done so he hired his brother Kenny. Then Georgy organized a big New Year's party at his place. We were all ordered to go to the party and couldn't leave until Kenny had finished his job. It was the perfect alibi until Johnny Johnson went batshit crazy with a shotgun." Bertie giggled.

"Or until you and Eddie started a brawl in the middle of the street," Pete said.

"That too," Bertie said, nodding in agreement.

"Almost the perfect alibi," John said aloud but to no one in particular. "What about you, Bertie, what's your role in the Independent Posse gang?"

"I'm a full-patch member of the gang," Bertie replied.

"What do you mean by that? Are there different levels of membership?" John wanted Bertie to describe the structure of the street gang; this intelligence was vital in the war against this gang and others like it.

Bertie raised his sweatshirt and showed a tattoo of a shield with the letters I-P in its center and the words Independent Posse at the bottom of it. All the words were in a Gothic type font. "Do you see how the background in my shield tattoo is shaded in a lighter color than the letters?" Bertie pointed to his tattoo.

"Yeah, what about it?"

"That means I'm a full-patch member, with all the privileges that comes with that. A junior member or an associate member can't have the background of the tattoo shaded in until he gets permission from the council."

"How do you become a member of the gang?" John asked while Pete was frantically making notes.

"You must know someone who is already in the gang at some capacity, either a full member or an associate. Then you get beaten in." Bertie looked at the two detectives, knowing there was a question coming.

"What do you mean beaten in?" Pete asked.

"You have to run through a gauntlet of ten or twenty fellas and they're all punching and kicking you. Make no mistake, they're trying hard to hurt you. It's a tough initiation. Then you can get the letters I-P tattooed on your knuckles. You can only get a chest or arm tattoo after you've worked in the shacks or in a Dial a Dealer car or done some missions. Again, you must get permission from the council before you get that tattoo."

"What exactly is this council?" John asked.

"There are actually two councils, maybe more." Bertie took a sip of his cold tea and asked for another cup as he started to explain. Pete left the room to fetch another tea.

"Let's wait until Pete comes back," John said, glad of a short break. The two men stared at each other in silence, neither wanting to comment on the way the interview was going. After a few awkward moments, Pete returned with large Styrofoam cup of hot tea.

Bertie sipped the tea. "It's like piss water," he said, grinning at the cops.

"You should be glad of it. How much afternoon tea would you get in Maghaberry Prison?" Pete said.

"The main council is on the street," Bertie continued. "The president is in charge. Tyson is the president now. It used to be Mikey G before he went to jail. There's also another council in Cork Prison.

Sometimes there may be a smaller council in another prison like Limerick, depending on the number of members that are locked up there."

"Who is the head of the council in Cork Prison?" John asked.

"I don't know. It used to be Walter Sheldon but he got moved to Limerick and, well you know what happened then. It will probably be Mikey G, but, for now, he's maxed out in Midlands or Mountjoy."

"What is the role of the president?" John enquired.

"On the street, Tyson is in charge of everything. He handles all the drug purchases and all the weapon stashes. He also handles all the money. The prison council works with him to get drugs into the prison and Tyson is supposed to get money to the members' families while they're locked up," Bertie said.

"How do you make money?"

"I sell drugs. I operate two crack shacks and I have a Dial a Dealer business on the go too. I get all my drugs through Tyson and pay him for them and I also have to pay a tax on what I sell."

"Do you make any profit?"

"There's never a time when I don't have at least sixty thousand euros in a plastic bag in my closet. I do OK." Bertie looked proud of what he had just told the officers.

"Are you ever worried that you'll get raided by the police?"

"The cops don't worry me too much. What really stresses me out is getting raided by another gang, like the M-W's. That's when things get really dangerous." Bertie stopped; he looked conflicted. He took a couple of short, deep breaths before he decided to go on. "That sort of thing gets out of hand very quickly. My shack in Mayfield was raided by M-W a few months ago. I think I killed someone! You can't use this against me, right?"

John smiled across the table, "That's right Bertie. Anything you say in this interview cannot be held against you. Please go on."

"It was after the time that Archie shot that fella on Manor View and before B.T. and Olly shot the Guppy on Dominick Street. I was at the shack in Mayfield and a bunch of Guppies raided us. Eddie was with me and we managed to beat them off. The shack was in an abandoned flat near Glenamoy Lawn. There was a narrow lane and a green space near it and that's where most of the fighting was." Bertie paused and he was struggling with this confession. "I came face to face with this big fucker. He pointed a gun right at me. It was one of those Hitler guns. He cocked the fucking trigger and was going to shoot me. I had my revolver with me and I pointed it at him. I shot him first. He fired then but missed me."

"Why do you think you killed this guy?" John asked.

"We were six feet apart when I shot him. I hit him in the chest and saw him fall down. He had to be dead."

"Did you move the body?"

"Fuck no, we grabbed our shit from the shack and legged it before the cops arrived," Bertie said sheepishly.

"You are sure of the time that this shooting happened?" John asked.

"Yeah, I'm sure because I think this is the reason that Tyson organized the hit on the Guppy on Dominick Street. To stop them coming across the river."

"I remember that shooting, Bertie." John smiled, and continued. "That fella's name was Herchell. He didn't die. We thought he would, but he survived and didn't want anything to do with the cops, when he woke up in hospital."

Bertie Flynn went on to talk about a few other shootings and beatings that were carried out by members of the Independent Posse under the direction of Tyson Rolland. After a long day of interviewing the prisoner, it was finally time to wrap up the interview. "Bertie, you've given us an awful lot of information here today. Now it's down to us to ensure that it's all true. That means that you're going to have to sit in Maghaberry until we sort through every single thing you said." John closed his notebook and put his pen in his shirt pocket.

"How long will that take? I swear to God it's all true." Bertie replied.

"It will take as long as it takes. I would say at least a few months. Sit tight. Nobody in Maghaberry Prison or anyone in the Republic knows that you spoke with us today. As long as you don't tell anyone, it will stay that way." Bertie looked dejected upon hearing this. Nevertheless, he was resigned to his fate. He had no choice but to wait.

"We will probably have to come and see you again. I'm sure there are a few things that we'll have to clarify, once we delve into this," John said, tapping the cover of his notebook. Bertie nodded. Part of him hoped he would be leaving Maghaberry Prison in the very near future. Now he knew he would have to wait patiently for the police to do their job.

John and Pete left Bertie alone in the interview room and returned to the monitor room. Detective Sergeant Charlie Brennan came to join them. "Is he going to be useful?" Charlie asked, sounding enthusiastic.

"If everything he told is true, he could be very useful," John replied, looking across at Nancy O'Dwyer.

"I don't know how much of that is true," Nancy said. "I'm very sceptical. He makes it sound like T.R.is the devil incarnate and is responsible for everything bad that has happened in Cork City in the last few years. I'm surprised he didn't implicate him in the J.F. Kennedy assassination."

"Just about everything he told us can be checked," John replied.

"Oh well, it's two days out of the office, if nothing else," Nancy said as she put her notebook into her brief case.

Meanwhile, Pete Sandhu was clicking away on his laptop. "One of the people he mentioned in there exists and is in our system as an Independent Posse associate." Pete turned his laptop to show his boss a photograph that he had up on the screen. "This is Herbie Okereke. He is fifteen-years-old and lives in Knocknaheeney. His alias is listed as 'Burnt Toast.'" The photograph was of a young black male with a short corn roll hair style.

"What did Bertie call him? Herbie Okie Dokie?" Nancy tried not to laugh out loud.

"That's pure Cork." John didn't even attempt to hold in a laugh.

Charlie Brennan took Bertie Flynn back to Maghaberry Prison and, of course, had to stop on the way to get him a double cheeseburger.

John thanked Charlie Brennan's detective chief inspector for the use of the police station and praised Charlie for going above and beyond in the assistance that he provided in this investigation. Then he drove Pete and Nancy to the hotel near the Titanic Museum in Belfast.

ONCE SETTLED INTO THEIR rooms, John called Jules.

"How was the interview?" she asked, being careful not to mention any names, on the off chance that someone overheard.

"I thought it was great. He gave us a name of someone I never heard of for the Woodsworth murder. He also gave us the people who facilitated it and the person who ordered it. He had information on two other murders and a few shootings. It's going to take a concentrated effort to prove everything he told us but I think we're on the right track."

"Oh, that's great! Will he get a deal?"

"Nancy O'Dwyer is very sceptical but she's slightly optimistic as two of the things he talked about are already starting to line up. There was a shooting that happened a couple of hours before Woodsworth was killed and Bertie identified the second shooter in the Dominick Street murder of Graham Hogan."

"That sounds promising. What are you doing tonight?" Jules asked.

"We'll get something to eat here at the hotel and then I'll go and see Fred and Janet. Pete and Nancy want to see the museum next door. What about you?" John answered.

"It's raining here so I'll take a drive into Clonakilty and pick up some groceries. I'll take the dogs down to the beach when I get back if the rain lightens up." Jules said.

After they said their goodbyes, John headed down to the hotel restaurant to meet Pete and Nancy for dinner. Then Pete and Nancy visited the Titanic Museum and John drove a few miles north to the Hollywood area to visit with the Nesbits.

Janet looked well. Her health was improving daily and she was feeling as well as she could. John noticed that some of her usual spark had diminished but knew, in time, it would come back. Janet told John that she went for walks along the Sea Front Park almost every day and gradually was beginning to feel more like her usual self. John returned to the hotel around midnight and slept well after what he believed to be a good day's work.

The following morning John, Pete and Nancy caught a flight from Belfast City Airport to Cork.

Chapter 28

John and Pete dropped Nancy at her office. Now the plan was to verify everything Bertie had said. John knew that they would probably have to meet with Bertie again as there were bound to be things that needed clarification. The two cops headed back to Garda Headquarters on Anglesea Street. Pete went to the incident room while John stopped in to see Superintendent Paddy Collins.

The rest of the team were in the incident room when Pete walked in. "Well? How did it go?" Mike Williams was first to ask.

"I think we got Tyson!" Pete said as he beamed with delight. "I'll let the boss fill you in. He's just popped in to bring the super up to speed. But I'll tell you one thing. This gang is organized, way more than we thought they were."

Pete didn't want to elaborate but he had no choice after dropping that bombshell; he began to describe the Independent Posse's disciplinary board and the punishments they dished out.

Meanwhile, in the superintendent's office, John reported on the interview. "There's a pile of forensic work to be done and we are going to end up reinterviewing a bunch of people. I'm confident that this fella is being truthful. After all, he confessed to two murders that he really believed he had committed. I better get back to the incident room before they start to torture Pete into telling them what happened."

John returned to the incident room and briefed the team on the Bertie Flynn interview. Everyone was excited at the prospect of not only solving the Woodsworth homicide but also everything else that Bertie spoke about. "Give me a day or two to dissect his statement.

Then we'll get down to work and there's going to be tons to do. But first of all, Pete will get a search warrant for Bertie Flynn's crack shack. He stashed the other shooter's gun there after the Dominick Street murder."

Pete was already busy typing the affidavit. It wouldn't take him long. An hour later, Pete was ready to go to see a judge to get the search warrant for Bertie's shack in the lane that ran off Dominick Street. Tim Warren went along for the ride. "Do you think the gun is going to be there?" Tim asked, as they drove to the main courthouse on Washington Street. "If we get this gun, then I think every other thing Bertie Flynn told us will fall into place," Pete said, as he found a parking spot near Saint Francis Church on Liberty Street. "This is his crack shack and nobody else has been in there since he got arrested. I am cautiously confident that the gun will be there."

Tim and Pete waited over an hour for a judge to read the affidavit and grant the search warrant. As soon as Pete had the paper in his hand, he called his boss. "We got the 'ticket'. Can you call forensics and have someone meet us at the address?"

"Sergeant Martens is ready to head out and meet you. Go by Martina Fitzpatrick's place in The Glen and ask her for a key. Bertie's already told her we'll be coming by. Otherwise, you'd have to break down the door," John said. "Don't talk to her about anything else at this point, no matter what she asks. Play dumb."

Tim and Pete drove to Mourne Avenue in The Glen and eventually pulled up at Martina Fitzpatrick's house. She was expecting them and handed them the key to the crack shack near Dominick Street. "He said you were going to get something at that house. He didn't tell me what it was but he said you knew where to look," Martina said in her strong flat northside accent. Tim took the key and thanked her, offering no information.

When they got back in the car, Tim turned to Pete. "She's a very pretty girl. What the fuck is she doing with a savage like Bertie Flynn?"

Pete laughed. "Money, what else can it be? She keeps a really tidy house too. I always expect these gangsters to be living in squalor."

Tim drove the police car down to Blackpool and along the Watercourse Road. He turned onto Gerald Griffin Street, continued on to the top of the hill by the cathedral and down the other side to Shandon Street. He turned right onto Dominick Street. "It's a good job we don't have a bigger car. We can barely pass here with cars parked up on the footpath," Tim said, navigating the extremely narrow street, while checking his side mirrors to make sure he didn't scrape the side of his vehicle. He passed an old impressive historic circular building.

"What's that place?" Pete asked.

"It's the old Butter Market. It's a relatively new building for this area. I think it was built around 1850." Tim smirked. Pete looked at the impressive round building as they slowly drove by.

After a few more meters, they arrived at the even narrower lane that ran off Dominick Street. "You could barely ride a bike down this lane," Pete remarked, as Tim let him out of the car and then parked, jamming the car against the wall of a house to avoid blocking the street. Seconds later, Sergeant Jennifer Martens from the Forensic Unit arrived and did a similar parking job.

The three police officers made their way to the front door of Bertie Flynn's crack shack. As Tim placed the key in the lock, an older man came out of the house next door. He looked Jennifer up and down as she was the only one in uniform. "Hmm, the law is here. It's about bloody time!" the old-timer said. He turned and went inside, but stretched his neck as he peered out his front window.

The narrow stairs were just inside the front door. Tim counted four steps from the bottom. "It should be this one," he said, stomping on the bare wooden step.

Jennifer reached into the gym bag that she carried and retrieved a long thick flathead screwdriver. She handed it to Tim. "Here, you can do the honors." She then pulled her camera from the bag and snapped a few photographs of the step before Tim pried it open. Once the photos were taken, Tim slipped the flat head of the screwdriver under the lip of the step and pried it up. It opened easily as if it had been done many times before.

Sitting in the empty box of the step was the cold grey Tokarev pistol. Tim went to reach in to grab the gun when Jennifer yelled, "Don't you dare!" She waved him aside and began to furiously photograph the weapon from every possible angle.

After a few minutes, Jennifer gently picked the gun up with her gloved hand. She expertly examined it, keeping the muzzle pointed into the empty box of the step. She located the magazine release mechanism, on the left-hand side of the pistol, between the trigger guard and the top of the black plastic plate on the handle. She pressed the button and popped the magazine out. Then she slid the mechanism back and forth a couple of times in order to eject any live rounds that may have been in the chamber. Nothing flew out of the ejection port. She looked at the magazine; it was also empty. The forensic sergeant now photographed the gun and the empty magazine.

When she was satisfied that she had taken enough photographs, Jennifer placed the gun and the magazine in a large brown paper bag. She wrote an incident number on the bag and photographed that too.

Pete called the office and put the phone on speaker mode. "We found the gun! It's a model TT-33 Tokarev with a magazine. Both empty, no ammunition."

"YES!" John reached up and punched the air. "Do you know what type of ammo fits that magazine?"

On hearing the conversation, Jen Martens looked at the magazine and read off the engraving, "7.62x25," she said, grinning from ear to ear. "Just like the shell casings we found at the scene. This magazine had a capacity of eight and I believe we found eight empty 7.62x25 casings."

"What's next Jen?" John asked, from his office.

"I 'll swab for DNA and dust for prints. Then we'll test fire it and compare the markings on the shell casings from the scene to our test fire. We'll also compare the striations from our test fire to any of the slugs we recovered from the victim's body. We are about half-way there to proving this was the other murder weapon."

"Right!" John said. "You know this is a priority?"

Sergeant Martens let out a long loud sigh. "Don't worry. I'll do most of the work myself."

"We'll take a look around here for anything of interest and then lock it up and bring the key back to Martina," Tim shouted into the speaker on the phone.

John walked to the superintendent's office and informed him of the find in the crack shack. "It looks like your 'supergrass' is going to be useful," Superintendent Collins said, making a note of the news in his notepad.

"Don't call him that boss! If the media resurrect that nickname, they'll blow it out of proportion and any trial down the road will fall apart. He's a witness, plain and simple. Not an informant!" John shook his head. He had seen the aftermath of major prosecutions falling apart in Northern Ireland, before the Good Friday Agreement, because material provided to police by informants known as supergrasses had been proved questionable. Occasionally, in the past, the Royal Ulster Constabulary had relied on information provided by informants to prosecute cases, without having any corroborating evidence to back up the evidence. This practice led to numerous acquittals and successful appeals.

"I suppose you're right. We will call him what he is. I'll make sure that we refer to him as a witness in every communication with the chief super and the assistant commissioner. They are going to be all over this, if it goes the way you expect it to."

"Don't give them too much too soon. We must protect Bertie Flynn and his family. Right now, only a hand full of us know that he has spoken to us. From now on refer to him by his initials, in all communications, B.R.F., for Bertie Robert Flynn. They know better than to ask more questions. I'll let Nancy O'Dwyer know the 'code name' when I update her about today's find."

Paddy Collins smiled when John left his office. He was excited about the opportunity to cut the head off the snake and take out the leadership of the Independent Posse, but he knew his inspector was right. This had to be kept low-key for now. Cops were notorious for gossiping, even in the higher ranks, and they needed to protect their witness.

John had just updated Nancy O'Dwyer on the find of the Tokarev pistol when Pete, Tim and Jennifer returned to the office. "We'll brief with everyone, first thing in the morning. I'll bring you all up to speed on the witness interview in Northern Ireland and our plan, moving forward with the rest of the investigation. Jen, can you be here first thing tomorrow?" Jen nodded.

"OK, I'm going home. See you all tomorrow." John turned the lights out in his office, grabbed his coat and headed to the door, leaving his team wanting more information, but they would have to wait.

IT WAS MIDAFTERNOON when John arrived home to Inchydoney. The sky was overcast but it wasn't raining. Jules was still at work so John let the dogs out of their crates. Lucy headed straight for her water dish and drank like she had been without liquid for an eternity; Molly went to the back door to go in the back paddock. When Lucy finished drinking, John let her out in the back to join her buddy. He refilled the water dishes. Lucy, the larger of the greyhounds, panicked if her water supply was low. Before she retired to life with the Cahills, she had been a racing greyhound and would have been deprived of water before races or time trials. She obviously did not enjoy this aspect of her working life. John joined the dogs in the paddock and walked to the side of the house, looking west, over the vast Atlantic Ocean. He could see a large container ship on the horizon, possibly heading to Britain, Europe or Africa. Seconds later, the dogs perked up. They could hear Jules' car, long before it turned into the driveway.

John returned indoors and had coffee made by the time Jules came into the house. She hugged her husband and told him that she had missed him. "You can tell me all about it when we take the dogs out later," she said, sitting at the kitchen table drinking her coffee. "I have to tidy up around here first."

Later they walked the greyhounds on the West Beach. The tide was in, making the East Beach difficult to reach. The dogs didn't appear to be interested in racing each other and just sniffed through the seaweed. Occasionally Molly would stop and frantically dig a hole approximately fifty centimeters deep, then leave it and just trot off along the beach. John told Jules all about the interview with Bertie Flynn and how he planned to dissect every piece of information and either prove it true or a lie.

"But surely he's telling the truth, now that you've found the gun in the crack shack," Jules said.

Every single thing he said must be true. There's no room for error. If there is a lie to be found, we have to find it. Because, I will guarantee you, the defence lawyers will find it if we don't." John kicked a piece of driftwood along the beach. "He has told us about fourteen serious incidents. Seven of them are homicides. Granted, a few of them are already solved, but he is adding unknown information about those ones too. If it's all true, this is going to be huge."

"What kind of a deal will he get?" Jules asked, holding her husband's hand as they strolled along the deserted beach.

"He'll get a second chance. A chance to start over and put gang life and drug dealing behind him. But it will be up to him to make it work. It will probably be a lot of hard work and he is a gangster and a drug dealer so hard work is not a concept he's too familiar with. The good thing is, he will not have to do it alone. There's a good program in place to help him along the way. I just hope that his wife supports him. Otherwise, he'll never make it." John whistled for the dogs as they turned for home.

As they walked through the sand dunes, John's cell phone rang. Jules sighed; she hoped he didn't have to go back to work. John looked at the number on the call display, "That's a Northern Ireland number," he said to Jules and answered the phone. A recorded voice asked him if he would accept the charges from a caller in Maghaberry Prison. John pressed 1, agreeing to accept the charges.

"Hi, it's Bertie Flynn," the caller said.

"There's a surprise! How are you, Bertie?" John laughed; he nodded his head at Jules. She relaxed now, hearing who was on the phone and knowing that it was not a call that was going to drag him away for another endless day.

"Did you find it? Did you find the gun in the step?" Bertie sounded really excited. "I was on to Martina. She said Pete and some other fella came around to get the key."

"Bertie, I can't discuss what we did or didn't find with you. All I can tell you is that we are still working with you, but it's going to take time."

"OK, so you found the gun. That means that I was telling the truth so why can't I get out?" Bertie said, pleading his case for an early release.

"Bertie, if I found a gun, then I must do a load of tests on it to prove that it's the gun that you said it is. That takes time. You must be patient. I know it's hard but you must be patient. This will take as long as it takes." John tried to reassure the prisoner on the other end of the phone.

"I suppose so. I was just excited when Martina said you went around for the key. I knew you would find the gun there. Nobody knew about that plank except me." Bertie sounded a little deflated.

"Look, call me anytime," John said, laying on the Cork accent more than usual. "I will not be able to tell you much if things are going well, but if things start to go bad, I'll tell you very quickly. OK?"

Bertie said goodbye and they ended the call. "Call me anytime! I hope he's not going to be a pain in the ass, is he?" Jules asked. "And I notice you really piling on the accent when you're talking with him." she giggled.

"I have to keep him on board so I don't mind talking to him. Anyway, he can only call when he gets access to the phone, so he can't call at all hours of the night. And the accent puts him at ease," John said and they turned into their driveway at the top of the hill overlooking the beach.

Chapter 29

When John arrived at work the following morning, the rest of the team was already there, bright and early, eager to hear about the Northern Ireland interview. Jennifer Martens from the Forensic Unit joined them for the briefing as did Superintendent Paddy Collins.

John laid out the interview with Bertie Flynn in sixteen points:

1. The Woodsworth homicide at Manor View Estate
2. The Parklands shooting
3. The Manor View Estate shooting before the Woodsworth homicide
4. Eddie Flynn's murder
5. The shooting of Liam Mahony by Eddie Flynn
6. The shooting of Frankie Spillane by Eddie Flynn
7. The Graham Hogan homicide near Dominick Street
8. The shooting at Hibernian Buildings
9. Archie Cambridge's arrest and the seizure of the second Tokarev
10. The Limerick Prison murder of Walter Sheldon
11. The New Year's Eve murder of Jason Kimberly at Manor View Estate
12. The New Year's Eve murders of Julian Hodnett and Alvin Pomeroy
13. The shooting of Tommy Herschel
14. Two Tokarev pistols
15. One Glock pistol

16. The structure of the Independent Posse

The briefing took the entire morning and a couple of coffee breaks. When he was finished outlining the information that Bertie Flynn had provided, John believed he had not seen his team look so excited and engaged for a long time. They were on the brink of solving all of their outstanding cases and a few more they didn't know about.

"Jen, the brunt of the follow-up work is going to fall on you, I'm afraid," John said, looking over at Sergeant Martens.

"I can't wait!" This time there was no sarcasm in her voice, only excitement.

"For everyone else, there are a lot of interviews and reinterviews to be done. We need to prove everything this fella said is true, but if there is any doubt about any point at all, bring it to my attention. It is very important that we do not bury anything," John instructed his team.

"What are we going to do about this fella, Archie Cambridge?" Mike Williams asked.

"I'm glad you asked that, Mike. Because in a few weeks, once we have made sense of some of this, you and Eddie will have to go and speak with Archie. I think we will have to charge him with the murder of Anthony Woodsworth, but maybe the Director of Public Prosecutions will be willing to offer him something, if he turns on Tyson and the others. Are you two OK with that?" John asked.

"Fucking right we are!" Eddie Jenkins said, beaming from ear to ear, glad of the opportunity to interview the gangster.

Jeff Rafter raised his hand and John pointed to him. "Is there any truth to the rumor that the superintendent will take us all out for dinner if we solve two of the murders?" Jeff asked, keeping a straight face.

"The superintendent is a Kerry man, what do you think?" John replied. "Maybe he'll take us to the chip shop on the Bandon Road." Everyone laughed.

Paddy Collins stood up. Time for me to go!" Then he stopped in his tracks and pointed at the white board. "I'll tell you what..." the Superintendent said, in his thick Kerry accent. "If you get a positive result in all sixteen points, I will take you all out. Maybe we'll have a barbecue at John's 'villa' in Inchydoney. I'll buy the burger buns." Paddy nodded at the inspector, grinned and then left the incident room,

John let the team go to lunch while he went over the information with Jennifer Martens and she made a plan of what she needed to do. It was not going to be easy and certainly not quick. Jennifer needed to compare the shell casings from different events and reexamine just about all the forensic evidence in the incidents that Bertie Flynn spoke about.

After lunch, John doled out the assignments to his investigators. There was an air of excitement in the office again. For months now, the Woodsworth investigation looked unsolvable; now they were confident they would get the shooter and the person who ordered the hit as well as the two people that facilitated it by driving the shooter. A nice tidy package.

There was no new business for the Serious Crime Unit for the next few weeks; that perfectly suited everyone as there was an enormous amount of work to do in checking everything Bertie Flynn had said in his statement. All the investigators had watched the video recording of the interview and knew what they had to do.

Jennifer Martens had ordered several ballistic reports from the various cases. She had also requested more DNA analysis and she was particularly interested in what is known as low count DNA results. Low count DNA is DNA that is located on a particular exhibit but is below the standard threshold that is acceptable in court proceedings.

Should there be a low count DNA match from an exhibit to an offender, it is not as conclusive as a 'definite' match but it is still a match.

For DNA to be entered as conclusive evidence in a trial, there must be an unambiguous match between the DNA found on an exhibit to an offender's DNA; the results are usually in the billions or trillions to one that the DNA could be from someone other than the offender. In a low count DNA match, the results may be in the hundreds of thousands or a million to one that it is someone other than the offender. In the eyes of the courts, these odds are not good. Nevertheless, John figured that they were still pretty good odds and requested the tests. If they got a hit, it would be up to the prosecutor to argue it in court with a team of experts.

THE RESULTS OF THE Woodsworth case were the first to be concluded. Jennifer Martens reported that no DNA was located on the shell casing that had fallen from Anthony Woodsworth's clothing in the resuscitation room at the hospital. John was disappointed with this but not surprised. Shell casings were often extremely hot when they were ejected from a pistol after being fired. This often destroyed any DNA that may have been present on the shell casing.

Nonetheless, Sergeant Martens had the laboratory weigh and measure the bullet and fragments that were recovered from inside the victim's skull and they were a perfect match for a .40 caliber bullet fired from a Glock pistol.

And the news from the further forensic tests just kept getting better. The markings made by the firing pin on the shell casing found at the hospital, in Anthony Woodsworth' clothing, were an exact match to the shell casings found at Peter Doyle's house in Parklands. There was no doubt that the gun used to kill Anthony Woodsworth was the same gun that shot out every window in Peter Doyle's house. Another win for Bertie Flynn's credibility.

Jeff Rafter and Len Benoit interviewed the Doyle family in Parklands. They confirmed that none of the family had any criminal involvement. Peter's daughter, Lisa, was reluctant to speak with the officers in front of her parents and agreed to speak with them outside in the back yard while she smoked a cigarette. Lisa confirmed that Jenny O'Callaghan, Tyson Rolland's girlfriend, was her best friend. Lisa said that Jenny only moved back with Tyson because she feared what he might do to Lisa's family next. She did not know that Tyson was responsible for shooting up her house but wouldn't be surprised if he had.

John and Tim headed into Mahon territory and interviewed the two other occupants of James Maloney's white Nissan that was shot at by Bertie Flynn, a couple of hours before Anthony Woodsworth was killed. They both confirmed James' statement and provided the same description of the man who had shot at their car. It was a perfect description of Bertie Flynn.

"THREE OF BERTIE'S POINTS are confirmed, only thirteen to go," John said to Jules that night, over supper. "Those are the easy ones. The next few are going to take a bit more work but I have a good feeling about this. I think it's all coming together."

"It's good to see you excited again. You were starting to get depressed about not making any headway. Has your man called again?" Jules asked.

With that, John's cell phone rang. He looked at the number. "Speak of the devil! It's the Northern Ireland operator."

John answered the phone and accepted the reverse long-distance charges on the call. "How are ya, Bertie?"

"I'm grand, any news?"

"No news yet. We are plugging away. There is a lot to be done and when I'm finished with my investigation, then the lawyers will get involved. It's out of your hands. All you can do is wait." John tried to keep the prisoner calm.

"Sure, I know. I'm getting bored here. I hate fucking jail."

"Well Bertie, it's your own fucking fault that you're in there. You're a drug dealer!" John chuckled and Jules shot him a stare across the table.

There was silence on the other end of the phone for a couple of seconds. Then Bertie laughed. "I suppose you're right. I shouldn't have got caught!"

"I'll tell you what, I'll come up and see ya again in a few weeks. I have to show you some photographs and maybe get some clarification on a couple of things, OK?"

"That's grand, I'll be here waiting for ya. Can I call you again in a few days?"

John thought he actually sounded lonely. "You can call me anytime, but like I said, it will be the same answer every time. I can't tell you what's happening in the investigations," John answered and they ended the call.

Jules smiled at her husband. "You have a new best friend?"

"I think so. He sounds forlorn. He has no one else to call except Martina and he must use a calling card to phone her."

"What did he say when you called him a drug dealer?" Jules asked.

"He knows what he is. He only laughed."

Chapter 30

Mike Williams and Eddie Jenkins had reviewed the new information that Bertie had provided and now were assigned to review the Eddie Flynn murder investigation to see if anything had been missed.

They confirmed that B.T. or Herbie Okereke called 999 a week before Eddie's murder. They obtained a recording of the 999 call and learned that B.T. did indeed report that his mother had been assaulted by her partner. When police showed up at the address, B.T. had left and his mother played down the incident, saying there was no assault, just some raised voices. No arrests were made and the responding officers did not track down B.T. to take a statement from him.

Being thoroughly efficient, Jennifer Martens tested the two knives found at the Eddie Flynn homicide scene for DNA. The lab identified a profile from an unknown male on the handle of the broken knife. This meant that the contributor of this DNA profile was not in the National DNA Databank. Sergeant Martens was like a dog with a bone and kept after the lab to make her requests a priority. As always, the squeaky wheel gets the oil. The lab developed a low count DNA profile for an unknown male from the handle of the Tokarev pistol that was found hidden in a step on the stairs in Bertie Flynn's crack shack. The lab confirmed that the low count unknown male DNA profile from the Tokarev was the same as the unknown male DNA profile found on the broken knife that was used to kill Eddie Flynn.

Sergeant Martens presented this information to John, Mike Williams and Eddie Jenkins. "Yes! This is brilliant news." John knew that the unknown male was B.T. Because he was a youth and had not been convicted of a serious offence, B.T.'s DNA profile was not in the National DNA Data Bank. Darryl Lyons, who John suspected of being the other person involved in Eddie Flynn's death, had a DNA profile in the National DNA Data Bank.

"We should bring B.T. in now," Eddie Jenkins suggested. Mike Williams looked at John for direction.

"Not yet. We still have a lot of work to do. Let's leave it awhile and see if we can get the entire rat's nest and bring them all in," John said. He had a worried look and good reason for it as Eddie Jenkins pointed out.

"I hate to state the obvious, boss, but this fifteen-year-old has killed two people. The longer he is on the street, the higher the odds are that he will kill more."

"I agree, Eddie. However, if we get enough to arrest the two adults who directed him, we'll save a lot more lives. If we bring him in now, we run the risk of losing everyone else. I'll wear this, if it goes south. Put it in your notes that I directed you not to arrest B.T. until we make more progress in the investigation. I'll also make a note in my investigative summary. It's a risk that I'm willing to take right now." John wasn't sure if it was the right thing to do; only time would tell.

He found this type of risk management very stressful. He could arrest the fifteen-year-old gangbanger for two murders now or keep gathering evidence and try to get enough evidence to charge and convict Tyson Rolland and Darryl Lyons and, hopefully, shut down the Independent Posse once and for all.

"WHAT WILL HAPPEN IF they send this kid out to do another murder?" Jules asked, during their evening walk on the beach with the greyhounds.

"I guess we would be back in Belfast as quick as a flash and I would be crucified in an enquiry," John said, picking up a small piece of driftwood and throwing it out of his way. The dogs stopped and looked at the stick but had no intention of chasing it; they weren't those kinds of dogs.

"Shouldn't you tell the superintendent about this?" Jules knew John was struggling with this.

"Deep down, I know this is the right thing to do, to leave this kid out on the street for another while until we finish the entire investigation. If I had any doubt, I would tell the superintendent about our predicament. But right now, I'm not going to put this on him."

John fell asleep thinking about the risk of B.T. being sent out to kill someone else before he was arrested for the murders of Graham Hogan and Eddie Flynn.

WHEN HE GOT TO WORK in the morning, John decided to cover his bets and get some help. He picked up the phone and called the Anti-Crime Unit.

The Anti-Crime Unit was a semi-covert Garda Unit that operated out of a clandestine building on Stable Lane, several blocks from Garda Headquarters. The Anti-Crime Unit primarily dealt with property crime, with a focus on serial offenders. They worked in the shadows and few criminals knew they were being targeted by this unit, until they were caught red-handed, ripping off a warehouse full of high-tech equipment or stealing a truckload of cigarettes or liquor. The officer in charge of this unit was Inspector Sean Harrington.

Harrington was an expert in physical surveillance and trained his crew to be patient and confident in the art of following their prey.

"Sean, I need a favour. Can I come over and see ya?" John asked.

"As long as you bring some snacks for Percy and me. We're the only two in the office right now," Sean Harrington answered, sniggering down the phone line.

John walked up Anglesea Street towards the Victoria Hospital and stopped at a small café. He bought a half-dozen pastries and four coffees that he carried in a Styrofoam tray. He turned down Copley Street and headed towards Stable Lane. When he arrived at the old run-down building, he put the box of pastries on the step and rang the doorbell next to a battered old steel door. He looked up to the top of the door frame and smiled. He knew someone was watching him from a covert camera on the door frame. Seconds later, he heard the electronic click on the door and he pulled it open. Picking up his bribe, he walked up the concrete staircase and stood at another steel door. Another click and this door was also unlocked.

Madge Eastwood, the civilian clerk, greeted John and asked after Jules. John handed one of the coffees to Madge and offered her a pastry. He learned a long time ago that keeping a good relationship with the civilian staff was paramount. If the civilians didn't do their job in managing all the office and clerical work, it would be next to impossible to accomplish any police work.

After exchanging pleasantries with Madge, John made his way along the corridor of this run-down disheveled building. From the outside it looked like an abandoned warehouse and from the inside it looked like it should have been condemned. Nevertheless, despite its appearance, this building held millions of euros worth of electronic surveillance equipment and was more secure than most banks.

John walked into the Anti-Crime Unit's office. Detective Sergeant Percy Jones was sitting at his desk, typing on a computer. He looked up when he saw the homicide inspector. "Hey, it's our pal from the North," Percy said, as Sean Harrington came around a corner from the back of the office space. "Do you have something fun for us to work on?"

John sat down between Harrington's and Jones' desks, took his own coffee from the tray and had a sip. He opened the box of pastries. "Help yourselves. I need your help to keep an eye on a target. He's good for two murders but we're not quite ready to bring him in. But I'm concerned that if I leave him, he might be sent out to kill again. Can you put him under surveillance for a week or two while we try and wrap this up?" John did not give the others the entire story yet; he wanted to see if they would bite.

And they did! "He sounds like a real bad ass," Harrington said. "This could be fun. Where does he live and what type of car does he drive?"

"Hmm, that's the problem." John took another sip of his coffee, followed by a deep breath. "He is one of the I-P's child soldiers. He's fifteen-years-old and doesn't drive a car, unless he steals one. He has a BMX bike."

"You're fucking kidding me!" Percy Jones looked horrified. "How sure are you he's good for two murders?"

"Right now, I'm pretty sure, but if you guys get me some cast-off DNA and it matches, I'll be one hundred and ten percent certain," John answered.

"This is going to be a nightmare," Sean Harrington added. "We might need some extra help. It's not going to be easy following a young kid on a bike."

"That's going to be a problem," John responded. "If I go to Paddy Collins with this, he's going to have to let the chief super know and they won't want to take any risks. They'll order us to bring this little fucker in right away. If I leave this for another couple of weeks, we can probably get another three people for murder, maybe some more."

The three cops talked about the issues of trying to conduct surveillance on a kid riding a BMX bike and the pros and cons of bringing him in now for the murders. Then Sean Harrington had an idea. "What if we catch him doing something while we're watching him, maybe get him selling drugs or stealing a car. We can get him in front of a judge and you can try and get him detained, while waiting for bail."

"I like that, Sean. That's a great idea. Hopefully he will do something serious enough to get locked up for a couple of weeks but not serious enough that he kills or maims someone else," John replied. He loved this idea; if it worked out, it could be the answer to his prayers.

"We'll set up on him first thing in the morning," Percy Jones said, as John was leaving.

"That's the best ten euros I've spent in a long time." John was thinking about the coffee and pastries as he walked back to his office on Anglesea Street.

Back at headquarters, Jeff Rafter and Len Benoit had brought Eddie Flynn's victim, Liam Mahony, in for an interview.

"The only car I remember seeing was a white Fiesta. It drove by slowly a few times before I was shot," Mahony told the detectives.

He provided a perfect physical description of Eddie Flynn and when Len Benoit asked if he saw the shooter's face, Mahony replied, "I'll never forget that face. It's burned into my mind. I still have nightmares when he stood right in front of me and pointed the shotgun at me and fired it."

Jeff Rafter showed Liam Mahony a photo lineup, one of the ten images being a photo of Eddie Flynn; the other nine men looked similar to him. Mahony didn't hesitate for a second and picked out Eddie Flynn. "That's him! That's the fucker that shot me and blew my fingers off," he said, holding up his right hand that was missing three digits.

Rafter and Benoit briefed John on the interview. He was elated, another major part of Bertie Flynn's story confirmed.

Eddie Jenkins had requested time off; therefore Mike Williams and Tim Warren drove out to Ballincollig to interview Frankie Spillane who had been shot in the face by Eddie Flynn. Tim led the interview, and, as usual, Mike had fun with the subject. "Have you remembered anything else about the night you were shot?" Tim asked.

"*Som fuckerr sot* me is all I can *member*," Spillane said, barely able to manage the sounds as his jaw and cheek bone had been shattered by the bullet.

"What's that, Frankie? Can you say it more clearly?" Mike asked, giving his partner a conspiratorial wink.

"No, all *da bones* are smash to *sith* and I *los ten teet*." It was obviously paining Frankie to speak.

"Do you remember anything about the fella who shot you?" Tim asked.

"A big *fukker* with a *mast*."

"A mast? Like on a boat?" Mike asked. Tim almost fell off his chair at this point, trying not to laugh.

"No fuck! A fuck'n *mast*, covern his fate," Frankie sputtered and held the neck of his T-shirt over his face to show a mask.

"Oh, I have you now. A mask covering his face, gottcha," Mike said, keeping a straight face.

"What about the gun? You must have seen the gun?" Tim asked.

Frankie nodded; he wasn't going to speak unless he really had to.

"Can you describe the gun?"

"Big, old *look'n* gun. A *revolvr*. Looked ancient. I can't talk no more, too sore." Frankie put his hand up to the right side of his face.

"What's that, Frank? I can't understand you," Mike said.

"Fuck off!" Frankie replied as plain as day.

Tim showed Spillane four photographs of pistols, one of them being Bertie Flynn's old Webley revolver. Frankie pointed to it and gave the thumbs up.

"You were a little hard on him, Mike," Tim told him on the drive back to the station.

"That fucking parasite is a drug dealer. I was only having fun with him," Mike said and they both laughed.

John made a note that Frankie Spillane was unable to identify who shot him as the shooter was masked; however, he identified the old Webley revolver as the weapon used by his attacker. It was a positive result.

The next day Eddie Jenkins was back at work and the entire team headed to Hibernian Buildings to locate the group who had the altercation with Darryl Lyons and the Flynn brothers. The detectives had reviewed the entire report and were hoping that someone might have remembered something new or they may be able to extract some more information, now that they knew who was responsible for the shooting. One of the young men, who was involved in the initial fight before the shooting, identified Eddie Flynn from a photo lineup. None of them could positively identify Darryl Lyons, until the man who had been shot looked at Lyons' photograph and tapped it with his index finger. "The fella that shot me had a red bandana pulled up over his nose but he had a birthmark just like that fella. Just under his right eye. It looks kinda like a teardrop tattoo but it's a birthmark."

"You're sure of that?" John asked.

"As sure as anything," the man responded. "I'll never forget that as long as I live. I thought I was going to die."

"That couldn't have been better," John said when the team returned to the station. They picked Eddie Flynn out and a positive identification on Darryl Lyons as the shooter.

"I think Mister B.R.F will be getting a deal," Pete Sandhu said. Everyone nodded. It was all coming together.

"Mike, Eddie, start preparing to go to Limerick to bring Archie Cambridge in. It's time," John ordered before sending the team home for the day.

"HOW DO YOU THINK CAMBRIDGE will be?" Jules asked, as she and John walked along the beach with the greyhounds that evening.

"Bertie thinks he will be OK and want a deal once he knows that he's getting charged with the Woodsworth homicide. But you never know with these guys. This fella has flown under the radar for a long time. But still, Bertie said that Tyson Rolland was worried that he could take over leadership of the gang. It all depends on what he wants." John called the dogs; they were falling behind while sniffing through piles of seaweed.

"I spoke with Janet today," Jules said, changing the subject.

"How is she?"

"She's good. She's doing her best to make her life normal again but she's been through hell and it's taken its toll." Jules reached out and held her husband's hand as they walked towards the channel at the west end of the West Beach.

"I hope things will get better in time." John, squeezed his wife's hand, thankful that they were both healthy.

Chapter 31

Mike Williams and Eddie Jenkins were ready to drive the one-hundred kilometers to Limerick to arrest Archie Cambridge for the murder of Anthony Woodsworth. They were sitting at their desks, checking that they had the correct paperwork before heading out, when Sergeant Martens walked into the incident room. "Are ye going to Limerick now?" she asked.

"We are heading out the door in five minutes. Do you have something for us?" Eddie said.

Jen Martens held up a sheet of paper she was carrying and waved her arm for the two men to follow her as she walked into John's office.

"Good morning, Jen," John said, smiling at the forensic officer.

"I got the ballistic report back on the Tokarev pistol that was seized from Archie Cambridge when he was arrested," Jen said, pausing for effect as she liked to do. Once she was sure she had everyone's attention, she continued, "It is the same gun that was used in the Hibernian Buildings shooting."

"That's the one near Albert Road?" Mike asked.

Jennifer turned and smiled at Mike. "Yes," she said, nodding.

"That's good to know that this has nothing to do with Cambridge." John pointed at Mike and Eddie. "He doesn't need to know anything about this gun. I hope he'll have a solid alibi for the night of that shooting."

Mike and Eddie returned to their desks and confirmed the date of the shooting; then it was time to make the trip to Limerick Prison and bring the infamous Archie Cambridge in for an interview. There wasn't a lot of information about Archie on PULSE, the Garda database. Although he had been arrested and charged several times during his young life, there was no real background information. His past crimes were mostly low to mid-level violence. This time he was looking at five to six years in custody for possession of cocaine and a loaded firearm. With the murder charge hanging over his head, he would be well past his prime when he got out of prison.

Mike and Eddie picked up a breakfast sandwich and a coffee from a gas station on the Mallow Road and arrived at Limerick Prison after a fast, one-hour drive.

On arrival at the prison, the detectives met with one of the Operational Support Group officers. The O.S.G. was a relatively new unit within the Irish Prison Service that had taken over internal security and intelligence. The unit may have been new but the office and the furniture were ancient and the room smelled musty. The O.S.G. officer was expecting them and knew they were arresting Archie Cambridge for murder. "Would it help your case if he didn't have to come back here? I can arrange for him to go to Cork Prison when you are finished with him if you want," the O.S.G. officer asked.

"That could be very useful. I suppose it depends on how much he wants to cooperate with us," Mike Williams replied.

A few minutes later, Archie Cambridge arrived in the security office. When he walked in the door, he immediately knew that Mike and Eddie were cops; he stood up straight and faced them. If he was scared, he didn't show it. Archie tilted his head to the side with a look of contempt. "What the fuck do you want?"

"Archie Cambridge, I am arresting you for the murder of Anthony Woodsworth in Manor View Estate in Cork City. Do you understand?" Mike Williams said as Eddie Jenkins pulled out his handcuffs and stepped towards Cambridge.

Archie took the news with a grain of salt. "Never heard of him! Fuck that, I'm not going with you." He took a step backwards towards the door.

"Now Cambridge, don't make an eejit out of yourself now," the O.S.G. officer added. "You have no choice. You can go quietly or we'll help them to drag you out and it's straight into the hole for you when you come back."

Eddie Jenkins stood next to Archie. "Put your hands behind your back." Archie complied and Eddie snapped the handcuffs on him. Eddie then double-locked the cuffs so they didn't tighten up and injure the prisoner.

When Archie was put in the back of the police car, his attitude changed; he did not have to act the tough guy anymore. He didn't say much for most of the journey back to Cork City until they arrived in Blackpool and began to drive into the city. "Ye must have spoken to Bertie Flynn. Is he OK?" Archie asked, while he shifted his body weight around in the back seat to take the pressure off his wrists that were tied behind his back.

"Bertie is fine. He said you are a reasonable person and will want to do the right thing," Mike answered.

"How can Bertie get a deal if he's in custody in The North of Ireland?" Archie asked, fishing for more information.

Mike Williams smiled at the question. The official name for the Six Counties was Northern Ireland but most people from the Republic referred to it as The North of Ireland, meaning one whole nation, not two separate countries on the same land mass.

"Bertie is looking out for Bertie. He said you should do the same. He said you two talked about this day." Eddie Jenkins watched Archie's face in the vanity mirror of the car.

When they arrived at Garda Headquarters on Anglesea Street, Archie Cambridge was taken directly to the second floor and placed in Interview Room # 1. Eddie removed the handcuffs and took

Archie's shoes, leaving him in his stocking feet. The officers left Archie alone after he requested a cup of tea. They had to hang up their coats and secure their pistols.

Archie stood in the middle of the interview room and surveyed his surroundings. The room was a typical interview room, approximately four meters by four meters, with a metal table bolted to the floor. There was one plastic chair, also bolted to the floor. The door was solid steel with a small window in the center. A shutter had been slid across the window and Archie could not see out. The fluorescent lightbulbs in the ceiling were enclosed with a thick metal grate to protect them from prying fingers. The inside of the door and the top of the metal table were covered in graffiti that had been scraped into the black paintwork by previous occupants, using rings and bracelets. Archie sighed and sat at the table.

Mike and Eddie returned to the interview room with a cup of tea and a chocolate bar for Archie. He devoured the chocolate and sipped the tea as he listened to Mike Williams read out his legal rights. When Mike was finished, Archie requested to speak with his lawyer from Limerick. Mike called the solicitor and she rudely told him that she had no intention to drive to Cork to speak with Archie; nevertheless, she agreed to counsel him over the phone.

After a forty-five-minute private phone call, Archie banged on the interview room door and told Eddie Jenkins that he was finished speaking with the lawyer. Mike and Eddie rolled two old office chairs into Interview Room # 1 and the fun and games began.

The recording equipment had been turned on and John and Pete Sandhu watched the interview anxiously from the monitor room.

"Archie, you are in a lot of trouble." Mike started. "You are being charged with the murder of Anthony Woodsworth. You were given a .40 caliber Glock pistol by somebody and you were driven to an address in Manor View Estate by two people. You walked up to Mr. Woodsworth and asked him how he felt about the Independent

Posse and when you didn't like his answer, you shot him point blank in the face."

For the first time since he was picked up at Limerick Prison, Archie looked worried and he shuddered when Mike described the shooting.

"Archie, the only person who can make this situation better is you. If you cooperate and tell us about the other people who are involved in this, you will most likely get a good deal," Mike said.

Archie did not reply right away and all three of them sat in an awkward silence for what felt like a lifetime. Finally, Archie spoke, "I want to call the solicitor back."

This time the call lasted only twenty minutes. On completion of the call, Mike and Eddie re-entered the room. Archie didn't waste anytime. "My lawyer told me not to say anything to you. All I can say is NO COMMENT!"

Mike and Eddie went over and over Archie's predicament with him for the next three hours. He sat in silence. At last he said, "I would rather do LIFE as a gangster than five years as a RAT!" Archie Cambridge never spoke again in the interview room.

"Well, that didn't quite work out how I wanted it to," John said to Mike and Eddie.

"What do we do with him now?" Eddie asked. "The O.S.G. said we can take him to Cork Prison if we want. We only have to let him know."

"I don't really care," John said. "Ask him if he wants to go to Cork or Limerick. And before you drop him off, make sure he knows he can come back anytime he wants to talk about a deal."

Archie Cambridge said he wanted to go to Cork Prison for now; it would be easier for family to come to see him. He knew he would be sent back to Limerick soon enough. He also told Mike Williams that he was looking for a new lawyer. Mike suspected Archie wasn't entirely happy with the advice he had been given and held on to a glimmer of hope, of turning this guy around. On the short drive up to Cork Prison, Archie asked Mike and Eddie if they could get him a book. He said that the prison service library wouldn't order it for him.

"What's it called?" Eddie asked.

"'The Art of War,'" Archie replied. "It's a really old Chinese book." Eddie made a note and said he would try and locate it.

When they returned to the station, Mike Williams looked up the title on the computer. "This book is about sixteen hundred years old but it's available online. I'll order it for him."

John just shook his head.

ONLY TWO NIGHTS AFTER the Anti-Crime Unit began following B.T. to ensure he didn't kill or maim anyone else, Sean Harrington's hopes became a reality. B.T. met up with another kid and they rode their BMX bikes through the North Side, until they reached Glenthorn Estate, at the top of Dublin Hill. They ditched their bikes under a tree in the green space at the corner of Glenthorn Road and Glenthorn Avenue and headed out on foot.

Both boys were unaware that they were under surveillance. This was no easy task for Harrington's crew. He had deployed officers in vehicles, on bikes and on foot to keep watch over their target.

And they didn't have to wait long. B.T. and the other kid walked casually along Glenthorn Drive, checking car doors. If the door was locked, they smashed a window and went into the car. They didn't try to steal the cars; they just rifled through their contents, looking for money or anything that they could turn into cash.

After damaging the first vehicle, Harrington called in uniformed support to capture B.T. and his accomplice. Although the uniformed crew were close by, the two kids had smashed the windows in five cars before they were arrested.

Herbie Okereke didn't spend long in custody but when released, he had to obey strict conditions. B.T. was given a twenty-four-hour curfew and had to remain in his home at all times unless it was a medical emergency.

John ensured that the local officers from Gurranbraher Garda Station conducted curfew checks on him several times a day and night. The kid complied with the curfew and hunkered down at home playing video games. Now, Inspector Cahill felt a bit easier about leaving the young killer out in the community for a little longer.

Chapter 32

John assigned Tim and Pete to make photo lineups of all the players. That included: Tyson Rolland, Darryl Lyons, Alfie Hastings, Lily Crawford, Olly Sullivan, Herbie Okereke and, of course, Archie Cambridge. That evening he told Jules that he had to go back to Maghaberry to show Bertie Flynn the photo arrays and get him to officially identify everyone he implicated in his first interview. "I'm hoping we can get up and down in one day. It shouldn't take long to show him a few lineups," John said while they drove through the rain to Clonakilty to get some groceries.

"Are you going to drop into P.S.N.I. Headquarters?" Jules asked with a mischievous grin.

John gave her a sideways look. "Are you kidding me! I'm not even telling them I'm going up there. Out of sight, out of mind. If they know that I'm there, they'll call me in and some high-ranking clown will have some stupid idea about something."

"They're bound to find out that you were there," Jules said, poking the sleeping bear.

"That's fine. They can find out two days after I get back here. As long as they let me alone here to do my job, I am fine and happy. I think I'm doing a wonderful job to strengthen the relationship between the P.S.N.I. and the Garda. Don't you?"

"You're full of crap, that's what you are," Jules answered.

Two days later, John and Pete were back on a plane flying to Belfast City Airport. Again, John had arranged to pick up an unmarked patrol car from the Airport Police Station and drove to Lisburn Police Station. When they arrived at the modern fortress,

Detective Sergeant Charlie Brennan met them. "I brought your pal in from Maghaberry earlier. He's in the interview room waiting for you. He's been fed and watered so he should be content," Charlie said in his strong Belfast accent.

Bertie's eyes lit up when the detectives walked into the room. He was thrilled to see a familiar face. "I'm worried about witness protection. I've been reading up on it in the library at the jail."

"What are you worried about?" John asked, sitting across from the big man.

"Well," Bertie paused and looked down at his feet, "I'll have to find a job. Sure, what can I do? I've never had a real job." Bertie was embarrassed, revealing this to the policeman.

"Bertie, you'll be fine." John smiled across at the gangster. "If it all works out, they'll retrain you. And don't sell yourself short. You've been successfully running a million-euro business! It may have been illegal but you ran it as a business. You had different levels of employees and you made a profit. You diversified when you had to and you stood your ground against the competition. Don't be a bit worried. You'll be grand."

"What do you mean by diversified?" Bertie asked.

"When you couldn't get crack cocaine, you sold meth or pills or whatever was available. But you always kept the business going. You'll learn how to use those skills honestly. Don't worry. You'll be grand!" John reassured him and Pete tried to keep from laughing.

"That's the problem. I have fuck all else to do but worry," Bertie answered.

Pete showed Bertie Flynn all the photo lineups and he positively identified everyone that he had implicated in the earlier interview. It was almost lunchtime when they were wrapping up the interview. "We'll ask Sergeant Brennan to get you a burger on the way back to jail. Was there anything else you want to talk to us about?" John asked.

Bertie squirmed a bit in his chair; John knew there was another disclosure coming. A sense of dread came over him. What more could Bertie have?

"One night, not long after I ended up in Maghaberry, I called Martina in Cork. She was really pissed off because Tyson and Darryl made her do some work for them," Bertie said, pausing for a breath. John and Pete ignored the pause and waited for Bertie to continue. "Martina said Tyson picked her up and brought her to Darryl's house in Manor View. She said there was a massive pool of blood on the floor in the utility room near the back door. Tyson and Darryl forced her, Jenny and Joan Carney to clean up all the blood. She was bawling when she told me this."

"When was this?" John asked, opening his notebook.

"A week or two after I got here. I spoke with Martina again about it. She doesn't say much over the phone but she's willing to speak with you about it."

"How much blood are we talking about?" Pete asked.

"Lots. A huge pool of thick dark blood is how she described it."

"Who's Joan Carney? John asked.

"She's Trish Langford's cousin. She's going out with John-Joe Cooper. He's a Dial a Dealer driver for Tyson and Darryl. Darryl was laughing at them when they were cleaning up the blood. Martina puked while she was doing it. Darryl was calling them the maids. She was kinda fucked up by this. She said she got nightmares after it."

"How well does Martina know Joan Carney?" John asked.

"They all know each other. They're all around the same age but Martina says Joan is flakey. John-Joe beats the crap out of her but she stays with him because she gets lots of coke. That's what Martina says anyhow. I only know her to see her."

"Did this John-Joe fella ever work for you?" John asked.

"Once or twice, but I ended up giving him a licking because he was shaving the rocks." Bertie grinned at the memory.

"What do you mean shaving the rocks?" Pete asked.

"He would have a bag of crack cocaine. You know how it's crystalized in rocks?" Bertie said and both detectives nodded. "He would open the bag and get a blade and scrape a little bit off each rock. Then he would soak the pieces in vinegar and join them together. That way, he would end up with a couple of small rocks for himself and Joan."

John shook his head in disbelief. At this point, Bertie had nothing else to add, apart from his continual asking about getting a deal and being released to the Witness Security Program.

It was a rush to get to the airport to catch the last flight to Cork; it was pouring rain in Belfast and the evening rush hour traffic was chaotic. Pete and John barely made it to the gate on time. They were thankful that they didn't have any luggage to check, only one briefcase between the two of them.

When they were sitting on the plane and taxiing down the runway, Pete turned to his boss, "You couldn't be up to them, could you? I mean, to sit down and open a bag of thirty or forty rocks and shave each one of them. How could you have the patience for that? Why wouldn't he just steal a rock?"

John thought about it for a minute. "Look what happened to Eddie Flynn when he was caught stealing product. I suppose he must account for every rock they give him so it's safer to shave them down than to steal a few." Pete nodded in agreement.

WHEN THEY LANDED IN Cork after the short flight, both John and Pete went home. Neither of them felt like going to the station at that late hour. The weather was better in Cork than it had been in Belfast. There was a cool dry breeze blowing in from the ocean when John returned to Inchydoney. Jules had left him a note. She had gone to Bandon to visit her Aunt Nan and his supper was in the fridge.

After he warmed his supper in the microwave, John took the greyhounds to the beach for their evening walk. The tide was out and he walked down the concrete slipway used by the lifeguard service during the summer months. He unleashed the dogs once he stood on the sand at the end of the slipway. They dashed off into the darkness. The beach was deserted and the only light was from the half moon that was trying to break through the clouds. John walked to the channel at the far end of the strand. It was completely deserted; occasionally the dogs would run up to him for reassurance and then take off on another adventure. He was deep in thought, wondering how to deal with this mystery pool of blood, when his phone beeped in his pocket. He looked at the text message. Jules was home. He whistled for the dogs to follow him and walked back to the slipway. He decided that he would have to interview Martina and Joan Carney and see where that led. He didn't want to speak with Jenny O'Callaghan just yet. She was too close to his main target, Tyson Rolland.

THE FOLLOWING MORNING, Pete Sandhu had accessed the profile of Joan Carney and John-Joe Cooper on PULSE. John studied the papers. Carney had been charged with shoplifting a few times but she had also been the victim of assault on three occasions. Each time, John-Joe was the suspect, but she refused to cooperate with police and the Director of Public Prosecutions so John-Joe had never been convicted of domestic violence. Cooper also had a conviction for possession of a controlled substance with intent to distribute. He had received a suspended sentence for that. PULSE also had Cooper listed as an Independent Posse associate.

John briefed the members of the Serious Crime Unit on the second interview of Bertie Flynn. They were thrilled that Bertie had formally identified everyone that he had implicated in his first interview; this was essential when it came to making arrests. The investigators were also intrigued about the pool of blood at Darryl Lyons' house.

John assigned Pete and Tim Warren to check all missing person reports from the time that Martina made the disclosure to Bertie in order to compile a list of potential victims. Tim was also to check the hospitals in and near the city for someone who may have lost a lot of blood. Mike Williams and Eddie Jenkins were assigned to interview Martina Fitzpatrick while Jeff Rafter and Len Benoit were to locate and interview Joan Carney.

Bertie had warned Martina in a phone call to expect a visit from the detectives. When Mike and Eddie arrived at her door, she asked them if they could drop the kids off at her mother's house on Brandon Crescent before she went to the station. Once Martina's children were safely stowed, she relaxed and chatted with the detectives on the drive to Anglesea Street.

Jeff Rafter and Len Benoit had no difficulty in locating Joan Carney. Joan shared an older apartment with another couple of girls on Belview Crescent, off Military Road. Jeff pushed open the wrought iron gate at the front yard and rang the doorbell on the ground floor suite. Seconds later the door was opened by a young woman. She was of average height and build and had dyed blonde shoulder-length hair but the dark roots were starting to grow in. The first thing that Jeff and Len noticed was the relatively fresh bruise under her left eye. "Yeah?" the woman asked, as she stood with her feet slightly apart and her left hand on her hip; she held the door with her right hand.

Jeff and Len recognized Joan Carney because they had looked at her police file photo before heading out. "Hi Joan, I'm Jeff Rafter, Anglesea Street Garda." He showed his Garda identification to the woman.

"Oh Jesus! I'm sorry. Boy, I thought you were the Mormons. They were up and down the street the other day. What do you want?" Joan smiled at her error.

Jeff and Len kept it vague and only told Joan they needed to speak to her at the station about an incident that may have involved her. She agreed to go with them.

On the drive to the station, Len Benoit gently asked Joan how she got the bruise on her face.

"I walked into a door," Joan answered, looking out the window as they drove down Summer Hill.

"No you didn't," Len said. "Was it John-Joe?"

Joan met Len's eyes in the rear-view mirror and she nodded her head. She looked down at her feet. She was embarrassed.

"Are you OK?" Len asked. "There's nothing to be embarrassed about. Nobody has the right to do that to you," Len was making sure that he wasn't accusing John-Joe Cooper of wrongdoing because, no doubt, this young woman would have defended him.

"I'm grand," Joan groaned, sniffing and wiping her nose with the back of her hand.

Chapter 33

Martina Fitzpatrick was cooperating with her interviewers in Interview Room # 1 at Garda Headquarters. Her only concern was her safety and the safety of her children. Mike Williams put her at ease and told her that they would not act on anything she told them without ensuring that she and the kids were safe. That, and the fact that Bertie told her they had to trust the cops, put her mind slightly at ease.

"Tyson showed up at me door that night and told me I had to come with him. I told him that I couldn't because I had to mind the children and he made sure that I understood that it wasn't an option. I had to call me mam to come over and stay with the kids," Martina said.

"Did he threaten you?" Mike asked.

"Not really, but I knew I couldn't say no to him, especially when Bertie or even Eddie weren't around. Not that he's scared of either of them, but at least they'd have stood up to him."

"What happened when you went with him?"

"He drove me up to Knocknaheeney and into Manor View Estate. He parked outside Darryl Lyons' house and told me to come inside with him."

"Who was there?" This was an easy interview for Mike; she was an awesome witness as long as he was asking all the right questions.

Martina thought about it for a few seconds. "Darryl Lyons and John-Joe Cooper were in the front yard. Joan Carney was standing at the back door and Jenny was inside in the utility room. Tyson told us all to get in the house and when I stepped inside the utility room, there was a massive pool of blood on the floor."

"How big a pool was it? Can you show me on the floor here?" Mike asked, pointing to the floor of the four-meter by four-meter room.

"It covered well over half of that floor and it was dark and thick in the middle of the pool," Martina said, shuddering as she recalled the horrific sight.

"What happened next?"

"Tyson said something like, '*You three fucking maids, clean that mess up. Use plenty of bleach and make sure every last drop of it is gone.*' Jenny was shaking. "I thought she was going to pass out. Joan turned to walk out and John-Joe grabbed her by the arm and pushed her back in. I just stood there. I didn't know what to do. Then Darryl got a few towels and two buckets and two big bottles of bleach. He told us where the mop was and started laughing," Martina told the detectives. The colour had now drained from her face after recalling this event.

"Can you keep going?" Mike's voice was low and calm because he saw the change in Martina's demeanour.

Martina looked up from the table at Mike; she nodded and then continued. "We had no choice but to start cleaning. I began to soak up the blood in a towel and I swear to God, I almost puked. And the smell! It was terrible, you know that metal smell from blood? And it was still warm and sticky." Martina closed her eyes and again shuddered. Eddie Jenkins thought she was going to puke this time. "Tyson, Darryl and John-Joe were talking out in the yard, I heard John-Joe say '*I can't do it on me own, someone has to come with me.*' Then John-Joe came into the utility room and yelled at Joan. He told her that she had to go with him and they had a job to do. Joan left then. It took Jenny and me about another two hours to clean the place. Then Tyson put all the towels, rags, paper towels and the mop that we used into a big garbage bag and took it away. Darryl gave me fifty euros, but I had to get a taxi home when I was finished and that cost fifteen," Martina said, sounding somewhat affronted.

"What else did you see in the utility room? Did you see any guns, knives, a hammer or a hatchet, anything like that?" Eddie asked.

"No, nothing like that. All that's in the utility room is an old washing machine and a clothes dryer."

"Was there any blood on the wall?" Eddie wanted to know.

Martina thought about this for a few seconds. "Yeah, there was. There were some smear marks on the floor going towards the back door, like something was pulled along the floor through the blood and there was a load of specks on one part of the wall."

"How high up were they?"

Martina held her hand against the wall, about a meter off the ground. "About that high."

"Did you talk to the other two girls about this afterwards?" Mike asked.

"No, Jenny and me would never talk about anything like that. We know what they're like. We don't want to draw them on us."

"What about Joan? Did you ever talk to her about it?"

"No, I hardly ever see her. Anyway, I can't fucking stand her. She's a flake." Martina grinned.

John had been watching the interview of Martina Fitzpatrick and was very pleased with how it turned out but he was confused. Someone had died or nearly died in the utility room of Darryl Lyons' house and he had no clue who it was. He switched monitor screens to watch the interview of Joan Carney.

Jeff Rafter and Len Benoit got on very well with Joan. She liked them and did not mind speaking with them. During the beginning of her recorded interview, she spoke freely about the latest beating she had received from John-Joe Cooper. Unfortunately, Joan was no different to many other victims of domestic violence because

Joan blamed herself and tried to make allowances for the man who brutalized her.

Jeff expertly steered the conversation to the night of the blood clean up at Lyons' house. "I had to do way worse than Martina and Jenny," Joan said indignantly. "They got off lightly and had the easy job."

"What did you have to do?" Jeff asked.

"I can't tell ya. John-Joe would fucking kill me."

"We're going to find out anyway, Joan. It's better to get in front of it now rather than get in trouble for it down the road. We found out about you going there to clean up the blood. We'll find out about everything else," Jeff said, reasoning with the young woman. "It took the other two girls hours to clean up all that blood. You didn't stick around to help them. Why? What did you do that could be worse than that?"

"Ya well, John-Joe made me dig a fucking grave for some fucker that he had wrapped up in the back of the van," Joan said, trying to one-up the other two cleaners.

John, watching the interview live, almost fell out of his chair when he heard this disclosure.

"Who were you digging a grave for?" Jeff tried not to look or sound as shocked as he was.

"I don't fucking know! John-Joe said Darryl shot some fella and Tyson made me and John-Joe take him away and bury him."

John had heard enough for now; they had to re-strategize. He left the monitor room, knocked on the door of Interview Room # 3 and called Rafter and Benoit out.

The three men looked at each other and all smiled. "Can you believe that?" John said. Len Benoit laughed.

"What are we going to do now?" Jeff asked. "Are we going to charge her as an accessory or with facilitating a murder?"

John thought about it for a moment; he rubbed his chin and then rubbed the back of his neck. He was incredibly tense. "OK, here's what we'll do. We'll treat her as a witness. She is a victim of domestic violence. She told us that John-Joe recently assaulted her and she stated that John-Joe made her dig the grave. She also said that it was Darryl who shot this mystery man. Go back in and get the full story from her. She is not a suspect. She's a victim and a witness. Let's make sure she's a damn good witness!"

Jeff and Len went back into Interview Room # 3 and John summoned Tim Warren and Pete Sandhu to the interview room. "Watch this interview for a while and then we're probably going to have to find John-Joe Cooper."

Joan Carney told Jeff and Len that John-Joe had called her over to Darryl Lyons' house. When she arrived, she found a large pool of blood on the floor. John-Joe told her that she would have to clean it up with Jenny and Martina. Neither of them was there at that time. They came over a little bit later. Joan didn't want to clean up the blood and when she went to leave, John-Joe pushed her back into the utility room. After a while, John-Joe told her that they had to go somewhere to do a job and she got into John-Joe's van. They drove for hours; she didn't know where they went because it was dark but it was in the country somewhere. During the drive John-Joe told her there was a dead body in the back of the van. She never saw the actual body. It was all wrapped up in plastic and an old piece of carpet. But she had to help John-Joe dig a grave and then help him carry the body through the woods.

"Can you tell me anything about the place where you dug the grave?" Jeff asked.

"It was in the middle of nowhere. We drove through a few villages and then down a twisty road. There was a big lake and a track up through the woods. I haven't a clue where we were," Martina said, shrugging her shoulders. "We smoked some weed after we finished covering him up and I fell asleep on the way home after that. When we got home, we smoked crack."

"What did John-Joe say about the body? You said it was a male?" Len Benoit asked.

"John-Joe said he went to Darryl's house to reload with crack. Tyson dragged this fella into the house and Tyson and Darryl were slapping him around. He was going door to door selling bunk weed." Joan took a breath; she didn't require any encouragement to keep talking. "He must be fuck'n mental to be selling weed in that neighborhood. Anyway, John-Joe said they made the fella get down on his knees and then Darryl shot him in the head. John-Joe said that he nearly shit his pants."

"John-Joe saw Darryl shoot him?"

"Yeah, that's what he said. Then he said that Tyson was pissing himself laughing because there was so much blood on the floor. They couldn't believe he bled so much. John-Joe helped them wrap him up and carry him to John-Joe's HiAce." Joan enjoyed the attention she was getting from the detectives.

"John-Joe drives a Toyota HiAce? What colour is it?" Jeff asked.

"Navy blue, it's an old piece of shit," Joan smirked.

"Go and find John-Joe Cooper and arrest him for domestic assault. Hopefully he'll have some dope on him too," John told Tim Warren and Pete Sandhu.

"What about this murder? Are we going to charge him with something?" Tim asked.

John let out a long breath. "Not yet. Bring a uniform crew with you and seize his van. Pete, you can get a search warrant and we'll see if we can find some blood in the van and identify this mystery victim."

Jeff Rafter and Len Benoit exited the interview room and made their way to the monitor room. "What did you think of that for a story?" Jeff asked his boss.

"I believe every word she said. Ask her if they cleaned up the back of John-Joe's HiAce. Then get her something to eat and hang on to her until Tim and Pete have John-Joe in custody."

Jeff Rafter went back to the interview room and asked Joan what she wanted to eat. A burger in batter and chips were her first choice. She told Jeff that the back of the van was filthy and she never cleaned it and doubted that John-Joe did.

When he was alone in the monitor room, John looked up the number for the Irish Prison Service Headquarters in Longford. He eventually got through to Finbarr Kinsella, the director of the Organizational Support Group. The O.S.G. were responsible for the security and gathering intelligence within the prison system in Ireland and often sharing it with other security forces.

After introducing himself, John got straight to the point. "We are about to arrest a gangbanger for domestic assault and he will be detained. He will probably be charged within the next two weeks with a much more serious offence, related to a murder. He might even be charged with the murder." John paused as he sensed Kinsella was making notes at the other end of the phone line. "It would really help us if this fella was kept out of the way for a week or two, and not in Cork or Limerick Prison where most of the Independent Posse members are."

The director asked a few questions about John-Joe Cooper and ran him through the I.P.S. database. Then he spoke, "After his first court appearance, I will have him shipped to the Midlands Prison in Portlaoise. I'll be able to hang on to him there for about ten days but his lawyer will probably kick up and I'll have to ship him back to Cork."

John could not believe how easy that was; Finbarr Kinsella was a very reasonable man to deal with and was happy to cooperate. This new O.S.G. Unit was a blessing. At last, there was cooperation between the different state bodies that had a common goal.

After the telephone call with O.S.G. ended, Tim Warren called to report that John-Joe was in custody. When he was searched, they found a baggie with four rocks of crack cocaine in his pocket. Joan was driven home after she downed her greasy food. John was relieved that she couldn't reach out to John-Joe and tell him what she had told the police.

Tim Warren paraded John-Joe in front of John when he was brought to the station. John-Joe was tall and thin. He had short curly brown hair but the sides of his head were shaved, He also had a noticeable scar under his right eye. The uniform crew organized to have the HiAce van towed to the police garage. Pete applied for the search warrant while Tim processed John-Joe for the assault and the drug possession.

When the search warrant was granted, Sergeant Martens entered the back of the van. She lightly sprayed luminol on the filthy floor. Then she turned on her blacklight. Immediately, spots of dried blood lit up like white patches near the wheel well. Jennifer Martens smiled to herself; she photographed the stains and then swabbed samples of each of them. She would send the samples to the National Laboratory and harass them until she got a fast result.

The harassment paid off and within a few days Sergeant Martens had a result. She walked into the incident room and directly into John's office. She placed a sheet of paper in front of the inspector and sat down. John read the paper. "Sam Falvey," he said and immediately ran the name through PULSE. "He's a small-time thief and druggie. He's not even reported missing." This saddened John. "His last known address was a flat near the intersection of Bakers Road and Harbor View Road." John sent a team to the address to make enquiries.

Sam Falvey's aunt lived in the run-down top floor flat. Although it wasn't yet noon, she was fairly drunk when she opened the door to Mike Williams and Eddie Jenkins. She told the officers that Sam stayed there occasionally but she had not seen him in weeks. "He sleeps rough most of the time. Sure he's a raging drug addict. I don't know when I last saw him." Liquor was emanating from her as she spoke. Mike and Eddie made some more enquiries with the shelters and soup kitchens but nobody had seen Sam Falvey for weeks.

Jules thought it was so sad that nobody had even reported Sam Falvey missing, when John told her about it, during their evening walk with the dogs on Inchydoney's beaches. "Can you imagine how awful that is, that nobody even noticed that he wasn't around any more? That poor man." John agreed with her; he was shocked by this, but unfortunately, he wasn't surprised. People like Sam Falvey were invisible to the rest of society. "What are you going to do now? This is like the case that will never end," Jules said.

"Its time to bring John-Joe Cooper back in. He'll be glad to be back in Cork for a while." John had made his mind up on how to proceed.

Chapter 34

The timing was perfect. Cooper had his next scheduled court appearance in Cork City Court House in two days. This meant that the Prison Service had to get him to court and the inspector didn't have to send someone on the 170-kilometer trek to the Midlands Prison.

After his court appearance, John-Joe Cooper was brought back to the cells in the basement of the courthouse. He was just settling down, waiting for his ride back to the Midlands, when John and Tim showed up and arrested him on suspicion of the murder of Sam Falvey. Cooper was brought to Garda Headquarters on Anglesea Street and put into Interview Room # 1. John-Joe was scared. His heart was pounding and he was gasping for breath. He spoke with a solicitor who told him not to say anything to the police and it would all be sorted out later. John-Joe didn't say it to the lawyer but he thought this was terrible advice. After all, he knew that he hadn't killed anyone.

John-Joe sat alone in the interview room. He did what every other desperate criminal who had been in the same position had done. He stared at the graffiti that had been etched into the steel table top by those that had gone before him. He saw the letters I-P scratched into the surface in a few places. He sighed, knowing that it was the I-P that had put him in this situation.

John-Joe heard the bolt on the steel door of the interview room being opened. He swallowed hard and the knot in his stomach tightened. Inspector Cahill held the door open while Detective Tim Warren rolled two mismatched office chairs into the room. Before sitting, John offered his outstretched right hand to Cooper. "How are ya John-Joe, I'm Detective Inspector John Cahill." John-Joe looked at the offered hand and shook it.

"Are ya alright?" John-Joe answered. John smiled at his prisoner, sat down and introduced Tim.

"I'm not going to spend a lot of time talking to you today because this case is cut and dry!" John said, looking directly at Cooper. "When you were arrested for beating the crap out of Joan and the crack cocaine you had in your pocket, we seized your van. We searched your van and found blood in the back. We analyzed the blood and it belongs to Sam Falvey." John paused and held John-Joe's stare. John then placed a police file photo of Sam Falvey on the table in front of Cooper. John-Joe stared at the photograph and looked down to the floor, then he sat back and folded his arms and stretched his legs out under the table, trying to look confident.

"So what? I never heard of Sam Falvey anyway," John-Joe said. He smirked and his voice was defiant.

"I'll tell ya what! Tim and I both know that Sam Falvey was shot dead and you wrapped up his body, put it in the back of your van and drove off and buried him. You are the last one with the dead body, so tag, you're it. You are going down for it." John was now the one smirking.

"I didn't fuckin' kill him!" John-Joe sat up and unfolded his arms. He was shocked that the detectives knew so much.

"Did you see anyone else here in the other rooms when we brought you in? No, you are the only one in here. You are left holding the bag, John-Joe. You killed him."

"I didn't kill nobody!"

"Well, who killed him?"

"I don't know what happened. He was dead when I got there," John-Joe pleaded.

"Progress!" John thought as he shot Tim a quick glance. "OK, John-Joe, I'm willing to listen to you, but I know you didn't find a dead body, wrap it up, put it in the back of your HiAce and then bury it."

"I don't know who killed him, but it wasn't me." There was now a slight quiver in John-Joe's voice. John knew that his prisoner was scared.

"John-Joe, I'm going to make this easy for you." The confidence in John's voice was unnerving the prisoner. "Sam Falvey was killed in Darryl Lyons' house in Manor View Estate. Start from the beginning and tell me everything. If you don't, you're going to wear this, I promise you that. You'll sit up in the Midlands Prison until you're an old man!"

John-Joe Cooper went pale. He was caught between a rock and a hard place. He could continue to play the gangster and be loyal to the gang or he could tell the cops the truth and risk the revenge of the gang. "I swear I don't know who killed him," he sputtered, hoping he could talk his way out of it.

"Yes, you do. But you are going down for it. We are going to leave you to think about that for a while. Do you want a cup of tea or coffee while you have a good hard think about your future?" John stood up and closed his notebook.

"Can I have a cup of coffee with milk and sugar? Any chance of a smoke?"

"I'll hook you up," Tim said as he walked out of the interview room.

A few minutes later, Tim handed John-Joe a cup of coffee in a Styrofoam cup. He also gave John-Joe another cup that was half filled with water. Tim gave John-Joe a cigarette and lit it. "You can use the cup of water as an ashtray." Tim turned to leave. He stopped at the door and looked at John-Joe. "You're going to get a life sentence if you don't smarten up." Tim left John-Joe alone to contemplate his future before he could answer.

John-Joe Cooper sat alone in the interview room for the best part of an hour. Occasionally he got up and paced around the small space like a caged wild animal. When the detectives returned to the room, John-Joe asked to speak with his solicitor again. Tim Warren dialed the number and handed John-Joe the phone while John turned off the recording equipment. After less than five minutes, John-Joe knocked on the door, signalling that the call was completed.

"Let me guess," John said when they returned to the interview room. "The lawyer said to keep saying 'No Comment,' am I right? Well, that's probably good advice but you are the one sitting here going to get charged with murder. Anyway, we are going to keep talking to you. It's up to you if you want to tell us anything."

After another hour of one-sided conversation, apart from John-Joe's 'No Comment' answers, John-Joe Cooper finally started to show signs of weakness. Although, he was defending himself, he was now engaging the detectives in conversation. John and Tim kept speaking to him and he was at the point where it was normal for him to converse with them. "Why would I kill this fella? Sure, he's nothing to me. I never saw him before."

"I agree John-Joe," the inspector said. "He is nothing to you and maybe that's why it was easy for you to kill him. OR you know exactly who killed him and why and you're afraid to talk."

"I am afraid to talk. I'm scared shitless. Wouldn't you be?" John-Joe answered, his voice trembling and he truly sounded scared.

"I know you're scared, John-Joe. I don't blame you, but it's time to look out for yourself. You can be charged with murder or facilitating a murder and go to jail for years. How old are you now?"

"I'm twenty-four."

"OK, think about this. You are twenty-four-years-old. You go to jail for at least twenty-five years. You haven't even been alive for twenty-five years! You will be nearly fifty-years-old when you get out. You'll be an old man like me!" John pointed to himself with his thumbs. He could see that this comment hit John-Joe hard and made him think. John kept going. "There is a big difference between moving a dead body because you're scared of the people who made you do it or being part of the murder. You must make a choice and you must make it right now." John slapped the table with the palm of his hand, snapping John-Joe back to the reality of the situation.

There was silence in the room. The silence seemed endless. Tim was about to speak when John-Joe beat him to it. "I did not kill him. I saw that fella a few times going door to door selling weed. It wasn't even real weed. It was shite. He told people he was selling for the I-P so when I saw him on Manor View, I told Tyson and Darryl." John-Joe stopped, hoping he had said enough.

"Yeah, go on," John said.

He did not need much encouragement, and John-Joe continued. "Tyson told me to bring him in to Darryl's house. I told your man that we wanted to buy his weed and he followed me in. Darryl and Tyson grabbed him as soon as he stepped in through the back door. Tyson grabbed him by the throat and Darryl punched him in the gut. I didn't touch him, I swear," John-Joe was pleading with them to believe him. "They made him kneel on the ground and Darryl shot him in the back of the head, execution style! The bang was so loud! My ears were ringing for two fucking days."

"What happened then?"

"They started laughing because there was so much blood on the floor. It was a huge pool of blood. You never seen anything like it! Tyson said that someone would have to clean it up. That's when he told me to call Joan."

"You called your Joan to come over and clean it up?" John asked, pretending that he didn't know this already.

"Yeah, my Joan. And then Tyson went and brought Martina to help and his old lady, Jenny, showed up. Me, Tyson and Darryl wrapped him up in plastic garbage bags and an old piece of carpet. We tied him up with duct tape and the three of us carried him out to my van. That's when me and Joan took him away."

"Who was there when you put him in the back of the van?" John asked.

John-Joe thought about it for a second and looked up to the ceiling. "Nobody but the three of us. The oul-dolls hadn't shown up yet."

"OK John-Joe, describe the route you took to bury him," John said.

"Did ye not find him?" John-Joe asked, looking puzzled.

"Not yet."

"For fucks sakes, I thought ye found him and that's why I was arrested."

"You may as well tell us where you put him because you'll get absolutely no leniency from the courts if you don't help us recover the body." John held John-Joe's stare. "I'd say you have no chance if you don't tell us where the body is."

John-Joe thought about it; he knew he was out of choices. "He's in the woods near Gougane Barra."

"Gougane Barra? How the fuck did you find that place?" The surprise showed in John's voice.

"My grandad used to take us there when we were small," John-Joe replied.

"Where is Gougane Barra?" Tim asked.

"Gougane Barra is a national park in West Cork. It's where the River Lee rises and is a beautiful peaceful place. There is a gorgeous lake, surrounded by mountains, and there is a tiny chapel, about eight-hundred-years-old, on a tiny island in the lake," John replied, sounding like a travel guide.

"It's where Saint Finbarr, the fella who discovered Cork City, came from," John-Joe added. John smiled at the phrase 'discovered the city.'

"Alright, describe the route you took," John said, now that the history and geography lessons were over.

"I drove out through Ballincollig to Macroom. Then I turned off and drove through Inchigeelagh. Next, we went through that village where they only speak Irish. What's it called?"

"Ballingeary?" John said.

"Yeah, that's it. It's only a couple of miles to the park from there. I drove past the chapel and up the dirt track to the car park. The gate was locked but I broke the lock with a hammer and drove into the national park."

"Where did you go once you were in the car park?" John asked, trying not to show his impatience with John-Joe.

"Do ya know the road goes around in a big loop? Well, I took the track to the right. I drove along the track past all the picnic tables until I came to the roundy turnaround area at the end. I stopped there. Do ya know that there's a little wooden footbridge right there?" John-Joe paused as he thought about where he went next. "Ya, we parked there and then Joan helped me drag him over the footbridge and up the hill. He weighed a fuckin' ton." John-Joe smirked and then continued. "We went off the track into the woods and we dug a grave and put him in it. I said a prayer for him before we went back."

"That was nice of you." John thought to himself and had to stop himself saying it out loud. "What did ye do then?"

"We smoked a joint back at the van and then I drove home. Joan fell asleep on the way." John-Joe looked around the room. Then he asked the question that was most important to him. "What's going to happen to me now?"

"Good question John-Joe," John responded. He hadn't quite planned on John-Joe being such a good witness. "You did not get bail today so you must go back to prison. You will probably end up back in the Midlands Prison for a while."

"Ah Jaysus, I hate that fucking place. It's full of fellas from Dublin," John-Joe interrupted.

"Give me a chance to finish, will ya?" John smiled at the prisoner. "I'm not going to charge you with any of this today, not with the murder or facilitating it. I will send the file to the Director of Public Prosecutions and they can decide. I will recommend that they keep you as a witness."

"Will I have to testify? I don't want to go to court and testify." John-Joe sounded quite concerned.

"Yes, you might have to testify. You can go to court either as a witness or as an accused. That will be up the prosecutor. But listen carefully. Nobody knows that you were questioned about this today, except you. It's up to you to keep it quiet. I will arrange to get you back to prison. If you get bail in the next couple of months, I suggest you leave Joan alone and stop using her as a punching bag or you're going to be locked up for a long time. She does not deserve to be treated like that." John stood up and turned to leave the room. John-Joe hung his head in shame.

Chapter 35

"What now?" Tim Warren asked his boss. The two men sat alone in the incident room. It was 7:00PM and everyone else had gone home.

John looked at his watch and sighed, "Let's take the weekend to think about it. We have to get inside Darryl Lyons' house to see if we can find any evidence of that shooting. I'll talk to the boss about organizing a ground search for Gougane Barra and hopefully we'll find the body. I cannot see those two ass clowns putting too much effort into dragging him into the woods. You can go home. Have a good weekend."

"This case will never end. It just keeps growing and growing," Tim said as he grabbed his coat.

John laughed. "We will be out of a job by the time we're finished. There will be nobody left to arrest for anything."

After Tim left, John called Jules and told her he would be at the office for another hour. Jules said she had kept his supper and he could warm it up when he got home. Her concern was growing because of the long hours John was working and the stress that he put himself under. She had recently read a book about work/life balance. She told John about the book and laughed. This was a completely unfamiliar concept in her house but deep down, she hoped that the situation would change in the near future.

John's next call was to Superintendent Paddy Collins. It was Friday evening and Paddy Collins was at a restaurant with his wife and a couple of their friends. John couldn't help feeling slightly envious. "I'll call you in the morning. This can wait."

"That would be much appreciated, Inspector," the superintendent said, with his thick rural Kerry accent. "Will you give me a quick hint as to what I will have to deal with tomorrow?"

"I know what happened in Darryl Lyons' house," John informed him.

Paddy Collins' wife kicked him in the shin, under that table, seconds before he would ask more questions. "That's grand so call me in the morning," he said, glaring at his wife.

John put on his coat and made the drive home to Inchydoney. On the way, he thought that Tim Warren was correct; this case was never going to end.

ON SATURDAY MORNING, after a walk on the beaches with the two greyhounds, John called Superintendent Collins. He apprised him of the interview with John-Joe Cooper. Although happy with the interview, the superintendent wasn't looking forward to his next task. Nevertheless, he said that he would organize a ground search of the area in Gougane Barra.

Saturday and Sunday were relaxing; John and Jules tried to keep their minds off the never-ending investigation, until Sunday evening when John's cell phone rang. It was Detective Sergeant Mike Williams. Mike had received a phone call from Limerick Prison. Archie Cambridge had been transferred back there and had reached out. Archie wanted to speak with Mike and Eddie. Archie hadn't said exactly what he wanted to talk about but he sounded very different on the phone to the person who Mike had interviewed a few weeks earlier.

"Things are looking up," John said to Jules, when he hung up the phone. "Archie Cambridge has asked to speak with Mike and Eddie again."

That night, yet again, John had trouble falling asleep. He was so close to taking out the leaders of one of the most violent gangs in the country but he was also very aware that he was one short step away from the entire house of cards collapsing. He stared at the ceiling and hoped that his luck would hold.

THE MONDAY MORNING briefing was abuzz with excitement in the incident room. When John told his team about the interview with John-Joe Cooper, the detectives were more enthusiastic than he had ever seen them. And when he told them that Archie Cambridge requested a meeting with Mike and Eddie, the other members of the team began to speculate on what Archie would say. That meeting was arranged for later Monday afternoon at Limerick Prison.

Paddy Collins walked into the incident room minutes before John concluded the briefing and announced, "We will be ready to begin the ground search at Gougane Barra tomorrow morning at 9:00AM. We will have about twenty uniform officers and another thirty soldiers to assist. Can you liaise with Sergeant Martens in the Forensic Identification Service? She will have to send someone to assist."

"Thanks boss. Are you going to come with us? We could do with all the help we can get," John asked.

"A day out in Gougane Barra sounds like just what the doctor ordered. We'll leave here around six in the morning," Paddy Collins said as he left the room.

MIKE WILLIAMS AND EDDIE Jenkins made the familiar drive to Limerick Prison. On arrival, they introduced themselves to the senior O.S.G. officer. He had a boardroom ready as both Mike and Archie Cambridge had made him aware of the meeting.

Mike and Eddie were surprised when they walked into the room; not only was Archie Cambridge present but so was his solicitor. This was a new lawyer. Mike recognized him from different court appearances and always thought him a fair man. If Mike was uncomfortable, he didn't show it and shook hands with Archie and the lawyer. They all sat around the huge oak table. The first thing that Archie Cambridge did was to thank Mike Williams for sending him the book, 'The Art of War.'

Then the lawyer spoke. "My client is ready to make a statement. Obviously, he is looking for some consideration from the Director of Public Prosecutions. I will deal with that later, but right now Mr. Cambridge wants to make a statement. I am aware of what he will tell you and he will answer most of your questions, if you should have any, and I'm sure that you will."

Eddie Jenkins was prepared for any development and had brought a video camera. He excused himself and ran to the car to fetch it. He called his boss on the way. "Archie wants to make a statement. We don't know what it's about yet, but it's looking good." John was speechless at this news. When Eddie returned to the room, he quickly set up the camera on a tripod and Mike reminded Archie Cambridge that he had been charged with the murder of Anthony Woodsworth and anything he said could be used against him.

Archie nodded and then he began. He described his entire actions on the night that he killed Anthony Woodsworth. When he spoke about the moment that he shot Woodsworth, he didn't show any emotion. "I asked him who he was down with. And I asked him what he thought of the I-P. He said 'Fuck the I-P' and I shot him in the face." The way that Archie described it was cold and indifferent It was just something that he had done. It was very clear that Archie Cambridge was only making this confession to save himself; he felt nothing for the victim. Archie told the officers how Tyson Rolland had given him the gun and sent him on the 'mission.' He described how he was driven to the scene by Alfie Hastings in Alfie's BMW and Alfie's old lady drove them. Archie's confession mirrored Bertie Flynn's description of the homicide.

When Archie was finished, Mike and Eddie thought they were done. Mike closed his notebook; however, the solicitor didn't budge. Archie smiled. "I'm not done yet. I have more."

Although Mike thought Archie was a cocky bastard, he liked him. "More? I can't wait to hear this." Mike opened his notebook again. He cautioned Archie again because whatever Archie was to tell them was a whole new offence.

"Most of the people on my range here in Limerick Prison are members of the Independent Posse," Archie said, looking around the table, making sure he had everyone's full attention. "Most of us are on remand but there are a few sentenced prisoners mixed in. A few weeks ago, one of the I-P council members was killed on the range. I was right there. I know what happened."

Mike Williams dropped his poker face and looked at a gobsmacked Eddie Jenkins. He then looked at the solicitor who raised his eyebrows and nodded at Mike. "Yes, it's true," the lawyer said.

Archie looked like he was bursting to go on and he looked impatiently at his audience. Mike nodded at him to continue and he did. "Things got stupid on the range when Walter Sheldon got transferred in from Cork Prison. Walter was out of control and was being a right prick. The other council members met a few times without Walter and issued him an ultimatum. Walter could either ask to leave the range or they would roll him off it." Archie once again paused for effect. No doubt, he was the center of attention. "Of course, Walter told them to fuck off and Ray-Ray Daniels decided to roll Walter off the range. Potsie told me to go up to Cell 22."

"Who told you?" Eddie asked and Mike shot him a glance for interrupting. There would be plenty of time for questions later.

"Jeff Brady, but everyone knows him as Potsie," Archie continued, without breaking his stride. "Then everyone on the range walked up around Cell 22. Apparently, there is a blind spot there for the cameras." Archie took a sip of water from a Styrofoam cup and went on. "The next thing, Walter was dragged into Cell 22 by Ray-Ray, Potsie and three other fellas from the council. Potsie stepped out and told me to stand six and not to look in. But I did. I looked in a load of times." Archie took another drink of water. "Ray-Ray and two of the others pinned Walter to the wall and Ray-Ray grabbed him by the throat. They were all yelling in there. When Ray-Ray let him go, Walter collapsed. Potsie said '*He's fucking dead.*' Then Ray-Ray got a towel and wrapped it around Walter's neck and pulled both ends, choking Walter more. Ray-Ray told the others to pull the towel in the same way and one by one, they all did. I watched the whole fucking thing." Archie took another drink of water and took a few deep breaths. "I thought for sure they were going to make me come in and pull the towel but when they came out of the cell, Potsie told everyone to fuck off back down the range and that's what I did."

Archie Cambridge looked at the two cops like he was expecting a round of applause. He almost got one. His lawyer looked at Mike Williams and said, "Nice story for you there." And it certainly was. In all of his career with the Garda, Mike had never heard a story like it and probably never would again.

Mike and Eddy spent the next hour asking Archie Cambridge clarifying questions and he answered each and every one of them. Archie also identified the other three other I-P Council members who helped strangle Walter Sheldon with the towel. When the interview was over, Archie went back to the range like nothing had happened.

Mike Williams called his inspector and told him about the confession and the revelation about the prison murder. John couldn't wait for them to get back so he could hear all the details.

"He's one cool customer," Eddie Jenkins said to his partner as they drove back to Cork City.

"Cool! He's an ice-cold killer. He didn't blink an eye when he described how he shot poor old Anthony Woodsworth in the face," Mike added, shaking his head.

When Mike and Eddie returned to Anglesea Street Garda Station, they retold the entire episode for John. John stayed late and watched the recording of the interview for himself.

WHEN HE FINALLY GOT home, he was bursting with excitement. He told Jules about the interview while they walked the dogs on the beach. "This will be the biggest case you ever worked on if you find the dead body in Gougane Barra tomorrow," Jules said, sharing her husband's excitement.

"I know. We'll have to wrap it up soon... before anyone else comes forward!" John said with a laugh.

MORNING CAME QUICKLY and was earlier than usual as John wanted to be at work early so they could make the drive to Gougane Barra to search for Sam Falvey's body.

Superintendent Paddy Collins walked into the incident room with an elderly lady who looked like she was ready for some hiking in the countryside. Paddy introduced his guest as a forensic anthropologist from University College Cork. Her role was to examine any burial site, should they locate one, before it was excavated.

Sergeant Martens took the professor aside and John updated the superintendent on yesterday's interview at Limerick Prison. The superintendent almost leaped for joy when he heard the results of the interview of Archie Cambridge. He would liaise with the investigating officers in Limerick regarding arrests and charges, but not today. Today was a day out of the office, in the National Park of Gougane Barra, and regardless of the fact that they were looking for a dead body, the superintendent was looking forward to the day away from headquarters.

Shortly after 8:00AM, the convoy of vehicles, including a busload of soldiers, made its way to Gougane Barra. After they turned off the N22, the main highway, the roads became narrower and more twisted, slowing things down for the larger vehicles. As they pressed farther west, the scenery became more rugged and typical of West Cork with rocky outcrops, bogs and forest all along the way. The sun was shining and the scenery looked spectacular. If the task ahead of them wasn't so grim, it would have been an amazing day out. The convoy drew a great deal of attention from the locals as they drove through the towns of Inchigeelagh and the Irish- speaking town of Ballingeary. Soon the lead vehicle, driven by Tim Warren, turned off the road into the Gougane Barra National Park.

Now the road shrank on the sides and the military bus and the Garda van took up the entire width of the road. Minutes later, they arrived at the gates of the forest park. The gates were unmanned and open. Tim drove along the tree-lined path to the car park; the convoy followed him. Within minutes they were set up in the parking lot. Superintendent Collins took charge and set himself up in the mobile command center with a very young-looking military officer and a tired, battle-weary sergeant. The larger vehicles were too big to navigate the track that John-Joe Cooper took when he buried the body.

The lake in the park was like a sheet of glass and the mountain on the far side of the lake was spotted with sheep, grazing on the slopes. There were six white swans swimming on the lake; that was the only disturbance on the reflection of the beautiful little chapel on the island.

"We're following the directions given to us by some junkie who wouldn't know north from south, let alone east from west," the superintendent said as he pinned a map of the park on a board in the command center. "But he did say he dragged the body up the hill from the footbridge which is about a kilometer from here."

The military sergeant tactfully suggested that they divide the area into grids of two-hundred-meters squared, from the edge of the footbridge and fan out from there. Paddy Collins then addressed the group as a whole; the military officer and the N.C.O. organized the grids to be marked off with different coloured flags and split the group into smaller search teams.

A little after 3:00PM, one of the search teams found a mound of earth that looked out of place. A police search dog attended and indicated that something was buried there. Then the anthropologist came in. She donned gloves and a face mask; very carefully she began to remove the top of the mound of earth with a small trowel and what looked like a paint brush. After an hour, she stopped, "It's a new grave," she said, getting to her feet. Paddy Collins ordered everyone else to stop searching.

The professor consulted with Sergeant Jen Martens who had her team set up a canopy tent and bright lights, powered by a small generator, over the grave. They continued to carefully remove the earth from the grave until part of the old carpet, around the victim's face, was revealed. The superintendent, the inspector and the military sergeant stood at the edge of the canopy, looking in. Under the direction of the professor, Jen Martens removed the wrapping to reveal the decomposing human face. And like a scene from a horror movie, a large black beetle crept out of the victim's mouth and into the light. Paddy Collins gasped, turned and took a step backwards. "Jesus, Mary and Joseph!" The superintendent crossed himself and looked around slightly embarrassed. Nobody said anything. Nobody blamed him for reacting in that way.

"So, are you going to dig him up?" John asked Sergeant Martens.

"Eventually, yes. We're going to be here for two or three days. We don't want to lose any evidence," Jen said. It was her scene now and she was going to do this properly.

As much as he wanted to know if this was, indeed, Sam Falvey, John agreed with the F.I.S. sergeant. She was the expert and this was her domain. The forensic team stayed at the burial site and two uniform crews were assigned to remain with them. Everyone else, including the military, returned to Cork City.

John was quiet on the way home. It was time to wrap this caper up. He was coming up with a plan to finally stop the Independent Posse and put Tyson Rolland and Darryl Lyons in prison for the rest of their days.

Chapter 36

For the rest of that week, John shut himself away in his office, putting the entire investigation in chronological order, so that he could present it to Brian McCarthy and Nancy O'Dwyer, the two lawyers from the office of the Director of Public Prosecutions.

At the end of the third day, having returned from Gougane Barra, Sergeant Jen Martens knocked on his door; John waved her in. "We knew all along that the body in the shallow grave was Sam Falvey. But now, it's confirmed by dental records," she reported.

"What was the cause of death?" John asked.

"The full autopsy is tomorrow and it will be a long one due to the decomposition. But right now, it looks like a gunshot wound to the back of the head."

"Ah, the poor fella," John sighed. "Thanks Jen, that is very helpful."

Nothing changed after the autopsy. Sam Falvey was killed by a single gunshot wound to the back of his head. The trajectory of the bullet suggested that he was on his knees when shot, just like John-Joe said, typical execution style.

By the end of the week, John was ready to present the entire case to the prosecutors. There it would be decided who would be charged with which offence and who would get a deal.

Before leaving the office for the weekend, John called Brian McCarthy and made an appointment to see him on Monday morning. "You had better put a few hours aside on your calendar. This will take a while," John said, knowing McCarthy would want all the facts before he authorized any charges.

ON SATURDAY MORNING, Jules called John to the front window that overlooked the West Beach and the Atlantic Ocean. "Look, someone is unloading four horses from a truck down at the beach."

John picked up his binoculars; he always kept them near the window to look out at the seascape in front of him. This time he focused on the horses on the beach. "They look like racehorses. They must be going to school them on the beach. Will we go down to watch?"

"How do you know they're racehorses?" Jules asked.

"Look at the shape of the saddle flaps and the knee pads on the saddles, and those horses look nice and fit," John said, as he reached for his coat.

As soon as the greyhounds saw John and Jules grab their coats, there was no way that they were going to be left behind. Lucy and Molly came to life from their deep slumber on the sofa and insisted on walking too.

It takes you back, doesn't it?" Jules said, philosophically, as they walked out of the sand dunes onto the beach. "It was a lifetime ago when you were schooling our horses on the beaches here."

"They were certainly simpler times. But were they better or worse?" John asked, as he cast his mind back to the days when he was training and riding racehorses on this very beach.

"Well, we didn't talk about mayhem, death and destruction all the time! That's all we do now. I'm sick and tired of hearing about the Independent Posse and having your new best friend in Maghaberry Prison call you every night." Jules was laughing but part of her was very serious.

John also laughed but he knew she was right. He also knew he was so lucky that Jules supported him in every way and put up with his job and the craziness that came with it.

The tide was completely out and the riders were walking the four horses along the seafront. One of the horses was shying from the waves. Walking the horse next to the waves would soon settle him when he realized that the sound and the water were not going to hurt him. Two men stood on the sand watching the horses. The older one had a pair of binoculars around his neck; the younger one, in his mid-thirties, was obviously the trainer. John asked the men if they could watch the horses being schooled. There were no objections. "The beach on the other side of the headland looks a lot wider. Is there any easy way down to it?" the trainer asked.

"There's access from our place. A path leads you directly to the dunes over there and it's suitable for the horses too," Jules said, pointing up to their house.

"It's suitable for the horses?" the trainer asked.

"We used it all the time for horses, twenty odd years ago. It's a little overgrown now but it's still very accessible," Jules answered. "You have much more scope on the other beach when the tide is like this."

The trainer walked down the beach to consult with the riders. When he returned, he asked John and Jules to show them the way to the East Beach. They walked back to the house on top of the hill, followed by the four horses and riders. The greyhounds were disappointed because they thought that was it for an outing.

As they walked around the back of the Cahills' home, the owner and trainer were surprised to see six empty stables and a large paddock. "Do you keep any horses or ponies here?" the owner asked.

"Not anymore. We kept a few here over twenty years ago. Now these stables are only used for storing junk." John opened the gate at the back of the yard that led to a little used, common pathway to the East Beach. "What brings you here today?" he asked, as the horses meandered their way along the narrow trail.

"We train a small string of horses near Innishannon and our gallops are half flooded at the moment. The Bandon River is unusually high for this time of year and two of the horses are declared to run at Clonmel next week," the trainer answered. Within five minutes the group had arrived at the sand dunes above the East Beach. "I see what you mean. This is twice the size of the other beach," the trainer added, looking up and down the vast, flat, deserted beach.

"You only get about an hour a day when the tide is like this," John replied. "The water comes in faster here than the other side and it gets smaller very quickly."

The horses were now trotting along the beach as the riders checked for any hidden debris that may cause them problems when they started to gallop. There was nothing. Two of the horses were four-year-olds; the other two were much more mature. The plan was to run them approximately two miles. "That would be about three loops," John said.

"You've done this before?" the horse trainer asked.

"Once or twice." John smiled.

The horses lined up with their backs to the rocky outcrop, known locally as The Virgin Mary Bank. Then they started at a slow canter for the first few hundred meters. They picked their speed up to a decent gallop after one circuit of the beach. The two younger horses were pulling hard. Their young riders were struggling to keep them back. One of the four-year-olds, a handsome looking horse with a chestnut-coloured coat, was actually jumping in the air every few strides to try to get away from the others and run as fast as he could. By the time they had started the final circuit and picked up the pace another notch, the chestnut horse had run out of steam. He finished in third place and was fading more than any of the other three when they pulled up.

The horses were blowing hard. Their nostrils were flared and they had white foamy sweat on their necks and between their hind legs when they walked back to the audience. "Sorry about that, boss," the young rider of the chestnut said to the owner. The rider was also gasping for breath. "He nearly pulled the arms out of me sockets for the first mile and when I asked him for more, he had nothing left to give."

"He looked like he was going to get away from you a few times," Jules said to the jockey.

"He nearly did, mam. Sure, didn't he kill three men before!" The jockey answered with a sly grin.

"Three men? Sure, how did he do that?" Jules was playing along.

"Didn't he pull the lungs out of them," the young man answered, patting his horse affectionately on the neck and turning him back towards the water's edge.

"Maybe try him in blinkers," John suggested to the trainer when the horse had walked away. "They'll keep him focused on what is in front of him and not what's coming behind him."

The trainer looked at John. "That's not a bad idea. I might try him in blinkers at Clonmel races next week," the trainer said to the owner. "Cool them off now." The trainer pointed to the ocean and the four horses cantered slowly to the water. The riders ran their horses through the waves, soaking each other and cooling their mounts at the same time.

As they headed back to the homestead along the trail, the trainer asked John and Jules why they didn't keep horses in their stables anymore. "Life happened and things changed," John said, sounding very philosophical. "We are way too busy for that now. But anytime you want to access the East Beach, you are more than welcome to go through our place. One of the stables is empty too, if you need it while you are here."

The horse trainer was thrilled with the opportunity to access the larger beach and he and John exchanged phone numbers. Later, when the trainer returned to the stables, he researched John Cahill on the internet and realized that he had just met an experienced horse trainer and jockey who had abruptly disappeared from the industry many years ago.

MONDAY CAME QUICKLY and John filled a banker's box with files and reports from the never-ending investigation in order to try to explain it to the two senior prosecutors. When he walked into the musty boardroom at the prosecution offices, Brian McCarthy laughed on seeing the box. However, he changed his tune when he saw that the box was almost full.

John spread its contents on the large table, looked at the two lawyers and said, "I hope you're not in a hurry today." He smiled and sat down. "I will start chronologically with the offences as they occurred and then present the evidence for each one. You will see that the source of the evidence is often from the same person or persons." John took a breath. "Nancy, you will be familiar with some of this as you were present when we interviewed B.R.F. in Northern Ireland." Nancy O'Dwyer nodded and opened a large notebook.

"I received a call last week from a solicitor representing Archie Cambridge. He told me you would be presenting me with his statement. He is looking for a good deal. But I don't know what we can do for him. Anyway, we can talk about that later. Let's hear what you got," Brian McCarthy said, anxious to get going.

"Sure, I'll start with the killing of Anthony Woodsworth." John picked up the first folder in front of him.

It was 6:30PM, with only a half-hour break for lunch, when John finally closed the cover on the last folder. He had presented strong evidence on ten serious incidents.

- The Anthony Woodsworth homicide at Manor View Estate
- The Graham Hogan homicide on Dominick Street
- The shooting of Tommy Herschel at the crack shack in Mayfield
- The shooting of the Doyle family home in Parklands
- The shooting at Hibernian Buildings, (Jewtown)
- The attempted murder of Liam Mahony by Eddie Flynn
- The attempted murder of Frankie Spillane by Eddie Flynn and Darryl Lyons
- The Eddie Flynn homicide at a vacant house in Mahon
- The Walter Sheldon homicide in Limerick Prison
- The Sam Falvey homicide

Nancy O'Dwyer and Brian McCarthy looked frazzled. They had been making frantic notes all day, while they listened to the presentation of evidence by the detective. "The common denominator in all of this is that it all started with Bertie Flynn's statement," Brian said. "I must say I thought it was a load of garbage when I first watched the recording. But now, you have corroborated every single thing he said, right down to the blood on the floor in Darryl Lyons' house."

"I thought the same, Brian. When we first took Bertie's statement, he made Tyson Rolland sound like the devil and I really thought he was embellishing some of it," John replied.

"Some of it?" Nancy O'Dwyer said. "I honestly thought the whole thing was bull shit! Until now."

"When can I expect an answer on your decision on charges for these desperados?" John asked. "You know it will go nowhere if you don't give Bertie Flynn a deal and you will have to come up with something for Archie Cambridge too."

"Give me a couple of weeks," Brian McCarthy replied as he prepared to stand up.

"Bertie phones me every day. He's getting anxious sitting around in prison. I can only appease him for so long. John's cell phone buzzed in his pocket. He looked at the familiar number on the call display. "Speak of the devil!"

"Hi Bertie, how are ya? Bertie, before you ask, the prosecutors are looking at all the evidence as we speak. I expect we will hear back from them very soon and only then can I tell you what is going to happen next." John looked across the table at Brian McCarthy who had sat down again.

Bertie Flynn was happy enough with the news; he really only called John for someone to talk to and break the monotony of being in prison, but John was not about to tell the lawyers that. He wanted to keep the pressure on them too. "If I didn't know better, I would say you had that call planned," McCarthy said with a sly smile.

The rest of the week was uneventful, apart from the result of the four-year-old Maiden Hurdle at Clonmel Horse Races on the Thursday. The chestnut horse, 'Dirtyharry,' won by a neck while wearing blinkers for the first time. The trainer texted John the following day and thanked him for suggesting the blinkers.

Chapter 37

After a peaceful weekend, John was back at his desk on Monday morning. He was tempted to send an email to Brian McCarthy but decided against this. It did not help when the first thing that the superintendent said to him was "Any news from the lawyers?" John kept telling himself that no news was good news. However, as he prepared to head home at 4:00PM, an email popped up on his computer screen. It was from Brian McCarthy. *'Can you come over here on Wednesday morning at 10:00AM?'* John kept his answer short and sweet. *'Yes, see you then.'* "Fuck! You could give me a hint at least." he said to no one in particular as he shut the computer off.

ON MONDAY NIGHT JOHN and Jules braved a gale force wind blowing in from the Atlantic as they walked the greyhounds on the beaches. He told her about the upcoming meeting on Wednesday. Jules knew he was nervous. Everything depended on the word of two drug-dealing gangsters. What they had said in their statements was proven true over and over again, but, at the end of the day, they were unsavoury witnesses that any smart defence lawyer could easily discredit.

ON WEDNESDAY MORNING after their morning briefing, the members of the Serious Crime Unit wished John good luck as he headed to his meeting with the two senior prosecutors. On arrival at their office, he was shown into the same boardroom. John sat down and looked around. The shelves along one of the walls were full of cardboard boxes with file names and Garda incident numbers written on them. One of the boxes stood out; it had the name David Perry written on it. Perry was one of three accused that John had investigated in his first homicide case in the Republic of Ireland. He smiled to himself, knowing that Perry would be in prison for a very long time.

With that, the door opened and Nancy O'Dwyer and Brian McCarthy walked in. They both carried cardboard folders. Brian sat down and put his hands on the closed folder. He looked across the table at Nancy and then at John, who was trying to hide his anticipation and hold his poker face. "How are ya?" John said to both.

"Oh, we're fine. How are you?" Nancy answered. John thought he detected a crafty grin on her face.

"I'll be much better when you put me out of me misery and authorize charges on a whole load of people." John tapped the table with his hand.

"Let's go through these incidents one by one," McCarthy said and finally opened his folder. John opened his notebook and picked up his pen.

"For the Anthony Woodsworth homicide, you can charge Archie Cambridge and Tyson Rolland with murder." John smiled across at the lawyer. "You can also charge Alfie Hastings and his girlfriend, Lily Crawford, with facilitating a murder," Brian said, pausing and looking up. "We are negotiating with Archie's solicitor. He wanted a manslaughter charge in return for his testimony. We cannot do that. It must be murder. We will work out suitable parole eligibility and he can take it or leave it."

"Let's hope he takes it. Bertie, on his own, isn't great," John commented while he scribbled notes in his notebook.

"Moving on," Nancy O'Dwyer said, "to the Graham Hogan homicide on Dominick Street. Olly Sullivan is already charged with murder. Now you can also charge Herbie Okereke. Unless Okereke implicates Rolland and Lyons, they will not be charged in this case."

"Are there going to be other charges for B.T.?" John asked.

"Patience," Brian McCarthy said smiling. "Now the shooting of Tommy Herschel at the crack shack in Mayfield." Brian paused and took a breath. John was worried that the lawyers would charge his star witness with this offence but said nothing. "Mr. Herschel had plenty of opportunity to tell the investigators what happened to him. He decided not to and he has recovered from his injury. We will not be charging Bertie Flynn."

John didn't say anything but he smiled as he made a note.

It was now Nancy's turn. "Charge Tyson Rolland with discharging a firearm and causing criminal damage to the Doyle family home in Parklands."

"And you can charge Darryl Lyons with attempted murder for the shooting at Hibernian Buildings. Bertie's evidence in that incident is compelling," Brian added.

John was ecstatic as he made his notes. This was much better than he could have hoped for.

"For the next two incidents, the attempted murder of Liam Mahony and the attempted murder of Frankie Spillane, there will be no charges. We have no doubt that Tyson Rolland and Darryl Lyons are behind it but without anything to corroborate Bertie's statement, we will not proceed," Nancy informed John.

"Only three to go," John replied, looking across the table at the two lawyers.

"Do you need a break? Is your hand getting tired?" Brian McCarthy said with a sarcastic grin.

"Keep going before you change your mind," John shot back.

"OK, moving right along," Brian McCarthy continued, "charge our 'child soldier' Herbie Okereke with the murder of Eddie Flynn. With his DNA on the knife and Bertie's statement, we are good here but we will not charge Darryl Lyons unless Okereke implicates him."

"We will address the Sam Falvey homicide next and finish up with the shenanigans in Limerick Prison," Nancy O'Dwyer said. "Charge Tyson Rolland and Darryl Lyons with murder! Charge John-Joe Cooper with facilitating the murder for assisting with disposing of the body. We will likely offer him a deal, down the road, for his cooperation." Nancy pushed her notes away, signaling that she was finished her part.

"So that only leaves the murder of Walter Sheldon in Limerick Prison," John said. He was tempted to start counting the charges but he was also anxious to see how this one would play out.

"What do you think?" Brian McCarthy asked.

"Charge them all and let God sort them out," John answered.

"Exactly," Brian said. "Charge Raymond Daniels and Jeff Brady with murder. We were going to charge the other three with manslaughter but we decided to go with murder and see how it plays out." Brian smiled with satisfaction. He was obviously confident; otherwise, he would not have authorised so many serious charges.

John looked at his notes and did some quick calculations. A few seconds later he spoke. "That's eleven murder charges, three facilitating a murder charge, one attempted murder and one discharging a firearm. Did I get that right?"

"We'll be prosecuting twelve murder charges if you include the charges already laid against Olly Sullivan for the Hogan homicide," Brian McCarthy answered. "That should be enough to keep you busy for a while." He laughed and closed his folder. "We're prosecuting twelve individuals for homicide related charges. Some of them are facing multiple counts. Let's see where the chips fall when we get to court."

It was lunchtime when John returned to Garda Headquarters on Anglesea Street. His first stop was the superintendent's office. "They authorized a few charges." John had a glint in his eye and grin on his face. The super caught it and knew it was good news.

"I suppose you haven't told your crew yet. I'll walk up with you and you can tell us all together." Superintendent Collins got up from his desk and put on his suit jacket.

There was silence when John walked into the incident room. The entire team were present and turned to look at him. Paddy Collins did not stand at the back this time; he walked to the front of the room with the inspector. "Come on, will ya? Don't keep us all in suspense," the superintendent said.

John was enjoying himself and decided a little bit of suspense wouldn't hurt. He took his time, taking off his jacket, unholstering his pistol and placing it in his desk drawer. When he knew his audience could not take any more of the anticipation, he began. "We have a few arrests to make in the next few days." He tried to pause but he couldn't play it out any longer. He read out the list of charges for each individual. The only one who was trying to keep count was Pete Sandhu.

The team were overjoyed with the result of their hard work. What had begun as an impossible homicide investigation had ended up being one of the most successful investigations in the history of the state. Now they had to formulate a plan to round up all the suspects at the same time.

Chapter 38

"I'll spend the rest of today and tomorrow putting an arrest plan together. Friday will be our 'Takedown Day,'" John said to the superintendent.

"That will probably run into the weekend, will it?" Superintendent Collins asked.

"It probably will but what choice do we have? Do you want to leave these savages out for another weekend? God only knows what they will do."

"I hear ya," Paddy Collins replied. "I just know some bean counter will have concerns about overtime. But I have never denied you overtime and I agree with you. They have to be taken off the street as soon as possible. What do you want me to do?"

John decided it would be best to leave the Garda in Limerick to deal with the arrests in Limerick Prison. They would be the easiest to manage as everyone was already in custody. Paddy Collins arranged for his counterpart in Limerick and his detective inspector to attend Anglesea Street on Thursday morning for a briefing.

"YOU'LL PROBABLY BE working all weekend," Jules said to her husband as they were out for their evening walk with their greyhounds.

"It can't be helped. I couldn't get to see the prosecutors until today. There are only so many days in the week."

"I know but you look awful. You need to slow down. You have that awful grey color about you. How much longer can you do this to yourself? You're well and truly at the wrong side of fifty now." Jules was concerned for his health.

John smiled; he hadn't thought about his age. He knew she was right. "Maybe another two years if we can. Then we can retire and walk away from it all. I think they will keep me here for another two years." Jules looked sceptically at him as they headed for home in the bright moonlight.

AT 7:00AM THE NEXT day, John told his crew that the morning briefing was being delayed until 11:00AM as they were being joined by a team from Limerick. "If that's the case, I propose we have a pre-meeting over breakfast," Jeff Rafter said.

"Now you're talking," Mike Williams agreed, grabbing his coat from the back of his chair.

John stayed in the office, deciding who was going to arrest which of the suspects, while his team went for a well-deserved breakfast. He did not expect to get too many statements or confessions but he didn't really need them. He had physical, scientific and witness evidence against each and every one of the suspects. "This is a great case." he thought as he typed up his plan.

At 11:00AM, Paddy Collins brought the officers from Limerick to the incident room. Sergeant Martens from F.I.S. was also present.

For the benefit of the Limerick officers and his own superintendent, John went over the entire investigation from the beginning, when they were first alerted to Anthony Woodsworth's body in front of his mother's house. An hour and a half later, he finished up with the murder of Walter Sheldon in Limerick Prison. The Limerick officers were impressed. All the difficult work in the investigation had been done for them; all they had to do was arrest the five gangsters who were easy to find as they were all inside Limerick Prison.

John told his audience that he had arranged with the Organization Support Group of the Irish Prison Service to remove Archie Cambridge from Limerick Prison. For now, he would be kept in isolation in another prison for his own safety. He would remain there until he accepted whatever deal the Director of Public Prosecutions offered him. If he turned down the deal, he faced life in prison as a 'rat.'

"Bertie Flynn has made a deal and he has been accepted into the Witness Security Program. We don't need to know the details of that but he will testify in any court proceedings that he is required at," John said.

"What about Martina and the kids?" Tim Warren asked.

"They're gone too," was all that John said. Tim knew better than to ask anything else. "OK, down to the wire now. Tomorrow, once and for all, we get to put an end to this street gang. Pay attention while I tell you who gets to arrest who, tomorrow!"

This is what everyone was waiting for. They all knew everything about this case and each one of them wanted to interview the worst of the worst. Some of you will end up with two interviews. "Pete, I'm going to draft you in to do an interview too. I know you usually don't do interviews but we need you tomorrow." Pete nodded in acknowledgement. John then handed out the assignments.

- John and Tim would arrest and interview Tyson Rolland
- Mike Williams and Eddie Jenkins would arrest and interview Darryl Lyons
- Jeff Rafter and Len Benoit would arrest and interview Herbie Okereke, better known as B.T.
- Jeff and Len would also arrest and interview Alfie Hastings
- Tim Warren and Pete Sandhu would arrest and interview Lily Crawford

When the briefing was over, the detectives began reviewing the evidence against each of the persons they were to interview. They wanted to be ready for the big show the next day. The superintendent for Limerick turned to Paddy Collins, "Where did you find your man?" as he nodded his head in John's direction.

"He's from Blackpool. But we found him in Northern Ireland," Paddy answered.

"Do they have any more like him?" the Limerick super asked.

"They broke the mould after him, and keep your eyes off him. He's not going anywhere." Paddy grinned.

John spent the rest of the day putting the final touches to his plan. Once Rolland and Lyons were in custody, search warrants would be executed at their homes. The police would look for the Glock pistol at Tyson Rolland's house and they would search for any traces of blood from the Falvey homicide at Darryl Lyons' home.

By 3:00PM, everyone from the Serious Crime Unit had gone home, including their inspector. As John drove across the causeway to Inchydoney, he hoped that there was no 'new business' for the next few days. That would really interfere with his plans.

WHEN HE PULLED UP AT the top of his driveway, he turned the car to face the ocean. It was a beautiful clear day with a strong breeze blowing in from the sea. He sat there for a few minutes watching the waves. About every third wave crashed into the rocks of the Virgin Mary Bank between the two beaches. The water sprayed at least ten meters into the air from this rogue wave. John smiled and got out of his car. The dogs were standing at the front window, waiting for him to get out of the car. When he walked to the back door, they dashed through the house at a speed that only they could do and were waiting for him to come in.

"They were watching you sitting in the car," Jules said, when he walked into the house, while the dogs were nuzzling him. "Were you on the phone?"

"No, I was just sitting there looking at the scenery."

"Is everything OK?"

"Couldn't be better. Hopefully we get a quiet night and tomorrow should go off without a hitch."

As usual, before a planned arrest, John had trouble getting to sleep. He heard every creak in their old house and heard the dogs moving around in their crates. He fought the temptation to get up and watch television or surf the net on his tablet. Eventually, he must have fallen asleep because he woke with a start when the alarm went off. He got up, took the dogs out to the yard, had a coffee and cereal and got ready for work. Before leaving, John brought Jules a cup of coffee; he kissed her on the forehead and she stirred. As he left the bedroom, he heard her usual cheer, "Kick ass today!" He smiled as he left the house.

BY 8:30AM A TEAM FROM the Armed Support Unit was set up around the corner from Tyson Rolland's home in Churchfield. Another team was in Manor View, close to Darryl Lyons' house. Surveillance teams from the Anti-Crime Unit had kept watch on both locations overnight and they were certain that both targets were in their respective homes.

At the exact same time, both teams from the A.S.U. moved closer to their targets. They had decided on a controlled approach on Rolland's house because his girlfriend and their baby were present. However, 'shock and awe' was the order of the day for Darryl Lyons who was home alone.

The team-commanders from both A.S.U. teams were in constant communication with each other and the order to go and get Darryl

Lyons was given. It was now 9:00AM. The street was quiet as all the school traffic had passed. The officers, in their grey uniforms and Kevlar helmets, moved silently to the front door in a stack. The Garda officer, second in line, carried the battering ram, a heavy piece of steel, weighing approximately eighteen kilos. The Garda in front stood aside and the one with the battering ram smashed the front door. It wasn't just the silence of the morning that was shattered; the door burst open and the frame splintered as the locks smashed to little pieces.

The officer with the ram stood aside and two flashbang percussion grenades were thrown into the house, one on the main level and another up the stairs. The grenades, less lethal devices, were used to temporarily disorientate their target. Seconds later, the six A.S.U. members entered the residence shouting '*Armed police, search warrant,*' several times. Two of the officers held shields in front of them and pointed pistols through a slit in the shields. The other four officers were armed with MP5 carbine rifles. The grenades did their job. Darryl Lyons fell out of bed. Three of the officers rushed up the stairs and saw Lyons on all fours. He was pinned to the floor with the shield, taken into custody and handcuffed.

Over in Churchfield, things were a little bit more sedate. The team commander called Tyson Rolland on the phone and a negotiator called out to him on a megaphone, instructing him to answer his phone. Tyson woke up in a daze. He thought he was having a nightmare until he heard the megaphone again. He looked at his cell phone next to his bed and saw it was buzzing. He picked up the phone and cautiously made his way to the window. Tyson peeked out through a gap in the curtains. The first thing he saw was the Garda Armed Response Vehicle that looked like a small tank. Knowing that there was nowhere to go, Tyson answered the phone. The commander instructed Tyson to stand in the front window with his hands raised and send his girlfriend and the baby out first. Tyson called out to Jenny and told her to get out of the house with the baby as he stood in the upstairs window with his hands up.

Once Jenny and the baby were safe, Tyson was ordered to exit the house. As soon as he stepped out the front door, he lay down in the prone position on the pathway. He was handcuffed and taken into custody.

Jeff Rafter and Len Benoit, along with six uniformed Garda officers, attended to Herbie Okereke's home. The uniformed officers took up various points around the house. They were prepared in the event that B.T. tried to bolt from the residence. B.T.'s mother opened the door. Jeff Rafter identified himself and informed her that he had a warrant to arrest her son. Rafter and Benoit stepped inside. The woman looked sickly and exhausted. She barely asked the officers anything apart from, "What has he done now?" Len told the woman that her son was being arrested for two murders. Her eyes filled with tears. "I really did try with him," was all that she could say.

"I know you did," Jeff Rafter said to the woman, trying to console her. She then showed the officers to a downstairs bedroom.

"He's in there. He never gets up until the afternoon."

Len Benoit called out to B.T. in a loud and stern voice. The kid shot up in the bed. For a moment he looked like he didn't know where he was. B.T. was told that he was under arrest and was taken into custody without incident.

Chapter 39

The three prisoners were taken to the Serious Crime Suite in Anglesea Street Garda Station. All three called lawyers. Herbie Okereke did not want his mother with him. He was entitled to have her there because, in the eyes of the law, he was still a child. Instead, he requested his solicitor to stay with him during his interview. B.T. showed no emotion; he did not look worried about the serious charges he faced. In fact, he looked like he hadn't a care in the world.

Darryl Lyons was the opposite. He looked scared when he was told that he was being charged with murder and attempted murder. Lyons wanted to know who else had been arrested. When Mike Williams told him that he shouldn't worry about that at this point in time, he panicked even more. Mike thought that Darryl believed he was being used as a scapegoat and suspected Tyson ratted on him.

Tyson Rolland behaved exactly the way that Detective Inspector Cahill thought that he would. He remained calm and cool. He answered basic background questions without hesitation and asked if he could call one of the most expensive solicitors in town. This woman specialized in drug cases but, if the fee was right, she wouldn't hesitate to take on a murder case. She preferred the drug cases because the dealers always had cash.

IN LIMERICK CITY A similar situation was playing out. Ray-Ray Daniels showed no reaction when he was arrested in Limerick Prison and taken to the Garda Station.

Jeffrey (Potsie) Brady was anxious; he had never been charged with such a serious offence. The other three who were charged were nervous wrecks as they imagined the next twenty years of their lives in Limerick Prison, or worse, Mountjoy in Dublin.

When the interviews started in Limerick, the three junior council members sang like canaries; their solicitors told them it was the best thing to do as they would probably get their charges reduced to manslaughter. They had no problem implicating Ray-Ray and Potsie Brady.

Potsie panicked during his interview. He tried to talk his way out of it, saying that only Ray-Ray had assaulted Walter Sheldon and nobody else touched him. He even denied being present in Cell 22 when it went down. He lied his face off to save his neck.

Ray-Ray Daniels was a logical offender. He wanted to know what evidence the investigators had against him. When he was informed that he had been implicated by five people, he wondered who the fifth person was as there had only been four others in the cell with him and Walter. After an hour of back-and-forth questions, Ray-Ray said that he did not mean to kill Walter. After all, they were old friends. He only wanted Walter to move to another range and he was just trying to scare him when he choked him. Ray-Ray would not say anything about the other four people in the cell, even though they all strangled Walter with the towel when he lay on the floor. Ray-Ray knew that they had all ratted him out. He certainly was an O.G., an 'Original Gangster.' Anyway, he would deal with the rats at a later time.

BACK IN GARDA HEADQUARTERS in Cork, the interviews were getting underway. Jeff Rafter was trying to build a rapport with fifteen-year-old Herbie Okereke. "What should I call you? Herbie or B.T. Jeff asked.

"Call me B.T.," the kid answered, trying to sound cool and tough. Nevertheless, Jeff detected a crackle in his voice.

B.T. answered all the easy questions. When it came to talking about the two murders he was responsible for, he tried to shut down. "No comment!" he said, over and over.

Jeff Rafter still had not presented B.T. with the DNA evidence or the fact that they had recovered the gun from the hidden space under the step in Bertie Flynn's crack shack. He wanted to see if he could get the kid to come around. "You do know that Tyson and Darryl used you, don't you?"

"What do you mean?" B.T. said in his strong African accent.

"Let me explain," the policeman said very calmly. "They know you and Olly are kids. You are both fifteen-years-old. I bet they told you that you would get a slap on the wrist if you were caught." B.T. nodded his head, ever so slightly, but the detectives saw it and knew they were on the right track. "I don't know what the courts will do with you, but I do know it will not be a slap on the wrist. You can ask your solicitor here. He'll tell you that." Jeff looked at the solicitor.

"If you are convicted of these charges, you will receive a custodial sentence," the lawyer said. "But for now, my advice remains the same. You should not make a comment to these officers."

Jeff Rafter didn't answer the lawyer; in fact, he ignored the last comment and focused on the kid across the table from him. "B.T., we know you and Olly shot that man in his car on Dominick Street. Do you know what his name was?" B.T. could not help himself and shook his head. "His name was Graham Hogan. He was only a few years older than you, just a kid as well." Jeff stared into B.T.'s eyes. "You both went to the crack shack in the lane and waited for the signal. Then ye ran down to Dominick Street and opened fire on that kid. He didn't have a chance. Olly ran off towards Mulgrave Road and you ran back to the crack shack and hid in the attic." Jeff paused as he held B.T.'s stare. He could see the kid was thinking about everything he said. It was time to turn the heat up ever so slightly. "We found the Tokarev."

"What's a Tokarev?" the solicitor asked, interrupting Jeff.

"The gun!" B.T. answered. The lawyer glared at his client; he knew he should not have asked that question and B.T. definitely should not have answered. Len Benoit couldn't hold back the smile that crept across his face. He hadn't said much in this interview so far. It was best to keep it to one person asking the questions for now.

"That's right, the Tokarev is one of the guns used to kill Graham Hogan. We have tested it for fingerprints and DNA. We have a male's DNA on the gun."

"Has the DNA been matched to anybody in your database?" the lawyer asked.

"No. The donor isn't in the database yet," Jeff answered, slightly smirking. "But we found that exact same DNA on one of the knives that was used to stab Eddie Flynn to death in Mahon." The lawyer made frantic notes in his notebook. "Tyson Rolland and Darryl Lyons and the rest of the Independent Posse treat you and Olly as 'child soldiers!' " Jeff slapped the table to make his point.

"I am not a child soldier!" B.T. raised his voice, showing real emotion for the first time in the interview.

Jeff knew he had hit a nerve. He figured he had nothing to lose by going down this rabbit hole. "You know what a 'child soldier' is? You know how those kids are abused in places like the country you came from? Are you being treated any differently by the I-P to the way those kids get treated? No! You're not! When you're not around, Tyson calls you his best 'child soldier.' He's taking advantage of you. He's using you!" Jeff leaned forward when he said this. "Who sent you to kill Graham Hogan? Who was with you when you killed Eddie Flynn?"

B.T. looked like he was about to answer but instead looked at his lawyer for direction. "Can we have five minutes please?" the lawyer asked.

Jeff and Len left the room and turned off the recording equipment. "He knows that he's caught," Len said. "That was hilarious when he told the lawyer that a Tokarev was the gun." Jeff laughed along with his partner. A minute later the lawyer knocked on the door to signal that they were ready to continue with the interview.

Jeff turned the recording equipment on and returned to the interview room. "We are going to take a sample of your DNA today. You and I both know that it will match the DNA on the gun and the knife," Jeff said.

"My client wants to make a brief statement," the lawyer announced. He looked at B.T. and nodded his head.

"I admit that I shot the man on Dominick Street and I stabbed 'Big E,' in a derelict house in Mahon. That is all I have to say. I will not speak about anyone else," B.T. said. He folded his arms, sat back in his chair and stretched his legs out under the table.

"You don't want to tell us who gave you the gun to shoot Graham Hogan or who was with you when you stabbed 'Big E'?" Jeff asked.

"That is his statement. He will not say anything else about these incidents. I suggest that you take it and go," the solicitor replied.

"I think you're right," Jeff Rafter said, closing his notebook and standing up to leave.

IN ANOTHER INTERVIEW room, a petrified Darryl Lyons sat across from Mike Williams and Eddie Jenkins. He was still shaken after the 'flashbang' grenade went off near his bedroom. One minute he was sweating and the next he was shivering. Lyons had asked

Eddie for a blanket and when he was given one, he wrapped himself up in it. He covered his head, leaving just a small opening for his face. It was as if he was trying to hide from the detectives who were interviewing him. But, regardless of how scared Darryl was, he knew better than to answer any questions.

Mike and Eddie spoke nonstop to Darryl for over three hours. He listened to every word they said but when it came to answering questions, he stuck to his mantra of, 'I have no comment to make.' Mike tried several approaches. He attempted to appeal to Darryl's sense of humanity, trying to get him to feel sorry for the victims and their families. That didn't work. Mike then tried to blame Tyson Rolland, saying that Darryl was under pressure to play the role of Tyson's right-hand man. That did not work either.

In the end, Eddie Jenkins tried the last play in the playbook. He started yelling at Darryl, trying to draw him into an argument, hoping that Darryl would say something incriminating in anger. All they got was, 'I have no comment to make.' In the end, they gave up. They did not need a confession from Lyons but it was always good to get one. As their boss always said, '*There is no such thing as too much evidence.*'

Chapter 40

The interview with Tyson Rolland was the strangest interview that John had ever conducted. Tyson answered all the background questions without hesitation. He even admitted his role in the gang and was proud to be the gang leader. He was smart enough not to admit to selling drugs or to the human trafficking of exploited women, but admitted that he was president of the Independent Posse. He proudly showed off his I-P tattoos and explained what they meant and how he received the different tattoos as he progressed through the criminal organization. John and Tim were both shocked when they saw that Tyson's entire body was covered in tattoos.

"How many tattoos do you have?" John asked.

"Hundreds, I have them everywhere." Tyson stood and remove his shirt and turned around.

"Do they all mean something? Or did you get random tattoos?"

"They all mean something to me," Tyson answered with a sly grin. Tim found that disturbing and wished he could wipe the smirk from his face.

"What do they mean?" John continued.

"That's my son." Tyson pointed to a tattoo of a fetus on his left pec over his heart. John looked closely at the image and he saw that the fetus was holding a pistol. He didn't comment.

"What about that one?" John pointed to a red tattoo in the shape of a bleeding bullet hole on Tyson's right temple. Next to the bullet hole was a hand holding a semi-automatic pistol.

"That's to remind me what to do if it all gets too much."

"Are you suicidal now?"

"Fuck, no!" Tyson laughed.

"What about that one?" John pointed to a tattoo on Tyson's right bicep. It was an image of two men carrying the body of another man towards the back of a HiAce van. This tattoo looked new and the skin around it was still red.

Tyson sniggered, "That's a new one."

"So what does it mean?"

"I can't talk about that one right now," Tyson said and laughed again.

Tyson engaged the detectives in conversation but he never admitted to anything. In fact, Tyson asked a lot questions too. He knew somebody had spoken to the police and he was desperate to find out who the rat was. He suspected Bertie Flynn but never suspected Archie Cambridge. The detectives never confirmed his suspicions. He would find out soon enough when his lawyers were provided with disclosure for the upcoming court case.

After two hours, John looked at Tyson, "You're not going to admit to anything, are you?" Tyson shook his head and laughed. "Well, I have news for ya. We don't need a confession. You're pretty much fucked!" John closed his notebook and he and Tim left the room.

Once out of the interview room, John sent Tim and Pete to pick up Lily Crawford and Mike and Eddie went to get Alfie Hastings.

They found them both at Crawford's house in Knocknaheeney. Alfie was furious when they told him that both he and Lily were being arrested. "What are ya lifting her for? She didn't do nothin.' It'll be alright Lily. Say nothin' to them," Alfie yelled when he saw Tim Warren put handcuffs on Lily.

When Alfie and Lily were brought into Garda Headquarters, John ensured that the names of the other three prisoners were visible on the doors of the interview rooms when they walked by. It wasn't

Alfie's first time in a Garda station and he looked at each door when he passed by. By the time he reached Interview Room # 4, he was certain that one of the others had ratted him out.

Lily Crawford, was less perceptive. She did not look at the names on the doors; in fact she was in a bit of a daze when she was led into Interview Room # 5.

Alfie sat alone in the interview room. Mike and Eddie had gone to lock up their pistols and get their notebooks. Alfie sat in the plastic chair that was bolted to the floor. He looked at the top of the steel table also bolted to the floor. The tabletop was covered in graffiti; he ran his fingers over one engraving in particular, 'I-P'. Then he punched the letters with a hammer punch. "For fucks sakes," he said out loud and shook his head. When the detectives returned to the room, Alfie asked to call a solicitor. He was provided with a phone and after a brief conversation, Alfie knocked at the door and told the cops that his lawyer would be along soon.

Lily Crawford hadn't really grasped the gravity of the situation and she was very open with Tim and Pete when they sat down to speak with her. Although Pete explained the severity of the charges she was facing, Lily did not appear to be perturbed. She answered all the background questions and when confronted about driving Alfie and Archie Cambridge to Manor View Estate the night that Anthony Woodsworth was killed, she kept talking. "I remember that. We were all at a party. The only thing I did wrong that night was I was half pissed when I drove Alfie and that skinny fella up near Darryl's house in Manor View. We heard a shot and your man came running back to the car and I drove them back to the party. Alfie never got out of the car."

Tim and Pete pressed her for more information. She vehemently denied knowing why she drove Alfie and Archie to Manor View Estate. She told them that Alfie said they needed a ride there and back and that's what she did.

Meanwhile, Alfie met with his solicitor in the interview room next door. After half an hour of consultation, the solicitor summoned Mike and Eddie back to the room. "Mr. Hastings will tell you what he knows about the incident that is under investigation. In return, you must release Miss Crawford and not charge her. My client will state that she had nothing to do with anything that happened that evening," the solicitor said, with a posh Cork accent, a complete contrast to the man that he was representing.

Mike told the lawyer that they could not make that deal and it looked like there might be a stalemate. Then John knocked on the door and called Mike out of the room. "Lily has already made a statement and she probably didn't know why she drove them to Manor View. Tell Alfie and his brief that we'll release her tonight but it will be up to the Director of Public Prosecutions as to whether she gets charged or not. Either way, he's going to jail tonight."

Mike returned to the room and told the lawyer and Hastings what the inspector had instructed. Alfie Hastings was happy with that and provided his account of what had occurred. Alfie stated that he was at a house party in Knocknaheeney with Lily. "There was a load of 'Posse' members there." Alfie said Tyson Rolland took him aside and told him that Archie Cambridge was being sent on a mission and Alfie was to go with him to make sure he carried it out. "Then I asked Lily to drive us up to Manor View. Archie got out and Lily and me stayed in the car. We heard a shot and Archie came running back to the car. He got in and said '*go,go,go,*' and we took off back to Knocknaheeney." Alfie claimed that he never asked Archie what he was ordered to do and they never discussed the mission on the way back to the party.

John called Brian McCarthy and Nancy O'Dwyer and updated them on the arrests and subsequent interviews. "Nancy and I will attend all their court appearances and bail applications. We'll see what happens as we prepare for the trials," Brian said, not sounding as confident as the inspector would have liked.

Chapter 41

It was after 2:00AM when John returned home. It had been another late night, and although exhausted, he felt good. They had finally cut the head off the snake by locking up the leaders of the Independent Posse; hopefully, that would bring an end to the violence that had raged uncontrollably through Cork City recently. He silently entered his home. The greyhounds, sleeping in their crates, lifted their heads to see him. "Hi girls," he whispered and they put their heads back down on their beds. He showered and crept into bed beside his wife. "How did it go?" Jules asked in a quiet sleepy voice.

"Great! In fact, it couldn't have gone better. It went off without a hitch," he answered as he pulled the covers over himself. Jules put her arm around him, kissed him gently on the shoulder and they both fell asleep.

In the morning John had coffee with Jules before he left for work. He had granted his team a later than usual start. He told her about the interviews and the reactions of the accused persons when they were arrested and presented with some of the facts. The only one that Jules felt sorry for was Herbie Okereke, the 'child soldier.' "What's going to happen to him?" she asked.

"It's hard to say," John answered. "They have a crap youth criminal justice system here in the Republic although it's not much better in the North. He'll probably get a life sentence but who knows how much time he will actually spend in prison. He's one messed up kid. I hope he comes out of this with some kind of a future because his past has been horrific."

Jules looked at her husband. "You and the police are only one small part of the system. You did your job. You found out who killed those people and put them before the courts. It's up to the rest of the system to do their jobs now. It's not your fault that some of the same system already let that kid down," she said, stepping towards him, kissing him on the cheek.

WHEN HE ARRIVED AT work, he went to see Superintendent Collins. A few hours earlier, before he went home, John had sent him an email briefing him on the outcome of the arrests and interviews. "I have already been up in the ivory tower to see the assistant commissioner and the chief superintendent. I even got an email from the commissioner in Dublin. They are all thrilled with the outcome of this investigation. I told them that we have been ignoring these street gangs for far too long and this is what happens. Things get completely out of control."

"What did they say to that?"

"What do you think? I am only waiting for them to craft some sly press release about these arrests. Mark my words! There will be no mention of gangs or criminal organizations. It will be made to look like a few homicides were solved at the same time. That's politics for ya!" the superintendent said.

"Oh well, you, me and my team know what really happened and the bad guys are still locked up. It just goes to show what can happen when we ignore a problem. It festers into something massive and dangerous," John replied as he went to brief his team.

All that was left to do was to complete reports and make sure that everything was ready to be disclosed to the office of the Director of Public Prosecutions. It was up to them to navigate these cases through the court system. However, one daunting final task remained, the notification to the families of the deceased victims. They had to be told that people had been arrested and charged.

Mike Williams and Eddie Jenkins met with Sam Falvey's aunt at her flat in Gurranabraher. Mike tried to explain to the woman that two people were charged with killing her nephew; she didn't appear to be interested until the men went to leave. Then she sighed and Mike saw a tear run down her cheek. "Did she seem to be more pissed than the last time we were there?" Mike asked his partner when they got back in the car. Eddie shrugged his shoulders.

Not too far away, John and Tim met with Anthony Woodsworth's family at the house where he was shot and killed in Manor View Estate. John explained that two people had been charged with Anthony's murder and a third charged with facilitating the murder. Caroline Woodsworth did not have any questions and was grateful to receive the news. She looked tired and worn out and was obviously having a difficult time adjusting to life without her husband. On the other hand, Brenda Woodsworth, Anthony's mother, had a lot of questions. She wanted to know why it took the police so long to make arrests. She wanted to know what would happen to those that were charged. This was a tough question for John. He knew that Archie Cambridge would likely get a good deal for helping with the other incidents. However, that was up to the prosecutors to deal with. They could tell the family about the deal and explain why it was necessary to make it.

"Where to now boss?" Tim Warren asked when they got back into the car.

"Drive across town. Let's go to Mahon and see Graham Hogan's family again." When they pulled up in front of the house, there were two vehicles in the driveway. "Looks like she has visitors," John said.

Mary Hogan opened the door. She recognized the detectives immediately and invited them in. Her sister and brother-in-law were visiting. John was happy; at least she would have some support after they delivered their news. John explained that a second arrest had been made and another fifteen-year-old boy had been charged with Graham's murder. This brought it all back for Mary Hogan and she wept uncontrollably. Her sister tried to comfort her but to no avail. She could not wrap her head around the senselessness of her son being killed by two children.

John and Tim drove back to headquarters in silence. "Do you find it weird?" Tim asked his boss when they were walking to their office.

"What's weird?"

"We pull out all the stops to get a positive result in these investigations. When we finally make arrests, we are over the moon! It's high-fives all around and we're on top of the world. Then we go and make a notification to the family of a victim and we come away feeling like crap." Tim looked at his boss for an explanation.

"That's not weird, Tim. That just means that you're human. The shit that we deal with is awful. We bring what we think is good news to these families but it doesn't change their predicament. Their sons are still dead and their lives are changed forever," the inspector said. "But don't let that take anything away from what we did. We had a rotten tough job to do and we did it well. You are entitled to be excited about that."

THAT EVENING, WHILE they walked the dogs on the beaches, John told Jules how the families of the victims reacted to the news of the arrests. "I can't imagine what they must be going through. They never had a chance to say goodbye. Their kids' lives were just snatched away for no reason at all," she said.

Later that evening, John woke up with a start. The 'dead parade' came to him in a dream. It usually happened when he closed a case. They were all there again... all the grotesque corpses, associated to every homicide he had investigated. This time Sam Falvey led the procession. His body was partly decomposed, with pieces of earth and mud hanging off him and the huge beetle scurrying around his neck and shoulders. In the nightmare Sam Falvey fumbled his way into John and Jules' bedroom. Walter Sheldon followed Sam Falvey and all the others lined up along the hallway. In the dream John stood at the foot of the bed and met each one of them. They whispered something to him, turned and disappeared. He could never figure out what they said. When he woke, this was the thing that disturbed him the most. "What did they say?" he whispered to himself. He looked over at Jules and instantly knew it was all a bad dream.

The next few days were quiet at work. Everyone was busy with the endless paperwork that followed every case. The weekend arrived and the members of the Serious Crime Unit, their families and their superintendent came to Inchydoney for a barbecue on the beautiful sunny Saturday afternoon. It was a perfect day; everyone relaxed and had a good time.

On Sunday morning at 10:30AM, John's cell phone rang. Jules looked at him and shook her head. She knew what the call was and, of course, it was NEW BUSINESS.

The End

The Strongest Web

A novel by John O'Donovan

Epilogue

Archie Cambridge *pleaded guilty to murder in a private courtroom. The only people present were Archie, his lawyer, and the two state lawyers, Brian McCarthy and Nancy O'Dwyer. Cambridge agreed to testify against Tyson Rolland, Alfie Hastings, Ray-Ray Daniels, Jeffrey Brady and the other three gang members in Limerick Prison. Archie Cambridge was sentenced to life in prison; however, he would be eligible for parole after serving ten years of his sentence. Archie was provided with a new name by the Witness Security Program, had his tattoos removed and served his sentence in a minimum-security prison. Archie kept a low profile and was a model prisoner.*

Brenda Woodsworth and Caroline Woodsworth, *the mother and wife of Anthony Woodsworth were furious when they were informed of the lenient sentence that Archie had received. Brian McCarthy tried to explain the bigger picture to them; they could not understand it and felt cheated by the system. Brenda, in particular, could not see that the prosecution of Tyson Rolland had the appearance of having a higher profile than the prosecution of her son's killer. This broke her heart and in the years after the court proceedings, Brenda's physical and mental health declined. She never fully recovered.*

Alfie Hastings *pleaded guilty to facilitating the murder of Anthony Woodsworth. He agreed to testify against Tyson Rolland. Alfie was willing to sacrifice his loyalty to the gang for his girlfriend's future and only pleaded guilty to keep her out of jail. Alfie Hastings was sentenced to two years in prison, with the last six months suspended.*

Lily Crawford was not charged for her role in the Woodsworth homicide, as the person who drove Archie Cambridge and Alfie Hastings to kill Anthony Woodsworth. Lily's addiction to street drugs worsened while Alfie was in custody. Lily died after overdosing on cocaine, three years after the killing of Anthony Woodsworth.

Oliver (Olly) Sullivan was convicted of the murder of Graham Hogan. He was dealt with in the courts as a child, but not a 'child soldier.' Because Olly was only fifteen years old at the time of the shooting, he was sentenced to life in prison, with his sentence set for a review by the courts after eight years. The sentencing judge described Olly as a victim of circumstances, as he was groomed by ruthless self-centered individuals to carry out the horrendous execution of another young man.

Herbie Okereke (Burnt Toast or B.T.) was convicted of the murders of Eddie Flynn and Graham Hogan. Like his co-accused, Olly Sullivan, B.T. was only fifteen years old when he killed both men. He was also tried in Youth Court. However, unlike Olly, B.T. showed no remorse during his trial. He was sentenced to life in prison. The sentencing judge ordered a review of the sentence after ten years. The judge did not refer to B.T. as a victim, but more as a willing participant.

Mary Hogan, the mother of Graham Hogan collapsed during the trial of Okereke and Sullivan. In the months after the trial, her health continued to decline. Unable to live with the pain caused by the senseless killing of her only son by two child soldiers, Mary Hogan eventually took her own life.

Liam Mahony and Frankie Spillane, the two low-level drug dealers who were shot by Eddie Flynn, both recovered from their ordeals. Liam Mahony got out of the drug dealing business after he was shot in the hand by Eddie Flynn. He felt he was lucky to be alive and used his experience to help youth in the area to stay away from drugs. Frankie Spillane didn't learn his lesson after his near-death experience when he was shot in the face. Spillane continued to live on the edge. He continued to sell drugs but aligned himself with the Mahon Warlords in order to benefit from their 'protection.'

William McSweeney *was unfit to stand trial for killing his cousin Agatha McSweeney and for stabbing his father, Padraig McSweeney. At the time of the incident, William was in a severe state of psychosis brought on by undiagnosed schizophrenia. William was not a drug user nor a heavy drinker but rather extremely ill. He was taken into care at a hospital where he would receive the treatment and care that he required. The McSweeney family came to terms with William's illness and forgave him, knowing that none of it was his fault. They visited him weekly, although he rarely recognized them. William's mother blamed herself for not knowing he was mentally ill, despite being reassured by many doctors and her family that there was no way she could have known.*

Sam Falvey's *remains were cremated by the state. Nobody mourned him. In fact, when he was alive nobody even cared enough to notice that he was missing and alert the Garda. The only ones who cared about Sam Falvey were the police officers who investigated his death and the lawyers who prosecuted his killers and brought them to justice.*

John-Joe Cooper *pleaded guilty to interfering with a human body and was sentenced to eighteen months in custody, with the last six months being suspended. In exchange for leniency, Cooper agreed to testify against Darryl Lyons and Tyson Rolland.*

Joan Carney *was not charged. Tired of being a punch bag, Joan left Ireland to work in London, shortly after John-Joe was sentenced. However, Joan went from one bad relationship to another.*

Raymond (Ray-Ray) Daniels *was arrested by detectives from Limerick for the murder of Walter Sheldon. Initially Daniels played the tough guy and refused to comment. He changed his tune in the months leading up to his trial and tried to work out a deal for himself by talking about other violent crimes. However, the Director of Public Prosecutions decided that Raymond Daniels was far too violent to be* *given any type of consideration. He was sentenced to life in prison, with no chance of parole for twenty years. Everybody knew that Ray-Ray tried to save his own skin and he lost all the 'respect' of his fellow inmates.*

Jeffrey Brady (Potsie), *like Ray-Ray, was arrested for the murder of Walter Sheldon by the Garda in Limerick. Brady attempted to cooperate in return for judicial consideration but was caught out in a lie in his statement. Jeffrey Brady was convicted of murder and sentenced to life in prison with no chance of parole for seventeen years.*

The three other men *who pulled the towel on the neck of the unconscious Walter Sheldon pleaded guilty to manslaughter and were sentenced to seven years in prison.*

Darryl Lyons, *the unaspiring second in command of the Independent Posse, pleaded guilty to the murder of Sam Falvey and attempted murder for the shooting at Hibernian Buildings (Jewtown). He was sentenced to life in prison with no chance of parole for twenty-five years. Lyons served his sentence in the maximum- security wing in the Midlands Prison. Lyons easily settled into prison life and was glad of the routine of being told when to sleep, when to wake up and when to eat.*

Tyson Rolland *pleaded guilty to two counts of manslaughter relating to the deaths of Anthony Woodsworth and Sam Falvey. He also pleaded guilty to the shooting of Peter Doyle's house in Parklands. Tyson was sentenced to life in prison with no chance of parole for twenty years. Brian McCarthy agreed to this plea because he knew that Tyson would never be granted parole as his crimes were all related to gang activity. Tyson began his life sentence in the maximum-security wing in Mountjoy Prison in Dublin. It did not take Tyson long to adjust to prison life and before long he controlled much of the illicit drug trade within the prison Five years into his sentence, Tyson overdosed on a lethal amount of his own poison and died.*

Bertie Flynn pleaded guilty to possession of cocaine and possession of a firearm in Northern Ireland. The Director of Public Prosecutions in the Republic worked out a deal with Prosecution Services in Northern Ireland and Bertie was sentenced to two years in prison. He spent six months in custody while the Serious Crime Unit confirmed his information. The rest of his sentence was suspended. Upon his release from Maghaberry Prison, Bertie was reunited with his wife, Martina, and their children. They entered the Witness Security Program and with the assistance of Europol they were relocated.

Bertie testified at the trial of Olly Sullivan and Herbie Okereke. Brian McCarthy and Nancy O'Dwyer spent days preparing him for trial and it paid off. The judge and jury believed his every word. The defence lawyers in Cork took notice and advised Tyson Rolland and Darryl Lyons to plead guilty. Bertie and his family were relocated to a small village within the European Union. He retrained as an electrician and, although he sometimes missed having thousands of euros in a plastic shopping bag in his closet, he was glad of the second chance. Before long, Bertie, was running his own legitimate company. Both he and Martina were forever grateful for the advice Bertie received from an old cop about using his business acumen for good and not evil.

The Independent Posse were broken and the gang lacked leadership and direction when Tyson Rolland went to prison. Violent crime in the North Side of Cork decreased dramatically. Drugs were still readily available but the tyranny of Tyson Rolland and his gang were gone for now.

Janet & Fred Nesbitt: Because of the early medical intervention when Janet suffered a stroke, she fully recovered from her ordeal. Even though it took a long time for her to come to terms with the harrowing experience, she defeated it and lived a long and happy life. Fred was forever grateful that his wife survived and was relieved that she received immediate medical intervention.

The Real John and Julia Cahill and Paddy Collins.

John Cahill was born in 1878 in the tiny hamlet of Rathbeg, in County Kerry. He joined the British Army and served as a Sapper in the Royal Engineers, in Gillingham. He left the military around 1911. For those who don't know what a Sapper is, it is probably the least prestigious job in the Engineers at that time. The Sapper dug trenches, tunnels and probably latrines, all by hand. After leaving the military, John Cahill returned to Ireland and got a job as porter in the Metropole Hotel, on McCurtain Street in Cork City.

Julia Crowley was born in 1890 in the hamlet of Ardfield near Inchydoney in West Cork. She moved to Cork City and worked as a maid in the Metropole Hotel on McCurtain Street, where she met John Cahill.

John and Julia married and had six children. They raised their family in a small red-bricked terraced house on Suttons Buildings, in the Rathmore Park area of Cork's North Side. In 1946 John Cahill lost his job in the hotel because he won a bet! Another porter bet him that he could not drink a bottle of whiskey in one gulp. John won the bet and lost his job. The year was now 1946 and at the age of sixty-eight, John Cahill returned to London to find work to support his family. The construction business was booming as London was being rebuilt after World War 2. John found a job as a night-watchman on a construction site in Tunbridge Wells. As a migrant worker, John Cahill sent his meager paycheck home every week, until he died alone, in his room in a boarding house in Tunbridge Wells, London in 1947. John Cahill was buried in a numbered grave in London because his family could not afford a marker or to bring his body back to Cork.

Julia Cahill raised her family in Cork City. They all grew up to be hard-working law-abiding responsible citizens. Julia walked to the City Center three times a week until she was 85 years old. Laded down with a couple of shopping bags, Julia walked up Richmond Hill and then Rathmore Road, back to her home in Suttons Buildings. These are some of the steepest residential hills in Ireland. In 1977, in Cork City, Julia passed away, surrounded by her family at the age of 87.

JOHN AND JULIA CAHILL WERE MY GRANDPARENTS. They went about their very ordinary lives without fuss. This is my chance to honor them both.

I do not know much about Paddy Collins, because nobody spoke much about him after he died in 1970 at the age of 42. Paddy was married and had four children. The family lived on the Model Farm Road and Paddy ran a moderately successful insurance brokerage. In September 1970, Paddy took his family on holidays to Kerry. Paddy had a heart attack, in the bedroom of the guest-house, where the family stayed. He was found unresponsive by his oldest daughter, Mary. Paddy died a short time later. When Paddy's daughter found him, she was only ten years old. In 1970 nobody thought that Mary should receive any form of counselling or help to cope with the shock of discovering her father's body. Fifty years later, Mary clearly remembers the day she found her dad. Throughout her career as an Education Assistant, in a high-school, Mary was a fervent advocate for children who have been exposed to shock and trauma. Now, Mary volunteers with children at a Therapeutic Riding Center. PADDY COLLINS IS MY FATHER-IN-LAW. The few people who remember him, knew him as a kind, honest and fair man. I wish I had met him; I think we would have been great friends.

Acknowledgements

First of all, Manor View Estate is a fictitious housing estate that I created. If such a place existed, it would be situated between Knocknaheeney and Nash's Boreen. I created Manor View because it is a hell-hole and although places like it exist in every city on the planet, there are good and great people everywhere and they should not be judged or have their reputations tarnished by the gangsters that live among us, in every neighbourhood.

After "*THE DEADLY STEPS*" was published, in January 2023 and "*ALIBI FOR AN ALIBI*" in August 2023, I received many positive emails and phone calls from people who had read both books. This made me extremely happy, because, without you the reader, this is just the ramblings of some retired 'oul fella.' And, although I have said many times, that I write to download the ugly data that is stuck inside my head, it is truly an inspiration to keep going, when I receive the positive feedback from you, the reader. From the bottom of my heart, I thank you for taking the time to read this book.

The inspiration to write the '*THE STRONGEST WEB*' came from the great people that I was lucky enough to work with during my twenty-five years as a police officer. The emotions that I try to describe here are emotions that we experienced while working through the most tragic of circumstances. I was so lucky to have worked for the best of the best. I took a little bit of your empathy and experience from each one of you, and used it, when it was my turn to lead a case. No matter what the outcome of an investigation, we could always say that '*WE DID THE BEST WE COULD!* There are very few careers, where you start your day, not only waiting, but expecting something awful and tragic to happen. And when it does happen, (and it always does), the world looks to you, the cop, to fix it, right now! And you are the first one to be blamed, when it doesn't turn out perfect. That is why police officers everywhere inspire me and I am so proud to have been one of you.

There were others who also pushed me along with '**The STRONGEST WEB**.' These were people that I worked with over the years and, I not only trust their opinion, I trusted them with my life more than once. I will name them alphabetically, Ron Bilton, John Burchill, and Kelly Harrington. You guys were amazing and gave up so much of your time to read my story and point me in the right direction. From the bottom of my heart, I thank you.

The title, '**THE STONGEST WEB**', came to me as I searched for a suitable quote for the epigraph. I found a quote by the Irish scholar, Johnathan Swift, who died in the eighteenth century. He said, "*Laws are like <u>cobwebs</u>, which may catch small flies, but let wasps and hornets break through.*" Unfortunately, its true and it's obvious we need a stronger web. There were often times, during a complex investigation, where I felt that we were never going to succeed and catch the killer we were hunting. Just as there are times, when I felt the court system let us down. But in the long run, I thing the web we weaved caught a lot of '*Wasps and Hornets*', and that's due to the hard work of the detectives and the prosecutors that caught our files.

I will continue to write the 'Inspector John Cahill' series. I have at least five books in mind, who knows maybe more. If you like them, please leave me a review, and keep going through the series. If you hate them, tell me what you disliked.

If my editor, Maureen Steinfeld, hadn't dedicated so much time to this story, it would be just a jumble of poorly punctuated words. Maureen has spent so much time, using her expertise and command of the English language to turn this document into a manuscript. I named a couple of characters after Maureen and her husband Leo; they are neighbours of the Cahill's at Inchydoney. And as you would expect, they are an awesome couple and the perfect neighbours. Thanks for everything Maureen, what a terrific teacher and a brilliant friend!

I dedicated this book to a few people, who worked on, what became known as 'Project Guillotine.' It was an amazing team effort and I am proud to have been part of that team. So many lives were saved and so many evil people were incarcerated. And it wasn't all cops, there were also a few remarkable lawyers, that were instrumental in making the project a success.

My stories tend to show the darker side of humanity that really exists among us. But the dark side doesn't take over, it will never win. Look around, our future is bright and positive. For every child soldier that is exploited, there are a thousand happy, healthy children who will guarantee that bright future for all of us.

Also, a special thank you to Bolen Books, in Victoria, BC, Canada, and Volume One bookstore in Duncan, BC, Canada. They graciously accepted 'The Deadly Steps' and 'Alibi for an Alibi', for sale in their stores. They both have dedicated shelf space for local independent authors.

Finally, thank you, Mary, my beautiful wonderful wife. You are always the first to read what I write and your opinion and judgement is invaluable. You always encourage me to continue writing regardless of what other commitments life throws at us. I really don't know how you put up with me. I disappear into my 'cave' for hours on end, writing a few thousand words, or working on a podcast, or with one of the True Crime production companies that continue to find me, to work on their documentaries. Mary, you never complain. You always find time to read the latest story and point me in the right direction while you pick up the slack that is part of everyday life. You are my inspiration and my rock. The feelings are real and I had to write them. Thank you, I love you.

TAKE CARE AND STAY safe. O'.D.

Be On the Look Out

BOLO

B E ON THE LOOKOUT FOR the next book in the Detective Inspector John Cahill series, *TIME TO BE SCARED* (Expected in the fall of 2024.)

TIME TO BE SCARED tells a story that starts in Amsterdam, then travels to Dublin and ends up on the streets of Cork City. Gang violence is at an all time low but drugs are still flowing freely. Where there is money, there are drugs, and where there are drugs, there is violence.

Meet two cousins from Cork who are living the lives of the rich and famous, as they run their lucrative international drug courier business for one of the largest drug cartels in Europe.

When the cartel is double-crossed, a hit squad is dispatched to Cork City to get answers, collect their debt and salvage what drugs are left. This story of deceit, greed, kidnapping, torture, and murder will keep you turning the pages to find out what happens next.

Read on to discover how the P.S.N.I. inspector, who is seconded to the Garda, navigates this trail of destruction. What will Detective Inspector John Cahill and the Serious Crime Unit have to do to find those responsible for these brazen murders in the ancient city?

Don't miss out!

Visit the website below and you can sign up to receive emails whenever John O'Donovan publishes a new book. There's no charge and no obligation.

https://books2read.com/r/B-A-OSGW-VWZAD

Connecting independent readers to independent writers.

Also by John O'Donovan

The Detective Inspector John Cahill Series
The Deadly Steps
Alibi for an Alibi
THE STRONGEST WEB

Watch for more at https://johnodonovanbooks.blogspot.com.

About the Author

John O'Donovan grew up in Dublin Hill, on the North Side of Cork City, in Ireland. He married the love of his live, Mary Collins, also a native of Cork City. John was never a police officer in Ireland.

However, in 1989 John, Mary and their young children emigrated to Canada. Five years later, John joined one of the largest municipal police forces in Canada. After a short period as a uniformed officer, John was transferred into a Detective Unit.

As a detective, John excelled and soon transferred into several different specialty units. John transferred to the Homicide Unit and eventually became the Supervising Officer. During his career, John has been involved in the investigation of over 255 homicides and hundreds of sudden and suspicious deaths.

John O'Donovan served as a police officer for twenty-five-years and served in a Government Investigative Agency for another three years. Like Jules Cahill, Mary O'Donovan supported her husband and helped him deal with the carnage and violence that became part of normality. Without Mary's support, John could not have been a successful investigator.

After retirement, people often asked John if he missed the job. John always said no. However, there were parts that he missed. He missed the joy of outsmarting the killers and the elated feeling when an arrest was made. He missed the energy that was required to drive a complex investigation forward, even when physically and mentally exhausted. And he missed working with a dedicated team.

What John did not miss outweighed these things. He did not miss the exhaustion from working non stop, for days at a time. Neither did he miss the horror of violent sudden death. He did not miss the agony and sorrow of the families of victims when they were told their loved one had died suddenly and violently. And he did not miss the sight of the mutilated corpses and the stench of death.

The writing of this series of books is in many ways cathartic for John, who has the utmost respect for Police Officers all over the world carrying out their duty under tremendous stress. Sometimes balancing several complex cases at once, as described in this book.

EVERY INVESTIGATIVE TECHNIQUE described in this book has been successfully deployed in an investigation that the author was involved in. All of these stories are based on real live experiences.

Read more at https://johnodonovanbooks.blogspot.com.

About the Publisher

Publisher of the *Detective Inspector John Cahill* series of Police Procedural novels.

Milton Keynes UK
Ingram Content Group UK Ltd.
UKHW030648130824
446895UK00001B/56